DARK ANGEL

Martha Morgan has finally found love, after weathering many storms of the heart. She agrees to marry Owain and all the family are delighted, but just as she starts to believe that she can have a quiet, calm life, Martha is terrified by a ghostly apparition, which the servants start to call The Nightwalker. Further troubles await her, and finally, Owain, her anchor, disappears. For the first time since she became its Mistress, the Plas Ingli estate is in serious trouble, and it is up to Martha to lead the family out of dark times, testing her to her limits...

DARK ANGEL

by

Brian John

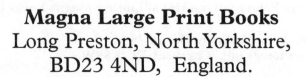

Magna Large Print Books
Long Preston, North Yorkshire,
BD23 4ND, England.

British Library Cataloguing in Publication Data.

John, Brian
    Dark angel.

    A catalogue record of this book is
    available from the British Library

    ISBN   978-0-7505-2777-4

First published in Great Britain in 2003 by Greencroft Books

Copyright © Brian S. John 2003

Cover illustration © Nigel Chamberlain

Brian John has asserted his right under the Copyright, Designs and Patents Act, 1988 to be identified as the author of this work

Published in Large Print 2007 by arrangement with Transworld Publishers

Magna Large Print is an imprint of Library Magna Books Ltd.

Printed and bound in Great Britain by
T.J. (International) Ltd., Cornwall, PL28 8RW

Every effort has been made to obtain the necessary permissions with reference to copyright material, both illustrative and quoted. We apologize for any omissions in this respect and will be pleased to make the appropriate acknowledgements in any future edition.

To Inger and all those who
commune with Angels

Acknowledgements

I am happy to acknowledge the generous support which I have received in the writing of this book. First, I thank the many readers who have willingly entered the fantasy world of Angel Mountain, and have urged me, after reading the first two volumes of my saga, to keep writing about the adventures of Mistress Martha Morgan! I have also received great encouragement from reviewers and from the book trade in Wales, and I thank them for all that they have done in promotion and marketing. My literary sources are too numerous to mention, but I owe special thanks to David Howell for his perceptive and erudite works on the social conditions of early nineteenth-century Wales. Within my own family Alison, Martin and Stephen have all spurred me on, and my wife Inger has acted unstintingly as editor, referee, proofreader, and adviser on the female psyche. And finally I have to record my great debt to my readers' panel of Irene Payne, Ian Richardson, Robert Anthony and Lis Evans. They have read carefully over drafts of the manuscript, and have acted as my technical and literary advisers and referees. They have helped me to remove inconsistencies and anachronisms from the text, and they are the ones who have ultimately given me the confidence to see this book into print. To them, and to my other helpful friends, grateful thanks.

THE MORGAN FAMILY OF PLAS INGLI

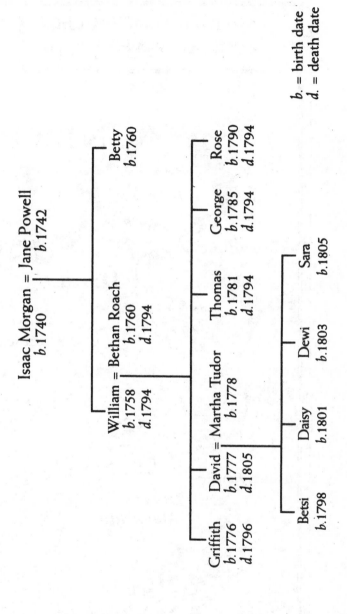

Isaac Morgan = Jane Powell
b.1740   b.1742

Betty
b.1760

William = Bethan Roach
b.1758   b.1760
d.1794   d.1794

Thomas
b.1781
d.1794

George
b.1785
d.1794

Rose
b.1790
d.1794

David = Martha Tudor
b.1777   b.1778
d.1805

Griffith
b.1776
d.1796

Betsi
b.1798

Daisy
b.1801

Dewi
b.1803

Sara
b.1805

b. = birth date
d. = death date

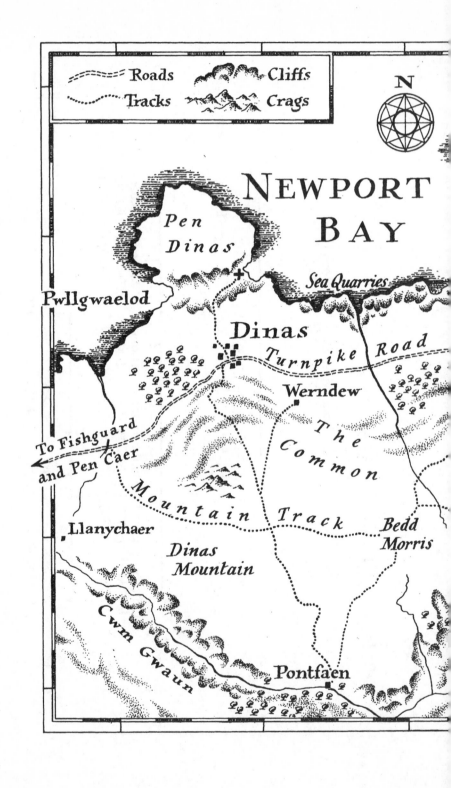

Roads
Tracks
Cliffs
Crags

N

NEWPORT
BAY

Pen
Dinas

Sea Quarries

Pwllgwaelod

Dinas

Turnpike Road

Werndew

The
Common

To Fishguard
and Pen Caer

Mountain Track

Llanychaer

Bedd
Morris

Dinas
Mountain

Cwm Gwaun

Pontfaen

To Moylgrove

One Mile

To Cardigan

Nevern

Cwmgloyn

Henllys

Llwyngwair

R. Nevern

To Eglwyswrw

Pentre Ifan

Newport

Ty Canol Wood

rningli

Mill

Chapel

Carnedd
Meibion
Owen

as Ingli

Cilgwyn

annog

Church

Brynberian

rhiw

Llannerch

Gelli Fawr

To Haverfordwest

©Neil Gower

PROLOGUE

Red Fire Burning

Abandoning her instinct for leading her admirers on a merry dance, the Mistress of Plas Ingli came to see me for a third time, and made herself available without requiring any effort on my part. It was unusually easy, and I was almost disappointed.

I remember the day, for it was mid-March, with the sun warm on my back as I climbed the mountain and a cool dry breeze from the east. The mountain was on fire. Red flames obscured the familiar skyline of bluestone crags and boulders, and the tangled gorse bushes which were green and golden yesterday spat and crackled as they were consumed. There were four separate fires, and I knew that if the wind maintained its strength throughout the day and the sun continued to shine, the mountain would still be burning after dusk.

Abraham Jenkins and five other commoners had started the fire, and they were observing their handiwork from a safe distance, a little way uphill from the Dolrannog road. They, and their cottages, were quite safe so long as the wind did not swing from the east towards the north, which it hardly ever did in March. They were talking about the progression of the lambing season when I approached them.

'Good morning, young man,' said Abraham.

'Good morning all,' said I. 'Fine day for it.'

'Yes indeed. Couldn't be better.'

We chatted about this and that, as one does, and then Abraham called me to one side and left the others to carry on with their discussion of farming matters. Once we were a safe distance away, he said in a conspiratorial voice: 'You know that Martha Morgan?'

'Yes indeed,' I replied. 'I know her well – almost as well as you. You aren't going to tell me, are you, that she has appeared again?'

'Now there's a funny thing,' said Abraham. 'Four days ago, early in the afternoon, I left the lambing for a while and came up here on the common to see if the gorse was dry enough for burning. Nice day it was, just like today. Had my two dogs with me. We went up towards the ruins of the Plas and damn me if the dogs didn't refuse to go past the place. The older one went down on the ground, facing the old ruin, and growled. The hairs on her back were standing straight up, and her ears were flat. The younger one got into a right panic. She whined and simply ran around – too scared to go far from me, but absolutely determined not to go any closer to the Plas. She was too frightened to bark, even.'

'How very strange. Did you see anything or hear anything yourself?'

'Not a thing. I went up to the ruins, climbed over the gate, and looked around. The dogs stayed where they were, whining and growling. Nothing to be seen, but I did get a feeling that I was not alone. You know how it is sometimes, when you feel that somebody is watching you, and you just feel a bit uncomfortable?' I nodded. 'Well, it was like that. And there's another funny thing. Once I was over the gate and scrambling over the collapsed walls and rotting timbers, I noticed that there was total silence. No lambs bleating in the distance, no blackbirds in the wood or buzzards mewing overhead, not even the sound of the breeze rustling the bare branches of the ash trees.'

'Mistress Martha Morgan?'

'Of course. She was there all right, watching me quietly. I knew it, although I could not see her.'

'Weren't you afraid?'

'Good God no! The dogs were, but as you and I know, my friend, she is not a frightening person. I never once thought that, from reading her diaries.'

'Interesting. But still, she was wilder than many women today – and she died a hundred and fifty years ago!'

'Perhaps,' said Abraham, with a grin on his face. 'But remember how young she was when we last had any contact with her? Still only twenty-seven, and trying to cope with lust, brutality, avarice and assorted other vices. She was a mere slip of a girl. When she died she was seventy-six, and probably more comfortable with life.'

'One would hope so,' I agreed. 'But from what we know of her, she seems to have attracted trouble as a pot of honey attracts angry wasps.'

'Well, there was another peculiar thing. When I had finished looking around the ruin I suddenly noticed that there was a big old raven sitting on the topmost stone of the old chimney stack, with her head cocked slightly to one side. I am sure she hadn't been there a minute earlier. She was just looking at me, perfectly calm and quiet.'

'What do you mean, "she"? It might have been a male raven, for all you know.'

'Come, come, my friend. Where is your common sense?'

I grinned and nodded. 'Point taken. Maybe common sense is the last thing to use in such circumstances. Sixth sense, more like.'

'Sixth or seventh, who cares? I have it, although it is sometimes more of a problem than a blessing. One member of the family in every generation. My father, his uncle Richard, and then Richard's mother Annie, who was always thought of as a witch. Not very much further back – three generations maybe – Shemi Jenkins, who was one of Martha's faithful servants at the Plas.'

Suddenly the wind started gusting, and Abraham could soon tell that it was shifting round to the south. 'Boys!' he shouted. 'That fire behind New England is a bit too close to town for comfort, and if it catches hold in the high gorse near Carn Llwyd we will have problems. Better go and keep an eye on it.' And off we all went, Abraham, Billy Howells, Tom Lewis, Gethin James and me, following the flames. There was no disaster, but the people of Newport saw only a thin sun through smoke for the rest of the day, and careful and continuous monitoring of the fires was needed. We had some beating to do, and the commoners of Cilgwyn ended up well sooted and smelling of burnt kippers. Abraham and I had no further opportunities for conversation. But he did manage to say to me before we parted, 'I'll call in and see you tomorrow morning. I've got something to show you.'

After dark the breeze dropped, and the red flames against the skyline gradually diminished in size and intensity. By the early hours of the morning all the fires had run their course and the blackened ground was ready for the green shoots of spring. I did not sleep well, since my mind was too full of speculations about ravens, ghosts and angels. My wife, angel that *she* is, was resigned and more than a little amused, for both she and I knew that Martha was about to enter our lives again. I was up early on a bright warm morning, and fidgeted about until Abraham arrived. He turned up at eleven, as I knew he would, just in time for a cup of coffee. We settled down in the sunshine and exchanged pleasantries while the kettle boiled. In the warmth of the back yard there was not a breath of wind. Then Abraham pulled a little cardboard box out of his jacket pocket and placed it on the bench in front of me. It was maybe eight centimetres square, and it had no markings on it. 'Martha Morgan's latest gift to the world,' he said with a smile. 'Can you guess what it is? No touching, mind. It is very precious.'

My wife and I made various incompetent guesses as to the contents of the little box, and at last we had to give up. I went and made the coffee, and then, as we sipped from our mugs, Abraham, not for the first time, delivered enlightenment. 'This little box,' he said, 'contains something called a microfilm. It is on a metal reel, and it looks for all the world like a 35-millimetre film negative, except that it is very long indeed.'

23

He took it out of its box and showed it to us, with a beaming grin upon his face. 'No sticky fingers, mind. It has to be handled with great care.'

'Used for recording old documents for posterity,' said my wife. 'Surely it can't be...'

'Indeed it can. Here we have the further scribblings of the Mistress of Plas Ingli, in a wholly new form.'

'You mean she has written more notes, diaries, stories or whatever?'

'Another diary, by all accounts. Not that I can be certain about it, mind you. I haven't been able to look at this film yet, for want of the right apparatus.'

'How on earth did it come into your possession?' I asked.

'Isn't it obvious?' said my ever-helpful wife. 'A black raven flew down from the summit of the mountain in the middle of the night, left it on Abraham's bedroom window sill, and tapped on the glass to draw his attention to it.'

'If only!' chortled Abraham. 'Nothing so romantic, I'm afraid. But to begin at the beginning, after that strange episode up at the ruins I knew that something was going to happen. Sure enough, as soon as I set foot inside the house again the phone rang. Strange voice, speaking in Welsh. Mr Abraham Jenkins? Yes indeed. The one who translates Dimetian Welsh manuscripts? Yes indeed, but as seldom as possible, since my eyesight is failing. Well, can I encourage you to look at something for us? To cut a lengthy story short, the lady on the telephone was from the National Library in Aberystwyth. She did not say whether she had been encouraged to ring by a black raven, but she did say that she had picked up on my involvement in translating Martha Morgan's diaries, *On Angel Mountain* and *House of Angels*, and that she had recently been doing some interesting detective work.'

'Well that's what libraries are for, finding things out.'

'Indeed. It transpires that this Catrin Mathias read *House of Angels* a few months back, and was greatly taken with the adventures of Mistress Martha. And then a little worm of a memory started wriggling around in her head. Had she not come across some battered old tome many years ago during her years as an archivist? Did the names of some of the characters in the story not ring a bell faintly in the back of her mind?'

'I see where this is leading, Abraham,' I said. 'But when our friend Ben Phillips spent an age hunting for Morgan family records with the staff in Aberystwyth they found nothing at all. Martha and her family might as well never have existed.'

'Well, their problem was that they were all looking in the wrong places. Young Catrin – very nice lady, I have to say – remembered that maybe twenty years ago, shortly after she started work at the library, she was given the task of preparing hundreds of old documents for microfilming. Most of them were handwritten ledgers, farm records or diaries, and many of them were in a parlous state. They were from various estates in West Wales, but Plas Ingli was not among them; if it had been, it would have shown up in their index. Anyway, Catrin went back to the collection of nineteenth-century microfilm records and started looking through them. She had remembered seeing one particular volume which she – as a Welsh scholar – could not read at all...'

'Dimetian Welsh?'

'Precisely ... so had merely noted on the index card. At last she found the right card. It related to the Price family papers and the Llanychaer estate.'

'The Price papers?' I could hardly believe my ears, for I knew that the Prices of Llanychaer were numbered among Martha's enemies, and I could not conceive of any circumstances in which one of her diaries could have found its way to Plas Llanychaer. 'Are we quite sure that this was one of Martha's accounts?'

Abraham nodded. 'Quite sure. This young lady Catrin had written onto the card, when she was first involved in this indexing business back in 1983: *Diary written by unknown person, member of Price family or servant, dates 13 January 1807 to 4 September 1822. Considerable gaps. Mostly indecipherable – written in code or old Welsh dialect? Dimetian Welsh as used in Cwm Gwaun? Personal reminiscences? Further work needed. Assessment: probably limited social value but no historical or political value.* Catrin got out the microfilm, put it onto this apparatus with a big screen, and looked over a few pages. She couldn't make much sense of it, but certain names kept on cropping up over and over again.'

'And they were...'

'Richard Fenton, Matthew Lloyd, Caradoc Williams, George Price, and various others. Then there were people only referred to by Christian

26

names, including Owain, Sara, Betsi, Grandpa Isaac, Dewi, Joseph, and Brynach. Of course she remembered that these were mostly names from the Morgan family.'

Now I was quite convinced, and had to share Abraham's conviction that Martha Morgan, Mistress of Plas Ingli, had indeed written another diary. We knew from her previous literary efforts that Richard Fenton, Squire of Glynymel, was an old friend of Martha's who had once saved her from seduction by his son John. Matthew Lloyd was one of the men who had murdered Martha's husband David in 1805. George Price was the Squire of Llanychaer, and Caradoc Williams was a tenant farmer. Sara, Dewi and Betsi were three of Martha's four children. Isaac was David's grandfather, the wise and worldly old gentleman who guided Martha in the management of the Plas Ingli estate. Joseph was the Wizard of Werndew, Martha's friend and mentor; medical practitioner, herbalist, amateur sleuth, philosopher and student of the human condition. He had, according to Martha's earlier diaries, saved her from life-threatening situations on several occasions. And Owain Laugharne of Llannerch, younger son of the Squire of Pontfaen, was the man Martha was planning to marry as she ended the second volume of her diary. I knew of no Brynach in her household, but a Celtic saint by that name had once made it his habit to pray on the summit of Carningli, and Martha had mentioned him often in her earlier writings.

'Did Catrin Mathias manage,' I wondered, 'to look again at the original manuscripts from which the microfilm was made?'

'Yes indeed. She got permission to call them up, and says that there were three volumes, nicely bound originally but now in a poor state of repair. She thinks that they must have got damp at some stage. She could find no further clues inside the covers of the books, or anywhere else, as to the name of the author. She says everything is on the microfilm, including copies of the endpapers.'

'What about provenance? How did the books find their way to Aberystwyth?'

'All she can find out is that the books were included in several cardboard boxes passed over to the National Library by a solicitor called Elwyn George when the estate of Plas Llanychaer went into administration around 1970. At that time the house was called "Cwrt" and had been in the hands of the Gwynne family for maybe a hundred and fifty years.'

'So the Gwynne family had been in possession of all these Price family papers over several generations? Isn't that a bit strange?'

'I asked Catrin about that,' said Abraham. 'She replied that it would not be at all unusual. If there had been a succession through from one family to another – for example, if a Price daughter had married a Gwynne and the house had been a part of the marriage settlement – there would have been no reason to tip all the old family papers out of the place.'

'So in the end the papers were only removed when the last of the Gwynne family went bankrupt and had to sell the whole estate – or what was left of it – to a total stranger?'

'Precisely what happened. I remember it well. Now the old house is in the possession of jackdaws and bats, the National Library is in possession of the third part of Martha's diary, and we are in possession of this strange thing called a microfilm.'

We fell silent for a while, serenaded by a blackbird on the topmost green shoots of a spruce tree across the river. A black raven circled high overhead, looking down on us from a wide blue sky. White water roared over the waterfall in the rocky woodland at the far end of the garden. Daffodils glowed and nodded as the gentlest of breezes breathed in from the west. 'Let me make more coffee,' said my wife. 'It looks to me as if you two have got some work to do.' She took the cups and retired to the kitchen.

'We do indeed,' said I, trying to assess Abraham's mood. 'Are you up for it, Abraham?'

'Of course I am. I want to find out what happened next, just as you undoubtedly do.'

'But a microfilm is no good without a microfilm reader. And the nearest one, so far as I know, is in the reference library in Haverfordwest. I can't expect you to travel back and forth, sit there for days on end, and translate another long manuscript over the summer when you have a smallholding to run. Besides, you haven't even finished lambing yet.'

'My dear fellow,' Abraham reassured me, with a chuckle, 'you underestimate both my enthusiasm and my ability to get things organized. How do you think I got hold of this microfilm? Well, by the time I had finished talking to young Catrin, she had promised to send me not only the microfilm, but also a fancy new microfilm reader which is more portable than the one they have in the library.'

'You mean you can work at home?'

'All fixed. I got the microfilm by special delivery, as arranged, two days ago. The microfilm reader is coming in a van tomorrow, for me to borrow for as long as it takes.'

'But that's fantastic!' I enthused. 'So you can work on the text whenever it suits you, just as you did with the earlier diaries.'

'And not only that,' said Abraham. 'I have had a letter from Catrin's boss, the Curator of Records, appointing me as an official National Library translator and saying that they will pay me two thousand pounds for doing the job. Apparently there are only three or four of us left who are conversant with Dimetian Welsh, and I am the only one who has a good command of English. The others are very old indeed.' His face was lit up with delight. 'Suddenly, at my age, I have become a valuable commodity!'

Just then my wife returned with some more strong coffee and said: 'Abraham, as far as we are concerned, you have been a valuable commodity and a dear friend for a good many years. You deserve some recognition for your work in bringing the writings of Martha Morgan into the light of day for the enjoyment of a new generation.'

So we toasted each other with our mugs, and talked about Martha, and the Plas, and the bluestone mountain of Carningli, as the spring sun soared to its zenith and the black raven continued to circle high overhead. We watched her as she rode on a thermal, higher and higher, until she was little more than a speck far above our heads. Then she disappeared.

'Back to the angels,' said Abraham, rising to his feet. 'I have twenty ewes still to lamb, and I must get home and keep an eye on them.' And thus we said our farewells.

The microfilm reader from Aberystwyth arrived on schedule, and when Abraham had finished with the lambing, a few days into the month of April, he began work. The months passed. I met him now and again, and on a couple of occasions he allowed me into his cottage to watch him at work. He professed to dislike intensely the business of working off a screen and winding little handles to move up and down on each page, and said that he missed the physical contact with the old paper pages of Martha's books and the scratchy marks made by her dozens of quill pens. He said he could not make the same contact with her spirit through a brightly lit screen, and I think I know what he meant. But he knew her writing style and the peculiarities of her phrasing and vocabulary, and he moved on rapidly.

By December the job was done. Abraham returned the microfilm and the accompanying apparatus to the National Library, together with his original handwritten translation, scrawled out onto almost two reams of lined A4 paper. I got a photocopy of the whole thing, and at Christmas we enjoyed a little celebration. Abraham joined us for Christmas dinner, having lost the old cousin with whom he normally celebrated the festive season. He was on wonderful form, as full-blooded and sprightly as a man forty years his junior, but he would say little about the story which he had so painstakingly transcribed. I was desperate to know more about the happenings between 1807 and 1822 within the walls of Plas Ingli and within the heart of Mistress Martha. He played little games with me, scattering a few clues, over the Christmas pudding, about a dark presence on the mountain, and about the loves and losses of the heroine. And then he said, 'In the New Year, get to it, my friend. You may be surprised by this next period in Martha's life. She learns some very hard lessons.' And with these enigmatic words, he raised his glass to give a toast to the Mistress of Plas Ingli, and would not say another word.

It took me six months of hard work to complete the editing of the manuscript, but just before midsummer the diary was ready for publication. On the longest day of the year, beneath a milky blue sky and a hazy sun, I walked up the lane to Blaenwaun and called in to see Abraham. We celebrated the completion of the task with Welsh cakes and a cup of tea. Abraham announced that he was planning to spend some of his money from the National Library on a holiday in western Ireland, learning Gaelic, walking on the hills and drinking Guinness. 'Brynmor Brithdir will look after the dogs,' he said, 'and the sheep and the lambs can look after themselves for a fortnight. First holiday in twenty years. I reckon I deserve it.'

Then I walked up onto the mountain. It was hot, since there was not a breath of wind. The air was full of bird-song. The new green bracken was still uncurling and thickening, and was already knee-high, so I had to watch my step when crossing the rocky areas. On a sudden impulse I tracked westwards towards Plas Ingli, crossing the Dolrannog road and then following the derelict driveway to the old house. I climbed over the gate and sat on the grassy bank adjacent to the ruined walls, in the shade of one of the tall ash trees which have taken up occupation of the site. Skylarks tumbled and celebrated midsummer high above my head. I heard the Gelli tractor in one of the bottom fields, and felt pleased that somebody at least was still cutting hay in an age of high-energy fertilizers, silage harvesters, and black polythene bags. Three small rabbits ran towards me, spotted me, and rushed away again.

Then I saw her. The old black raven was there, no more than twenty feet away from me, perched on the highest stone of the ruined gable end. She looked at me, and I looked at her. She was bigger than I had anticipated, for I had never before been so close to a full-grown raven. Her plumage was jet black, but in the sunlight it gleamed and glistened with all the colours of the spectrum, like a cut crystal rotating in a beam of light. She preened her feathers with perfect nonchalance, as I sat watching her for maybe twenty minutes. In spite of her great age she was still very beautiful, and she knew it. I smiled at her. Then, without a sound, she launched herself into the air and flew off towards the summit of Angel Mountain.

MARTHA MORGAN'S STORY

EXTRACTS FROM THE PAGES OF HER
DIARIES FOR 1807–1822, TRANSLATED
FROM THE DIMETIAN WELSH DIALECT
BY ABRAHAM JENKINS

PART ONE: 1807–1808

Black and White

14 January 1807

He screamed and screamed again, unceasingly, with the certainty of a man who knew that he was being dragged down to Hell. No words. Just screams. He looked at me with wide and wild eyes, pleading for the help which he knew I could not and would not give him.

Inexorably and mercilessly the stinking water and the morass of rotten vegetation on the surface of the Clydach bog sucked John Fenton into its black depths. His legs sank deeper and deeper, and then, as he lost his balance and tried to support himself on all fours, his arms sank in to the elbows. Frenetically he struggled, and then his chest was on the surface of the bog. His screams were those of a man about to die and terrified beyond comprehension, and then those of a dying man, loud at first, and then weaker, and at last stifled and silenced by the stream of filthy water entering his throat. At the last moment of life, his eyes caught mine, and there was a curse in his glance. His terror became mine.

Soon nothing was visible of him but the top of his head, and then that was gone too. The surface of the bog moved slightly and then became as placid as it had appeared for centuries, with no trace of either the man or the struggle.

Nightmare or wild daytime fantasy? Neither – but simply a recollection of events that occurred less than one month ago as I watched my worst enemy's terrible and futile fight for survival. To be sure, I have had pleasant enough days over Christmas and New Year. But latterly I have found it impossible to get these sights and sounds out of my head during the hours of daylight, and when at last I have subsided into sleep I have suffered from nightmares so appalling that I cannot face the prospect of describing them.

I pray that tonight God will decide that I have had torture enough, and tomorrow allow me the privilege of rehabilitation.

15 January 1807

It is midwinter, and twenty hours of continuous snowfall have transformed this place from a province of Hell into a little corner of Heaven. Dusk is falling, and as I look out from my bedroom window I can see clear skies to the east, with a faint white moon and a scattering of early evening stars. The *cwm*, and the ridge of Carnedd Meibion Owen beyond, and the old hills of Mynydd Presely beyond that, are covered beneath an even blanket of snow about twelve inches thick. There has been no wind, and there will be none tonight, and the temperature is falling fast. Twenty minutes since, as I stood at the back door of this beloved house, I could see the last of the leaden snow clouds far to the west as they were melted into gold by the rays of the setting sun.

Transformation was needed, for yesterday my mood was as black as the heart of John Fenton and my mind's eye saw nothing but the image of that evil creature as he travelled to Hell. So preoccupied was I that I heard not the happy laughter of the children, or the comfortable domestic sounds of the kitchen, but the screams of a dying monster. And I was not spared the nightmares...

Then, thank God, came the new day, with four small children rushing into my room as soon as it was light, leaping onto my bed and shouting 'Mam! Mam! It's snowing! All night it has been coming down, and the whole world is covered!' So I was dragged out of bed, feeling (and probably looking) a thousand years old, and forced to open the shutters. Together we looked out towards the *cwm*. It was, of course, quite invisible, obliterated by a gentle and continuous cascade of snowflakes swirling and fluttering earthwards from a leaden sky. I pulled on my dressing gown and then sat in my comfortable chair by the window, with children draped around me. With wide eyes we watched, and the silence without encouraged a lovely tranquillity within. Neither the children nor I had ever seen such large snowflakes before. There was no wind, and although the sun was blocked out by the cloud so much light was entering the room that we were temporarily dazzled. 'Oh, just look at that!' whispered Betsi. 'I can see a million angels dressed in white, and all dancing.' I pulled her closer, and thus was my black mood banished by the innocence of a child.

'Mam,' said Dewi, 'why are you crying? Are you sad?'

41

'No, *cariad*. I'm anything but sad. I'm shedding a happy tear because the world is so beautiful, and because I love you all so much. Now then, come and make me even happier by giving me a kiss.' And, much to my surprise, he did.

Then there were heavy footsteps on the stairs and Bessie and Sian came bursting in. Bessie was carrying a bucket of small coals and kindling for my bedroom fire, and Sian had an armful of children's clothes which she had been warming in front of the *simnai fawr* in the kitchen. 'Good morning, Mistress Martha! Good morning, children!' they sang out in union.

'Now then, Mistress,' said Bessie, on her knees in front of the fireplace, 'there's snow we are having. If it goes on like this it will be up to our necks by dinner time. But we will all have a lovely day, so long as we keep nice and warm. Better get this old fire going. Cold outside will never win so long as we have flames within, as my old mam used to say.'

Sian went through my room like a wild west wind, heading for the nursery and calling over her shoulder: 'Come along, children. The old folks are already up and about. Hot water is in the tub in the kitchen. Betsi and Daisy first. Come along now! Down the back stairs with me. Dewi and Sara, you wait here a minute with your mam, and then we'd better get you scrubbed up too. Quickly now, you big sisters, if you want to put your winter clothes on while they are still nice and warm.'

And so began the happy day, with giggles and groans and squeals and laughter as the business of washing and dressing and eating breakfast got under way. I listened to the four little ones, and to the cheerful chatter of Bessie and the exhortations of Sian in the nursery, as I sat before the window. Love belongs in this place, I thought. How foolish that I should allow myself, all too often, to be dragged down into misery and introspection when I have so much kindness and happiness around me.

'Mistress Martha,' said Bessie, breaking into my reverie, 'you are very slow this morning, if I may say so.'

'Yes, I know it. I fear that I did not sleep very well. I was troubled once again by nightmares.'

'I am sorry to hear it, but not entirely surprised. You were in a very dark and pensive mood yesterday, and hardly aware of what was going on around you. The weather does affect the soul, Mistress. Perhaps the buildup of snow clouds was to blame?'

'No. You know me well enough, dear friend, to notice my demons when they creep up on me. The unpleasant events of the past weeks have afflicted me more deeply than I would have liked, and now and again they threaten to overwhelm me.'

'Come now, Mistress,' said my faithful maid. 'If those evil monsters could not defeat you in head-to-head conflict, they will certainly not defeat you in the form of phantoms and remembrances and nightmarish visions. Put them all behind you! You have better things to think of, including Master Owain, and your four beautiful children, and a world cleansed and sanctified by snow-flakes scattered from heaven...'

I had to laugh. 'Dearest Bessie!' said I. 'You are

very poetic this morning. And before breakfast, too. I do not think I can cope with any more metaphors on an empty stomach. Now then, would you please fetch me some warm water for my morning wash?' She grinned, and gave a sweet curtsy, and did as I asked.

So the hours have flown by, with the Plas quite cut off from the rest of the world. It snowed until the middle of the day, causing the servants to grumble and curse as they went about their tasks. But in truth it was not so cold as to cause great difficulties, and with no wind there has been no drifting. The cattle and horses are all under cover, and the sheep are close to the farm, and Billy says that there have been no losses. Water and hay have been carried to cowshed and stable, and other tasks have been completed under cover in the barn. The children and I have been out and about, disturbing the gentle contours of the snow blanket, playing silly games, rolling giant snowballs and building a snowman six feet high. By midday we all looked like snowmen ourselves, with thick layers of fresh snowflakes accumulating on our hats, coats and mufflers. By the time we came inside for our dinner at one o'clock, Dewi and Sara were quite overwhelmed by all the excitement, and were too exhausted to eat, so Sian packed them off to their warm cots for a little sleep.

With the clearing of the sky in the afternoon I decided that we should all pitch in with shovels in an attempt to clear the yard and the entrances to all the buildings. I knew that any change in the weather could lead to difficulties, with slush and streaming water, or sheets of ice, or further accumulations of snow liable to make life much harder than it was already. Billy, Shemi and Will did most of the hard work, but Bessie and Sian assisted with vigour, as did the two older children and I. Even Grandma and Grandpa joined in. By the time the light started to fade we had, between us, built a most satisfactory assortment of snow mountains and ridges, with wide pathways passing between them. Tomorrow we will have to start digging our way out along the driveway down as far as the Dolrannog road; but nothing was moving down there today, and it may be several days before we can reach the town on horseback or with wheeled vehicles. No matter. We are used to being snowed in, and I like it here when no news can find its way in and no news of the Plas can filter out.

Now Mrs Owen is banging on her gong and calling us to supper. Our daily routines have been disrupted because of the snow, and we will all eat supper together – six servants, Grandpa Isaac and Grandma Jane, four children and myself. We will eat *cawl* and crusty bread with butter and cheese, followed by a spicy oatmeal pudding and raspberry jam. With thirteen people of all shapes and sizes seated round the kitchen table there will be pandemonium. Sara and Dewi will get covered with food, and Daisy will probably have a tantrum at some stage during the meal, and Grandpa will scowl and think that I am a terrible mother. Mrs Owen will get very flustered, and Grandma Jane will simply raise her eyes to the heavens. Billy will feed a few scraps to the cats under the table, and Shemi will talk about horses and harnesses. Bessie will quietly get on with serving food and moving dishes. Will and Sian will talk about great snowfalls of the past. I will love every moment of it.

17 January 1807

Yesterday the thaw started when a warm westerly breeze sprang up, and today we have had rain on top of snow. So our snowman has gone and our ridges and mountains of snow have almost dissolved away. We have had avalanches sliding off our roofs, and the ice has disappeared from the duckpond. There is slush and running water everywhere, and since it cannot all escape there are pools and ponds in all sorts of places where they should not exist, much to the delight of the children. They have been out in the rain, slipping and sliding and falling over, and throwing heavy snowballs at each other, and by mid-afternoon they were all so wet that I had to call them inside for fear that they should all catch a chill. They were stripped of their sodden clothes and each given a warm bath in the big tub in front of the kitchen fire, and now they are in the nursery with Sian, rosy-cheeked and happy, listening to a fairy story.

I have made a decision. It is that I will continue with this diary-writing until such time as I have my new husband in my bed. When my beloved David died almost two years ago, the act of writing something in my little book (on those evenings when I had a mind to do it) brought me much consolation, and helped me to drive away my demons. The act of putting words together in a sensible sequence helped me greatly in the midst of my grief, and even though I am now older and wiser the act of writing still strikes me as a worthwhile activity. From the very beginning I have carried in my breast the expectation that sometime in the future somebody will unscramble my words and actually read them, long after I am gone – the idea of leaving my diaries as a memorial appeals to my sense of vanity. We all need to be loved and valued, and to leave the world a little better than we found it. So says my friend Joseph Harries the Wizard. Thus will I find my salvation.

I have completed two diaries so far, and I have no wish that either should be read by anybody while I am alive, for they both contain dark secrets and descriptions of terrible events. The first diary is in a box in the attic of this beloved house, and there it will stay until I am dead and gone. The second, which was recently completed, is now safely tucked away in the library at Plas Pontfaen as a result of a subterfuge which has given me much pleasure.

Five nights since, on the evening of *Hen Galan*, we made one of our essential annual expeditions. Every year the Morgans of Plas Ingli visit the Laugharnes of Plas Pontfaen, to celebrate the old New Year in style. I travelled with Grandma Jane and Grandpa Isaac in the small carriage, on a winter evening which was unexpectedly mild. I carried my last diary with me secretly, wrapped up in a silk cloth and buried in the depths of my evening bag. The journey took an hour, and the time flew by since Grandpa was in one of his jovial and expansive moods. He enjoys wicked gossip a good deal more than his long-suffering wife, and he was minded to pass on many tasty titbits about the local gentry families which caused my jaw to drop. Grandma had to rebuke him for his indiscretions over and again, but I found their good-natured banter thoroughly diverting. It kept my mind off my beloved Owain for a little while, which was no bad thing, since I do not cope with anticipation very well. So far as I was concerned, the evening was significant not for the celebration of the Old Calendar but because Owain and I would announce our betrothal in the presence of his family. I was therefore more than a little on edge, and the old folks knew it. Wise people that they are, they had kept me well away from the brandy bottle in the hours leading up to our departure – it has been my undoing in the past.

As we clattered up to the front door of the big house, the whole place was glittering with candlelight. There were branched candlesticks in all the windows, and gleaming storm lanterns were strung out across the yard. The whole place was as magical and welcoming as a fairy castle. And Prince Charming was on the doorstep, with his father John, his mother Olwen and his older brother James.

Owain opened the door of the carriage, helped me down, and kissed my hand. 'Welcome to Plas Pontfaen, my dear Martha,' he said, looking deep into my eyes. I wanted him to embrace me and kiss me long and hard upon the lips, but I knew that in the presence of his parents decorum would not allow it; and so I had to be patient. As

48

the evening went on, I trusted, the opportunity for a little time alone together would arise, as indeed it did. But for now there were warm greetings all round, and we three visitors were ushered into the depths of the old house to meet assorted other guests. Among them were the Higgons of Tredafydd and various relatives, some of whom I had not met before. Owain's sister Liza was there, and it was a pleasure to meet her again, for I do not know her well. My dear friend Mary Jane, Owain's older sister, was present with her husband Dafydd and little boy William. Once the little fellow had been packed off to bed Mary Jane and I found a corner, and a few minutes, to talk about the state of the world – but so much has happened since we last met that I hardly knew where to start and finish, so serious conversation had to be deferred to another occasion.

The evening was quite perfect, our hosts attentive and my future husband at my side, keen to indulge me at every opportunity. What loving glances! What sweet words in my ear! All given with love and received with love, and with such frequency that both Owain and I felt that our self-indulgence was bordering on the very edge of bad manners. But our blessed families smiled and forgave us. They have seen love before, and I pray to God that they will see it again.

Before the evening was too far advanced, I made an excuse to visit Mistress Laugharne's dressing room in order to powder my nose, knowing that it was just along the corridor from the Squire's library. I knew that the library was never locked, for I had explored its contents several times before. Without being observed by anybody, I took my old diary wrapped in its silken cloth. Then with a candle to light my way, I went into the library, made my way to the shelf of Master Shakespeare's plays, and made some small rearrangements. It was tempting fate, but I felt a compulsion to place my book between *Two Gentlemen of Verona* and *The Merchant of Venice*, and I noted with some satisfaction that the volumes were of very similar dimensions and appearance. I sent out a quick prayer that nobody would discover the diary until such time as I was with the angels. And so, having placed my description of past appalling events right in the heart of the house in which my sweet Owain had grown up, I washed my hands and tidied my hair, and returned to the fray.

We all ate well and drank well, and enjoyed old and beautiful harmonies from Grandma Jane's harp. We laughed and reminisced and talked of the future. Squire Higgon played a very loud tune on his *pibgorn*, not terribly well. And then, late in the evening, Owain held up his hand and called for silence. He was among his dearest friends and closest family, and although he is naturally a shy man he did not appear to be at all inhibited. He smiled at me, and then asked Grandma Jane if he might borrow her harp for a minute or two. She was only too delighted, for she already knew something of his musical talents. He tuned the instrument for a few minutes, in total silence, and then he looked up and smiled at me again, and said 'For Martha.' He started to play. His fingers swept across the taut strings and then with the most delicate of fingering he embarked upon the loveliest performance of 'The White Lilac Tree' that I have ever heard. His clear tenor voice rang around the room and penetrated to every corner of the building, stopping the servants in their tracks and demanding – and receiving – the rapt attention of all. I listened to his fingers and his voice, and was entranced and enchanted, and loved him with a passion I had never felt before. I could not take my eyes off him, but in my mind's eye I saw him floating quite naked in that deep pool near Pandy, singing that same song at the top of his voice on a hot and lazy day last summer. It was no fantasy, but a remembrance as clear as a crystal spring. On that day, now and for ever inscribed on my heart, I had chanced upon him and watched him as I crouched, quite hidden, in a little copse of bushes, until he dried himself, and dressed, and went on his way. One day I will tell him of my espionage, and see how he reacts...

'Martha! Moved to tears you may be, but Owain wants you to join him by the fireplace!' So said Grandma Jane, holding my hand and giving me a little kiss on the cheek. Thus was I dragged back into the real world, to realize that Owain had long since finished his song. All eyes were upon me, and tears were rolling down my cheeks. I immediately became flustered, and blushed the colour of ripe cherries. But then I realized, with some relief, that those present could not see into my head or share my impure and beautiful thoughts, and I remembered also that I was among friends. They all laughed, and so did I. I wiped away my tears and went to join Owain. As we held hands by the roaring log fire, Owain announced to the assembled company that I had agreed to become his wife, and that in a few short months, at the beginning of June, the Laugharne and Morgan families would be united. He announced that his parents had given their blessing, as had Grandpa Isaac and Grandma Jane and my own dear father and mother at Brawdy. Nobody was in the least surprised, but in any case there was clapping and cheering and embracing all round, and little speeches, and toasts, and more singing. Mistress Laugharne brought in the family's magnificent Ewenny Pottery wassail bowl filled with spiced apple cake, which was anointed with brandy. The servants were called in, and they all shared in the ceremonial, which I found greatly touching. I know that they are all very fond of Owain, and I dare to hope that they will grow fond of me. Then, between us, we despatched the alcoholic and delicious cake with due ceremony. Soon there was not a crumb nor a drop left in the bowl.

In the midst of all this excess Owain and I managed to find a few minutes together in the privacy of the music room, where at last we could embrace and protest our undying love for each other. He kissed me with a passion which quite literally took my breath away, and when we returned to the parlour I was so weak at the knees that I would have fallen over had it not been for the strong arm that supported me.

It was one of the happiest evenings of my life. I confess to feeling quite reluctant to go home, but for all of us the morrow was another working day, and Billy, our head servant and occasional coachman, needed a couple of hours' sleep before getting up to milk the cows. Owain promised that he would call at Plas Ingli within the week, and I told him that I would die of loneliness if he did not keep his promise. 'Loneliness?' He laughed. 'My dear Martha, with four little angels, and an assortment of larger ones, beneath your roof, I should have thought that loneliness is a perfect impossibility.' We said our farewells and the coach rumbled back eastwards along the Cwm Gwaun road, illuminated by starlight and the flickering flames of our candle lanterns.

19 January 1807

Today, Tuesday, Owain came to see me and the children, and we have had other visitors too. I needed company, for it is precisely one month since the death of John Fenton. If I had been simply left to the tender mercies of the children for the whole day, I do not think that I could have coped. I have come to recognize my tendency towards introspection, and so I engineered the distraction of a house full of visitors.

Some days since I received a note from Squire Richard Fenton of Glynymel, near Fishguard. In it, he asked whether he might pay a visit in the company of his wife in order to congratulate me and Owain on our recent betrothal. Tuesday, he wrote, would be perfectly suitable from his point of view. I replied, for better or for worse, that I would be delighted to welcome him and Mistress Anne on that day for afternoon tea, and that I would encourage Owain and Joseph Harries the

Wizard – who had done so much to bring us lovebirds together – to join us. As soon as the Glynymel manservant rode off down the drive with my message in his pocket, I sat at my desk writing out invitations to Owain and Joseph requesting the pleasure of their company also.

So it came to pass that I spent the morning in the kitchen with Mrs Owen and Bessie, baking currant cakes and scones, and generally keeping my mind off John Fenton. I should explain at this point that the reason for my apprehension was simply that John Fenton – may he rot in Hell – was the oldest son of Squire and Mistress Fenton. They have no idea that he is dead, and I suspect that they have no great concern one way or another, since last year, on the occasion of the Squire's Autumn Ball, the old fellow threw the wretch out of Glynymel and told him that he would kill him with his own hands should he ever return. He also cut him out of his will. The reasons for the enmity between father and son are many and complex, but suffice it to say that John Fenton's dissolute life in London in the company of the Prince of Wales and his cronies had long been an embarrassment to his father, beside which the fellow had wasted the whole of his inheritance, and a good deal more, to the point of almost bankrupting the family. The last straw came at the Glynymel Autumn Ball, where, for reasons which still cause me to grow pale when I think of them, he enticed me into his bed and attempted to use me most grievously. His father rescued me at the very last second, and ordered John out of the house; and to this day his

intervention is a secret shared only ⌐ ⌐⌐⌐⌐⌐ ⌐⌐⌐
us. Nobody else knew, or knows, that J⌐⌐
his father's house, for he came and went ⌐
back door unseen by guests or servants.

Neither do the Squire and his wife know the
full extent of the evil that infected John Fenton's
soul. They do not know that only three months
ago the monster tortured Owain without mercy,
spilling his blood and inflicting such pain upon
him that he lost consciousness, and then dumped
him on the mud of the Nevern estuary, leaving
him to die. That he did not perish is due in no
small measure to the combined efforts of my
friend Patty, and Joseph Harries, and those who
reside in Plas Ingli. Some of us know what he did
to Owain, partly out of jealousy, partly out of the
sheer pleasure of inflicting pain, and partly out of
the mad desire to extract from Owain's lips the
location of the Plas Ingli treasure. Owain knew
nothing about it, and swore so on oath, but that
did nothing to deter John Fenton and his cronies
from their unspeakable work with a bloodied
knife upon the flesh of the man I love. They
carved stripes upon his chest, and in so doing
guaranteed their passage to the fires of Hell.

Only two people, Owain and myself, know that
John Fenton is dead. We saw him die following his
abduction of my sweet daughter Sara and his
attempt – for the second time – to possess me. It
happened in a lonely hut deep in the valley of the
Clydach, about a mile from the Plas. I had been
forced by Fenton to go there alone, in an attempt
to save the life of my child. This time my rescuer
was Owain, who risked his own life in order to save

55

...e and that of little Sara. Although he was still weak from his injuries and quite unarmed, he confronted Fenton and managed to get the better of him in a fearsome struggle, and when Fenton fled he ran straight into the peat bog which consumed him. Owain and I could only look on in horror, and we could do nothing to save him. Luckily little Sara was spared the sights and the sounds of this terrifying encounter, for she had been given some sedation by her abductor. She may, in years to come, remember the fact of her abduction; but she will remember little else, and for this I thank God. In spite of the sheer horror of our ordeal, Owain and I had the presence of mind to clear the hovel in the wood of all traces of Fenton's occupation. Within minutes the bog had swallowed his body and all of his possessions without a trace being left on its slimy stinking surface. Owain and I have sworn that while we live we will never divulge to another soul what happened on that fateful day precisely one month ago. I pray that my written record will not be read until I am in my grave.

Enough of morbid recollections. I have a life to live, and a love to celebrate. On a sunny winter afternoon enlivened by a westerly gale and scudding black clouds, Squire and Mistress Fenton arrived in the Glynymel coach. It was a pleasure to welcome them and to see that they were both in the rudest of health. Grandpa Isaac and Grandma Jane, who are old friends of theirs, were delighted to see them, and ushered them inside. As we went in, I was struck, not for the first time, by the Squire's distinguished presence. He is not

56

particularly good-looking, but he has eyes of the deepest blue and a kind mouth; and although he must be around sixty years old he has a spring in his step and an alertness about him that is very appealing even to a young woman such as I. He has a fierce intellect and shows a great interest in everything and everybody, and I have heard it said that in Fishguard he has the reputation of a *dyn hysbys* or 'knowing man'. Perhaps this is why Joseph and he get on so well together. Dear Joseph arrived on his white pony, having taken the mountain track, and my darling Owain came along the Dolrannog road on his chestnut hunter. I kept the warmest of my welcomes for the man who is in possession of my heart, but in truth I love all four of our guests, for they are the kindest and most faithful of friends. Between us we have seen much brutality and experienced much pain, and through shared tribulations we have forged close bonds of friendship.

With much excitement and laughter we led our guests into the parlour. If we had hoped for a little decorum such hopes were dashed when the children came tumbling down the stairs as delicately as a herd of Welsh Black bullocks, and welcomed Owain and Joseph as if they had not seen them for a century or more. These two are indeed their favourite men, and I have thought more than once that since the death of their father they have acquired two most excellent substitutes who can do perfectly well most of the things that are expected of fathers, apart from the imposition of discipline. Well, nobody is perfect. The older girls were a little intimidated by Squire Fenton, for he does look a somewhat forbidding figure in his red jacket and black breeches, with spectacles upon his nose, a powdered wig upon his head, and shiny buckles on his shoes. But he has a twinkle in his eye, and much to my surprise Dewi hopped up onto his lap almost as soon as he was seated, and before I could admonish him my son had engaged his new friend in earnest conversation. The Squire, who has no grandchildren of his own, was thoroughly delighted with this unexpected attention, and listened intently as Dewi explained, at great length, that he would very soon be four years old. And little Sara, who is all innocence, took hold of the hand of Mistress Anne and would not let it go, while chattering nineteen to the dozen in her own made-up language which even I could only occasionally understand.

At last I banished the children to the nursery, for I was not prepared to allow them to dominate proceedings for too long, or to vie for the attentions of the guests. Sian took them off happily enough, each of them transporting a special treat of currant cake and fruit cordial. So calm descended, and Bessie brought in our best Wedgwood china, our silver knives and spoons, and our most beautiful linen napkins, and we enjoyed a civilized afternoon tea free of black bullocks. The fresh scones, served with clotted cream and strawberry preserve, and the currant cakes made to two of Mrs Owen's ancient recipes were greatly appreciated, and there were many queries as to the name of the tea blend which we had used in our largest silver teapot. I had to be honest and tell my guests that it had been acquired, at a very special price, from Dai Darjeeling just a few days since, and that I had no idea what it was called. 'He calls it his threepenny blend,' said Grandma Jane, 'and he mixes it himself with leaves and dried blossoms and secret essences. But the real secret of our famous tea at the Plas is not the tea leaves, but the water. I declare that there is nothing on this planet to match the taste and the health-giving properties of the water from Ffynnon Brynach.' And who was I, or anybody else, to disagree?

We all had a most convivial time, and I noticed with pleasure that Joseph made several return visits to the plate of scones and to the currant cakes. I caught his eye and then winked at him, almost causing him to choke, which gave me a good deal of amusement. Living alone in his cottage at Werndew, he spends so much time looking after others and investigating esoteric matters that he neglects himself. I thought he looked too thin, and determined that I must play a full role in seeing him well fed through the coming hungry months. We chatted about politics and music and literature, and the only difficult moment came when Grandma Jane asked about the health and the whereabouts of the rest of the Fenton family. I exchanged quick glances with Owain, and then, on meeting Joseph's eye, realized in an instant that the Wizard of Werndew knew all, even though he had been told nothing. 'Oh, they are well enough,' breezed the Squire, 'so far as I know. Samuel, our youngest, is studying in Oxford, and shares the studious instincts of his father. Richard, the middle one, is set upon the life of a cleric, and has found a comfortable living in the south of the county. And as for John, I do not know and I do not care.' His countenance darkened. 'He should be in London, working in the War Office. But last time I heard of him he was here rather than there. I gather that he lived on the Parrog for a while, kept very bad company, and was involved in that treasure hunting business in Parc Haidd. Stupid fellow! And then, as we all know, a warrant was put out for his arrest some months ago. If he has any sense he will never show his face in this county again, and he will certainly find no refuge at Glynymel from his creditors and from the many others whom he has wronged.'

At this, Mistress Anne looked pained, and I could understand why. I caught the Squire's eye, and he understood that it was time to change the subject. But his wife took the initiative. 'My dear Richard,' said she in her delightful French accent, 'shall we not talk of more pleasant things? Do not forget that we have come here with a little celebration in mind.'

'God bless my soul, Mistress Anne, you are quite correct! We are here among dear friends to celebrate young love! And could there be anything more worthy of celebration?' He did not expect a reply, but fished about in his pocket and extracted a little wooden box tied with a red ribbon before rising to his feet and coming over to where I was sitting. He motioned to Owain to come and join us. Then he presented to us the little box, and said: 'For you, Owain and Martha, my favourite young people, on the occasion of your betrothal. From Mistress Anne and myself, as a little token of esteem. May the time fly by until the day of your wedding, and may you find a long lifetime of happiness together.' And he bent over and kissed me on the cheek, and then gave Owain a hearty embrace.

'Open it! Please do!' interjected Mistress Anne, with all the excitement of a small child who has made a little worthless but wonderful gift for its mother.

I untied the red ribbon and opened the box gingerly. Inside it there were two gold rings, one a man's signet ring with a single ruby set into it, and the other a more delicate and very feminine ring with three small diamonds. They were quite beautiful, and neither Owain nor I knew what to say. I tried to express my gratitude, but also to protest that they should not have spent so much money on us and we had not expected even the smallest gift; but my words got tangled up and I ended up spluttering and stuttering. Owain did no better, and the Squire roared with laughter. 'No protests, if you please!' he boomed. 'We will take your disjointed sentences, dear friends, as thanks. It is our desire that you should accept these rings, as it is our desire that you should find perfect happiness.'

'Oh, how romantic,' said Grandma Jane, with tears in her eyes.

'Try them on! Do!' said Mistress Anne, with her eyes gleaming. 'They come from India. If they are too small or too large, Gethin Goldsmith will make adjustments.'

So we tried them on, and were delighted to find that they fitted perfectly. The rest of the afternoon swept by with all of us in the best of humour. Servants and children inspected the rings, and their gasps of admiration were enjoyed by donors and recipients in equal measure.

Now our guests are gone. My ring is still on my finger, where it will stay. It is late at night and the house is quiet as I sit at my desk by the window. The embers of my coal fire are glowing in the grate. I have not yet closed my shutters, and I can see a few faint lights flickering down in the *cwm*. It has been a quite wonderful day, and the bond between Owain and myself is strengthened and drawn ever tighter. I ponder on what might lie ahead. After the tragedies and terrors of the past, dare I hope for a straight and smooth road scattered with rose petals and stretching to the far horizon of old age? Perhaps that is too much to ask for. But I beseech God in his wisdom to give the children joy and peace, to bless the union between Owain and myself, and to speed the day when he and I can share the same bed.

25 January 1807

It has been a tiresome business, but I have spent most of the day involved in discussions about the marriage settlement. At first Owain and I wished to have nothing to do with it, in the secure knowledge that we are both driven towards the altar by love and mutual respect and not by any desire to increase the wealth of our estates or to enhance our standing in the community. But both Grandpa Isaac and Squire John Laugharne, Owain's father, have insisted upon the drawing up of a lengthy document, on the grounds that there is no knowing what will happen in life and that secure provision is needed for the sake of the children in particular.

So it was that shortly after breakfast George Lewis Legal arrived. He and I sat down with Grandpa in the parlour to make some preliminary assessments of the wealth of the Plas Ingli estate and to talk over our strategy for obtaining what Master Lewis called 'the best deal that might be achieved in the circumstances'. I said that I found this very distasteful, and that in my personal view marriage was a union of two loving partners rather than a competition between two estates.

'My dear Mistress Martha,' he said, gazing at me over the top of his spectacles, 'there is no doubt in my mind, or anyone else's, that the forthcoming marriage between you and Master Owain is indeed the natural consequence of a mutual romantic attachment. I see it in your eyes as I see it in his demeanour. But do not forget that the Plas Ingli estate is bigger than the Llannerch estate, and that the Laugharne family will, as a result of this marriage, benefit far more than the Morgans of Plas Ingli. To put things crudely, most women seek to marry up, and have to pay for the privilege in marriage settlements; but you are marrying down, and for the sake of you and your children careful provision has to be made.'

At this, I could feel my cheeks flushing, and if I had had the opportunity I would have said something very haughty to Master Lewis. But Grandpa Isaac, who knows me far too well, placed his hand upon mine and said: 'Now then, Martha, you know that George is not being condescending or unkind in any way, and you know that he has the greatest respect for the Laugharnes. But what he says is quite correct. Owain and his father are the most honourable of gentlemen, and will never seek to take advantage of us after all the troubles we have had in the past. But as he says, provision has to be made. Have you thought about what might happen if God forbid you were to die, perhaps in childbirth, a year after you are married? Have you thought about what might happen if you and Owain have three children? Is it your wish that their inheritance should be greater than that which would fall to Betsi, Daisy, Dewi and Sara?'

I admitted, with some shame, that I had not even thought of such things. Master Lewis nodded. 'Quite so, quite so,' he said. 'And indeed there is no reason, Mistress, why you should have devoted your time to dismal thoughts about the future. You have had quite enough to deal with in past months, with evil men hunting for imaginary treasure on your land, court cases the like of which I have never seen before, plus four small children to entertain and educate, while you run an estate. It is a wonder to me, in the circumstances, that you have managed to retain your composure, and may I say your beauty, to the extent that you have, and that you are able to find the time for two old gentlemen here this morning...'

I laughed. 'Behave yourself, Master Lewis. Flattery will get you everywhere, as you well know. Shall we now get down to business? I accept what you say, and I am also aware that I have responsibilities towards dear Grandpa Isaac and Grandma Jane, who must never be left destitute whatever happens to me or the estate. And then there are the interests of our tenants and servants, who smile with us and cry with us. I insist that they too must be looked after.'

Bessie brought us some tea, and we got down to work. I knew a good deal about the affairs of Plas Ingli, but not nearly as much as Master Lewis. He informed me that the estate is now worth £1800 per year, about three times as much as the Llannerch estate which fell upon hard times under the management of its past owner, the late and unlamented Alban Watkins. About half of our income derives from the tenancies of the five farms which have been acquired over the years by the Morgan family – Gelli, the two Dolrannogs, Brithdir, and Penrhiw. The rest comes from an allowance paid by my own dear father from his estate at Brawdy, as agreed (unknown to me) prior to my marriage to David in 1796, and additionally from various small rentals on labourers' cottages, and from the sales of produce and animals. But as Master Lewis explained, and as I know from experience, our estate is very different from the grand estates in England in that very little money ever changes hands, with most of our rental income being paid in the form of sheep, eggs, bacon, corn and labour. If we were to insist on cash payments, our tenants would simply not be able to pay, and would be forced into destitution. There are enough destitute people around as it is, as I know full well from my contributions to the parish poor rate.

According to the law of the land, little Dewi will inherit the Plas Ingli estate when I die or when he comes of age, leaving the girls to receive substantial sums on the attainment of their twenty-first birthdays or on the dates of their marriages. Master Lewis confirmed that according to David's will, made only two years ago, I am the sole owner of the estate. I therefore have absolute discretion in the matter of disposal of assets, marriage settlements for the girls, and the designation of income and any savings that I might have under the bed when I die. Such power brings with it an awesome responsibility, and also a terrible confusion in my mind, for I have to decide whether I want the income for my daughters to be assured simply for their lifetimes, or for the lifetimes of their husbands should the latter outlive them, or indeed for the lifetimes of their children. 'I would advise against making arrangements for theoretical grandchildren,' said Master Lewis. 'No doubt they will come along in due course, but if you place too many encumbrances on the estate you will reduce your options for the future, and make the estate unattractive to others should you fall upon hard times. I advise you to allow your four children to make provision for their own, when the time comes. More to the point, how do you wish to provide for any offspring of your union with Owain?'

I knew not how to respond to this direct question, and spluttered into my teacup. Grandpa Isaac helped me out.

'Martha, my dear,' he explained, 'a great deal depends upon your new husband. Remember that from the date of your marriage the estate will be enlarged, to the benefit of both families, and especially Betsi, Daisy and Sara. Owain may be happy for Dewi to be heir to the whole of the new estate, but I cannot imagine his father agreeing to this. The Squire may well feel that any future son named Laugharne should inherit your combined properties, leaving Dewi with a cash settlement. There are many possibilities, and George and myself may not even be able to guess at all of them. The income from the new estate, whether it be paid in cash or cabbages, may have to be split seven or eight ways...'

At this, I instantly saw in my mind the image of a large pile of cabbages being apportioned between seven or eight small children, and my capacity for concentration, flimsy at the best of times, disappeared at a stroke. Men are serious creatures, but in fairness to Grandpa and Master Lewis they also saw the funny side of things and roared with laughter when I explained. I could not possibly return to weighty matters after that, and decided that I would leave the experts to it rather than cause confusion through my own ignorance. I rose to my feet and said to Grandpa Isaac: 'Grandpa, you know my mind better than I know it myself. Will you please help Master Lewis to draw up something which we might discuss later in the day? Of course I want the best for my children, born and unborn, but I also insist on written provision for the future comfort and security of you and Grandma Jane, should anything unpleasant happen to me, and also for the well-being of my tenants and all six of my servants.'

'Most irregular,' said Master Lewis.

'Irregular it may be,' said I. 'But that is what I want, and I will not sign any piece of paper unless

67

I have my way.'

The two gentlemen rolled their eyes in perfect harmony, if such a thing is possible, and then grinned and nodded. We agreed to discuss a draft settlement at lunchtime, and so I left them to their calculations and convoluted legal phrases, their inkpots and quill pens and piles of paper.

I spent the rest of the morning with the children, indoors because it was a cold and blustery day with occasional sleety showers driven down the slopes of the mountain. By midday the two gentlemen had something they were happy with, and they called me in to examine it with them. I made a few adjustments, and then agreed that they could discuss the draft document with Owain, Squire Laugharne and his attorney in the afternoon. We ate a convivial dinner. Then, by prior arrangement, the Pontfaen coach rolled into the yard at two o'clock and disgorged Owain, his father and Master Hopkins Legal, who has dusty rooms in Haverfordwest. We ushered them inside to the warmth of the house, and Owain gave me a warm and loving embrace. Much to my surprise and delight, his father insisted on doing the same. We chatted about the weather and the effects of our winter snowfalls, but there was work to be done, and wording to be agreed before darkness fell. As we talked, my apprehensions disappeared, and I realized that agreement would come easily. Master Hopkins was a very stiff gentleman, but it transpired that he and Master Lewis are old friends, which boded well for the discussions that were to follow. The Squire was also in a benign mood, and Owain explained that the three of them had shared a most excellent dinner in the Blue Boar in Newport prior to their arrival at the Plas, and that his father had enjoyed more than a few glasses of excellent red Portuguese wine alongside his roast beef.

Owain and I left the four gentlemen to it, and sat together in my dressing room for a while. We did at least manage a few moments of privacy, although we expected the children to come rushing in at any moment, following the end of their afternoon lessons. Owain explained that he and his father and Master Hopkins had sat together all morning, working things out and preparing a draft settlement; and he said that he was now thoroughly tired of the whole business. 'My dear Martha,' said he, with his arm round my shoulder, 'if this is what is involved in the business of getting married, I hereby declare to the whole world that I will do it only once. Promise me that you will never leave me!'

'Of course, Master Laugharne. I will remain at your side for ever, until the old blue rocks of the mountain are all rolled down into the valley, and the stars fly away, and the sky turns green.'

'A rash promise indeed,' he whispered into my ear. 'And what will you do if these prognostications come to pass? Will you leave me to my lonely fate, with an empty bed and a broken heart?'

'Oh no, Master Laugharne. We will go together. If the mountain is destroyed, and the bluestones roll down its slopes, they will surely sweep this old house away during the cataclysm. And at the time we will surely be in our bed, in each other's arms, and we will go to our fate in a state of blessed union. We will have much to answer for, for we ourselves will have been responsible for the shaking of the foundations of the universe...'

Owain followed my drift perfectly, and raised his eyebrows in amusement, his laughter blending with my own. Then, somehow or other and entirely without aggression or presumption on his part, his lips were upon mine, and his hand was upon my breast, and decorum was forgotten. Passion flooded through me as irresistibly as a warm spring tide. Suddenly there was a loud hammering upon the door. 'Mam! Mam! Can I come in?' said a little voice that belonged to the heir to the Plas Ingli estate. Owain and I re-arranged ourselves while I thanked the flying stars for my foresight in training the children to knock before entering my dressing room. At last I replied, as calmly as I could: 'Come in, *cariad*, and tell me what you want.' In the little fellow came, to inform us that we both had red faces, that he had not seen Uncle Owain for a very, very, very long time, and that he had come to play with him. Owain realized at once that there was no further prospect of playing with me for the time being, and acquiesced. He agreed that piggy-backs round the kitchen table would be in order, so long as Dewi promised not to tell his sisters. So the two of them tiptoed off down the stairs to the kitchen, hand in hand, whispering conspiratorially to each other like Guy Fawkes and his henchman heading for the basement of the House of Commons. I sat back with a sigh, and smiled to myself and at the world, and vowed to hold the memory of that moment close to my heart for ever.

Then the girls came back from their lessons with Sian, and my moment of calm was over. They wanted to know why all these people were in the house, and I had to explain that arrangements were being made for the wedding of Owain and myself. Then Bessie came in and said that Master Lewis Legal would be grateful for a minute or two of my time so that he might 'take instructions'. We found a private space in the office, and I instructed Bessie not to allow anybody to disturb us. We had a brief conversation during which it became clear that there were no real points of disagreement between the parties. It was very plain, said my sharp-witted attorney, that Owain had instructed Master Hopkins to seek whatever was in the best interests of me and the children, notwithstanding the instincts of his father. All were agreed, he said, that Plas Ingli should be the estate mansion house, and that Dewi should be heir to the estate even if I should bear Owain one or more sons. However, Owain asked that the oldest son to be born to us in the name of Laugharne should be allowed to succeed to the Llannerch estate as it is presently constituted. That would mean splitting the estate again in the next generation, but I thought it perfectly equitable, and said as much to Master Lewis. There were a few other minor matters to agree upon, including the provisions for Grandpa and Grandma and for the tenants and servants. Then I said: 'Thank you, Master Lewis, for all your efforts on our behalf. I trust that all is now agreed, and that Owain and I need have no further involvement. Can I leave matters now in your competent hands, and those of Hopkins Legal, until such time as you require signatures upon a piece of paper?'

'Well, yes and no, Mistress Martha,' replied Master Lewis, and I saw that there was a shadow on his face.

'Whatever do you mean?'

'If I am to act on your behalf in this matter, my dear, I must be certain that I am aware of all of the assets of the estate. And I mean *all* of them, except for future inheritances and so forth that might come from your parents, which are difficult to predict.'

'I am sure, Master Lewis, that from your ancient knowledge of our estate, and from everything that Grandpa Isaac and I have told you, you are indeed in possession of all of the facts.'

'Very well. But is there anything that you wish to tell me about the Plas Ingli treasure?'

This came at me like a thunderbolt, and I fear that colour surged into my cheeks. He noticed, of course. Attorneys always do. But I regained my composure, and said: 'There is absolutely nothing more to say. You know, Master Lewis, that in the silly business in Parc Haidd last year, assorted treasure hunters who had worked themselves up into a frenzy fought over a deep hole in the ground that proved to contain nothing other than sand and stones. You know, and we all know, that there was no treasure there.'

'I accept that. You invented that story, and put it about, and caught them in a trap that was thoroughly entertaining for all of us. But I have noticed, throughout all our conversations on this matter, before, during and after the court case

72

that sent those men to their various fates, that you have always chosen your words with the greatest of care. You will not tell a lie, and I admire you for it in these days of deceit and dishonesty. You are a worthy mistress of a fine estate, and it is a privilege to work on your behalf. But now I am afraid I have to ask you another direct question. Please, my dear, give me the blessing of a direct and truthful answer. Is there, to the best of your knowledge, a treasure buried somewhere on the Plas Ingli estate?'

For several minutes I looked at the floor, for I could not meet his eyes. My mind was in a turmoil, with attempts at rational thought disrupted by raw emotions and the remembrance of past pledges made to myself and to the angels of Carningli. But I could not lie to this good and intelligent man who had done so much for the estate over the years. So in due course I looked at him, with as much composure as I could muster, and said: 'Yes, I believe that there might be.'

'I thought as much. But I observe that the knowledge of it is a mixed blessing, and that you came to know of it in circumstances which still give you pain.'

'You are quite correct, Master Lewis. I wish that you had not reminded me of the occasion.'

'Dare I ask what the value of the treasure might be?'

'I believe it to be worth two thousand pounds at the most.'

'Very well. Do you know where it is?'

'I have a rough idea. I do not have enough information to go to it directly, and considerable

73

excavation over a wide area might be necessary in order to uncover it.'

'Do you want to tell me how you came by the knowledge of this treasure?'

'No. I am sworn to secrecy, and the person who told me is now dead. I will never divulge to a living soul either his name or the circumstances in which I came by this information.' Then, I fear, I began to shake as the memories of an appalling episode in the cave on Carningli swept over me, and as I saw the lifeless eyes of Moses Lloyd gazing into mine. Tears started rolling down my cheeks. Attorneys know how to deal with tears, and Master Lewis came over to me, sat beside me and put his arm round my shoulder.

'There now, my dear,' he said, transforming himself in an instant from attorney into friend. 'I apologize for my crass questioning. I should not have asked you so much. Here, take my kerchief, and then return it to me so that I may carry your tears far away.'

I managed a weak smile. 'Master Lewis,' I said, 'you are a true friend, and I beg that you will never repeat to a soul what I have just told you. You may think me foolish, but the approximate where-abouts of the Plas Ingli treasure is known only to me. Only I know where it came from. Please accept that it is rightfully mine. It is my security, and the security for my beloved Morgan family, in the event that the world collapses around us. Neither famine nor plague will encourage me to dig it up. I will not touch it unless the continued existence of Plas Ingli is in jeopardy, and I will not recover it unless all other avenues for the saving of my family have been explored without success. Perhaps, one day, I will lose my resolve and undo my vows. If my instinct for secrecy disappears in the comfort of old age, I'll tell Owain or the children about the gold coins in the ground, and perhaps we will then have an exciting day and do some excavating.'

'I understand you, my dear Martha. You are driven by the same imperative as a squirrel, which secretes hazel nuts as a means of combating a harsh winter when it gets the first sniff of autumn frost upon the air. I will not press you further, and I promise you that my lips are sealed. An attorney never breaks a confidence. In any case, this matter has no bearing upon the marriage settlement, and leaves nobody disadvantaged. Whoever benefits from the treasure in due course can treat it as a pleasant surprise. But please, my dear Martha, do not go to your grave before you pass on the secret to your nearest and dearest.'

'I will endeavour to follow your advice in that regard, Master Lewis,' I said, and our consultation was at an end. We smiled at each other, but said nothing more. He kissed my hand, bowed, and strode out of the room.

In due course I recovered my composure and went downstairs to join the others. Owain was still playing with the children in the kitchen. A cold dusk was beginning to settle across the *cwm*, and the sleet was turning into snow. The meeting in the parlour broke up with everybody in good spirits, and our guests left promptly so as to avoid the use of candle lanterns and shovels upon their journeys.

Supper came and went, and the children were

bathed and entertained and settled down to sleep. My recollections of the evening are hazy, for I felt utterly exhausted by the emotional and intellectual exertions of the day. I tried to relax by playing for a while on my harp, and as ever that did help me. Once again I have been bobbing about like a cork in the midst of a raging torrent, but I am still afloat, and I think I know where I am going. I hope and pray that my destination is the Ocean of Peace, where I can drift lazily upon a calm sea beneath a high sun and an azure sky.

26 January 1807

We had only a sprinkling of snow in the night, and woke to a cold day with a thin veneer of ice upon the pond. As the sun came up there was a rapid thaw, and this gave me the confidence to ride into town in the middle of the morning on my favourite pony. I had a wedding mission to complete, not on behalf of Owain and myself, but on behalf of two other good people who wish to be married in the church of St Mary in Newport.

Some days since, I received a letter from my friend Patty who lives on the Parrog in a little cottage alongside the shore not far from the lime kilns. A frequent caller to her cottage is one Jake Nicholas, the man she wishes to marry. A good fellow recently arrived in this community, Jake owns a share in a herring boat. He is a seaman who has seen the world, but the place he loves best is the sea front at Parrog, because that is where Patty is. And why should he not feel a mad passion for Patty? Such a thing is entirely natural, for she is well spoken and more intelligent than most of the gentry hereabouts. She is also very comely, with the most beautiful blue eyes, a fresh complexion, blonde hair and a shapely figure. Her hair used to be very long, but when she was freed from being a prostitute three months ago she cut it short as a sign of respectability, which made Jake very miserable for a while. But signs and signals are all important in a little village full of wagging tongues, and the handful of Nonconformists who live on the Parrog continue to whisper, with malice in their words but envy in their hearts, about the fact that Jake and Patty shelter under the same roof and share the same bed. Let them whisper.

I know a good deal about Patty and Jake, and consider them to be dear friends. In the past, they have saved me from the depredations of wicked men and have helped me to bring them to justice; and for that I will always be in their debt. Jake was instrumental in the capture, some months back, of the most nefarious of my enemies, one Alban Watkins. It was he who owned the Llannerch estate before its acquisition by the Laugharne family, he who persecuted me without mercy during the conduct of a feud against the Morgans of Plas Ingli, and he who helped me to understand through observation the full meaning of depravity. Now Watkins is dead, murdered by a vengeful Irishman, his corpse first left to rot on the shore of the estuary and finally buried (what was left of it) beneath lime in an unmarked grave. As for Patty, she too knows all about persecution. She was a respectable and well-educated servant girl before a minor indiscretion led her into the clutches – quite literally – of one Joseph Rice, another enemy of the Plas Ingli estate and one of those who was driven by lust for the treasure supposed to lie beneath the soil in the field called Parc Haidd. It was he who forced Patty into prostitution and lived off her earnings. He was one of the men who murdered my beloved David two years ago. He was a cowardly and cunning creature who lived on the proceeds of his criminal activities, and made so many enemies in his life that his death, at the hands of fellow prisoners in Haverfordwest gaol, came as no great surprise to me or anybody else.

I return to Patty's letter. This is what it said:

Parrog, 20th day of January 1807

My dear Mistress Martha,

Jake and I send you our greetings from the seaside, and report that we are both well. Food is short, but we have some small savings, and we will survive until the herrings come in. Jake and his confederates spend most of their days, weather permitting, repairing and tarring the lugger and making ropes and sails. He is very happy, and so am I, for he is a good hard-working man who will not let us starve.

Thank you for your message about your betrothal to Master Owain. Of course there was no doubt that such a thing would come to pass! He is a true gentle-man and very worthy of your love; and indeed he is lucky too, for there are many others who have dreamt of winning your hand in marriage during the time when you have had to struggle without Master David at your side. Jake and I obtain some small pleasure from the knowledge that we have helped to bring you and Master Owain together, and we wish you two, and the children, a long life of happiness together.

This brings me to the one little sadness in my life. I cannot complain, for I am at least rid of that devil Joseph Rice, and I can stay in the cottage so long as I can find the rent. But I am living with Jake, and I wish sin to be a thing of the past. I hope to find virtue as a bedfellow, and to deserve a reputation on the Parrog as a worthy and respectable citizen. I have my past to cope with, and too many men who walk around the streets of Newport know more about my body than I might have wished, but by the same token I know more about their strengths and weaknesses than they might have desired, and this knowledge may yet help in the process of my rehabilitation. Most of my neighbours know about the cruel manner in which Rice engineered my downfall and used me to earn the money that kept him alive. So there is a degree of sympathy for my plight, and there are good people urging me and Jake to get married.

Martha, my wisest and closest friend, will you please go to Rector Devonald and plead on our behalf for us to get married in church? This is my dearest wish. I fear that if I go to talk to him myself I will lose the power of speech, for he is fierce and intimidating. He will likely say that I am doomed, through fornication and other past indiscretions, to burn in the fires of Hell. But in my estimation he has a liking for you, and if anybody can persuade him to agree to giving us a church wedding, it has to be the Mistress of Plas Ingli.

Will you do it? I dare to hope that you will oblige. I will call in to see you and the little ones soon.

Your loving friend, Patty

What else could I do for a dear friend, other than make an appointment to see the Rector? Besides, I relish a challenge. Before I set off I read Patty's letter again, and could not resist a quiet smile at her skill in the arts of diplomacy. She may be a retired whore on the verge of destitution, but she writes a good letter, combining gentle compliments and felicitations with straight words where necessary, and with subtle reminders that I am in her debt and she now wants the debt repaid. I myself have used feminine wiles and reminders of indebtedness in the past, on more than one occasion, to get out of difficult corners, and why should not she? She deserves a good deal more out of life than that which is currently before her, and if I had it in my power I would find her a lucrative posting in His Majesty's Diplomatic Service.

So it was that I arrived at the Rectory at eleven of the clock, to be helped down from my horse by Master Devonald's man. I felt apprehensive but not afraid, and a good deal more confident than I might have done even a year ago in a similar circumstance. The Rector and his wife appeared at the front door to greet me, and when we had exchanged pleasantries she went off to fetch some tea while he and I settled into the study for our conversation about matrimonial matters. 'Well, well, this is very pleasant,' said he. 'I am delighted to hear of your betrothal to Master Owain Laugharne. An excellent match, if I may say so. Two good old families coming together in harmony. Very good. Very good. Now then, on the matter of the arrangements?'

'I am sorry to disappoint you, Rector, but those particular arrangements can wait for a little while. The settlement has still to be finalized, and no date is set. I have come to discuss another wedding.'

'Oh, indeed? Well, well, let us see if we can help. And who might the happy couple be?'

'Patty Ellis and Jake Nicholas, from the Parrog.'

I watched Master Devonald's face with more than a little interest. First it registered puzzlement, then comprehension, apprehension, and finally horror. His face reddened, and his eyes started to bulge. Breathing deeply, he sought to control his own emotions. With his eyes closed, he brought his hands up to his chin in a gesture of prayer. The ticking of the clock on his study wall grew very loud. I knew that I had a problem and a challenge on my hands.

'Are you surprised, Rector?' I asked. 'I presume you know the good people on whose behalf I am here?'

'Yes, I know of them,' he replied in a strangled voice. 'The one is a fisherman by trade, and the other is a common...'

Buffoon that he is, he could not bring himself to mention the word. So I helped him. 'A common whore?'

He nodded like a frail old man carrying the weight of the world's sin upon his shoulders. At last he steeled himself to face the problem which now confronted him. He straightened his back and looked me in the eye. 'I cannot possibly allow it,' he said, as masterfully as he could. 'It is absolutely out of the question for a prostitute to be married in the House of God. Maybe a licence can be arranged, but I will never marry those two in church.'

'You disappoint me, Rector.'

'Your disappointment, Mistress Morgan, is a small price to pay for an irrevocable decision which is based upon a respect for the Ten Commandments and my desire to encourage virtue among my parishioners.'

At that moment Mistress Devonald came in, served tea and cakes with a sweet smile upon her face, and then retired to the warmth of the kitchen when she sensed a chill in the air.

I worked out my strategy while I nibbled and sipped. Then I played my opening card. 'On the matter of Patty Ellis's profession,' I said, 'may I remind you, Rector, that it is a thing of the past? She is a reformed character, as many of your parishioners will attest, since they now have to travel all the way to Fishguard to visit Moll Liberal Favours when they have a few pennies to spend.'

The Rector flushed to a beautiful shade of crimson. 'Whatever do you mean?' he spluttered.

'You know perfectly well what I mean. I do not need to elaborate. And are you aware, Rector, of the circumstances which drove Patty into prostitution?' He shook his head, and I continued. 'Then let me explain. It will be no bad thing, in my view, for you and other gentlemen in authority to know what happened to this poor girl; we might then move from condemnation towards compassion, and from punishment towards rehabilitation. We might even seek to move towards an understanding of the word "forgiveness", since that is a

82

word we do not hear very often from your pulpit.'

That, in retrospect, was very unkind of me, and also risky, since I have to admit to a somewhat haphazard attendance at church myself. But I calculated that since the Rector's attendance in church is also haphazard, I might get away with my insolence. And so I did. Before he could open his mouth to respond, I told him the full story of Patty's entrapment by Joseph Rice, and of her miserable life in the boudoir while he lived in some comfort as a pimp. The Rector is not very familiar with the details of a whore's life, and I dare say that he found my narrative more than a little enlightening.

By the time I had finished, Master Devonald was sunk deeply into his chair, with an expression of resignation on his face. Poor fellow, I thought, he is kind enough, and does his best, but he should really have been an attorney's clerk or a shopkeeper rather than a man of the cloth. I almost started to feel sorry for him, but then I remembered that I had a job to do, and that on occasion one must kick a man when he is down.

'I am not very practised in matters theological, Rector, but did not our good Lord have more than a passing acquaintance with a lady called Mary Magdalene?' He nodded weakly, for he could see what was coming. 'And did he not demonstrate, in his dealings with her, that those who are fallen can be saved, and those who are penitent and change their ways may enter the Kingdom of Heaven? Am I free of sin? Are you, Master Devonald, ordained as a priest, free of sin? But we poor sinners take comfort from the promise of redemption. Did Christ not also say that all of us, no matter what our station in life, obtain grace through forgiveness, and that we must seek to follow His will? My dear Rector, do you have the good grace to forgive this poor girl, and to extend the hand of friendship towards her?'

I dare say that this piece of sermonizing on my part was all very garbled, but it had the effect of keeping him quiet. Before he had had a chance to work out a theological riposte, and while he was still down, I thought I might as well kick him again.

'On more practical matters, Rector, how many allocated pews do you have in St Mary's church?'

He looked at first surprised and then suspicious. He knew that this question must be leading somewhere, but he could not work out the direction of travel or the steepness of the slope. 'About fifteen, I believe,' he said.

'I thought as much. You include, no doubt, the Morgans of Plas Ingli. That means that fifteen of the best families in this area contribute to your well-being, and to the upkeep of the church, as well as paying their tithes on time and making contributions to the poor rate?'

He nodded. Then I said: 'Would you like me to tell you how many of the squires who sit in those pews of a Sunday morning, all happily married and seen as the very pillars of society, have been regular clients of Patty Ellis in her cottage on the Parrog?'

'You would not dare!' exclaimed the Rector, with the look of a hunted man on his face.

'Indeed I would. I happen to be very friendly

84

with Patty Ellis, but in the days before her reformation her tongue was as loose as the associations into which she was forced to enter. I assure you that I know a great deal about her clients. And before I forget, may I ask you a theological question?'

'Oh, dear, I suppose so,' he said with an ill-disguised grimace.

'On the scale of things, when we are called to account, which is the greater sin, fornication or adultery? Is it not the case that adultery is mentioned in the Ten Commandments, but that there is no mention of fornication? And might that be because the former involves betrayal, whereas the latter simply involves frailty, and the sharing of a little pleasure by two like-minded people?'

Once again I perceived that I was in danger of getting a somewhat complicated and protracted theological response, so I continued after the briefest sip of tea. 'To return to your parishioners, Rector, would you like the names of those august gentlemen who sit before you in their paid pews and who have, to my certain knowledge, betrayed their wives and families and made adulterous visits to Patty's feather bed?'

'No indeed, Mistress Martha, please do not tell me. It is probably best that I do not know these things.' He squirmed in his seat, and wrung his hands like Pontius Pilate.

'Very well, Rector. I will keep their secret. But your part of the bargain will be to announce to the world that Patty is forgiven, that she will be welcomed into the bosom of the Church, and that you will give her and Jake a church wedding.'

'This sounds to me like blackmail, and black-mail ill becomes a lady.'

'No, no, Rector. What we are talking about is a course of action which brings mutual benefit. I make an oath of secrecy, you demonstrate Christian charity to your parishioners, and Patty and Jake get a church wedding. By the way, I will pay for it. Happiness all round.'

'And if I do not co-operate in this murky business?'

'Then I will give you the list of names, and await your response. A public denunciation of the adulterous squires from your pulpit should suffice.'

'Absolutely impossible! The Lord Marcher would probably take away my living, and my relations with the good families of this area would be at an end!'

'But you would be a hero with the poor people, as well as showing yourself to be a true man of God. You must decide, Rector, which may be the lesser of two evils.'

The poor fellow groaned and slumped deep into his chair once again. Time for one final kick with my booted foot. 'Incidentally, I forgot to mention that my father, whose estate is at Brawdy, is on the most amiable of terms with the Bishop of St David's. They dine together frequently, and share many confidences. Having given you the list of adulterous squires, I will of course ensure that the Bishop is informed of the scandalous situation that has developed in Newport. He will no doubt keep a careful eye on your actions in upholding virtue and condemning vice.'

The Rector was now entirely at my mercy, and

he knew it. I have to admit to enjoying the situation, but to feeling more than a little sorry for him, for he is by no means a bad fellow. He follows his calling moderately well, and ministers to his flock appropriately enough, when occasion demands it. However, he does like a peaceful life, just like the rest of us. He had no option but to agree to my proposal, and he admitted as much.

'Will you now go to visit Patty and Jake in their cottage as a gesture of forgiveness? The locals will take note, and will be very impressed. There is a lot of sympathy for the couple on the Parrog. There will be some wagging tongues, especially among the Baptists, but you can deal with them, and if I get the chance I will defend your actions and express my admiration for your magnanimity. Others will do the same. Your standing in the community, Rector, will be greatly enhanced. You may take it from me.'

He brightened up considerably. 'Do you really think so?' he asked.

'Absolutely. And you will also make the Nonconformists, in their complaining, look mean-spirited and vengeful in the eyes of fair-minded people. Will you now fix a date with Jake and Patty, and arrange for the reading of the banns?'

'Yes, very well. But what if I receive objections from my congregation on the basis that Patty is – or was – a loose woman?'

'I doubt that you will. The squires who are Patty's past clients will certainly not say a word, and if anybody else does, I am sure you can deal with anything that might be raised. You have the final word, Rector, on whether any objection is serious enough to be a true impediment to the marriage, and I have every confidence, considering the interests of all those involved, that it will go ahead.'

I smiled at the Rector, who managed a weak smile in return; it was clear that we understood each other. Then I stood up. 'Thank you so much, Rector, for the delightful refreshments and for our most interesting conversation. We must talk again of theological matters one day, since I am keen to know more about the scriptures.'

'Heaven forbid, Mistress Morgan! Of course you are always welcome at the Rectory, but may I suggest that you leave the scriptures, and the interpretation of them, in my hands?' And to his credit he chuckled at his little joke, and then gave a great roar of laughter, and I had to follow suit. And so we parted eventually on the best of terms.

Twenty minutes later I knocked on the door of Patty's cottage on the Parrog. After my triumph I was grinning with glee, and she welcomed me with open arms.

'It is all fixed!' I declared. 'You and Jake can have your church wedding!'

Patty could hardly believe it, and before long the pair of us were dancing around her front room giggling and screaming like a pair of little girls. I fear that the neighbours must have been very shocked, for sound travels easily on the Parrog. At last we calmed down enough to talk, and Patty insisted that I gave her all the details of my conversation with the Rector. As I spoke she looked more and more surprised, and at last she intervened, and said: 'But Mistress Martha, who are all these worthy squires who are supposed to have paid me visits in the past? I declare that I cannot remember a single one.'

'Oh dear, is that so?' said I. 'What a pity. Perhaps I have misheard something, or misunderstood the matter. I really must concentrate more in the future, and ensure that I get my facts right.'

As we embraced, with another fit of girlish laughter, Patty wept tears of unadulterated joy.

2 February 1807

I have been up onto the mountain. For the last few days the weather has been cold and clear, and there has even been a little warmth in the sun. The days are lengthening perceptibly. Jack Frost is still in control of the landscape, and no doubt we will have more snow in the weeks to come, but spring cannot be far away, and this blessed day was a reminder of the fact that the sun will eventually win the battle of the seasons.

After a chaotic breakfast at which the children were very ill behaved, causing Grandpa Isaac to display his irritation more than once, I had to do some work on the estate accounts. Sian took the children on a brisk walk down to Gelli, to deliver some eggs and cheese to her parents Caradoc and Bethan. Poor Caradoc is confined to bed just now, having suffered a heavy fall in the sea quarry near Aberfforest a few days back. Nothing broken, says Havard Medical, but many cuts and bruises which will only be healed by the passage of time. Caradoc is fretting a good deal, not so much because of his injuries as because of his lost income and because he fears that while he is away the quarry will degenerate into a shambles. I think he is well out of it for a while. The sea quarry is a dangerous place, with ropes and pulleys and flimsy wooden platforms teetering over the water. Those bleak faces of flaky slate, just above the waves and exposed to the full force of the north wind, sap the energy and the health out of men who already have to suffer enough from poverty and hunger. Eight quarrymen have died young in the last two years – four from accidents, two from the effects of breathing slate dust, and two from pneumonia. At any rate, the children will cheer Caradoc up for a while, and he will no doubt amuse himself, and them, by telling them stirring tales of pirates and smugglers.

By ten o'clock the Plas was quiet. Grandpa and Grandma had taken the trap and set off for a morning of social visits and shopping in Newport. The men were busy outside, mucking out the cowshed, feeding the sheep, and repairing stone walls. Mrs Owen was in the dairy, churning thin winter milk and dreaming of buttercups and summer. That left only Bessie and myself in the house, and she wanted me out of there so that she could clean my dressing room and bedroom. She noticed that I was in no mood for record keeping.

'I see that scribing and mathematics do not appeal to you greatly this morning, Mistress,' said she.

'Quite correct, Bessie. I do not feel inspired by figures today. I am thinking too much of other things. The children were very naughty at breakfast. Grandpa and Grandma are more than a little short-tempered these days, and Shemi and Will were exchanging harsh words over the best way to repair the wall near Parc Ganol. I am getting worried about Billy's liking for brandy and tobacco. And I do not seem to be able to tear my mind away from wedding arrangements, and churches, and reverend gentlemen.'

'The winter sickness, Mistress.'

'I beg your pardon?'

'Maybe in past winters you have been too busy with the little ones to notice it,' said Bessie. 'But the miserable weather, and the pitch blackness of the evenings, and the bare trees and frozen soil, and all of us cooped up together like chickens sheltering from a storm – it all leads to misery and short tempers. Two suicides last month, one near Brynberian and the other on the mountain above Gelli Fawr. Loneliness is the chief culprit, Mistress. Not that that is your particular problem. Too many of us under the same roof, more like.'

'You are probably quite right, Bessie. It has been a long winter, stretching back to those terrible events of November and December which almost tore our family to pieces. What happened then probably drained more vitality out of me than I have been prepared to admit.'

'Have you got enough energy left to get up to the top of the mountain?'

Thus, once again, did my blessed handmaiden demonstrate that she knows me better than I know myself. She knew that I had not been on the summit of Carningli for several weeks, and that the wild winds, wide horizons and crusted boulders were calling me. I felt ashamed that I had not heard them myself. Of course, I had to go. So I put down my quill pen, closed my account book, and replaced the lid on the inkpot. I embraced Bessie, as I always do when she demonstrates her genius, and asked her to put out my warmest woollen dress, shawl and stockings. Ten minutes later, with stout boots upon my feet and furry mittens on my hands, I was on my way, inhaling the heady breath of freedom deep into my lungs.

I followed the water pipe up to Ffynnon Brynach. The pool had ice round the edges, but in the centre the clear clean water was gushing out from beneath the mountain with its usual force. Grandpa says that the stream has never stopped, and never will. I anointed myself, as I always do when I pass the sacred spring, as Saint Brynach did in days of old, and on I went, through crackling dead bracken and dusty heather until I reached the first tumbled boulders. I passed three mountain ponies and a few Brithdir ewes which must have managed to escape the autumn round-up. They were thin, and I thought it a miracle that they had survived the heavy snows of last month.

Up I went onto the jagged terrain where banks of broken boulders and bluestone crags are interspersed with little grassy hollows. Past the last of the stunted holly trees. Carefully across the outermost of the ruined stone walls that once protected animals and people from the ruthless tribes that hunted in the *cwm*. Gingerly through the little circular enclosures which, according to Squire Fenton, were the sites of crude thatched shelters back in the days of the Druids – taking care to step only on stones and to avoid placing my feet where greenery might cover crevices deep enough to break a leg. Now following sheep tracks, then following a route that I could have walked blind, across wide sloping slabs and boulders as big as labourers' cottages. How many times, I wondered idly, had I passed this way since my arrival at the Plas more than ten years ago? And how many times had my little pilgrimage calmed my troubled breast and washed away the nonsense from inside my head?

It was my decision for today not to stop until I was on the summit, and ten minutes later I scrambled breathlessly up over the last of the rock faces and stood there, with my arms held wide and the world beneath my booted feet. The sun was up, still low and hazy over Mynydd Presely, and there were no clouds but for a few smudges on the western horizon. The familiar landscape faded into the haze in all directions. There was no wind, and out in the bay the surface of the winter sea was disturbed only by some long slow swells rolling in from an invisible storm far out in the Atlantic Ocean. They piled high as they came into the shallows of Berry Sands, and crashed onto the beach, throwing white foam at the wading birds along the water's edge and sending thunder to the top of Carningli.

I looked down at the roof of the Plas, and reminded myself how much I loved the place. Smoke was drifting up from all three of the chimney stacks. The north-facing slate roofs of the big house, stable and cowshed were all in shadow, glistening white with hoar frost. The big door of

93

the barn was wide open. Billy was walking from the coach-house to the dairy, carrying something heavy. He was whistling an old Welsh hymn tune, which I found amusing since he never goes to church or chapel. Shemi was feeding the sheep in the paddock behind the rickyard. Bessie appeared, carrying the carpet from my bedroom, and started to beat it with a big stick. Will was struggling with a heavily loaded wheelbarrow along the mountain track, transporting the stones needed for the repair of the Parc Ganol wall.

I began to feel cold, and decided on a short visit to my cave. So I scrambled down across the frosty south-facing crags, found my secret route between the bluestone boulders, and slipped away from all contact with the outside world. Nobody could see me here, even with a spyglass trained on the mountain, as I squeezed through narrow gaps, ducked under overhanging rock faces, jumped across chasms and wriggled along a gully hardly wide enough to take a sheep. Then I came to the grassy passage bounded by walls of blue rock, saw the little rowan tree that shows me where the entrance of the cave is located, and found the two rough pillars split by cracks and crusted with lichen. I brushed aside the dead fern fronds and white grasses that masked the slit in the rock, and slipped inside.

It was surprisingly warm, and pitch black. In the summer, some light filters in when the sun is high, but not now. I did not need to see, for I saw with my mind's eye every inch of the rough walls, every undulation of the roof, every patch of gravel and bare rock on the floor. Crouching down and minding my head, I made my way to the back of the cave and settled onto my mossy bed close to the beating heart of the mountain. I pulled my knees up to my chin, and closed my eyes, and listened to my own breathing. Cares and concerns floated away, to be replaced by a deep and lovely serenity. Over the course of a minute, or an hour, recollections of the terror which I have experienced here in the past drifted into my mind and drifted out again without causing me distress. I wondered how many others had sat on this bed of moss in years gone by. Moses Lloyd, for one. And little Daisy last year, when she wandered off and was saved by the raven and – according to her – by fairies and elves. And then, of course, old Saint Brynach, who came here when he needed to escape from the bustle of monastery life. He found shelter here from the elements, and according to the old legends sat on the grassy patch near the mountain summit in order to commune with the angels. He did not need to do that, I thought, for the angels are surely here too, in this dark warm cave, visible to those who have a mind to see them. My angels.

I know not how long I sat there, but realized with a jolt that time was passing. When I popped my head out into the fresh air I could not see the sun, but I could tell from the shadows that it was sliding gently westwards. Mid-afternoon, and I felt hungry. Time to go home.

Ten minutes later, as I scrambled down the slope of broken rock fragments leading to Ffynnon Brynach, I saw the old raven. He was perched on the topmost branch of a dead ash tree, maybe twenty yards away from me. He looked at me, and I looked at him. We know each other very well, I thought, and have shared many experiences together. He cocked his head, preened his feathers for a while, and then, without making a sound, launched himself lazily into the air. He flapped his great black wings, displaying the battered and ragged feathers of his wing-tips, and spiralled effortlessly upwards, higher and higher above the mountain, as I stood and watched. Soon he was but a speck in the sky, maybe two thousand feet over my head. Then he was so high up that I could not see him any more, no matter how hard I strained my eyes.

I wondered how old that ancient raven might be. Decades, or centuries? What things has he seen in his time? He surely does not miss much. He knows everything – every stone on this mountain, every whispering blade of grass, every purple blaze of heather, every scuttling mouse and burrowing rabbit, every ephemeral bank of snow and streaming gully and sunlit bank. He knows everything about the Plas, and everything that goes on beneath its roof. Is he real, or does he exist simply in my mind? I cannot be sure. No matter. If it should fall to me to decide my fate in years to come, I think that I should like to be a raven.

3 February 1807

Euphoria one day, and desolation the next. Such seems to be the pattern of my life. News reached me this afternoon that three men are dead, having been strung up on the gallows in Haverford-west gaol. I was the one who sent them to their deaths. It happened yesterday morning, by a cruel irony at exactly the time when I was immersed in serenity on the top of the mountain.

How am I supposed to feel at the receipt of such news? True, those men deserved to die, and died because the heavy wheels of justice had finally rolled over them. They were arrested, incarcerated, tried in a court of law according to the traditions of our land, and allowed to defend themselves. They were duly sentenced to death by a fair-minded judge. The King was given the opportunity of exercising his royal mercy, but chose, in the light of the gravity of their crimes, not to do so. Their miserable lives were extinguished, one after another, in the courtyard of Haverfordwest gaol, in front of a crowd of silent onlookers. Within that crowd was my brother Morys, Baptist minister and Christian gentleman, who had given the three of them the last rites and had, for the last six weeks or so, ministered to them in their filthy cells. He will never tell me what passed between them, but I have to admire the charity of a man whose faith is strong enough to offer the love of Christ to three of the men who killed his sister's husband.

John Howell of Henllys, Ifan Beynon of Berry Hill, and Matthew Lloyd of Cwmgloyn were three of the men who murdered my beloved David on the sands of Traeth Mawr during the annual *cnapan* contest on the 12th day of February in 1805. The date is carved into the very depth of my heart. They, together with their fellow conspirator

Joseph Rice, were playing in the mighty throng for the Nevern side, while David, Billy and Shemi played for Newport. The murder of my dear man involved a bizarre combination of chance and opportunism, and I am still not entirely sure of the motives behind it, but there can be no doubt as to their guilt. They also tortured and tried to kill Owain Laugharne, my new love and the man who has restored my sanity. They might have got away with their heinous crimes had it not been for the dogged determination and extraordinary intellect of my friend Joseph Harries, who sees things that other men do not see and who knows things that would tip others over the precipice of insanity. Many allies, including Lewis Legal, played their part in bringing the murderers to justice. But I know that it was I who was responsible for bringing them to court and for placing the hangman's noose round their necks. While they thought that they were pursuing me and seeking the Plas Ingli treasure in the field called Parc Haidd, I was in reality pursuing them. I laid a trap for them, and they fell into it with such naivety that I still feel a degree of sorrow and disappointment at their stupidity and the ease of my own triumph.

Should I, if I were older and wiser, now be capable of setting emotion to one side? Late at night, as I sit at my desk, I still feel as I did this afternoon when I opened and read Morys's brief letter. I had not expected it, and it left me speechless. No exultation, no pleasure – not even satisfaction. Just an emptiness in my stomach and a sense that my heart had turned to ice. Three men now dead because of me. Three more corpses to be laid out on the stony verges of the road to Hell, alongside those of Moses Lloyd, Alban Watkins, John Fenton, Joseph Rice, George Howell, Benjamin Rice and Mistress Maria Rice. Only I know that they are all dead, and how they died.

Ten people dead over ten years because of me. Am I some sort of Dark Angel of avengement, swooping over the bleak winter landscape of Pembrokeshire intent upon the destruction of whole families? For every death, there are probably another ten people – parents, siblings, children – whose lives are blighted and who will live out their days in misery. I fear that I will not sleep tonight, and I pray to God that in the morning, when I open my shutters, some light will be let into my soul.

4 February 1807

Last night, absorbed as I was in my private world of grief and guilt, I forgot that today is Dewi's fourth birthday. I was awake for most of the night, sometimes with my head resting on a pillow dampened by tears, and sometimes wrapped in my warmest dressing gown and gazing out through my unshuttered window into the impenetrable darkness. I could not wait for the dawn to come, but at last I heard the sounds of Mrs Owen and Bessie in the kitchen. Then I heard low voices and heavy feet stamping on the kitchen flagstones as Billy, Will and Shemi emerged from their rooms and prepared for the day. Doors creaked open and slammed shut. An hour later little Sara woke up in the nursery and started to cry. Sian, ever attentive, was at her side in an instant, giving her a cuddle, making her comfortable and putting a cup of warm milk to her lips. I could, and should, have done all that myself. However, terrible mother that I am, I had no heart for it and no strength in my legs for a walk across the landing to the nursery. Sian must have known it, as they all know it, for they all saw my reaction yesterday when I read the letter from Morys.

The first streaks of light illuminated the underside of the cloud bank far away over the eastern horizon. Dawn at last. As soon as it was light enough to see properly, I heard horses' hooves clattering on the slate slabs of the yard, and somebody went off at the gallop along the mountain track to the north. I wondered idly about the identity of the rider, but I was so tired that my mind was working at the speed of a slow-worm, and I cared little for anything outside my own head and heart.

Then, whether I welcomed it or not, the world burst in on me. Dewi, with his blue eyes gleaming and his cheeks aglow and his blond locks as unruly as ever, rushed in without knocking. I had no time to scold him for his lack of good manners, for he ran across the room and flung himself into my arms. 'Mam! Mam! I am four years old! Soon I will be as old as Daisy and Betsi! Can we have a picnic today, or a big party? I want to eat lots of cakes and play funny games! Have I got any presents, Mam? Have I?'

'Calm down, child!' I laughed, as he bounced up and down on my lap, banishing my self-obsession

100

and misery at a stroke. 'First things first, if you please. For a start, a picnic is out of the question, since that heavy sky tells me that snow is on the way. And yes, we will have a little party with cakes and games. And yes, there might even be some presents for you later on, once you are washed and dressed and have eaten your breakfast.'

Then the three girls came in, followed by my two female servants. Sian ushered the girls, and their excited brother, off to complete their morning ablutions, and Bessie saw from my haggard face and dishevelled looks that I had been awake all night.

'Too much thinking about that letter from Master Morys, Mistress?' I nodded as she settled down on her knees at the hearth with fire lighting in mind. 'Well, as Grandma Jane said yesterday, it doesn't do to dwell at great length on the deaths of evil men. Mourn the deaths of good people, by all means, she said, but those who get their just deserts must make their peace with God. You did your duty and brought them to justice, Mistress, and if they had still been free men today we would all be living in terror, and so would lots of other innocent folk.'

I nodded again. Without looking up from her arrangement of kindling and coals in the fireplace, Bessie continued: 'I saw that you were in some distress last night, and was not surprised by it. I thought you might appreciate a little visit from Master Joseph. I imagine that he will not have heard of the hangings yet. So Shemi has gone off over the mountain to tell him the news. I trust, Mistress, that you will not be upset by what I have done?'

I had to smile. 'On the contrary, Bessie. Thank you for your consideration, and for appreciating that wise words from my old friend will be very welcome in the circumstances.'

So it was that two hours later Joseph and Shemi pulled up their ponies in the yard just as the first flurries of snow started to fall from a lowering sky. It was very cold, and I looked at the weather glass and saw that it was dropping fast. I knew that a blizzard was on the way, and that Joseph would not be able to stay for long. I welcomed him with all the affection I could muster, and gave him a mug of steaming tea to warm up both his hands and his gullet. 'Much as I love to be here with you, my dear, I must return after an hour,' he said, 'or the blizzard will trap me. Bad business about the hangings. Shemi told me. Justice has been done, but I am not surprised that you are upset. Shall we talk in the parlour?'

'Yes please, Joseph,' said I, leading the way. 'We will have a little privacy there, for the children are busy with their lessons. And before you go you will have a bowl of potato broth to remind you that it is one of my tasks in life to ensure that my friends are well fed.'

We talked and talked. I was very emotional at first. Joseph perceived that I was tired, but he put his arm around my shoulder and then held my hand, and in a way that I am at a loss to understand (although it has happened many times before) strength flowed from his body into mine. He has a cool and clear perception of the world which I can only envy. As he talked I realized that my dear friend is not simply a *dyn hysbys;* but a *wise* man as well. He has a wisdom which I fear will for ever elude me.

Over the course of our conversation he convinced me that I could not have acted in any other way than to bring three murderers to justice, and that responsibility for their deaths must be shared between the villains themselves and the law of the land. It is the duty of all citizens, said Joseph, to uphold the law at all times, so long as the law is just. There is an additional moral responsibility placed upon the strong to assist the weak and upon the rich to help the poor. In all respects, said Joseph, I had done what was right. What, he asked, might have been the depredations upon the weakest and most vulnerable members of our community had those three men been allowed to go free? What terror might they have inflicted upon my own beloved family? So we talked of morality and responsibility. But I knew that I had rejoiced in the hunting and the capture of the villains, and that I had felt an almost sensuous pleasure in seeing them flung into the Newport lock-up and then sent to the dungeons of the county gaol. 'Was that not some sort of perversion?' I asked. 'Dear Joseph, how could I have felt such joy through the visitation of misery – and ultimately death – upon other human beings?'

'I understand it, dearest Martha, all too well. I have felt such emotions myself. We all get caught up in the excitement of the chase, and because we are frail we sometimes react in ways which later bring us shame. Have you not observed the disgraceful behaviour of mourners at a wake, indulging in laughter and drunkenness and other lewd behaviour precisely at a time when one might expect silence and decorum? It is all to do with the tightening of a bowstring inside the body, and then the sudden release. Tension cannot be maintained for too long, Martha. Release has to come, and sometimes it brings unexpected consequences.'

'I think I recognize that, Joseph. But it chills me, and I fear that when I was in pursuit of those men I was driven by the imperative of vengeance and by a sort of blood lust.'

'Blood lust, no. I never observed that in you, although I watched you closely. You kept yourself admirably under control. Vengeance – maybe. You were hunting down the killers of your husband and the torturers of your new suitor. But I do not believe that your thoughts of vengeance ever reached obsession. And I sensed that after the capture and condemnation of the prisoners you stood back, breathed deeply, and worked in your heart in order to find that elusive quality called forgiveness.'

My eyes widened. 'That is precisely what I tried to do,' said I, 'but without notable success. How did you know that?'

'Martha, my dear, you are not the first or the last of my friends to have travelled this particular journey. You have tried, and that is all that matters. You have moved farther along the road than many whose names I could mention. Be satisfied with what you have achieved. Keep working on your heart, if you will. Owain will help you more than I, since love and forgiveness go together. A loving heart is a heart enlarged, with room for forgiveness within it.'

'Should I go to Owain and share my distress with him?'

'You must decide that for yourself. He may not yet know about the hangings. News travels slowly to Llannerch, and he is not a great one for gossip.'

I smiled. 'Yes, I know that. I fear that I am very indecisive in this matter. Owain suffered far more than I at the hands of those monsters, and I am concerned that a deep discussion about my emotional state might bring all sorts of horrors flooding back into his mind. On balance, I incline to the view that I might be wiser to deal with this alone.'

'Dear Martha!' said Joseph. 'Always the martyr! But your kindness and consideration in seeking to protect those you love are blessed virtues. May those virtues protect you from evil. Write Owain a little note, if you will.'

Then he gave me a kiss on my cheek and sprang to his feet. 'Now then, my dear friend, I can smell the vapours of good potato broth wafting in from the kitchen. That Mrs Owen is a miracle worker. If I were older, I would marry her myself. May I tackle a bowl before I go? In twenty minutes I will be off, and the blizzard will strike just as I get home.'

When he left I have to say that I felt a good deal better, calmed and reassured exactly as Bessie knew I would be. The wind growled and prowled around the house for an hour, trying to decide in which quarter it should settle. Then it made up its mind that a few degrees north of east would do, and built up to a climax until it was whining and screaming at the house and the other buildings ranged around the yard. We were ready for it, and the animals were all quite safe. The snow came, horizontally, not in gentle fluffy flakes but in grains as hard as sand, assaulting everything that dared to stand in its way and insinuating itself into every crack and crevice in doors, windows and eaves. We did not care, since we were cosy enough indoors, and besides, we had a birthday to celebrate. Guests from near or far would have been risking life and limb had they been foolish enough to try to reach us for the occasion; but there were enough of us anyway, and little Dewi had a wonderful time as the centre of attention. He has a pile of new toys, all of which have been manufactured beneath this roof over the past weeks from wood, paper and fabric. Now he and his sisters are in bed and fast asleep, having had their fill of silly games, cakes and custards, sweetmeats and jellies. I too have eaten too much rich food, and I trust that I will not lose too much sleep as a consequence. Life is very complicated. Last night I struggled with guilt, and tonight I will surely struggle with indigestion!

5 February 1807

The blizzard did not last long, and had blown itself through by the morning. It remained very cold. There were heavy drifts of powdery snow on the lee sides of walls and buildings, but by the early afternoon the men had cleared them away and contact was re-established with the world.

This morning I shut myself away for half an hour and penned a short note to Owain, telling him about the executions. I explained that I had been greatly upset when I received the news from Morys, but that I had now accepted the deaths with the help of wise words from Joseph. I hoped that he himself would not find the news too distressing. I told him that I loved him and longed to see him again, and asked him to call in soon. After dinner Shemi took the bay pony and delivered the letter to Llannerch. He brought back a loving reply from the lord of my heart, and that made me feel a good deal better. He said that he would be greatly involved in the Pontfaen barley threshing for the next few days, but promised to call in within the week.

Sian and Will walked down to town with some eggs, bacon and milk for Hettie at her lodging house, and returned just before dark with further news about the hangings in Haverfordwest. Apparently John Howell and Ifan Beynon were buried in unmarked graves somewhere outside the town walls, since their relatives refused to take the bodies home. But Meredith Lloyd, having received notification of the date and time of the hangings, travelled personally to the county gaol with the Cwmgloyn pony and trap to fetch the body of his brother Matthew. He could not bring himself to watch the executions, but afterwards he took the body while still warm, wrapped it in a blanket, and drove it all the way home across the mountain to his estate. The vicar of Bayvil would not allow burial in the parish churchyard, so

107

Meredith had his men dig a grave in the rose-garden close to the big house, and they buried him there yesterday morning, in a coffin made by Davy Death. According to Sian, who heard it from Hettie, who heard it from the driver of the Haverfordwest mail coach, the vicar at first refused to say a few prayers before the filling of the grave, but Meredith insisted upon it, and said that he would give the Bayvil living to somebody else if the man did not co-operate. So prayers were said, in the presence of Meredith and two of the estate labourers, and the grave was filled and marked with a simple wooden cross.

I cannot explain why, but I was greatly touched when I heard this tale. It confirmed my belief that Meredith is a good soul, and it showed me something of the love that can exist between a man and his brother, no matter how far that brother may have fallen from grace. It taught me something also of what it means to belong to an old patch of ground and to an old family, and I greatly admired Meredith's capacity for remaining dignified in the face of public humiliation and disapprobation. The thought of his quiet resolution brought a lump to my throat, and I determined that when this miserable spell of weather is over and done with I will make a visit to Cwmgloyn and seek to further improve relations between our two families and our two estates.

7 February 1807

Terror has returned to my life, and not just

108

because of happenings inside my own head. I am stretched on a rack of fear not because of my reaction to events reported by others, but because I have seen something with my own eyes which I can hardly believe even now, six hours later.

It happened like this. In mid-morning the snow returned, having threatened to do so for the last two days. We did not have to put up with a full-blown blizzard this time, but there was a north wind rolling down off the mountain, and the eddies of bitterly cold air swirled the snowflakes around in all directions, piling them up here and removing them there, and then rearranging them all again. The children loved it, and spent the afternoon playing in the clean whiteness of the yard and the orchard.

By four of the clock the dusk was settling in, and I called the little ones back to the house so that they could thaw their frozen fingers and chapped cheeks and get changed into dry clothes before supper. They came inside, under protest, and Sian stripped off their snow-covered coats, hats, scarves and mittens in the kitchen. Then they sat in a row like four rosy-cheeked cherubs in front of the eternal kitchen fire, gazing at the flames and clutching mugs of steaming, creamy milk. Leaving them to it, I decided on a walk round the farm buildings, to check that the animals were secure and all gates and doors safely shut for the night. I said that I might be out for an hour. The men were still at work with the feeding and milking, and I exchanged pleasantries with them as I went along my way. The snow was swirling and dancing on the wind, and I could see no more than fifty yards in any direction. I felt light-hearted, as one does sometimes in a fog, contained as one is within a little world of one's own.

Then I saw it. An unrecognizable creature, standing in the semi-darkness on the bank behind the house, no more than thirty yards away from me. It stood absolutely still, almost as if it were a statue made of stone, black from tip to toe. A heavy black cloak covered the whole of its body from neck to feet. It had a tall wide-brimmed black hat upon its head, and its face was hidden behind a black muffler. I could not see its arms, and assumed they were folded under the cloak. The creature just stood there, with snowflakes settling on its shoulders, the brim of the hat, and the folds of the cloak. It was watching me, and made no attempt to move. I was so surprised, and so instantly terrified, that I staggered backwards, feeling my way towards the wall of the dairy without taking my eyes off it. I was too frightened even to scream. As I retreated, I knew that its gaze was fixed upon me. After some minutes I found the sanctuary of the wall, and slid along it until I reached the corner. Then I turned and scrambled towards the kitchen door of the house. I was about to enter when I remembered that the children were lined up contentedly before the fire, and I knew that my wild eyes and shaking hands would frighten them out of their wits if I should go inside. So I determined to hide in the dairy instead. I lifted the latch, slipped into the cold darkness within, and closed the door behind me.

This, in retrospect, was the worst thing I could have done. There was no light in there, and not even a dead candle or an empty lantern, since this was a place of damp slate slabs sluiced with icy water twice every day. I huddled into the corner, and although I was well wrapped up I realized after a while that my teeth were chattering through a combination of cold and fear. The wind moaned through the gap between the house and the dairy, and there was just about enough light to see flurries of snow blowing through the cracks in the door. Had the monster seen me coming into the dairy? Would it follow me? Just to make sure of my safety I felt my way along the wall to the place where the two butter churns are kept. I identified the smaller one on its wooden frame, and pushed and dragged it in the darkness over to the door. I jammed it into position and then collapsed onto the floor, quite exhausted. Gasping for breath, I crawled back to the far corner and sat there with my knees drawn up to my chin, my eyes fixed upon the door and my ears pricked for any faint sound which might be out of the ordinary.

I have no idea how long I sat there, getting colder and colder. I began to fear that I might freeze to death. But at last I saw lights through the window and heard voices. Billy, Shemi and Will were all out in the yard, waving their lanterns and searching for me. They sounded very alarmed. 'Mistress Martha! Mistress Martha!' they shouted.

At last I felt safe, and yelled out as loudly as I could: 'Over here! I am in the dairy!' Luckily, Billy heard my voice above the wind, and I saw the light of his lantern approaching. He tried to open the door, but my barricade proved very effective, and it would not budge. So he went to the window, and waved his lantern, and looked inside. I declare that I have never ever seen anything so beautiful as his grizzled and weatherbeaten face, dusted with snowflakes, as I saw it then.

'Mistress, are you in there?'

'Yes, Billy. Thank God you have come.'

'Are you all right?'

'Yes, I am quite unharmed.'

'Duw Duw, that's a relief, Mistress, I can tell you. We were quite convinced that you were buried in the snow. What are you doing there? Why won't the door open?'

'Because I have jammed the butter churn against it. I shall see if I have enough strength left to move it away.'

I was stiff with cold, but helped by the light now coming in through the window I made my way towards the door and managed to drag the butter churn away just far enough for Billy to slip inside. He looked puzzled, and probably became even more so when I flung my arms round his neck and dissolved in tears. 'Oh, Billy, you are so kind!' I wailed. 'Whatever would I do without you?'

'There, there, Mistress,' he said in the most soothing voice that he could manage. 'You are quite safe. Don't you worry, now then. Everything will be all right.'

Then Shemi and Will turned up with their lanterns, having been attracted by all the noise. This was no time for explanations, for they could see that I was very cold indeed. Shemi took Billy's candle lantern, and my head man picked me up as if I were a small baby and carried me across to the kitchen door, lifting his feet high so as to negotiate the thickening snow. 'Are the children in bed?' I whispered in his ear.

'Oh yes, long since, Mistress. They are all fast asleep.'

When Billy delivered me into the sanctuary of the kitchen I was overwhelmed by light, and warmth, and love. I was shivering uncontrollably. My frozen outer garments were stripped off, and Bessie fetched my warmest woollen dress and my thickest dressing gown. I was wrapped up and placed in a chair before the glowing fire in the *simnai fawr*, and Grandma Jane and Bessie pummelled my hands and feet, which were blue with cold. Then I was forced to eat lumps of wheat bread soaked in hot milk. I wanted a big glass of brandy, but Mrs Owen would have none of it, and said it would probably kill me.

At last I began to thaw out, and the situation was sufficiently under control for the interrogation to start. Questions flew at me from all directions, and I could tell that they were all angry with me. But all I could think of was the idea that the creature in black might still be standing outside in the snow.

'Have any of you seen it?' I asked.

'Seen what, Mistress?'

'The black creature. Outside, on the bank behind the house. It frightened me. It was standing there, looking at me.'

Billy and the other men looked at each other as if I was mad. 'No, Mistress,' said Shemi. 'If there had been anything there, I should certainly have seen it when I went across the north paddock to check the sheep just before it got dark. That was maybe ten minutes before you came by on your little walk in the snow.'

'Is it still snowing?'

'Yes,' replied Will. 'Still coming down. But less heavily than it was earlier in the evening.'

'Will, Shemi, Billy. I want you to wrap up well, take your lanterns, and see if the creature is still there. If there is no sign of it, please search carefully for tracks. The snow is soft and quite deep, so it might have left distinct footprints. Find out which direction they have come from, and follow them if you can. When it is light in the morning, if we do not get too much more snow overnight, we can undertake further investigations.'

The men shrugged and looked at one another. 'Very well, Mistress,' said Billy. 'We will see what we can find for you.' And they put on their heavy coats and boots, and their felt hats, and lit their candle lanterns once again, and went outside. I worked my way through my bread and hot milk while they were gone, and was in no mood for conversation with those left inside. After twenty minutes they returned, shaking their coats and stamping the snow off their boots on the kitchen doorstep.

'Nothing to be seen, Mistress,' said Shemi. 'No creature in black or any other colour, for that matter. We searched all over the bank, and up in the paddock and further afield. If it had been anywhere around, one or other of us would have seen it for sure. No tracks either. Not a trace. The snow was clean and smooth everywhere.'

'Perhaps, Mistress Martha, you imagined it?' asked Billy. 'Flurries of snow, and the fading light

114

at nightfall, can play strange tricks, as I know full well...'

'No, Billy, I did not imagine it. Thank you for your efforts, but I am sure of what I saw.'

And then I described for them all, in as much detail as I could, my sighting of the monster in black, its clothing and black hat, my reactions, and my flight into the dairy. They listened, engrossed, and there followed an animated discussion of what I might have seen. Bessie and Will think that I have seen the Devil, and that no good will come of it. Grandpa takes the view that the strange creature was human – a vagrant, probably starving, prowling about on the hunt for food, and then surprised when I appeared round the corner of the dairy. He thinks that the poor fellow was probably more scared by the encounter than I was, and that he has now fled, never to be seen again. But he is at a loss as to the lack of tracks in the snow. Billy and Sian think that I have seen the ghost of Matthew Lloyd or one of the others recently executed, and that it may return to haunt us again. Shemi thinks that I have seen an omen of hard times to come or some tragedy that might befall us.

Our discussions went on far into the night, but in truth many of the comments around the kitchen table over our belated supper were tongue-in-cheek, and I fear that the consensus may be that I simply imagined the sighting of the ominous figure, and that this might be a sign of some derangement in my mind.

Now I am in bed, and the house is quiet. I am calmer, and feel almost safe, but there is still apprehension in my breast, and I will leave a candle burning while I try to sleep. I am very tired, but my mind is so full of speculation that I hardly know black from white. I am beginning to doubt my own sanity.

Shades of Grey

10 February 1807

The snow has gone, and life has returned to some sort of normality. But my sighting of the figure in black is now accepted by the others who dwell beneath this roof, for five others have seen the apparition as well.

Two days since, at a time of improving weather and snow flurries, Sian walked down to Gelli to see her parents at dusk, while I told a story to the children and got them off to bed. Shemi went with her. I insisted on it, since I am concerned about people walking alone in the snowy darkness. They returned at about nine of the clock, looking considerably shaken, having earlier seen a shadowy black figure, exactly as I had described him, moving down the track towards Ty Rhos and the Cilgwyn road. Sian was terrified. Not many things frighten Shemi, but he was frightened too, and they hurried on to the safety of the Gelli kitchen. Later, on their way back to the Plas, they went to investigate the place where they had seen the mysterious figure, in the hope of finding alien footprints. But although the snow was soft and new, they found nothing. They searched over a wide area with their candle lanterns, and saw only the marks made by their own feet. This frightened them almost more than the sight of the figure itself, and explains their agitation when they got back to the Plas. What sort of creature, they thought, drifts across the landscape without leaving any marks of its presence?

Yesterday, as night was falling, Billy was on the common near the mountain track, on the south side of Carningli, looking for three missing ewes. There had been a thaw, and only a few snowbanks were left high on the mountain and behind stone walls. Suddenly he saw the apparition, standing quite still about three hundred yards away from him. It was dressed in the same heavy black cloak and the same wide-brimmed black hat, and it had the same heavy muffler over its face as I had described. The figure was standing quite still, looking down at the Plas. Billy thinks that it must have seen him, but it made no attempt to move. At any rate, Billy was greatly upset by the encounter, and retreated to the Plas without finding the ewes. When he looked back up the slope from the safety of the farmyard, the figure had disappeared into the gathering gloom. He came into the kitchen with a wild look in his eyes, and his hands were shaking, but he said nothing then about his sighting since the children were still running around.

And then today, for the third day running, the figure was seen among the dark evening shadows, this time by Mrs Owen, as she came in from the dairy, and by Bessie as she looked out of one of the back windows of the house. It was standing very close, on the bank inside our boundary wall. They were both very frightened, and I observed over supper that both of them were behaving in a distracted and erratic fashion. But neither of them said anything about their encounters until the children were asleep.

This evening we all sat round the kitchen table and held a conference. I no longer doubt my own sanity, since there are now six of us who have seen this strange phenomenon. But I am still very apprehensive, especially since the figure appears to have an interest in Plas Ingli rather than in any other residence in the neighbourhood. Even the sighting by Sian and Shemi fits this supposition, since they are convinced that the figure was moving away from the Plas, having been there unseen earlier in the evening. The servants have been talking among themselves, and they have started to call the creature 'the Nightwalker' since they think it manifests itself and moves about at night, and disappears off into the spirit world by day. They are quite convinced that it is not human, since it leaves no tracks, but when we talked round the table we could not agree on whether it is a normal harmless ghost or some denizen of the spirit world which manifests itself for some malign purpose. The prevailing view at the moment is that the creature is the ghost of one of the three men recently executed, restless and miserable, and come to haunt us in a feeble attempt to exact revenge. Perhaps there is not one ghost, but three? Maybe the shades of John Howell, Ifan Beynon and Matthew Lloyd are all

118

out there, attired identically, and each occupying a particular part of the landscape? Grandma Jane thinks we should get the Rector up to the Plas with a view to an exorcism, but I cannot agree with that, since the house itself is not haunted, and indeed feels as warm and friendly as ever.

The remaining theory is that the Nightwalker is indeed the Grim Reaper, come to call one or more of us to his cold bosom. That thought fills all of us with apprehension. Are all six of us who have seen him soon to die? Or are we, all six, to suffer loss and grief as a consequence of some other death? Is some plague, like the dysentery sickness that swept across the neighbourhood some years back, about to afflict us? In the past, when I have seen the Battle in the Sky, or after the hearing of the *tolaeth* or the sighting of the *toili*, terrible things have happened within a week or two – including my fateful encounter with Moses Lloyd in the cave on the mountain, the murder of David, and the abduction of my beloved Sara by that monster John Fenton.

If there is any comfort to be obtained from this situation, it is that the sightings of the mysterious Nightwalker have been shared between those who are ordinary folk and those who have special powers. Shemi and I see things that other people do not see, and the Wizard of Werndew has told me in the past that omens and signs may be given to us while others exist in a state of blissful ignorance. Common sense tells me that since such earthy folk as Mrs Owen, Bessie and Billy have also seen this strange black figure, maybe it would be a mistake to read too much into its

119

presence. We will await developments, and for the moment I will resist the temptation, in spite of the unease which inhabits the house, to call in my friend Joseph Harries for his advice. I am even less inclined to call in Owain, much as I love him, for a cold fear for his safety sweeps through my heart like a blizzard. Could he be the man whom the Nightwalker has come to claim?

12 February 1807

It is now exactly two years since the death of my dear David, my first sweetheart, gentle squire of the Plas Ingli estate, loving father of my children, passionate lover and wonderful husband. I have still not fully recovered from the shock of his death, or from the desolation that followed it, and occasionally I experience a deep melancholia which lasts for days on end. But every time it happens, I struggle out of it, and in truth the children will not allow me to be miserable for too long. Their good spirits and blue-eyed optimism are sources of wonderment to me – although I dare say I was the same when I was little. I must seek to learn from them, to catch hold of each moment, to smile at beauty when it shows itself, and to think of today and tomorrow rather than yesterday.

Today at breakfast time Owain's man arrived with a brief message. It contained a poetic remembrance of David, and said that he would hold me and the family in his prayers throughout the day. He is too sensitive by far to impose himself upon us at such a time, but I was greatly touched, and shed tears for both of these good men who have lightened my life. Later on the children and I, and Grandpa and Grandma, walked down to Cilgwyn church in order to place small posies of wood anemones and daffodil buds on David's grave. We spent a little time in silence inside the family enclosure, holding hands, each one of us lost in our own thoughts. Then Grandpa Isaac said a little prayer. For the old people – Isaac and Jane – each visit is especially poignant and painful, for there are many family members besides David buried here, including Isaac's grandparents Ezekiel and Sara and his parents Jenkin and Elizabeth Ann, as well as Isaac and Jane's son William and his wife Bethan, who were David's parents and died in appalling circumstances when the old Plas Ingli burnt down in 1794. David's brothers Thomas and George, and his little sister Rose, all died at the same time. And there is a plaque to David's brother Griffith, who was drowned at sea in 1796 and whose body was never found. Verily a place of memories, many of them sad but perhaps more of them happy, and linked to good people who led honest and cheerful lives. I talked to David sometimes about his parents and his siblings, and although he could never erase his memories of the fire he remembered well the days of his sunlit childhood, and valued them.

We spent some time in the enclosure, and Grandpa made a note of some repairs that are needed to the gate and the masonry walls. The children played among the old yews on the north side of the churchyard, and I noted with pleasure that the spruce trees planted along the south and west walls three years ago by Isaac were all doing well. There were seven of them, one for each member of David's family, and as I looked at them I dreamt that one day, when I am dead and gone, they would be tall enough to drop pine cones upon the church roof and indeed to be seen from the top of Carningli. Then Grandpa took the children to one side and told them that he had heard from his grandfather, who had heard it from his grandfather, that once upon a time Prince Henry Tudor had passed this way with his army of Welshmen on his journey from Dale to a place called Bosworth Field. They camped on the hillside to the south of the church, at a place called Fagwyr Lwyd, and the Prince worshipped in Cilgwyn church. Then next day they went on across the mountains of Ceredigion. At Bosworth, in due course, Henry and his troops defeated wicked King Richard in a great battle, and the crown of the realm was placed on his head. Thus he became the first Welsh King of England since the good old days of King Arthur. The children listened wide-eyed, and then Isaac took them inside the church and showed them the very spot where Henry had knelt in prayer before the altar.

Grandma Jane and I stood with our arms round each other and smiles upon our faces at the churchyard gate. Then we all walked home, with the children chattering incessantly about kings and battles.

Now the bright day has gone. We have had supper, and everybody but me is in bed. The house is quiet, and I am alone with my thoughts.

I thank God for David and for our time together. His loss was an appalling thing that I only just managed to cope with, thanks to Bessie and Joseph and my other friends and family members. But now I have given my heart to another – Owain Laugharne, artist, hero and romantic gentleman who thinks of flowers and poems and little gifts while other men might think of weather changes and rotten gates and the price of barley. He is truly a prince among men, and I love him with all my heart. I want to give every fragment of my being to him. And yet, and yet... What if I should lose him as I lost David? I do not think that I would be able to withstand that, even if all the angels of Carningli sought to hold me up and save me from tumbling into the slough of despond. Am I strange to harbour such fears in my breast? Or do they haunt every woman in every age? Can a second love ever be the same as a first? God only knows how I wish it. But maybe it is impossible, for there can never again be such innocence and such anticipation, such optimism and such wondrous discovery.

I will marry Owain, and I will love him tenderly and fiercely. But there is still apprehension and a cold fear somewhere within me that something could still go wrong, either before or after we stand together at the altar. And then there is the matter of the Nightwalker. I cannot get it out of my head that the creature has something to do with Owain, who may in his innocence be a marked man. Tonight I will go to sleep praying: 'Dear Lord, let it not be true. Let it not be true...'

22 February 1807

We adults have been much more relaxed of late, since there has been no further sighting of the Nightwalker for nigh on a fortnight. It has been very rainy, with one gale after another washing across the mountain from the west, and Billy jokes that ghosts do not like wet weather. Maybe the phantom has been out there, but we have not seen it.

Owain has been to visit me twice, and we have talked at length about the executions. He was very understanding of my emotional reaction to them, and was not so affected himself as I had feared. On other matters I was less forthcoming. All of us at the Plas adhered to our agreement that we would say nothing to him about the Nightwalker. The children do not know about it either. Eventually the news may creep out, but I dare to hope that the figure in black will never be seen again, and that in years to come we will look back on the encounters with some amusement while Grandpa tells ghostly stories about them. At any rate, we managed to put dismal matters into some sort of perspective. Both of the visits from my beloved man were full of laughter and affection, and we managed to steal enough time together in the privacy of my dressing room to confirm me in my desire to get him into the privacy of my bed as rapidly as possible.

Shrove Tuesday is late this year, and today we have been celebrating it as is appropriate, according to ancient tradition. We opened the shutters to find a bright and dry morning, which warmed all our hearts. The men were given the day off in order to participate in the annual *cnapan* contest between Newport and Nevern parishes on Berry Sands. I encouraged it, in spite of my own mixed feelings, since it was in the *cnapan* game of 1805 that David met his death. But I cannot allow my own misery to restrict the lives of others, and we must all seek to restore normality. So Will, Billy and Shemi saddled up three of the ponies and set off for the beach at nine in the morning, with the game planned to start at eleven on a falling tide. They were in good spirits. They clearly looked forward to the sport, having missed the contest last year out of respect for David's memory.

Since this is one of the greatest social gatherings of the year in the neighbourhood, I allowed Bessie and Sian to have the day off as well. They have little enough free time for meeting friends and families, and I knew that they would enjoy the mighty throng of townspeople and country folk who would congregate on the Parrog and at the Bennet on the north side of the river, as well as the music and dancing, and the stalls and booths erected by the vendors of food and drink, trinkets and fancy goods. The entertainment comes from jugglers and clowns and other street performers. Pedlars and gypsies always gather in good numbers, much to the disquiet of the Mayor and the Court Leet who seem to spend most of their time trying to prevent illicit trading. It would be better, in my view, if they and the Newport constables concentrated on catching the pickpockets and petty thieves who will have a thoroughly profitable day. Gambling is also part of the tradition, with large sums of hard-earned money being put down by the supporters of the two sides. This year, Billy told me, the safe money was on a Newport win, largely because he, Will and Shemi were playing together; but that is just bluster, since I cannot imagine how three fellows from the Plas could greatly influence the course of events with four or five hundred players on each side.

The children wanted to go and watch the contest, but I would not allow it. It goes on for far too long – four or five hours of watching hordes of semi-naked men rushing about in the distance is too tiring for little ones. There is also too much drinking and violence at *cnapan* contests for my liking. Maybe next year I will allow Betsi and Daisy to go. Bessie and Sian are old enough to look after themselves, and they know that if they have need of help in town they will find Grandpa Isaac in the corner of the upstairs room in the Royal Oak, where he will be drinking brandy with his cronies.

At any rate, by ten o'clock all the servants except Mrs Owen had departed, and Grandpa set off around midday. I dealt with the grumbles and sulks of the children by telling them that those of us who remained at the Plas would all have a wonderful day helping to mix the pancake batter, and that we would hear all about the game later on when the heroes returned. And so, with the redoubtable Mrs Owen in charge, Grandma Jane, the children and I all set to with flour and eggs, milk and buttermilk, vinegar and spices, measuring and mixing and whipping and pouring with gusto. Sara and Dewi got themselves into a terrible mess, and considerable quantities of batter ended up on the floor, but we all enjoyed ourselves. The cats under the table enjoyed themselves most of all.

By the time everybody returned, just after dark, there was a veritable mountain of pancakes on the kitchen table ready for consumption. Grandpa, Bessie and Sian carried with them enough gossip to fill every waking moment of the next fortnight. Shemi had a split head, Will sported a black eye, and Billy complained about bruised shins, but they were thoroughly elated since Newport had won the game by carrying the wooden *cnapan* to the Nevern goalpost after only two and a half hours of play. A mere formality, they said. They were of course rather drunk and unspeakably filthy, so we packed them off to the scullery where a large tub of hot soapy water was waiting for them. At last they emerged, with bright shiny faces and sore heads, and resplendent in clean dry clothes. Then the pancake feast began in all its chaos and ended the same way, with everybody talking and eating at once. The men were far too excited after their day of sporting endeavour to calm down, and it would have been unkind to dampen their elation. The principles of good manners sank without trace, and the sins of gluttony and grandiloquence were given free rein. I went to the pantry to fetch some more treacle, and thought that the sounds emanating from the kitchen must have been very similar to those made long ago by our ancestors who lived in caves and communicated with grunts rather than words. So much for civilization. But in truth I did not mind, and the evening was very entertaining. I dare say that tomorrow we will all be back to normal.

27 February 1807

Sunday today, and I have been to church in Newport, flanked by Grandpa and Grandma in our family pew. Normally we attend Sunday worship at Cilgwyn church, since it is closer and more convivial, and has fewer holes in the roof, but today it was necessary to go to town because the banns were due to be read for Patty and Jake.

Some days since, the couple were visited by Rector Devonald, which says a good deal for the reverend gentleman, given the tendency of Parrog tongues to wag at the slightest provocation. He went there at the invitation of Patty and Jake, to discuss the arrangements for the wedding. By all accounts Patty declared to him that she is a reformed person who now sincerely seeks to lead a sober and honest life devoted to good works and religious observance. I am not sure that even I believe all of that, but time will tell. Jake is a good man, besotted with love for Patty, and he will catch fish for her and seek to ensure that she sticks to the paths of righteousness. They got on well with the Rector, and no mention was made of Patty's past clients or indeed of my intervention in seeking to arrange a church wedding. So it is all organized. The reading of the banns will take place over the next three Sundays, and the happy couple will get married – God willing – towards the end of March.

Prior to the service and the first reading of the banns, I was very worried that somebody from the congregation would raise an objection and force the Rector to call the wedding off. There are those in our midst who disapprove of fornication. So on the assumption that there would be a good turnout by the forces of bigotry, I had made certain arrangements.

In the event, all went according to plan. When we entered St Mary's church there was a great crowd already present, and we saw that Patty and Jake were standing at the back. There was, as usual, a good deal of hat doffing and curtsying as we exchanged greetings with the other gentry and the regular churchgoers of the town. We found out at once that the Rector had absented himself and was away in England looking after one of his other livings, so matters were left in the hands of a young curate named Harry Maggs. I was not surprised. The Rector's courage stretches only so far.

The young fellow was clearly very nervous, and as he stood before the altar he looked like a rabbit surrounded by hungry ferrets. At last he came to the point in the devotions when he had to read the banns. He stepped up into the pulpit where he could see the whole of the assembled company, and read out the following words from a piece of paper: 'My dearly beloved brethren and sisters, I have received notice from two of my parishioners that they sincerely desire to be married in this church on the twenty-fifth day of March in the year of our Lord 1807. They are Mistress Patty Ellis, resident on the Parrog, and

Master Jake Nicholas, also resident on the Parrog. I have satisfied myself that there is no impediment to their union. However, if there is any one here present who knows just cause why they may not be joined in marriage, speak now or for ever hold thy peace.' Poor fellow. He was so nervous that he only just managed to get that last bit out, sounding more like a frog than a man.

There was a long silence. Then five gentlemen stood up together, three from the gentry pews and two near the back of the church, in what was clearly an orchestrated move. I recognized all of them as stuffy and mean-spirited men whose idea of happiness was to spread their own miseries as far afield as possible. One of them, Squire Solomon Huws of Bayvil, started to speak. 'Curate Maggs, I feel that it is my duty, in the interests of maintaining morality in this community, to say that–'

There was suddenly a great bout of coughing from the back of the church, where all the common people were standing. Everybody turned round to confront a sight that would have caused Goliath to quake at the knees. There was Joseph Harries in his tall black hat – outrageous enough, since no gentleman wears a hat in church – fixing Squire Huws with his stony gaze. He wore a bright red hunting jacket and a purple waistcoat, and held a long wooden staff in his hand. He looked perfectly grotesque, and I could not resist smiling to myself. Nobody crosses the Wizard of Werndew, and the Squire knew it. To make matters worse, flanking Joseph were about twenty of the roughest characters in town, assembled for the occasion by

Will and his friend Skiff Abraham. Not very nice people, most of them. They have heavy boots and light fingers. None of them had ever been seen in church before, and they were clearly here for a purpose. They too had their beady eyes fixed upon the Squire. The poor fellow shrank visibly, turned back to face the curate, and thought for a long time in total silence. Then he continued: '...it is very pleasing indeed to see that this church extends the hand of goodwill to all, and that past sins are forgiven, and that these two good young people will be joined in holy matrimony before this altar.' At this sudden change of strategy, the other four gentlemen had no option but to splutter and say 'Amen to that' and sit down, one after another. There was a murmur of approval from the congregation. The curate looked greatly relieved, and continued with the devotions.

At the end of the service we filed out, to find that the ruffians were all long gone. Sermons are not very much to their liking, and even with heavy boots or clogs on their feet they move very silently. To his credit, Joseph was still there, doffing his hat and smiling angelically at all the ladies as they passed by. We three from the Plas exchanged pleasantries with the curate and with various other acquaintances, and caught up with Joseph in the churchyard. 'Joseph!' I said with a fierce voice and a twinkle in my eye. 'You look absolutely disgraceful! Where did you get that jacket and waistcoat? We must get you something decent to wear next time you come to church.'

'My dear Martha, I thought that my attire was perfectly splendid,' said he. 'Borrowed it for the occasion from young Master Laugharne of Llan-nerch, whom you might know. A very accom-modating and understanding young man, if I may say so. He and I have very similar dimensions.'

'Well, you might have taken your hat off in church, as a mark of respect.'

'Respect? I have no respect for the Church, as you well know. Inhabited for the most part by very silly people. In any case, I was there in a theatrical rather than a religious capacity today. I thought the performance went remarkably well.'

Grandpa and Grandma and I all laughed, and encouraged him to come back to the Plas with us for dinner. I encouraged Patty and Jake to do the same, and they were happy to accept our invitation. Later on, in the dining room, we all had a very agreeable time, and we knew that there would now be no further impediment to the wedding on the 25th day of next month. The second and third readings of the banns would pass without incident, even if Joseph and his friends should be absent from church.

I am now in debt to Skiff and his friends, since they were packed into the back of the church at my request. No doubt they will call in the debt at some stage. I do not care, since the day's enter-tainment has been thoroughly worthwhile, and two good young people will be made happy because of it.

1 March 1807

We have been celebrating the feast day of our

patron Dewi Sant, in a fashion which is not to everybody's liking since it involves abstinence, and the consumption of nothing but bread and water before sunset. Saint David was, according to the ancient texts, a very ascetic fellow who looked upon a dish of sorrel leaves as a veritable feast. He lived and died in great poverty, and in remembrance of him we do ourselves no great harm by setting aside some of our excesses just for a day.

However, the poor people of Newport have chosen to celebrate the day with something more than symbolism, for there has been a food riot in the town centre. According to Mrs Owen, who knows everything about everyone, about a hundred men ran amok down Market Street and Long Street, waving placards, smashing windows and chanting: 'We want bread! We want bread!' They hurled stones and abuse at the residences of three or four of the biggest merchants in town. Then they made their way to the Parrog, and laid siege to the warehouses of Hubert Harry and Jeb Wilson. They said that they were starving, and demanded that the merchants should release the barley that they had in store instead of holding it back for export and higher prices. This hoarding and price fixing has been done before, and will be done again, and it is still controlled by a ring of squires and merchants. David in his time would have nothing to do with it, and neither will I. Owain agrees with me and insists on fair trading and sales to local people. The price we have paid for this independence, year after year, is lost income, but instead we have gained a measure of respect from the families who simply cannot afford to buy barley when prices are as high as ten shillings per bushel.

Apparently the riot reached its height in front of Master Harry's warehouse when the silly fellow opened up the door and harangued the crowd. The men, who had consumed liberal quantities of cheap ale, became very incensed, and started throwing stones. At last they broke in and 'liberated' about twenty bushels of barley. Harry was furious, and sent somebody to fetch the constables. But by the time John Wilson and his timid confederates arrived there was not a single rioter to be seen, and the Parrog was bathed in peace and light. Later on, twenty empty hessian sacks were delivered back to the warehouse by a street urchin who claimed not to know the name of the fellow who gave them to him. He demanded, and got, a reward of five pennies from the warehouse manager.

Nobody will be arrested, and nobody will testify as to those who were involved in the theft of the barley. But there will be two hundred poor families in Newport who will have bread in their bellies very shortly. Mrs Owen says that Edwards Castle Mill has been hard at work this afternoon, milling small quantities of barley for the most unlikely customers. But it is not his job to ask questions, and he gets his cut from every stone of flour milled in any case. Tonight and tomorrow the poorer part of Newport will smell of freshly baked crusty bread, which is a great deal easier on the nose than the smell of raw sewage on the street.

I had forgotten, in the comfort and relative isolation of the Plas, about the difficulties of life in the labourers' cottages and hovels of this area. And the three barren months are still to come. April will be harder than March, and May is always referred to, with good reason, as 'the hungry month'. Then all the hoarded foodstuffs of the winter will be gone, and there will be nothing new in either fields or gardens. It has been a hard winter, with several snowy spells, which will have drained the energy resources of people who were already on short rations back in November. I have grave concerns about the future. I trust that there will be no further disturbances; if there are, the squires will not hesitate to pull in the militia to keep order. The ringleaders, whoever they are, will be identified and captured. They will end up in court, and may well find themselves incarcerated in the prison hulks of Portsmouth for seven years, or even transported to New South Wales. Billy, Shemi and Will know of my concerns, and I have told them that I will not tolerate any involvement in riots. Not that that is likely. They have dry beds, a comfortable place to live in, and good food in their bellies. But they have relatives and drinking partners who are starving, and people sometimes do silly things on behalf of their friends.

6 March 1807

Yesterday I saw the Nightwalker again. This time the creature was quite high up on the side of the mountain, standing among the rocky crags and piles of boulders. As before, it stood quite still, and it was watching the Plas. The afternoon was heavy and overcast, with flurries of rain spattering in from the west. I was the only observer, since I was up on the common inspecting the work which Will and Shemi and some of the other labourers have been doing on a new cart track. The phantom must have seen me, but appeared quite unmoved as I turned tail and fled back to the security of the Plas. As I approached the rickyard I looked back up the slope, and it was gone. This caused me some confusion. Had I actually seen it, or had it simply been some strange figment of my imagination? I needed to control myself, so I breathed deeply and sought to calm the heavy thumping of my heart. I determined that I would say nothing to anyone about the episode, and when I went back into the house it was obvious that nobody else had seen anything untoward.

And that was that. Or so I thought. It was still not dark, and suddenly there was a shout from the nursery. It was Betsi, and she yelled: 'Mam! Come quickly! Come and look!' So I ran up the stairs and found Sian and the four children all clustered round the window, looking up at the mountain. I thought they might be watching the Nightwalker, but no – they were watching the most enormous flock of starlings I have ever seen. The whole sky was blackened by thousands of them, swooping and wheeling around like clouds of gnats above a stagnant pond on a summer's evening. They moved at such tremendous speed that it was almost impossible to distinguish individual birds. We could not see the mountain, and even the top fields and stone walls were blotted out as the feathered multitude flew within a few feet of the ground, rising and falling in black waves. There was a sort of wild anger about them which I found unnerving. The air was full of their screeching, and a rain of droppings fell from the mad gyrating cloud. It was as if night had descended half an hour prematurely. I went and lit some candles, and when I returned to the window Sian and the children were still looking out, their mouths agape, transfixed by the spectacle.

And then they were gone, as suddenly as they had come. 'Oh my!' said Daisy. 'That was quite amazing! I wonder how many there were? A hundred or a thousand, maybe?'

'Far more than that,' replied Betsi, who knows all about everything. 'Thousands of thousands, more like. And quite possibly millions of thousands, as many as the stars in the sky or the sand grains on Traeth Mawr.'

And so the discussion went on during supper, and during bathing time and bedtime for the little ones. I noticed that Sian was not her usual self, and was going through the motions as if her heart and mind were elsewhere. I said nothing at the time, but when the children were all asleep I called her up to my dressing room. 'Now then, Sian,' said I. 'You are looking very distracted this evening. Did the starling swarm have anything to do with it?'

She looked at her feet, and was reluctant to reply.

'Come now, Sian. You and I are good friends, and have no need to hide anything from each other. Please be honest with me.'

At last she nodded. 'I did not like what I saw,

Mistress. I fear that no good will come of it.'

'Whatever do you mean? We simply saw a flock of starlings on their way to their night-time roost. A very large flock, I have to admit. The birds have probably settled by now in the trees of Tycanol Wood.'

Sian shook her head. 'No, Mistress. No good will come of it, just you mark my words. To see so many starlings all at one time is a bad omen. My grandmother told me that five minutes of starlings means misfortune, ten minutes means death, and fifteen minutes means disaster. Tonight we had twenty minutes, unless I am very much mistaken.'

'Nonsense, Sian!' I exclaimed, not very vehemently. 'You must not believe these old wives' tales. They come from another age, when people had very primitive ideas. A flock of birds cannot possibly tell us anything about the future.'

'I hope you are right, Mistress,' said Sian. 'I will try to cheer up. Please may I go now?'

'Of course. Off you go.'

And off she went, leaving me with my thoughts. I felt nothing like as brash and confident as my words might have indicated, and when I was alone my sense of foreboding increased. I too had felt a distinct unease under the shadow of those birds, and I reminded myself that they had come swooping out of the skies just a few minutes after my sighting of the Nightwalker. Were the two things connected? I knew not what to think. At last I said my goodnights to everybody, and settled into a fitful sleep.

This morning I woke late, to find that a raw red light was filtering through the shutters of my bedroom window. I was mystified, and scrambled out of bed with an even deeper sense of foreboding in my breast. I opened the shutters as I always do to let in the bright light of the dawn. But I was horrified by what I saw. The sky was as red as fire and blood and cocks' combs. Angry, raw and menacing red, in many shades, painted across the sky by wisps of high cloud. As I watched, the cloud swept and twisted, moving ever higher, from east to west. The shades of red changed and blended with purple and indigo and yellow and orange like the palette of a mad artist. Here was another omen, and I knew it.

When Bessie came in, she said: 'Bad sky this morning, Mistress. Billy came in from feeding the animals a few minutes ago, and said that they are all very nervous. The bull went for him, and almost managed to pin him to the wall of the stall. The cows are not letting the milk out, and the horses refuse to eat. Shemi says that some disaster is about to befall us.'

'Thank you, Bessie, for your optimism. I can do without it, since I had enough of it from Sian last night following the visit from those wretched starlings. Let us not forget that this red sky is in all probability affecting the whole of north Pembrokeshire, and that whatever disaster befalls us will also fall upon the head of every other member of this community.'

'You are probably right, Mistress. Do you have a mind to look at the weather glass?'

I nodded and went downstairs, into the parlour where Grandpa Isaac keeps his spyglass, clocks and other scientific instruments. He was there already, gazing at the glass and shaking his head. 'Trouble coming, Martha,' he said. 'The glass has been falling steadily since yesterday afternoon, and it is now almost as low as it was some years ago when we had the great flood in the *cwm*. It will not be snow, since the air is not cold enough, but it could be rain and it could be wind – more likely a combination of the two. We must get all the animals close to the house or under cover; and every loose thing must be battened down. All hands on deck, if you please!'

And he hurried out to the back passageway, pulled on his heavy boots, flung his greatcoat over his shoulders, and rushed outside. The three manservants needed no prompting from me or Grandpa, and they were already hard at work in paddocks, stables, barn, yard and rickyard. Bessie, Sian, Grandma Jane and myself followed suit, and the children insisted on helping too. By ten of the clock we were all outside, securing everything that would move, covering loose small things with oilskins and ropes, and placing all buckets and pots and tools inside the barn out of harm's way. Chickens and geese and ducks were all shut in, as were the dogs. As we worked the red sky turned to deep purple and then to black, and then blacker than black as the cloud grew heavier and thicker. It became almost as dark as it had been at midnight.

We went into the kitchen to get some dinner, happy that we had done all that we could do. As we went inside I sniffed a change in the air. Instead of the cool freshness of a typical March day my nostrils suddenly detected dry warmth and the temperature soared upwards. The wind swung in an instant from east to south, which is almost unheard of in these parts, and started to pick up in speed. From the gentlest of zephyrs it turned into a stiff breeze, and then into a strong and constant southerly wind, and then into a full-blown gale – all in the space of thirty minutes. Whispering was transformed into moaning and whining, and finally into mad howling and screeching. We sat inside with our bowls of *cawl* and slices of bread and cheese, and watched the storm develop as we gazed through the windows at the sky and the bare trees.

By mid-afternoon we could not have gone outside without risking life and limb. The scream of the wind became a roar, with the pitch descending from tenor to baritone and finally to bass. At last there was so much noise in the air that we could not communicate with each other in the kitchen except by shouting. The children were frightened, as indeed we all were, for there was so much banging and clattering from shutters and doors and roof tiles that we thought it only a matter of time before the roof itself was ripped off. Branches were coming down from the trees, some of them flying wildly through the air as if they were as light as feathers. Then one of the upstairs windows was blown in; and then another; and we had no option but to close all the shutters and sit tight in the back rooms of the house, out of danger, almost deafened by the thundering wind and with our faces illuminated by guttering candles.

It was as hot as a summer's day, but it did not rain. On the contrary, it became drier. We all felt that our throats were parched, and then we noticed that there was fine dust in our nostrils and in our throats. It was hard to breathe. We all drank fresh water from the jugs on the kitchen table, but in spite of that we all spent an hour or more coughing and spluttering. We noticed that the light around the candles was turning from white to orange and then to red. Daisy wiped her finger across the surface of the table and showed me that it was covered with fine red dust. How it got into the house, God only knows. And so we sat the hurricane out, frightened and immobilized, until about four in the afternoon.

And then, within the space of a few minutes, it stopped. We could hardly believe it. We waited for a while in order to be sure that it really was over, and then we started gingerly to open shutters and look outside. We were greeted by a scene of devastation. Two of our tallest ash trees were down, and there were heavy branches on the ground beneath three of the oaks along the driveway. When we went out into the yard, we saw that the buildings were intact, apart from some roof tiles which had disappeared without trace. We thanked our lucky stars for the care with which they had been built by David and Billy and the other estate labourers a few years ago to replace the old buildings lost in the fire of 1794. We feared greatly for our neighbours, whose buildings are old and ill repaired, and we knew that some of them would be faced this evening with disaster and ruination.

'That was very unpleasant indeed,' said Grandpa. 'I have never experienced anything like it. Wind and sand from the Sahara desert. I never expected a hurricane from the south. That is our most vulnerable direction, located as we are on a south-facing mountain slope. Thank the Lord for deliverance. Yes indeed. Thank the Lord.'

The most important man in our household in the aftermath of the storm was Shemi, who knows how to talk to animals. He went patiently and systematically from stable to cowshed, from pig sty to chicken coop, from kennel to goose house. He spoke to every animal in turn, in a quiet and soothing voice, using words which neither I nor anybody else understands. He did not come inside until well after dark, and I noticed that he was quite exhausted. I was intrigued, and determined to talk to him about his strange talent when things have settled down again.

Now we have had supper, and we are all off to bed early. Tomorrow there will be a great deal to do. The wind is cool again. The inside of the house is caked with red dust, and two rooms are full of shattered glass. Outside there is debris everywhere. Roofs and windows will have to be repaired. And once we have sorted out our own problems, there will be others to assist on the tenanted farms and in the labourers' cottages. Before I climb between my dusty sheets I wonder whether the omens and portents which concerned me yesterday and this morning were all pointing at this great storm. Is it now over and done with? Or are there consequences still to be revealed? I pray to God that neither my family nor Owain will figure in such consequences. And I trust that my dear man has remained safe and healthy during the buffeting of the desert wind.

8 March 1807

Skiff and his friends have called in their debt, and I hope that I will not get into deep trouble because of my willingness to repay them for services rendered.

It all came about because of the storm. Yesterday morning news came of a shipwreck on the cliffs adjacent to the river mouth, no more than a few hundred yards from Parrog. A small ketch called the *Pole Star* had been heading for New Quay from Bristol with general cargo on board. The captain had seen the storm coming, and had come in close to the cliffs near Aberrhigian to what he thought was the safety of a lee shore. He had put down his anchor and decided to ride the storm out. Although the wind was blowing offshore there were some big swells coming in from the north-east. According to those who watched the tragedy, the wind suddenly shifted to the west and the vessel was caught in a set of ferocious crossing seas. With the gale now blowing from an unexpected quarter she shipped several tons of water, dragged her anchor, drifted eastwards, and before the crew could get the sails unfurled was on the rocks near the Newport sea quarry.

Out of a crew of five, four were swept overboard and lost. Some of the locals who were brave enough to venture out in the choking red-coloured wind tried, without success, to get a line from the clifftop to the last remaining man on board. He was washed into the sea by a towering wave, but by some miracle he was deposited on a ledge halfway up a cliff on a rocky peninsula. He was quite badly injured, but like a mad thing he scrambled up the shaly rock face and got to the top, where the locals grabbed him and pulled him clear of the cataclysm. He passed out and was carried to Mistress Billings's lodging house, where he was attended by Havard Medical. He had a broken arm and a broken leg, and many other injuries, but when they pulled off his oilskins they found – miracle of miracles – that the ship's cat was there, also alive and apparently unharmed, in a deep pocket. When the sailor came to, the first thing he did was ask about the cat, and when he was told that it was quite safe he smiled and then fell into unconsciousness again. He is now under heavy sedation. He may or may not survive, but the locals are already calling him the Catman, and the place where he was dumped onto the cliffs will no doubt be known henceforth as Pen Catman. Four bodies are still missing, but they will probably come ashore in due course and will be placed on the cold slate slabs of the Parrog mortuary, where David was laid out after his death on Traeth Mawr.

Yesterday was relatively calm, but because all the roadways around Newport were blocked by fallen trees and branches, it was almost impossible for travellers to get in or out. The *Pole Star* had broken her back, and was stranded on a reef at the foot of the cliffs. Much of the cargo had been washed overboard, and was now littered all over Berry Sands. The locals took their chance, and since they assume that they have a right to

145

flotsam and jetsam nobody will ever know what exactly was spirited away. Ropes, timbers, bales of cloth, barrels of brandy and gin, packages of tobacco, pieces of furniture, boots and shoes, and even ladies' bonnets were by all accounts washed ashore on the first high tide after the wreck. Now all these items have found good homes and no doubt brought a little relief to those in need. Griff Hickey, the Excise man from Fishguard, was nowhere to be seen, which is not surprising since he probably had other wrecks to deal with; and the Newport constables and magistrates were also conspicuous by their absence.

When I had absorbed the news, I was of course saddened by the loss of life, but thought that the wreck was in other respects unremarkable. I assumed that the matter was closed. But then, after supper, Will asked if he could have a word with me. 'By all means, Will,' said I. 'Come upstairs into my dressing room, where it is quiet.'

Once there, we sat down and faced one another. I wondered what was coming, for Will has a chequered past, and for all I know he has a chequered future too. He looked nervous. 'Mistress, you know that ship that was wrecked?'

'Yes, I have heard all about it from your mother and others.'

'Well, you know about the stuff that came ashore?'

'Yes. Onto the beach at high tide and spirited away in a flash, as usual.'

'Well, that was not all there was.' He looked round to ensure that the two doors into the room were both closed. 'My mates in town went aboard

146

at low tide, when the waves had died down. The ship was in a terrible mess. The holds was smashed to pieces, and was almost empty but for some crates of tiles and fancy bricks. Too heavy to shift. But in the captain's cabin, or what was left of it, there was five small wooden boxes, very heavy and only a little bit damaged.'

'And what was in them?'

'Well, Skiff knocked the lid off one of them to have a look. Silver cutlery, very beautiful. Knives, forks, spoons, serving things like sugar tongs, all with heavy shaped and embossed handles. Destined for some wealthy squire in Cardiganshire, I dare say. Skiff says that at London prices we are looking at five hundred pounds at least.'

'But that is a huge sum! That cannot be correct!'

'Skiff knows his silverware, Mistress. Anyway, my mates could not get the boxes off in daylight, so they mounted a guard on the wreck and would not let anybody else get near. The next low tide was at three o'clock this morning, and I heard this afternoon that they managed to get the boxes off.'

'And the best of luck to them. The Cardiganshire squire will assume that they are on the sea floor, and he will probably manage to ride out the misfortune of their loss. But what has this got to do with me?'

'Skiff and his mates need a safe house, Mistress. The Catman will recover from his injuries, and he will tell of the boxes stored in the captain's cabin. Even if he didn't know they were there, some rich fellow from up north will soon enough come prowling about when he hears of the wreck, and he will be after his silverware. The magistrates will be informed, and that fellow Hickey will be here, looking out for anything that shines. That's for sure, that is. And the first doors he will be knocking on will belong to Skiff, Faggot, Abby, Halfpint and the rest of them.'

'Why should he do that? Why should he assume that the disappearance of the silver has anything to do with your friends?'

'Everything that happens in Newport has something to do with Skiff and that lot. What they haven't pinched, they know about. And what they don't know about is not worth knowing. The Excise men are well aware of that.'

'But surely they won't get any search warrants simply because they think Skiff and his friends might have information?'

'You forget, Mistress, that they guarded the wreck and kept other people away from it. Tongues will wag, and Hickey will hear what they wag about. Will you help?'

I thought for a long time. I was most unwilling to get involved in something that might be deemed to be theft or the receiving of stolen goods. Providing a safe house for tax-free goods is one thing, since the only one to suffer is the mad King George, and everybody trades in tax-free items anyway. But benefiting from the misfortune of others is another business altogether.

At last I said: 'I will not get involved in the hiding of valuable stolen goods. But I owe a kindness to Skiff and his friends. You were not here at the time of the French invasion, Will, but at the height of the crisis we hid all of our valuable possessions in oilskin bags in the middle of the dung-heap. If I hear strange noises outside tonight, on the driveway or in the yard, I might be minded to turn over and go to sleep again. Do you understand?'

'Yes, Mistress.'

'Right. Now, after all the hard work you have done today in sawing up fallen branches and so forth, I think I will give you the rest of the evening off. You might like to pop down to town for a drink.'

'Thank you, Mistress!' Will grinned and got to his feet. 'I will be off right away.'

And away he went. Tonight, he will be back very late, and there will be heavy footsteps and curses coming from the smelly area at the bottom of the rickyard. The dogs will bark and the geese will make a good deal of noise. I have told the rest of the household not to react.

We will all be awake, but none of us will lift a finger. And by the time the sun rises in the eastern sky, we will have forgotten everything.

11 March 1807

This morning, at about eleven of the clock, a very strange fellow came dancing and prancing along the driveway and into the yard. Daisy spotted him first, from the nursery window. 'Oh, look, Mam!' she said. 'There's a funny man coming up the drive. He looks as if he's galloping on a horse, but I think he's left his horse behind.'

We all gathered at the window, and there he was, just as Daisy described him. We were all mystified, except for Grandma Jane. She laughed and said, 'Oh, don't you worry about him. That's Gethin Gwahoddwr from town, come to do some bidding. He's as mad as a March hare, and likes to put on a bit of a performance. Sent by Patty and Jake I shouldn't wonder.'

'What's bidding, Mam?' asked Dewi.

'It's what happens before a wedding, Dewi, to announce the date and the time, and also to invite people to give nice presents to the happy couple.'

'Now then,' said Grandma, 'if we go downstairs to the kitchen we can welcome him when he comes inside.'

So we all tumbled down the stairs and along the passage into the kitchen, where we lined up beside the table. The children gazed at the door, their eyes wide with expectation. Then it burst open, without any knocking or any invitation to step inside, and in he came, galloping on his imaginary horse. He was a strange creature indeed, with sparkling green eyes, a weather-beaten face and a scrawny beard that might have been ginger twenty years ago. He was dressed in a long black coat with a substantial white apron tied in front of it, and a big leather bag slung over his shoulder. A white ribbon was tied to the lapel of his jacket, and on his head he wore a tall black wide-brimmed hat which was more or less encased within a wreath of daffodils, celandines and primroses. He carried a stout staff about seven feet long, and this too was decorated with daffodils tied on with hessian cord. The children screamed and giggled, and he neighed and chased them round the kitchen table three times.

Then he stood in front of the kitchen fire,

recovered his breath, and cleared his throat. He struck his staff three times on the flagstone floor, and then leaned it against the wall. He took off his flowery hat and placed it on the table. Then, with the panache of a magician conjuring up a white rabbit, he took out from a deep pocket a battered piece of paper, and read from it as follows, in a strange singsong voice: 'Good masters and mistresses, this is my *rammas*, and I have been desired to call here today as a messenger and bidder by the friends of Patty E. and Jake N., resident on the Parrog in this parish of Newport.

'The happy couple will make a bidding on the twenty-fifth day of March, at St Mary's church at three of the clock and afterwards at the cottage known as Bwthyn Bach for a goodly dinner. They shall have tender beef and cabbage, mutton and turnips, pork and potatoes, a goose if somebody will be so kind, a quart of ale for tuppence, a cake for a halfpenny, and sturdy chairs to sit upon and clean pipes and baccy.

'Good eating there will be, but if nobody comes to eat, I will eat as well as I can.

'There will be lusty singing to be sure, but if nobody will sing, I'll sing as well as I can.

'And fiddlers too, but if they will not fiddle I'll fiddle though you may not like it.

'And company of the best, but if nobody will attend I'll attend as well as I can.

'Good masters and mistresses, on such a day a great many can help one, but one cannot help a great many. I beg you to promise to come, but in any case to send a wagon or a cart, a horse or a colt, a cow or a heifer, an ox or a shoulder, a pig or

151

a fat hen, a cask of butter or an egg. If that is too much, a cartload of turnips will do, or a score of cheeses, or a blanket, or a sack of flour, or a needle and thread. Anything will do: a cradle or a pound, a tea-kettle or a frying pan, a dish or a ladle, a spoon or a mustard pot, a doormat or a pepper pot, a penny or a penny whistle.

'Ladies and gentlemen, and young masters and mistresses, I was desired to speak in this way so that all dues to the parents and grandmothers and grandfathers and brothers and sisters of the young people should be repaid without fail on the happy day. So bless my soul, enough is enough. And now, if you please to order your butler, or underservant or overservant, to give a quart of ale to the bidder, and a piece of bread and cheese for his bag, he would be most happy.'

Then Gethin gave a deep bow and wiped his brow with a vulgar red handkerchief while we all laughed and applauded. We sat him down at the table and gave him his quart of ale, although it was obvious that he had already consumed several quarts on his journey between Newport and the Plas. He ate some of his bread and cheese and stuffed the rest of it into his bag. Then he took out a little notebook from his deep pocket and wrote down the promises: ten pounds from myself and the children, ten shillings from the servants, three tapestry blankets from Grandma and Grandpa, and assorted foodstuffs and a barrel of ale for the feast from all of us, along with the offer to let them hold the wedding feast at the Plas if they wished. Then, with his mission completed and his energy restored, he gathered up his belongings, and leapt to his feet. He insisted on giving Grandma Jane a big kiss, right in front of Grandpa Isaac. She blushed, Grandpa scowled, and Gethin grinned from ear to ear. He said his farewells, mounted his imaginary horse, and went galloping off down the driveway towards Dol-rannog Isaf, where he would perform his next bidding and consume his next quart of ale.

When he had gone, and the children had calmed down enough to get on with their lessons, I managed to snatch a moment of peace and quiet with Mrs Owen in the pantry. 'What was that about, with Grandma Jane?' I whispered.

'You mean the kiss, and the blush and the scowl? Oh, don't you worry about that, Mistress. Gethin was in love with Mistress Jane once, back in the dawn of time. Still is, maybe. She might have married him too, but discovered in the nick of time, she did, that he is quite mad. Thank God that Master Isaac came along when he did, for indeed, if he had not, I do declare that none of us would be where we are today!'

And she slapped her ample thighs, and roared with laughter, and her bosom undulated like a magnificent pink jelly.

12 March 1807

The forces of law and order have begun to hunt for the boxes of silver cutlery. It has taken several days, but it was inevitable. As Will predicted, there is a strange squire in town, from an estate called Wervil in Cardiganshire. He owned the ship and he owned the silver, and he is very angry. To make matters worse, he is the cousin of Squire George Price of Plas Llanychaer, who by all accounts is not a very nice fellow.

Dai Canton called, as he does in the middle of every month, partly to see Bessie – whom he loves with a wonderful fervour – and partly to sell me some tea which he says is newly arrived from Bristol. 'On a vessel called the *Pole Star,* which came on the water and then went under it a few days ago?' I asked him.

'Come come, Mistress Martha,' said he. 'You know that commercial gentlemen like me never reveal their sources. Too much competition from those cheap fellows from Fishguard who sell floor scrapings. When you see me, you see quality and honesty from tip to toe.' I could get nothing else out of him, but I bought a pound of tea anyway.

I left him and Bessie in the kitchen, with a good deal of whispering and giggling going on. Bessie does not love him, but she is still young and still very pretty, and she enjoys the attention, and the posies and poems. When Dai had gone on his way to the Dolrannogs and Penrhiw, Bessie reported on the news from town. Apparently ten Excise men from Fishguard, under the control of Griff Hickey, have been searching high and low for goods washed up from the wreck. They are on horseback, and they move about quickly. They have recovered a few things including five boxes of oranges and two casks of brandy. But it is difficult for them to prove provenance, especially when the cottagers swear on oath that suspicious rolls of fabric or tins of sugar were bought last week at Newport market. In truth the Excise men are not very interested in these odds and ends, and it is hardly worth their time to search every cottage in town. Nobody has been arrested. But they are looking for some silver, and they have had a meeting with Squire Price and Squire Edwards from Wervil. They have offered a reward of ten pounds for information leading to the recovery of some boxes of silver cutlery, and they have already gathered information that has led them to Skiff and some of his fellow conspirators. They have searched their hovels, without success, and Skiff and his friends have protested vehemently that these searches have damaged their reputations as honest hard-working men. Skiff says he will take out an indictment against the Excise men for defamation of character. He will not, of course, but one has to admire his nerve.

Having relayed all this information to me, Bessie asked: 'Mistress, you know that noise in the yard the other night? It could not, by any chance, have had anything to do with–'

'It is best, Bessie, that neither you nor I know what went on outside. Will might know something, but he is old enough to look after himself.'

'Well, Dai tells me that Griff Hickey knows of the friendship between Skiff and Will, following various adventures in the past involving duty-free brandy and strange vessels and calm moonless nights.'

At this I blanched, for I recalled the incident less than a year ago when I rescued Will from the Newport lockup and made Hickey and his fellow Revenue officers look very foolish. Will was

155

caught in possession of two ankers of free-trade Nantz brandy following a landing at Aberfforest. I got him out of the clutches of the law by pretending that the brandy was duly paid for, and was being delivered to me at dead of night by Will's Newport Nocturnal Delivery Service. Nonsense, all of it, but it saved Will from appearing before the magistrates. At the instigation of his mother I then gave Will a job at the Plas, and have almost succeeded in my aim of making an honest man of him. But he still has dubious friends and a long reputation. Hickey has a score to settle with Will, and a score to settle with me. He will be here soon, as sure as omelettes is eggs.

13 March 1807

I have had a thoroughly bothersome day, and I am still not sure what the repercussions will be. Early in the morning, straight after breakfast, I took the precaution of sending Shemi and Will up onto the mountain to cut peat. I told them to go to the northern cutting on Waun Fawr, which is miles from anywhere and cannot be reached at this time of the year on horseback since the bogs are waterlogged. The weather was grey and drizzly, with low cloud settled on the mountain. I knew that they would not get lost, but that the Revenue men might, if they were foolish enough to go hunting for them.

Around midday the dogs started to bark, and we saw a considerable group of men coming up the driveway on horseback. They came straight to the front door, and I watched them from behind the curtains. Griff Hickey was in the lead, accompanied by a thick-set middle-aged man on a very beautiful black hunter. I had not seen him before. 'George Price from Llanychaer,' said Grandma, who was peeping with me. 'That means trouble.'

There was a great hammering on the door. Bessie opened it and said politely: 'Good day to you, sirs. Will you two gentlemen like to step inside? I shall announce your arrival to Mistress Morgan. Who shall I say it is?'

'Price Llanychaer,' said a loud bass voice. 'And this is Master Hickey from His Majesty's Excise Department. We will indeed step inside, whether you like it or not, since we have a search warrant in our hands.'

Bessie was somewhat taken aback by this aggressive reply, and so was I as I listened from the safety of the parlour. I felt my hackles rise, for I have an innate dislike of arrogant and over-bearing middle-aged squires, and when Bessie came in to convey the message Squire Price and I were already set on a collision course. I made him wait. When Bessie came to call me I told her to report that I would be with him shortly, since I was not used to receiving visitors unannounced and was currently involved in some pressing business. She did as I asked, and showed Master Price and Master Hickey into the office. Then she invited the other fellows to take their horses round to the yard, where Billy would look after them.

When I felt that sufficient time had elapsed to send both of them into a merry stew, I sailed in and gave a sweet curtsy. 'I do apologize for keeping you, gentlemen,' said I, poison dripping off my tongue. 'I am Martha Morgan. Delighted to meet you. Please sit down. Now then, what is it that I can do for you?'

'You know perfectly well why we are here, Mistress Morgan,' growled Squire Price. I widened my eyes in surprise, noticing from his flushed complexion and his writhing hands that he drank too much, had a tendency towards apoplexy, and was very agitated.

'I can assure you, sir, that I have not the slightest idea why you are here. Would you care to enlighten me?'

'We have reason to believe, Mistress Morgan, that certain items—' began Master Hickey, but he was cut short by a withering look from the Squire.

'We have reason to believe,' said Master Price, 'that five boxes of silver cutlery stolen from the wreck of the *Pole Star* by certain unsavoury fellows, are secreted in this house, and we have come to recover them.'

'What an outrageous accusation!' I exclaimed. 'I have to say, sir, that I take the gravest exception to those words. Will you withdraw them?'

'Indeed, madam, I will not!'

'Very well, I shall ask you to repeat them in the presence of witnesses.' I rang the bell from the desk, and when Bessie appeared I asked her to give my compliments to Grandpa Isaac and Grandma Jane with a request that they might step into the office. While we waited for them I noticed that Master Hickey grew more and more nervous, and that Master Price moved ever closer to an apoplectic fit. At last the old folks appeared, and settled themselves down onto the settle after the completion of frosty formalities. I asked the Squire to repeat his accusation, and he did so. Grandpa nodded, went to the desk, took out a clean sheet of paper, dipped a quill into the inkpot, and laboriously wrote down the exact words the Squire had used. 'Very serious words, George,' was all that he would say.

'Let us proceed,' said I. 'Would you now care to give us the evidence on which this scurrilous slander is based?'

'Master Hickey,' said the Squire, 'over to you.'

Master Hickey looked very surprised, and managed to find his voice again. 'Well now,' he squeaked. 'We have it on good authority that certain persons suspected of the crime are on familiar terms with certain persons resident in this house.'

I was beginning to enjoy this encounter, especially since Grandpa and Grandma were now present to support me. 'Do you call that evidence, Master Hickey?' I asked, not expecting a reply. 'I have heard the gossip from town about this missing silver. Nobody has seen it, so far as I know. All we have is speculation. It may be on the bottom of the sea off the Parrog cliffs. It may not even have been on the vessel in the first place.' Master Hickey started to slide deeper into his chair, and I continued the attack. 'Now then, sir, would you care to tell me which person or persons in this house stand accused?'

'Master Will Owen, whom we believe to be the son of your housekeeper.' At that point Grandpa coughed, and wrote noisily on his piece of paper again. Then he nodded to me, and I continued.

'How dare you, sir? William is a perfectly respectable fellow; if he were not, I'd certainly not employ him. But do you think that he has the run of this house, simply because he is my servant? Do you think he creeps around the place, secreting stolen goods at will, merely because he lives here? And am I supposed to be guilty by association, just because I employ him?' I did not expect replies to these questions, nor did I get them. I stared at both the Squire and Master Hickey, trying very hard to make my eyes blaze. Then I stood up. 'Gentlemen,' I said, 'I think this conversation is at an end. We have heard very serious accusations, witnessed and written down. We have not seen a single shred of evidence that a crime has been committed. Now, before you gentlemen sail into even more troublesome waters, may I show you to the door?'

Squire Price, who had been in a sort of trance, suddenly came alive. 'Mistress Morgan,' he said in a low voice lubricated by venom, 'I know your little game. I am a justice of the peace, and I know all about diversions and obfuscations. Now then, where is that rogue Will Owen?'

'He is up on the common cutting peat, if you must know. But even if he were here, I would not hand him over to you.'

'Very well. In that case, we will search the house. Master Hickey, the warrant, if you please.'

The poor fellow, looking more intimidated than ever, fidgeted in his pocket and produced a piece of paper. He handed it to me, and I handed it straight to Grandpa. He looked over it for a few moments, and then shook his head. He turned to

160

the Squire and said: 'George, you know perfectly well that this will not do. You disappoint me.'

'What do you mean, Isaac? Damn it, man, you know it is quite properly made out!'

'You are quite wrong in that, my dear fellow. Whose signature is this on the warrant?'

'Mine, of course!'

'George, we are both magistrates,' said Grandpa, perfectly calmly and quietly. 'We both know that your patch is Fishguard and Dinas, and mine is Newport. The Lord Lieutenant will not have magistrates signing warrants intended for execution on other people's territory. Neither will he have one magistrate signing a warrant for a search of another magistrate's property. And finally, may I ask you on whose behalf this search warrant is made out?'

'The complainant is Squire Edwards of Wervil. He is the one who has lost the silver cutlery.'

'And are you two related?'

'Well, yes. He happens to be my cousin.'

'Oh dear, oh dear, oh dear,' said Grandpa. 'Very naughty indeed. You know, George, that the Lord Lieutenant is very strict when it comes to such matters. At the last annual meeting of the magistrates' bench I think he used the word "corrupt" – and various others – to describe magistrates who instigate proceedings and use their influence on behalf of family members.'

Then he stood up, placed the warrant inside his desk, closed the lid, and locked it. He removed the key and placed it in the deepest pocket of his jacket. Squire Price looked on, quite incapable of either action or speech. His face became redder

161

and redder until I feared for his health. 'I will look after this piece of paper very carefully, George,' said Grandpa, 'just in case it should ever be required in court.'

I appreciated that the next move was mine. 'Gentlemen,' I said, 'I think that our discussion has reached its natural conclusion. Some minutes ago I invited you to leave. May I now so invite you again? I trust that we will hear nothing more of this business, and that henceforth we will be left in peace to get on with the little matter of running this estate. For our part, we can assure you that no mention of our discussion will pass outside these four walls. Good day to you, Master Hickey. It was good to make your acquaintance, having heard so much about you. And good day to you, Master Price. I trust that we will meet again, in more convivial circumstances. And may I wish you well in the future in the worthy work that you do as a justice of the peace. I am sure that the Lord Lieutenant will continue to value your contribution.'

Having put in the knife and twisted it to my satisfaction, I curtsied, and left the room, leaving Master Price and Master Hickey to assess the extent of their wounds. Grandpa remained with them while they recovered the power of speech, and Grandma Jane went to tell the other Revenue men, who were drinking contraband tea in the kitchen, that their leaders were ready to depart.

Now they have gone off back to town, and we will not see them again. When the coast was clear, we all collapsed in hysterics. I had found the encounter exhausting, but also exhilarating. I hugged Grandpa Isaac, who was very pleased

162

with himself, and laughed. 'Grandpa, you are a genius! I would never have thought of bringing in all that information about the magistrates' code of behaviour. Thank God you are one of them. It was all true, of course?'

'Good Lord, no! A load of nonsense, all of it. But he does not know that, since he never attends the Lord Lieutenant's annual bench meetings, and I dare say he has never tried to serve a search warrant on a fellow magistrate before.'

We enjoyed a most convivial supper, and I brought out a good bottle of tax-free Nantz brandy since I thought the occasion warranted it. The only sour note was struck by Grandma, as she went off to bed. 'Martha, my dear,' she whispered into my ear, 'just you watch that George Price. He is a bad-tempered bully who is used to getting his way. Today you have insulted him and done great damage to his pride. And in front of that fool Hickey. He will not forgive you. You have had fun, but I fear that no good will come of it.'

I hope that she is mistaken, but just as a precaution I will get a message to Skiff tomorrow, inviting him to get that silver out of my dung-heap just as quickly as he can.

17 March 1807

I thank the good Lord in his Heaven that things have quietened down. On the two days after that business with the search warrant, we had squally rain and wind, and the ground was too wet for spring ploughing. I checked with Grandpa that there was a good winnowing wind going through the barn, and then I ordered the threshing of the last of the barley. Some of it was done in February, when the market price was temporarily high, but a few days ago Billy reported that mildew was beginning to appear on the residual pile, and it is a principle of mine that I will not risk any reduction in the quality of the grain. It had to be done now, for merchants like Wilson and Probert can smell mildew from a distance of ten miles. So we set to it as a matter of emergency, with three pairs of threshers on the threshing floor, and six of the estate labourers providing assistance. All of the residents of the Plas were involved – most of the servants and family in the barn, and only Mrs Owen left in the kitchen to feed the dusted masses. The children love threshing time, which is like organized chaos for me but playtime and conviviality for them. The girls helped with the winnowing, and Dewi insisted on being head hummeller. Tucker Penrhiw and two of the Jenkins boys helped with the bagging, and Caradoc Williams and Tomos Huws did the carting. The occasion was very good-humoured, leaving us all thoroughly exhausted, covered with fine dust and little barley spikes, and fully informed as to the local news. The children, I fear, have learned some very rude songs that I would prefer them not to know.

In the event Grandpa rejected only six sacks of tainted barley, and those will be held back for planting or for animal feed. We have sixty bags of clean barley left in the barn to cover our own needs, and those of our labourers, and two hundred and sixty bushels have been sold. I could obtain no more than fifteen shillings per bushel, and was not happy with that, but in retrospect I should have threshed and sold earlier. No matter. We will survive.

The news from town is that Squire Edwards has removed himself from his comfortable lodgings in the Llwyngwair Arms and has gone back to Wervil in his carriage. He was apparently in high dudgeon when he left, complaining bitterly about the incompetence of the local Revenue officers and constabulary, and swearing that he will never again set foot in Newport. I dare say that Skiff will have been relieved to hear that particular piece of news. Hettie, who knows one of the serving girls at the inn, tells us that relations between the Cardiganshire squire and his cousin George Price are now very strained, following a blazing row between them in the upstairs bar. Griff Hickey and his Revenue men have also removed themselves from their lodgings and gone back to Fishguard.

Last night there was a lot of noise in the vicinity of the dung-heap at four of the clock. Luckily there was a bright high moon. When I came down to breakfast Will was there, looking like death and not exactly smelling of lilac blossom. I sent him off to the scullery in the company of three buckets of hot soapy water, and invited him to change all his clothes, and he obliged. When he came back, the other servants could not resist a little entertainment at his expense. 'Been re-arranging the dung-heap, Will?' asked Billy, with a big toothless grin. 'Very commendable, and outside normal working hours too. Indeed, there is no limit to your enthusiasm in the matter of hard work.'

Will gave Billy a withering look, and tucked into his bowl of porridge. In spite of various taunts from Sian and Shemi, and grinning faces all round the table, he would say no more. Afterwards I caught his eye and had a word with him in the passage. 'All gone, Will?'

'Yes, Mistress. But we did have a devil of a job finding them. The whole dung-heap had changed shape, what with all the new dumping that Shemi have done in the last few days. Too enthusiastic by half, that fellow.'

'He was simply following my instructions, Will. Incriminating evidence is best buried deep. I hope Skiff is not stupid enough to try to sell that stuff locally?'

'He was not born yesterday, Mistress.' Will grinned. 'He have borrowed a pony and a *gambo*, and five sacks of barley. Tomorrow he is off to Carmarthen on business. He knows a fellow there who buys barley, especially when it contains certain strange and heavy impurities.'

I patted Will on the back, and we went our separate ways. I dare say that Will will get a guinea or two from Skiff for all his trouble, and I hope that Skiff will take the advice that I have offered to him more than once and invest some of his earnings in a decent cottage and a horse and cart. He is a natural tradesman, and smart to boot, and with application he could even become a respectable merchant.

Over the last few days I have been longing for Owain, and have wished on a number of occasions that I had him by my side – to hold my hand, give me reassurance, and help in the making of difficult decisions. I had, before this morning, not seen him since the Sahara storm. Indeed, it must have been the best part of a month since we met. I was reminded of this when I received a little note from him, accompanied by a bunch of daffodils. The note read as follows:

Llannerch, 16th day of March 1807

My beloved Martha,

It seems like a thousand years since I last warmed myself in the radiance of your smile. I see your beauty before me wherever I look, and hear your soft words and your laughter whatever else it may be that I am supposed to listen to. I am a man distracted and overwhelmed by love, and I am not ashamed to admit it. I long for the touch of your lips, and long to fold my arms round you.

How are you? Are you well? And the little ones – are they happy too? Did the Plas survive the storm without too much damage? I assume so, and that if it had been otherwise you would have called upon me to help. I must know all that you have been doing, and indeed I have much to tell you about events at Llannerch and Pontfaen. Did you hear about the shipwreck?

I cannot sleep because of this ache in my heart and this longing in my breast, and I hate this time of separation. I must see you again, or I will surely die of a broken heart. I will call this afternoon at three, and hope that this may be convenient.

I love you. I love you for ever.
Owain

When I read this for the first time I laughed and cried at once. What a passionate and wonderful man! Can there be any greater joy in life than to love and be loved? And to be loved by a poet prepared to display his passions on his sleeve? Then I read it over and again, and felt myself to be greatly aroused. I was almost dizzy with the warmth of my passion. I folded the note up very small, and popped it on an impulse into my cleavage, presumably on the grounds (though I cannot be sure) that I needed it to be permanently fixed close to my heart and my breasts. I tried to concentrate on displaying the daffodils in a glass vase, but made a very bad job of it. Bessie came in and said: 'Now then, Mistress, it appears that notes from Master Owain have a serious effect upon your artistic abilities. If I may say so, you look like a sixteen-year-old who has just been invited to her first ball. You'd better sit down by the window and think beautiful thoughts, and leave the daffodils to me.' I followed instructions, and she arranged the flowers.

At three of the clock Owain strode into the yard. I like a man who walks, and is not afraid to get his boots dirty. He took them off and came into the kitchen, where I was waiting for him. We kissed and embraced with a degree of passion not normally seen in the kitchen, and Mrs Owen, who was baking Welsh cakes upon a griddle plate, averted her eyes in a state of some embarrassment. 'Good day to you, Master Owain,' said she, lowering herself about three inches in what passes, among large ladies, as a curtsy. 'Just you carry on. I am well practised in the business of seeing nothing and hearing nothing.'

'Good day, Mrs Owen,' said Owain when he had recovered his breath. 'I must apologize for that display of unbridled passion, but perhaps you can imagine how it is for a poor fellow who has not seen the Mistress of Plas Ingli for at least a hundred years.'

'I can well imagine, sir, what pent-up passions you must have within you after all this time,' said she, not batting an eyelid.

Owain blushed and I collapsed in a fit of giggles. 'Mrs Owen!' I scolded. 'You are very rude. Please remember that you are talking to a gentleman who is your future master. He may well have a mind, if you are not careful, to ask you to hold your tongue, and to reduce your wages.'

'Or indeed to increase them,' said Owain, grinning. 'Women who have such a good understanding of a gentleman's passions are to be valued, and given adequate remuneration.'

Now it was Mrs Owen's turn to blush, at which Owain bowed deeply, took me by the hand and led me to the parlour. We sat on our most comfortable settee and kissed, and embraced, and talked. I told Owain all about the storm, and about my efforts in securing a church wedding for Patty and Jake. He knew something about that, having lent his hunting outfit (which is never used for hunting) to our friend the wizard. Joseph had told him a certain amount, but there were some details that I had to fill in. I did not tell him about the Nightwalker, for I have a strange superstition in my mind that if I do it will somehow

169

substantiate my fear that Owain is a marked man, and he – and I – will be overtaken by tragedy. But I did tell him the full story of the silver in the dung-heap, which he found thoroughly entertaining. He was roaring with laughter at the idea of Will up to his neck in ordure when that young man's mother came in, quite unannounced and uninvited, with tea and Welsh cakes for the two of us, served on a silver tray. I was amazed, for Mrs Owen, as housekeeper, makes a point of never serving guests or anybody else, for that is Bessie's job. But I knew that this was the sealing of a new friendship between Owain and herself, springing out of a shared sense of humour and a mutual respect for the earthy realities of life. 'Oh, thank you, Mrs Owen,' said I. 'You are very kind.'

'Thank you indeed,' said Owain, bowing deeply. 'How did you know that when I smelt those fresh Welsh cakes on the griddle it was love at first sniff?' The good lady smiled demurely, lowered herself a good four inches, and went out backwards like a musician retiring to thunderous applause.

We enjoyed our tea and griddled cakes, and Owain told me about events at Llannerch. All very mundane, apart from some thefts of turnips and potatoes by vagrants who have been living rough in Cwm Gwaun. 'I fear, Martha, that nothing very much happens down in the *cwm*,' he said. 'Even the hurricane was but a whispering breeze round the house and farm buildings. By comparison, this place is a hotbed of intrigue and a hive of mad buzzing activity. I sometimes wonder if it is because of the children; but then I return to the inevitable conclusion that it is because of their mother. The sooner I move in here and calm things down, the better!'

'No no, my dear Master Laugharne,' said I. 'You are quite mistaken. It is because of the rarefied atmosphere up here on the mountain. The air is thoroughly invigorating. I advise you to try it sometime.'

'You forget, Mistress, that I have indeed tried it. Some weeks back, you may recall that I was well settled in your bed, in a state of considerable disrepair. The problem was that I was in that bed alone. I am utterly convinced that had you been in it with me, my recovery would have been greatly accelerated.'

'Poppycock, sir. If I had been between those sheets your recovery would have been in great doubt. Master Harries, the good doctor, informs me that certain activities are strictly prohibited for invalids...'

And so we chatted on, cuddling and kissing and talking utter nonsense. We laughed so much that I had to borrow Owain's kerchief to wipe away my tears. It had to end, of course, when the big children came tumbling out of their afternoon lessons and Sara finished her afternoon nap. Owain had to go to help with the evening milking, since his cowman has injured his back. But we agreed to meet again on the day after tomorrow, which is little Sara's second birthday. I pray that tomorrow will fly by without my noticing it, and that before I have recovered from today I will be in his arms again.

19 March 1807

Sara is two today, and we have had a very jolly time. My little angel is no longer a baby, which causes me some regret, for she is my youngest and I miss the warm and lovely baby smell that has been a part of my life more or less continuously for nigh on nine years. But she is very beautiful, and as cheerful and bubbly as her big brother Dewi. She has a mass of golden hair which she wears in ringlets, and she has David's blue eyes. She is an early and precocious talker, and is already almost as clever with words as Dewi. The two of them are the very best of friends, and do everything together. She adores him, and now that he is a manly four years old he defends her and assists her in all manner of things. Even if she is being very pestilential, as she can be with her big sisters, he will stick up for her through hell and high water, and it is interesting for me to observe how Betsi and Daisy have become very close as a counterbalance to the affiance of the little demons. Things are occasionally difficult, but for the most part they are, all four, a joy to be with. I declare that I could not manage without Sian, for she carries much of my mother's load, and indeed takes care, for the most part, of their education. But Betsi is ready for more challenging and stimulating activities than Sian can devise for her, and I am minded, before long, to take in a tutor and piano teacher.

I will have more children, and Owain will be the father. He will be master of my heart, master of my bed, master of my family, and master of my household. I need all this to happen, and soon, for I am not suited to the single and celibate life. I have an appetite that needs to be satisfied, and I have no time for the feeble females who see it as their role in life to be chattels and playthings to be plucked up and cast away by arrogant and cynical gentlemen. I am, after all, a widow and the owner of an estate in spite of the idiocy of the laws of this patriarchal land. Destiny has given me freedom and responsibility, and I hope to God that I have truly earned the trust which others now place in me. I could never live with a man whose purpose in life was to use me as a baby-making machine, an ornament to be paraded in front of his peers, and a means towards aggrandizement. Owain is not such a man, nor can he ever be. He is a true gentleman, and he will be my lover, and my protector, and my friend and companion. He has eyes one could drown in, and the form of Adonis, and the soul of an artist, and the grace of a prince. He is as perfect as a man can be; and that is why I love him and will have him all to myself.

Enough of romantic ramblings. It was my intention to write of Sara's happy day. But in truth, with my mind elsewhere, suffice it to say that it was a lovely occasion, with warm spring weather and sweet and sticky food suitable for small children and grown men, and silly games, and presents, and visitors. Joseph came, and so did Owain, and because the children love both of them dearly I fear that I was pushed out onto the margins of various energetic games on the muddy lawn. I did not mind. I looked on and loved them all.

And then Joseph realized that we two love-birds needed time together. 'Children, now just you listen to me!' he announced in stentorian tones. 'Who likes jelly?'

'I do! I do! I do!' shouted all four of them in harmony.

'Who makes the best jelly?'

'Mrs Owen!' 'Bessie!' 'My mam!' 'Grandma Jane!' shouted all four of them in disharmony.

'Oh dear,' said Joseph. 'We appear to have some disagreement. Wrong – all of you. The best jelly in the whole world is made by the magic frogs who live in Ffynnon Brynach.' There were exclamations from the little ones and protest-ations of disbelief from Betsi and Daisy. 'Don't believe me? Very well then, just you follow me. I will show you that the frogs can make magic jelly that comes to life!' Sara and Dewi jumped up and down and clapped their hands, but the two older ones displayed all the scepticism that comes with age. 'Come along! Come along! Perhaps Sian and Bessie will come with us? Yes? Good, good. Now then, stout shoes upon your feet and coats upon your backs. And you children must have hats upon your heads, if you please, since the wind is bitterly cold.'

There was pandemonium as they all got ready, and gathered up bottles and tin boxes for the collection of frogspawn. And off they went up onto the mountain without so much as a back-ward glance or a word of farewell, skipping and jumping and yelling like the infidel hordes at the gates of Jerusalem. For an hour Owain and I were left all alone in the blessed peace of the parlour, to continue with the process of learning to love one another. He holds me now in the palm of his hand, as I hold him in my heart. Does this place me in danger, or expose me to the slingshots of fortune? I declare in these pages of my little book that I do not care. Truly, I do not care, for this is my destiny.

20 March 1807

Today Owain has had to go to Carmarthen on estate business with his father in the Pontfaen coach, so I have not seen him. I have missed him terribly, for I have had to deal with very difficult news all alone. A messenger came up the drive in mid-morning with a letter, which proved to be from my sister Elen in Bath. I have seen too little of my eldest sister in recent years, since she has settled in Bath and is engaged as a music teacher by various elegant families of that town. I have not been as close to her as I have sometimes wished, and my relationship with my other sister Catrin has always been more intimate. That is perhaps natural enough, since she lives just a few miles away, at Castlebythe. But of course I love Elen dearly and long for her company, and I was therefore dumbfounded when I read the following:

Bath, on the 10th day of March in the year 1807

My beloved sister Martha,
  This is not an easy letter to write, and I fear that I may wet the paper with tears, so I must endeavour to

175

contain my emotions and try to be brief. I fear that this has to be a note which says farewell, for we will never see each other again. Some trouble has come into my life, and it would be too painful to describe it to you. Do not worry, for I am not ill and I am not about to die, either by my own hand or in any other way. But we will not meet again until we do so in Heaven.

I have to escape from here and leave my sadness behind. I must try to be brief. I will write more when I have the time. That is, if I have time before I go. Pray, do not worry.

I trust that you and the children are well, and that David's grandparents are in good health. Dear Martha, you have had enough trouble in your life, and you deserve happiness. Marry Owain, and do it soon. I hope and pray that your lives together will be truly blessed. And the little ones, too.

Do not try to contact me, for I am no longer at my old address. Nobody knows where I am, and I may not be here for very long anyway. I am very sorry.

Your loving sister, Elen

There were blotches and smudges on the letter. She had clearly been weeping as she wrote it. The ink used was not all the same. There were also crossings out and subtle changes in the hand-writing which suggested to me that she had written the letter in several different stages.

What could I do when I read this appalling and confused epistle? I could not understand it, and read it over and again. I sat in my chair for more than an hour, as if I had been turned to stone. What did it mean? What was the trouble to which she referred? Had she done something and been discharged from her employment? Had she hurt her hands, so that she can no longer make music? To Elen, that would truly be almost as bad as the death of a loved one. Had she been involved in some torrid affair of the heart, and been rejected? Had she gone out of her mind? My thoughts spun round inside my head until I was no longer capable of rational thought. I wept, and dried my tears, and was then overtaken by a sort of impotent panic. Elen, my elegant and beautiful elder sister, the one in whose warmth I had basked as a little child and whose accomplishments I had admired as a young lady – now reduced to such a state of despair that she could not write a sensible letter, or string half a dozen sentences together without repeating herself or losing her train of thought. Elen, who loved light and gaiety and the good things of life – reduced to misery somewhere in the stinking back streets of the most stylish town in England. My imagination ran riot, but I was also angry with her and with myself for the fact that we had grown apart. If we had been closer, maybe I could have helped her. We could have exchanged confidences, as sisters do.

On impulse I wanted to take the next mail coach to Bristol and Bath, but then I realized that I did not know where she now lived. Even writing was impossible, for I had no address. Impotence, frustration and rage washed over me.

I had to talk to somebody, so I went to the old people's bedroom and disturbed Grandma Jane. I read the letter out to her, and pleaded with her to tell me what to do. 'Do nothing tonight, my dear,' she said, with her arm round my shoulder.

'Sleep on it if you can. And do not forget that tomorrow is Betsi's birthday, and that Catrin and James and the children are invited. Tomorrow you must talk to your other sister, and decide together what to do.'

I will follow her advice. If I can sleep, I will sleep on it.

22 March 1807

I slept very little. It was a calm clear night, with a full moon sailing from east to west. I kept the shutters open and watched the shadows of my chair and desk as they moved, inch by inch, across the floor. I listened to the tawny owls in Gelli Wood, and then I listened to the dawn chorus.

I am in no mood to write about Betsi's birthday party, jolly as it was. Catrin and James came over from Castlebythe, as planned, with their little ones John and Mark. Suffice to say that I managed to put a brave face on it, and did all the things that a mother must do on the birthday of a nine-year-old daughter. Betsi's friends from the neighbouring farms came to play with her, and she had her presents, and she loved the silk dress and matching bonnet that I bought for her. She sang prettily for her guests, and then all the children made music together, with gusto and not much skill. We adults clapped and smiled. But my mind was elsewhere, and at last Catrin and I managed to find a space where we could talk for a few minutes.

It transpired that she too had received a letter from Elen, and been desperately worried by its contents. She felt that Elen's mind was quite deranged. Her letter was phrased differently from mine, but it expressed similar sentiments and gave us no additional information. We speculated, and discussed Elen's past history and relationships in an attempt to understand her current despair, but at the end of our conversation we were really no further forward. Then it was time for them to set out for home, with little Mark over-excited and very tearful. We embraced, and said our farewells. Tomorrow, as we agreed, she will write to brother Morys in Haverfordwest, and I will write to our parents in Brawdy. We will tell them what we have gathered from Elen's sad letters, and we live in the hope that they may know more. We will both propose a family meeting at Morys's home – the Bethesda manse in Haverfordwest – where we can discuss matters together. Elen must be saved. I only wish I knew what it is that she must be saved from.

24 March 1807

I am learning to deal with crises, and one of the lessons I have learned is that I must occasionally commune with my angels on Carningli. Today I have done just that. I could have gone to Owain at Llannerch, and I could have poured out my heart to him and left him burdened with my problems. But I knew that if I had spent an hour in his company I would have re-examined stony ground in the minutest of detail. I would have obtained his loving support and understanding, but would have come away exhausted and maybe even more miserable, and no closer to knowing what to do about my beloved sister. So I chose peace, and I chose the mountain.

As has happened before, the experience was quite magical. After breakfast I observed that it was a warm bright day, blessed by the benign hand of spring. It was far too beautiful, I thought, for the Nightwalker to be abroad. So I banished apprehension from my breast. I took some bread and cheese and an orange from the pantry, and placed them in my walking bag. I told Bessie and Mrs Owen where I was going, and why. Then I left the children to their morning lessons, put on my comfortable boots, and set off up the slope.

I carried my woollen cloak over my arm in the expectation that there would be wind on the summit. I stopped at Ffynnon Brynach, anointed myself with a handful of the sacred water, and made some close observations of the progress of the little tadpoles wriggling about in the frog-spawn which covered the adjacent pools, smiling at the thought of the children's recent – and very successful – jelly-hunting expedition with Joseph. Then I climbed onwards and upwards, across a landscape still dressed in its subdued and subtle winter raiment of grey, brown, buff and ochre. The old blue rocks which litter the land surface were easy to see through the lattice of brittle bracken stalks still standing proud in spite of the snows of the winter. I skirted round some of the scorched areas burnt by Billy and Shemi last year, and noted with satisfaction that some fresh grass shoots were already coming through the blackened debris of dead gorse and heather. It was wet underfoot, but I managed to keep my feet dry by hopping from rock to rock. Because the air was so still here on the lee side of the mountain I could hear birdsong everywhere, and skylarks were fluttering high overhead, noisily celebrating their arrival from foreign parts. Even higher up, over the mountain summit, there were five buzzards, tumbling and mewing in some family dispute.

Soon I crossed the first of the stone embankments. Like the others higher up, this appears now as a long ridge of relatively small stones, chosen presumably by the ancient inhabitants of the mountain because they were easy to move. Squire Fenton had told me that these banks were once impregnable walls ten or fifteen feet high, intended to protect families and their animals from the marauding bands which lurked in the woods below. I found a warm flat rock facing the sun, and lay on it and closed my eyes. In my mind's eye I saw tough women dressed in goatskins and rough woollen garments, carrying earthenware pots of water up from the spring. I saw a group of laughing children swinging from the branches of a stunted ash tree. I imagined I heard the tinkling of goat bells, and dogs barking, and the clanking of heavy stones placed in position by a group of men building a wall.

Then I climbed on, crossing sunlit grassy hollows, and heading for the steepest part of the mountain slope. I decided that today should be a day for solid rock rather than boulders. So I scrambled up rough rock faces, getting my fingers into small cracks and pulling myself up like an intrepid mountaineer. From below, my progress up the mountain must have looked very undignified, but I had a wonderful time. The old raven fluttered down, perched on a crag about twenty yards from me, and watched me with disapproval writ large across his face.

After my unconventional ascent I had to cross a steep bank of precariously balanced boulders to reach the summit, and negotiated it with more than a little apprehension. Twice I misjudged things, and sent boulders crashing down; and on other occasions several jagged rocks moved as I put my weight upon them. But with perspiration on my brow, and my heart beating wildly, at last I reached the summit where the angels dwell. I looked out towards the coast, and was greatly surprised because I could not see it. Neither could I see Newport or the Parrog. All was lost in a great bank of sea fog, which was insinuating its way in from the north. I was looking down on its upper surface, which had mysterious ethereal moving hills and valleys in it. It was very strange, because above me the sky was clean and blue, and to the south the sun was high and white. As I watched, I saw that the fog bank was thickening and rolling higher and higher up the northern slope of the mountain. Waves of white mist tumbled towards me and broke against the rocks and red bracken slopes in total silence, splashing translucent whitish fragments in all directions. There was magic on one side, and another sort of magic on the other.

I knew that the fog would soon climb over the summit, so I sat down on my folded cloak on a south-facing bank of bilberry and heather, with my back against the bluestone summit rocks. I ate my bread and cheese and drank the water that I had collected in a small bottle from Ffynnon Brynach. Dogs barked down in the *cwm*, and I heard children's laughter. Then I saw Betsi and Daisy playing with a skipping rope in the yard, enjoying the sunshine and a few moments of freedom from the little ones. My heart warmed and my cheeks glowed. Then I felt the first stirrings of the air around me, and the temperature dropped sharply. As I watched, the first wisps of fog started to curl round the flanks of the mountain, some way below me and on my left. Streamers of mist moved along the valley and into the *cwm*. Then I saw some indistinct smudges of vapour to my right, drifting in through the gap between Carningli and Carn Edward. Within a few minutes I saw the first traces of cold damp cloud passing directly over my head, driven on the gentlest of northerly breezes. As I looked about me, ragged and ethereal fragments moved silently through the little gaps between the summit crags. Inexorably the process of blotting out the landscape and the sun continued, with the fog thickening all the time, and individual rivers of vapour joining together into a silent flood that obliterated everything.

After twenty minutes the *cwm* below me was full of milky cloud. I was enveloped in damp sea mist, and could see nothing further than ten yards away. My little world closed in on me, but I was not at all afraid, rather entranced and almost intoxicated by this bravura performance from the spirits of the mountain. The sounds of dogs and geese and sheep from down in the *cwm*

183

were echoed and magnified, just as they are in the prelude to a thunderstorm. Then the warmth of the sun melted away the top of the fog bank. I was suddenly bathed in warm sunlight again, and looking down on an ocean of frothy milk. On the far side of it, the rocks of Carnedd Meibion Owen stood up like islands, and in the distance there were further sunlit islands on the rolling uplands of Mynydd Presely. Faraway Foeldrygarn was one island, and Foelfeddau another, and nearby Foeleryr yet another...

The sun was triumphant, and bit by bit the ocean of milkiness was melted away. It broke up into smaller seas and lakes, interspersed with bright patches of my familiar and beloved vista of trees and fields, stone walls and cottages. And then the fog was all gone. The sunlit landscape was as calm and soft as it had been when I had climbed towards the summit two hours since.

In a state of euphoria I gathered up my cloak and my walking bag, and skipped and danced my way down the easiest of the mountain paths. Had I been dreaming? Had that magical performance by sun and fog, rock and sky been arranged entirely for my benefit? Surely it cannot have been real? But I was reminded that it had indeed all happened, for the banks of heather and bilberry, and the lichens and mosses on the old blue rocks, were all covered with myriad glistening water droplets where previously they had been quite dry.

When I arrived back, breathless, at the Plas, Daisy and Betsi ran out from the back door to meet me. 'Hello, girls,' I said. 'Have you had a nice time while I have been away?'

'Huh!' said Daisy 'It was nice, but then it got all dark and damp and horrible. We have had a very miserable time indeed.'

I mused on giving them a little sermon on life's dark moments and the need to rise above them, but then thought better of it. The symbolism and the moralizing might have been more than they could have coped with. Anyway, I thought, why should I not keep this afternoon's moments of magic all to myself? So I said: 'Never mind. The weather is very changeable at this time of year. Let's go inside and toast some scones before the kitchen fire, and see if there is some of that nice raspberry conserve left.'

'Hooray!' shouted Daisy.

'Oh, yes please!' said Betsi. And we three held hands and skipped in step into the kitchen.

Now it is very late, and I need to sleep. Looking back on my day, I have suddenly realized that I have spent virtually all of it without devoting a moment's thought to troublesome letters, mysterious phantoms, dastardly squires or silver cutlery. I am well pleased with myself and with my mountain.

25 March 1807

Patty and Jake have had their church wedding. Their names are in the register, and they are respectable at last. I was heavily involved, since as promised I paid the Rector and the fiddlers; but the happy couple did not take up my offer of the use of the Plas for the wedding dinner since they are determined to be independent. So everything happened in the town and on the Parrog.

It was a thoroughly jolly occasion, with all of my family and most of the servants involved. Grandpa gave away the bride, since her parents both died long since and her only surviving relatives are some ancient aunts and uncles who have disowned her. The old gentleman was resplendent with his shiny bald head, fawn coat and black breeches – and indeed he looked every bit as proud as any doting father might have done. Owain was best man, and as the day went on it came as something of a surprise to me to discover how close he and Jake have become. Perhaps I should not be surprised, for Jake was heavily involved in the terrible events of last November, when Owain was almost killed and Jake played a prominent role in bringing his torturers to justice. Jake and Patty appeared very tidy at the very centre of attention, with the bride enjoying every moment and the groom looking nervous and dreaming of the wide acres of the ocean. Such is the way with weddings. I was at the front of the church too, in my capacity as Matron of Honour – a title which I will do my best to forget. At any rate, I wore my tightest stays and most daring silk dress, which will have served to demonstrate to all and sundry that I am not as matronly as all that.

To his credit, Rector Devonald conducted the ceremony, and then delivered a little homily from the pulpit – while looking me straight in the eye – on forgiveness. He even managed to weave into the message something about marriage. I gave him a grin, and he directed a subtle nod in my direction without anybody else's noticing. The fiddlers fiddled furiously, and there was some lusty singing from the large congregation. Skiff and his mates from the Parrog took great delight in sitting in the gentry pews which would otherwise have been empty. My friend Joseph took up sole occupation of the pew paid for and maintained by Squire Owen, as a means of reminding everybody that the wretched fellow has still not paid for an exorcism completed two years since at Gelli Fawr. He had better pay up soon, before Joseph's exasperation turns to anger, or he will find that his cattle will all lie down and refuse to get up. This was Joseph's second visit to church in less than a month, and as on his previous visit he refused to take off his tall black hat.

It was a walking wedding rather than a horse one, for most of the friends of the happy couple are poor people, but since the distance from church to cottage is only half a mile this presented no problem. Jake was thrown out of the house yesterday, under protest, and had to spend the night on the floor in a neighbour's cottage. He had then been kidnapped early in the morning and dragged off to the Royal Oak by his confederates for a few pints of ale to calm his nerves, while the womenfolk – including Mrs Owen, Grandma Jane and I – moved in to defend the bride and to prepare the feast. There were a dozen of us all told, including four tough fishwives from the Parrog who have grown very fond of Patty and make up a very formidable bodyguard. We worked away through the morning, but at last the men arrived, somewhat the worse for wear, in search of the bride. To reach the front door they had to clamber over assorted obstacles we had put in the way, including heavy ropes and timbers borrowed from the shipyard, for it would not have been seemly for the cottage to be perceived as a place of easy conquest.

After some scrambling and heaving away of encumbrances, Jake's fishermen friends reached the door and beat upon it with a staff. Mrs Owen, opening it, presented an obstacle substantially more impregnable. There was no way past her, and the men knew it. There commenced a protracted exchange of strange rhymes, some traditional and others invented on the spot, between the assailants and the defenders. Inside the cottage it was mostly Grandma Jane or Mrs Owen who shouted them out, and outside Grandpa Isaac and Daniel Jenkins Blaenwaun were the main spokesmen. The rhymes went something like this:

Women: 'Good day to you, kind gentlemen. And what might your business be? No beggars if you please, for we are near the hungry month.'

Men: 'No beggars, to be sure. We were bid to make an errand by a warm-hearted young fellow, to fetch the blue-eyed Patty, for to be his loving wife.'

Women: 'Then yours is the mistake. Be sure she will not have him. For who will have a fisherman, when just round the corner there may be a scholar and a poet?'

Men: 'A scholar and a dreamer? And where will he find the sovereigns to feed a wife and family? Our fisherman is a scholar of the sea, and a wealthy one at that.'

And so on, and so on, for over an hour, until both parties tired of the sport. At last Mrs Owen stood aside to allow the men entry, but by then Patty had escaped out through the back door and was wandering around the back passages of the Parrog disguised as an old crone, with a floppy felt hat upon her head, old boots upon her feet, and a tattered shawl over her bent shoulders. She was supposed to evade arrest, but in truth she did not try very hard, and soon she was captured, brought back to the house, and dressed up in her wedding finery before being paraded up the road all the way to the church.

She looked very pretty indeed, in a neat blue silk and taffeta dress and a wide-brimmed straw bonnet. In her arms she carried a big bouquet of daffodils and cowslips made up by Daisy and Betsi. The sun shone, and we all paraded together, enjoying the cheering and the laughter of all the good people who lined the route. Jake and the other men were in the church when we arrived, looking relieved, as men always do when they discover that women are actually capable of keeping their promises.

As soon as the ring was on Patty's finger, somebody blew on a whistle at the church door, and all the young men who had been standing at the back of the church stampeded out and went rushing off down the street. So began the race for the wedding cake. We all grinned and returned to the sedate conclusion of the ceremony, and it was a good deal later that we discovered that the race had been won by a skinny lad called Zeke Shobbins, who arrived at the door of the cottage on the Parrog a good fifty yards ahead of his nearest rival.

At the end of the ceremony, with the bells ringing out from the squat church tower, the bride and groom were carried shoulder-high by friends and neighbours down Market Street, along West Street and then all the way down Parrog Road, with cheers and good wishes all the way. I knew, in witnessing this rehabilitation and the opening of the community's heart, why the church wedding had been so important to Patty, my long-suffering and much-abused friend who was now Mistress Nicholas.

The feasting and singing and dancing was, I am assured, better than anything seen on the Parrog for twenty years or more. The cottages on both sides of Bwthyn Bach had been opened up for the celebrations by their inhabitants, and a hundred or more guests wandered back and forth, eating in one, drinking and singing in another, and dancing in the third. Owain and I had hardly a moment to ourselves, but that was no more than we expected, and we knew that our day would come. Outside, the lads who had raced for the cake consumed it on the sea wall and threw crumbs to the gulls. The children rushed about with their old friends and discovered new ones. The invited guests ate and drank until they were replete and incapable; other well-wishers turned up and bought their quarts of ale and griddle cakes in the knowledge that all of their coppers would go into the cottage savings, ready for the time when Patty and Jake would start a family. The music was unexceptional, but the noise level was utterly astonishing. The tide came in. Laughter echoed across the water, bounced against Morfa Head, and rolled back again over the Parrog, reminding those of us who were capable of the observance that this old land and fathomless sea have heard and seen it all before.

By nine of the clock the children were exhausted, and we took them home in the chaise, with Grandpa driving. We had said our fond farewells, and left Master and Mistress Nicholas to the tender mercies of the revellers. Later on they will be put to bed by their friends, but they will certainly not get a moment of privacy before dinnertime tomorrow. They will not worry. They have little new to discover about each other anyway, and when they come to count their gifts they will find that they are thirty pounds better off and a good deal better equipped than they were before to face the rigours of a life spent together ten yards from the water's edge and an inch from the edge of poverty.

Between the Lines

30 March 1807

A response has come from my parents to the letter which I penned about a week ago. It was a strange letter, very bland and complacent, telling me not to worry. That, I have to admit, made me angry. How can I not worry when my dear Elen appears to be suffering from derangement and delusions, and says she will never see her sisters again? Parents can be very silly sometimes. Perhaps my dear father, who was so direct and decisive in all his dealings, is beginning to feel his age? But I must not be uncharitable. At least he agreed that we should all meet soon at Morys's house in Haverfordwest, and said that he would immediately instigate some investigations through people whom he knows in Bath. He will also write to Great-aunt Lizzie in Bristol, who has been like a mother to Elen since she left home to be a student of music. He will no doubt write again if he receives any intelligence.

Closer to home, trouble is brewing over the hardships suffered by the poor people of the neighbourhood, and although I am not currently involved in any disputes I have a presentiment that I soon will be. I also had a powerful premonition last night that I will be drawn into further conflict with the bothersome Squire Price of Llanychaer. This causes me to feel considerable apprehension in my breast, for I have quite enough to deal with as it is.

The trouble is to do with the rent increases which some of the squires have been imposing this month on their tenants, and with the sudden enthusiasm Rector Devonald has developed for the collection of tithes. Several of the small tenant farmers on neighbouring estates have had their rents doubled or even tripled on their renewal dates, and have had agreements forced upon them which reduce their tenancies from three or four lives down to one. This means that their children have virtually no prospect of taking over the farms and fields on which they have grown up. These are the places that are imprinted on their souls, and little wonder that they feel betrayed. The squires and their stewards say that there is now such a demand for land that tenants have to pay the market rate, especially since the estates themselves are in dire straits. They say that if the sitting tenants are not happy with the terms on offer, they can move on, for there are others standing in long queues who are ready and waiting to take their place. But if the small farmers move, where will they go? Some, to my knowledge, have been forced into labourers' cottages and condemned to lives of poverty, their farming skills lost to the community. This cannot be in anybody's best interest, and I am certain, from my own observations, that those who have no security will abandon good husbandry and the repairing of walls and buildings, on the basis that a farm in good heart may simply be passed on to somebody else or attract even greater rent increases which they can never afford to pay. The insanity of the situation is obvious to me, and I will have nothing to do with this worship of the market which involves the sacrifice of good and worthy lives.

Matters are made worse by the new obsession with money which seems to be spreading like an epidemic across the countryside. In England, as I have reported, money is in widespread use, but here in Wales there is very little coinage or paper money to be had, and so payment for services rendered is made in the form of other currency – labour, sacks of barley, barrels of salt herrings, geese or fat chickens, butter and eggs. Labour comes from the tenant farmers and from the poor labourers, and even from their wives and children, and every day spent on stone walling, bird-scaring, hay-making or harvesting is duly recorded. We all need help from our neighbours, and we reciprocate. The system works well. At the Plas, we collect our rent from Blaenwaun in the form of labour, woollen stockings, and various offerings at Michaelmas and Christmas. The rent from Plain Dealings comes nowadays mostly in the form of eggs, and sewin from the River Nevern which are acquired in circumstances I would prefer not to know too much about. Thomas Tucker Penrhiw offers up wood pigeons and woodcock. Caradoc Williams Gelli contributes roofing slates and slate slabs from the Aberrhigian sea quarry. And, most bizarrely, Jeb Phipps from Brithdir pays part of his rent in smoked eels, part in willow baskets and another part in charcoal. These agreements, which are seldom written down, are based upon the needs of the estate, the skills and inclinations of the tenants and the labourers, and the nature of the land which they occupy. But the system breaks down when a squire suddenly demands cash on the nail at the time when the rent is due. The tenant can only obtain cash by selling his produce privately or at Newport market, often at a price lower than the valuation which the squire, in the good old days, might have given it. If he still cannot raise the fifty pounds needed, he must sell some of the food normally set aside for the needs of his own family; and if he is still short he will demand cash instead of labour from those who are indebted to him. So the obsession with cash trickles right down through every stratum in society from the squires to the tenants, from the tenants to the labourers, and from the labourers to the paupers.

And as if this is not bad enough, Rector Devonald has now decided, in keeping with the modern trend, to require the payment of tithes in the form of cash rather than produce. He is away from Newport so often, enjoying the comfort of various other livings, that he has grown tired of traipsing about at harvest time with his horse and cart collecting sheaves from here, there and everywhere. His changed view may have something to do with the fact that his visits are very unwelcome and are normally accompanied by arguments as to the size of the harvest and the number of sheaves reckoned to make up 10 per cent of it. The Nonconformist tenants do not see why they should pay tithes in any case to a largely absentee Rector who does virtually nothing for them, and they are especially incensed that he is now demanding annual inventories and valuations of their produce and presenting them with bills and final demands for cash. He has even employed an agent to act on his behalf, and in order to boost his commission this arrogant fellow pushes up his valuations and hence the tithe required, with nobody able to prevent this blatant display of greed and exploitation. In the last month there have been three distraints, and two tenant families on the Llanychaer estate have had everything taken away by the bailiffs – every piece of furniture, every farming implement, curtains, bedding, carpets and even cooking utensils. In one case, kindly neighbours bought everything at the distraint sale, and gave it back to the poor suffering victims; but in the other case there were no neighbours to help, and a family of five has been forced into paupery. The foolish Rector does not seem to realize it, but both he and his agent will get their throats cut one dark night if they do not mend their ways.

The greatest villains in all of this, apart from Rector Devonald, are Philip Owen of Gelli Fawr, Solomon Huws of Bayvil, and George Price of Llanychaer. It is a mystery to me why every community seems to acquire its quota of mean and snarling wolves that thrive on the misfortunes of others. I had thought that with the departure of Alban Watkins, Benjamin Rice and George Howell into the fires of Hell the world would be a kinder and gentler place; but no, there appear always to be new villains ready to take their places and keen to act out their roles as enemies of the people.

After dinner today we were all forced to remain indoors by heavy squalls rolling in from the west, and while the children were having their lessons I took Grandpa Isaac to one side, to seek his advice on my best course of action in the face of these unsettling changes. We sat in the parlour, gazing into the raw flames of a log fire. I was relieved to find that his views are almost identical to my own. He is a man who has a great respect for tradition and dislikes unnecessary change; but he also thinks about the future and has a considerable facility for predicting what will happen to those who, in his view, think more about profits than about the nurturing of the land, and care more about property than about people.

'Just you take heed, Martha,' he said, jabbing his bony finger towards me, 'this mad obsession with cash will not last. There are not enough bits of paper and gold coins to go round, and when people realize this we will all be forced back to the old and sensible way of doing things. It is all to do with wisdom, passed on from one generation to another. I know, because my father taught me, exactly the value of a child's day of bird-scaring, or a dozen summer eggs, or a dozen winter eggs, or a basket of field mushrooms. I know that a basket of Easter apples has five times the value of a basket of November apples. These men who learn about bookkeeping and sit in offices know none of these things, and I predict that when sensible squires learn that these silly fellows are maintained by deception, and by the dictates of fashion, they will simply be seen as aberrations, and will all become redundant!'

He slapped his knees and roared with laughter. Much as I would have liked to agree with him, I could not, and I said as much. I said that I feared that the old ways of farming and stewardship were under pressure, and that the men with money, real or imagined, would one day rule the world. 'But I promise you, dearest Grandpa,' I said, 'that I will keep faith with your beliefs and will always try to be sensitive to the needs of tenants and labourers alike. Owain sees things in a similar way, and this has already led him into dispute with Squire Price. But like it or not, I feel in my bones that one day I will need a good deal of cash to ensure that our estate is able to resist the assaults of a hostile world. I will find the cash, and the estate will survive.' I said no more about it, nor did Grandpa press me – but I know that the Plas Ingli treasure is still in the ground, in a place revealed only to me, and I feel sure that one day I will need it. I changed the subject.

'Why is it, dearest Grandpa,' I asked, 'that Price Llanychaer appears to be so intent upon antagonizing his tenants, his labourers, and even his neighbours?'

'Probably, my dear, because he is not a happy man. When men are unhappy, I have observed that they take actions which appear to be designed to compound their unhappiness.'

'But he is wealthy, and his estate is growing, and he has a respected family. Does that not add up to happiness?'

'Not always, Martha. I know a good deal about Price Llanychaer. The expansion of his estate is foolhardy in the extreme, for it is financed by borrowed money. Recently, I heard from my fellows that he has borrowed at least two thousand pounds at a rate of interest which makes me shiver when I think of it. And his personal life is sad, to say the least.'

'In what way? Does he not have three beautiful daughters and a loving wife?'

'Three daughters and a wife, certainly, but beauty and love are, in my estimation, conspicuous by their absence. Two of the girls were married off, not in particularly advantageous marriages, but both of their husbands are dead.

The last daughter, Fanny, is a sweet girl, but she is reputed to be a simpleton, and will probably never find a husband. And as for Mistress Susan, she suffers from some wasting ailment, and those of us who have seen her over the years are astonished that she is still alive.'

I had not heard this before, and was appalled by these revelations. 'Oh, the poor things!' I exclaimed. 'Perhaps we should not be surprised that Squire Price has a sort of anger in his breast, and that he seeks to vent his fury on those who are weaker than himself. But were there not two sons as well?'

'Yes indeed. But they were tragic figures, both of them. Herbert was a pleasant enough fellow, and should have inherited the estate. But he died in an accident on the farm three or four years ago. Iestyn, the other boy, was not at all interested in the estate, and was set on joining the army from the days when he was just a slip of a lad.'

'I know that. I recall that I met him more than once. A polite and very eligible young man, with looks to dream of. His eyes had magic in them, and I must admit that they caused a few female hearts to flutter, including mine!'

'And now that magic has gone too, for Iestyn is dead.'

'But that is terrible! How did it happen?'

'There is some mystery about it. I heard the news myself only yesterday. He was fighting against the French in some skirmish in foreign parts. From what I can ascertain, George Price has recently received a communication from the Army, informing him that his son was lost in action and that he was mentioned in despatches, having served his King and country with distinction.'

Seldom had I heard such a catalogue of distress and disaster, and Grandpa Isaac reacted to the horror that was writ large across my face. 'My dear Martha,' he said, placing his hand upon my shoulder, 'your sympathy does you great credit. The Prices of Llanychaer have indeed suffered, but no more than the Morgans of Plas Ingli. Now then, leave them to their own grieving, and leave the rebuilding of the Llanychaer estate to George Price. I suggest that you concentrate on the happiness of your own family.'

I nodded, for I knew that Grandpa was right. But I was intrigued by the manner in which huge misfortunes had been visited upon our two families, and acting upon a sudden impulse I said, 'Grandpa, I am minded to invite Squire Price and his wife and daughter to join us for afternoon tea. I know that he is no ally of ours, but even enemies are human, and deserve gestures of sympathy and kindness. Perhaps I can find a way to improve relations between our families and estates. What do you think?'

'I do not advise it, Martha.'

'And why not? Do you not think that he will appreciate the offer of the hand of friendship?'

'I doubt it. Remember, Martha, that you have very recently humiliated him, and sent him packing when he came here with that clown Griff Hickey on the hunt for the silver cutlery.'

'I seem to recall that you played a full role in that humiliation, Grandpa.'

'So I did.' The old fellow shrugged. 'He deserved it. And you needed assistance. But news of that event has spread all over town, and he has become something of a laughing stock as a result. He will not forgive you, no matter how pretty your dress or how much you seek to bewitch him with your eyes and your honeyed words...'

I laughed. 'Grandpa! You make me sound like a seductress and a sorceress, all rolled into one! I seek not to inflame passions but to calm them. At any rate, I am set upon this course of action. If I invite the Prices, will you join us for tea, and will you behave yourself?'

'Of course, my dear. I will attend, since you need somebody to keep an eye on you. I will, as ever, I hope, demonstrate what it means to be a gentleman. But be warned. I fear that the loss of his second son will have made the fellow bitter and vengeful – an enemy to compare with Alban Watkins and Benjamin Rice for cunning and brutality. Do not cross swords again with that man, Martha. Mark my words – no good will come of it.'

31 March 1807

For the first time in my life I have had a major altercation with Grandma Jane, and I am still shaking with emotion because of it. It happened like this.

After breakfast, with the men out and about and the children settled into their lessons with Sian, I asked Grandma if I might have a word with her. She appeared reluctant, but I failed to read the significance of the shadow across her face. None the less, I encouraged her to sit with me near the window in my dressing room. I explained that I wanted her blessing before writing to invite the Price family of Llanychaer to tea. I assumed that I would get it, and was quite unprepared for her response.

'Martha, what is your motive for asking them to call at the Plas?' she asked. 'I want the truth, if you please.'

'Why, Grandma, you must know perfectly well what my motive is. You must have spoken to Grandpa Isaac about our conversation of yesterday. Squire Price is a blustering bully of a man, and he is causing a deal of trouble in the neighbourhood just now. But you must know that I feel sorry for them after all their misfortunes. I simply hope to improve relations between our two families.'

'Is that the truth?'

'Why yes, of course it is.'

There was a pause, and I noticed that there was a flush upon Grandma's cheeks. When she spoke next there was a tremor in her voice. 'Martha, my dear, we love you dearly, but sometimes you are not entirely honest with yourself or with the rest of us. Have you really examined your motives in this matter? Are you absolutely sure that you are not engineering another situation in which you will be able to humiliate a gentleman?'

'Grandma! Whatever do you mean?' said I, feeling my temperature soaring.

'I mean, Martha, that I have observed something in you over the past few months that I do not particularly like. By that I mean your enthusiasm for arranging confrontations with gentlemen, humiliating them, and then taking great pleasure in their misfortune.'

'I refute that completely, Grandma!' I cried, my voice rising. 'I really do not know what you are talking about!'

There was now frost in the air. Grandma was perfectly calm, and as I looked at her this made me even more angry than I was already, for I knew and she knew that I was on the defensive.

'I take no pleasure in saying this, Martha,' continued the old lady, her voice calm and perfectly controlled. 'But it is not so long ago that you planned in elaborate detail that theatrical performance in Parc Haidd which led to the humiliation of more than ten men, including five gentlemen...'

'Gentlemen, you call them? Rice, Watkins, Lloyd, Howell, and Fenton – men of good breeding maybe, but gentlemen – never! They were evil through and through, all five of them. And do not forget, Grandma, that they murdered your grandson, my husband. Did you not desire justice, just as I did?'

'Indeed I did, Martha. And now nearly all of them are dead. You and I have had our pounds of flesh.'

'Yes, and the cause of justice has been served. I hope, Grandma, that we can agree on that, and acknowledge that we have in consequence been able to sleep a little easier in our beds?'

'Of course. That is not a matter of dispute. But I have to say, with hindsight, that in the aftermath of your triumph there was too much noise and celebration. Humility was conspicuous by its absence.'

I did not reply immediately, for this last comment cut me to the quick. Grandma was now being more cruel than she needed to be. I closed my eyes, breathed deeply and tried to control my emotions. At last I said, 'Grandma, that was not a kind thing to say. Hindsight is a wonderful thing. In the aftermath of the capture of those villains, we were all swept along by a wave of relief and even euphoria. Yes, the atmosphere in the house was triumphant, in spite of the fact that we were sending several men to the gallows. But how else could we have reacted? Were you not in our midst, Grandma? Did you not laugh, and cry, and dance and sing with the rest of us...?'

Suddenly I felt utterly weary. My voice trailed away, and I became aware that tears were rolling down my cheeks. Grandma came across to me and put her arm round my shoulders. 'Yes, yes,' she said. 'We were all swept along, and we all rejoiced in your triumph. I freely admit it. But afterwards we might have been wiser and more restrained in our celebrations.'

'Do you not think, Grandma,' I sobbed, 'that I have struggled with all this already? I have relived that episode in Parc Haidd, and other episodes that I have never revealed to you, over and again in my head and my heart. I have analysed my actions and my motives. I have tried to work out whether I was driven by dark vengeance or shining justice in my pursuit of those men. I have tried to learn about forgiveness, and I have tried to learn about humility... God only knows it, Grandma, but I have tried. I have tried.'

'I know, my dear, and I admire and love you for it. You are a good deal more aware of what is going on than the rest of us beneath this roof. And a good deal stronger.'

She kissed me on the cheek. We sat there, the old lady and I, for several minutes, holding hands. At last I pulled myself together and managed a weak smile. 'Now then, Grandma, while you are in the mood for honesty and I am your prisoner, is there anything else you want to say to me?'

'Just a little more. Two recent episodes have caused me concern. The first one was the occasion of your meeting with the Rector, when you convinced him to give Patty and Jake a church wedding. The second one was your encounter with Squire Price and Griff Hickey, when they came hunting for the silver cutlery.'

'Yes, I recall them perfectly well. Why should they have caused you concern?'

'On both occasions, my dear, you acted in defence of yourself and your friends when confronted by powerful men. So far, so good. I admire your courage and your steadfastness. But if I may say so, Martha, your quick wit and your lack of respect for authority led to the humiliation of those particular gentlemen. They will not forgive you for it, and there may yet be repercussions.'

I was no longer in the mood to argue, for I knew that her assessment was perfectly accurate. I nodded, and she continued. 'And then, following each conquest, you laughed a little too much, and talked a little too much in the presence of others who have big ears and wagging tongues. If I may say so, my dear, it appears to me that you actually enjoyed the discomfort which you visited upon Masters Devonald, Price and Hickey, and obtained further pleasure from boasting about it afterwards.'

I swallowed hard, and felt like a small child who had been ticked off for sticking a finger into a pot of honey. Of course Grandma was right. I had, in retrospect, taken too much pleasure in my small triumphs on behalf of womankind. I had been less than sensitive to the obligations placed upon gentlemen – even foolish ones – to maintain their pride and their reputations. For a gentleman to feel belittled by the words of another gentleman is one thing – but to be brought crashing to earth through the actions of a woman is to be damaged by quite another sort of shame.

'I am sorry. I am sorry, Grandma,' I whispered. 'I have been very insensitive. Please forgive me.'

'My dear Martha, there is nothing for me to forgive. I am thinking only of your best interests, and giving you a loving and gentle reminder as to how others might perceive you. You are greatly loved, and you deserve all the respect which may be accorded by others. But reputations are made and lost through the most subtle of words and the most innocent of deeds. Your high reputation is hard won; and it is my most heartfelt wish that you should enhance it rather than lose it.'

I squeezed her hand and smiled. 'Thank you, Grandma,' I said. 'I appreciate your honesty and your instinct for sniffing out trouble before it overwhelms me. I will think on what you have said this morning, and I will try to learn my lessons.'

So our interview was at an end. Grandma returned my smile. She smoothed my cheek with the back of her hand, nodded, and left the room without another word.

1 April 1807

There is a small postscript to my account of the hurtful encounter between Grandma Jane and myself, which I was too emotional to commit to paper last night. In the afternoon, when the children were outside playing in the garden, Bessie came into my dressing room to find me staring aimlessly out through the window.

'Mistress,' she said, 'if I may say so, you look a little careworn today and in need of some tidying up. May I suggest that a change of dress and a little attention to your hair might have the effect of lifting your spirits?'

I agreed, and Bessie put out my prettiest pink dress for me. When I had put it on, she sat me before the mirror and let down my hair. Pampering is something I enjoy, especially when I feel fragile.

'I could hardly help noticing that you were rather listless at dinner today, Mistress. Not feeling sick, I hope?'

'No, Bessie, I am quite well. Just thinking a lot at the moment.'

There was a long silence while Bessie continued to sweep away my tension with the aid of my softest hair brush. Then she said 'Raised voices this morning, Mistress.'

'Yes, I have to admit it. I hope I did not disturb the household too much. I have received a considerable admonishment from Grandma Jane.'

'Do you wish to tell me about it, Mistress?'

I did not know whether I wished to talk about it or not. For some time I dithered. Then I stood up and faced Bessie, and she must have seen that I was close to tears. 'Hold me, Bessie,' I whispered, and she did. I buried my face on her shoulder and wept into her collar while she smoothed my hair with her hand. I knew that I could not have revealed myself to such an extent, or in such a way, to anybody but my dearest Bessie – not even to my beloved Owain. She let me sob until the sobbing was done, and said nothing. She is very good at saying nothing, when that is what is required.

Then I stood away from her and held her hands in mine. I looked her straight in the eye. 'Thank God, Bessie, that you are here when I need you,' I said. 'I do not know how else I should survive. Now then, I want the truth. Do you think that I despise men, and that I have made it my mission in life to humiliate them?'

At this, Bessie's blue eyes sparkled, and she could not stop herself from laughing. 'What a very strange thing to say, Mistress!' she giggled. 'I do not think I have ever met anybody more passionate than you, or more eager for the company of a good gentleman. Who has accused you of this urge to conquer and humiliate? Not Grandma Jane, surely?'

'Well, yes and no. I have to admit that the idea does indeed arise from our conversation of this morning. She did not exactly accuse me of hating all men, but she did suggest that I have been making a habit of humiliating those for whom I have no respect, and that I have taken too much pleasure from their discomfort. Can that be true, Bessie? What do you think?'

Bessie paused, and swallowed hard. 'Since you ask me, Mistress,' she replied softly, 'I have to say that there is a grain of truth in it. I have noticed myself that you do seem to get some pleasure out of belittling the likes of Masters Devonald and Price, and this has caused me a little disquiet in my thinking moments. But then again, Mistress, they are arrogant and insensitive fellows, and they deserve to be brought down a peg or two. And if there is no man to do it, who better than Mistress Morgan of Plas Ingli?'

Then I laughed too, and squeezed her hands. 'You do not need to find justifications on my behalf, Bessie,' I said. 'I thank you for your honesty. You and Grandma are my two best friends, and the only two women who truly know my heart. You have both told me the same thing, and I would be insane not to take heed. Now then, I have red eyes and wild hair, and you have a wet collar. We had better continue with our tidying up operations before the children return from their games in the garden.'

2 April 1807

Having recovered my equilibrium, I took a walk this morning down to Llannerch in the company of Betsi and Daisy. Owain was delighted, as ever, to see us, and the girls demanded, and got, a good deal of attention from him. Then his shepherd took the little ones off to inspect triplet lambs born just three hours previously, and the two of us spent twenty minutes together in the privacy of the parlour. I needed his passionate kisses and his warm embrace more than he appreciated, and like a true gentleman he was only too happy to oblige. At last he came up for air, and said, 'My goodness, Martha! I perceive that you have felt the want of a man over these last few days! And I count it as my great good fortune that when you are in need of a man, you head for Llannerch.'

'Perfectly true, my dearest Owain. I have been up and down of late, largely because of female sensibilities which you may or may not understand.'

'Tell me. You may be surprised.'

So I told him everything, and to his credit he did understand. He had noticed my propensity for getting into difficult situations, and for puncturing the self-esteem of pompous squires and puffed-up reverend gentlemen, but he declared that he loved me for it. He said that he was indeed a little concerned about the possible repercussions of my actions, but declared that he would be at my side in any event, and would see that I came to no harm. I was intrigued to find that he loved me for my wilfulness, and was moreover excited by it, whereas for Bessie and Grandma it was a cause for concern and even anguish. For a man, it may be that a wilful woman is a challenge and a stimulus. But I had no time for deep thoughts about the instincts and behaviour patterns of the human species, for the children would be back at any moment.

I asked Owain if he would like to come to tea with the Prices of Llanychaer, and I was a little surprised when he declined. 'It would not be in your interest, or mine,' he said. 'I have a much greater dispute with George Price than you have, and one day I will explain it to you. It would make for a very complicated occasion if we all were to share tea together. I have to meet him soon, man to man, to sort out various grievances, and that meeting needs to be in private. No – you make your peace with him if you can. Master Isaac and Mistress Jane will help you, I am sure, and I would be a hindrance rather than a help in the circumstances. Keep it simple, Martha.'

Then the children came rushing in and insisted that we should all go and look at the triplets, and our few minutes of peace and intimacy came to an end.

As we walked home I realized that Owain had a very subtle appreciation of the ways of squires and the ways of women, and it was clear that he wanted me to deal with Squire Price on my own. That made me feel nervous, but I had to accept that when I dig a hole for myself it is best that I climb out of it unaided, even if the experience leaves me bruised and breathless.

So it was that this afternoon I sat at my writing desk and penned the following note to Squire Price of Llanychaer:

Plas Ingli, on the 2nd day of April in the year 1807
My dear Master Price,

It is the cause of some sadness to me that on the occasion of our previous meeting we had difficult business to conduct, and that we parted under conditions that were less than cordial. You had your duty to perform, and I should have paid you greater respect in recognition of that fact. I therefore offer you my unreserved apologies for my insensitive behaviour on that occasion, and trust that you will have the good grace to accept them.

I wish, in some small way, to make amends, and to seek better relations between our two families. All of us beneath the roofs of Plas Ingli and Plas Llanychaer have suffered a great deal, and as we have shared misfortune in the past it is my fervent hope that we can share more friendly relations in the future. It was only recently that I learned from Master Isaac of the tragedy that has afflicted you and your dear wife and daughter. If I had known at the time of our meeting about the loss of your beloved son Iestyn, I would not have behaved as I did – and I am truly sorry for it. May I express our deepest sympathy to you in your loss.

Would you and your wife and daughter care to join us at the Plas for afternoon tea at three of the clock on the afternoon of Friday the 10th of April? It will give me great pleasure if you accept this invitation, and I know that I also represent the views of Master Isaac and Mistress Jane in this matter. They send you warmest greetings.

I look forward to welcoming you to the Plas.
Yours etc.,
Martha Morgan

I went through several versions of this epistle before I was finally satisfied, and then I took it to Grandma Jane for her approval. I had already made my peace with her and thanked her for her timely intervention of a couple of days ago, and now I wanted to make sure that I was pitching my letter at just the right level. Too apologetic? Too fawning? Too direct or too oblique? 'No,' said Grandma. 'That will do nicely, Martha. I admire you for having the courage to apologize in such a straightforward way, but without compromising the rightness of your cause or giving in to his bullying. I hope he is gentleman enough to reply positively, and to accept the invitation. He will probably not trust you, and he will have his strongest suit of armour on when he arrives, but we must seek to win his trust. Send it, my dear.'

Now Shemi has gone off on the chestnut pony to deliver my envelope, and I hope to receive a reply tomorrow. In the meantime, I must get on with life.

4 April 1807

Today I have been to Haverfordwest with Owain, not on some frivolous expedition to buy crinolines and bonnets but in an attempt to get to the bottom of the business about my sister Elen. We travelled early, just the two of us, in the chaise, and got soaked by the squally rain, but we were together, and that made our suffering bearable. Prior to our departure I had told Owain about

213

Elen's strange letter, and on the way I gave him as much extra information as I could. I told him about the fears that were shared by Catrin and me about my sister's safety and indeed her sanity. He listened intently, furrowed his brow, but said little. As arranged, Catrin and James travelled over in the Castlebythe coach, and we all met up at the Bethesda manse. Sadly, my parents were not there, and they had sent a message to Morys to say that Mother was in bed with a severe chill. However, my brother and his dear wife Nansi were on the front doorstep to greet us, and soon we were seated in their well-appointed dining room, tucking into a very welcome hot meal of chicken pie and potatoes, followed by potted pears and custard. While we ate and downed a flagon of good claret, we talked.

We compared letters and found that we were all in possession of the same basic information, and all equally mystified. Neither Morys nor Catrin had any light to shed on Elen's finances, or on any affairs of the heart, and they both confirmed my suspicion that Elen has made a virtue of keeping herself to herself, communicating with her family only on the rarest of occasions. Since she has been in Bath she has become friendly with a young lady called Jane, the daughter of a certain Reverend George Austen; and she told me in a letter before Christmas that she had been saddened by the departure of that family to Southampton. But she did not seem particularly depressed or lonely at the time, and indeed her Christmas letter was full of good cheer. She even wrote that she would try to pay us a visit in the summer, since she was dying to meet this fellow Owain about whom I had written in such euphoric terms. Morys also reported that his Christmas epistle from Elen had been full of the joys of life, and had ended with these words: *My dearest brother, the world is glowing with good cheer at the moment, and I declare that I have never been happier.*

Catrin and I both thought that we could read romance in those words, but really we had to admit that our conclusion might just as well be based upon fantasy as upon intuition. 'And talking of intuition and instinct,' said Morys, 'you were always one for seeing things, Martha, which others could not see. Have you not seen anything regarding Elen? Have you experienced no premonition about her fate?'

I shook my head, but that was an unspoken lie, for I still have the image of the Nightwalker in my mind's eye, and I now fear that the creature is somehow connected to my sister's destiny. Owain looked at me, but I avoided his eyes. So I spoke truthfully and said, 'I have had no premonition about her, and no dreams. I pray to God that that means she is well, and that she will come to no harm.'

Then Morys produced a letter from our parents, and read it out in full. It was long and rambling, for my father's brain is not as sharp as it used to be. But he wrote that he and Mother have exchanged letters with Elen, and that they are reassured. He said that he was not aware of any medical or financial problems on her part, and that if she had needed money she would certainly have written to ask for it. At any rate, they are off tomorrow to Oxford and London for a few weeks, and promised that they would call in to see Elen in Bath on the way home, at the end of May.

Catrin was very irritated by the revelation that a letter had gone from our parents to Bath and had apparently reached our sister. 'That means that they have an address,' she said, 'but they will not divulge it to the rest of us. That is a cruel thing indeed. Do they not trust us? Do they not think that we can help her?'

'Calm down, Catrin *bach*,' said Morys, always the big brother. 'It is clear to me that Mother and Father know where they may contact Elen, but it is equally clear that Elen has asked them specifically not to divulge the address to anybody else – even to her beloved siblings. She clearly does not want the six of us, or even the three of us, to go rushing off to Bath on some errand of mercy. Let us take that as a positive sign.'

We could get no further in our discussions, and in spite of the shadow of uncertainty hanging over us we contrived to enjoy a pleasant few hours together. I was reassured to see how easily Owain slotted into our family circle, and delighted to observe how he was made to feel comfortable by Morys, Nansi, Catrin and James.

Then it was time to go home over the mountain before we were overtaken by darkness. We arrived at the Plas just as the last glimmer of light in the west faded away, and my beloved man stayed for supper. I could not concentrate on the buzzing conversation round the kitchen table, for my mind was elsewhere. This is all very well, I thought, with Owain taken to the bosom of my

Brawdy family as well as of my Plas Ingli family; this is all very well, and I love him for it all the more, but I need to take him to my own bosom, in my bed, sooner rather than later. Please God, make it sooner, for an empty bed is a place where dark thoughts and fears reside.

10 April 1807

Today the Prices came to tea. I have survived the experience, but the encounter was not an easy one for me or for them.

We were forewarned, for some days ago we received a brief note from the Squire by way of response to my laborious invitation. He kindly accepted my apology, and even admitted that his behaviour, on the occasion of our one and only previous encounter, had been 'somewhat lacking in finesse'. That represents progress, I thought, and I decided that a man who admits to even one of his many failings cannot be all bad.

The Llanychaer coach, drawn by four very beautiful black horses, pulled into the yard just a few minutes late. The old folks, myself, and the four children, were all lined up by the front door. He likes his black horses, I thought, for he was riding on one when he last came into the yard in the company of Griff Hickey. Grandpa welcomed them and helped Squire Price, and then Mistress Susan, and then Miss Fanny down onto the gravel driveway. I gave a deep curtsy, without lowering my eyes, and noticed that the Squire's eyes followed my cleavage down and then up again, suggesting to me that he enjoyed some simple pleasures other than the consumption of spirits. No alcohol today, I thought, but contraband tea and delicate cakes and pastries – I hope that he can cope. There was a welter of polite introductions, culminating in a little bow from Dewi and sweet curtsies from Betsi, Daisy and Sara. I was inordinately proud of them, but thought afterwards that it might have been better to have kept them in the nursery rather than showing them off in front of a squire and his lady who have suffered too little joy and too much grief in their own family life. One cannot think of everything.

I ushered the three of them inside, and Bessie took their cloaks and bonnets. The ladies used my dressing room for a few minutes to tidy themselves up, and Sian took the children off to their own private tea party well away from 'boring' adult conversation. Then we boring adults all settled into the parlour and tried to get to know each other.

Bessie brought in the tea and other refreshments, and as she served our guests I endeavoured to work out what was what. The Squire is a man of medium height, not particularly striking in appearance, with brown eyes and a ruddy complexion. It was clear to me that he was used to getting his way. He was well dressed in a dark grey coat and a light grey waistcoat, with black breeches and purple stockings. His cravat and cuffs were sparkling white, and he wore a good pair of black shoes with silver buckles. His wig was more elaborate than necessary, but he wore it with perfect ease and it was obvious that he wore it often. He would not sit on a comfortable easy chair, but preferred a high-backed wooden chair from which he could more easily control the social situation. He chatted quite amiably with Grandma and Grandpa, casting frequent glances in my direction. He looked nervous. His hands were never still, and they sweated profusely. I thought, with some amusement, that he looked frightened of me, but maybe it was just that he was uncertain as to how I might behave.

When I looked at the women I was reminded forcibly of Grandpa's words of a few days ago, and I was horrified by the misfortune visited upon the family. Mistress Susan appears a sad and wasted figure, dressed in an ill-fitting prim-rose-coloured silk gown with long sleeves, and a white lace shawl over her shoulders. Her hair is snow white, as is her complexion, and she carried a pair of white gloves as if they were her most prized possessions. Perhaps they were. She spoke hesitantly, in a thin voice, and never smiled. She was clearly very ill, and it was obvious to me that she was not used to spending time in the open air. Her husband showed her very little respect or consideration. Their daughter Fanny is about twenty years old, with a shapely figure, bright brown eyes and a healthy complexion. She was dressed simply in a lime-coloured cotton dress with elbow-length sleeves, and her hair was piled high and bound with red and yellow ribbons. But appearances were deceptive, for her tragedy was captured in her voice and her manner. She chatted incessantly, in an endless string of comments and questions addressed to everybody and

219

nobody, with remarks tossed into the arena which had nothing at all to do with the topic currently under consideration. When we talked about the weather, she spoke of little birds. When we discussed the latest ship to unload at the Parrog, she mentioned the spring flowers. When we spoke about the prospects for the hay harvest, she talked of her favourite doll. Her parents were in turns alarmed and embarrassed by her behaviour, but to their credit they never remonstrated with her. Grandpa, Grandma and I smiled and accommodated Fanny's whimsy, but in truth I found the conversation extremely distressing, and at the end of it I was quite exhausted.

My exchanges with the Squire, such as they were in the midst of Fanny's ramblings, went as well as one might have expected. Neither he nor I referred to our last encounter, or to my subsequent apology, for those were private matters between us. We studiously avoided any reference to the shipwreck that had caused us both so much grief, and the only subject which required circumspection on my part was the discussion of rents and land enclosures which Grandpa introduced without warning. It was almost as if he felt that we were all getting on far too well, and that a little chill was required in the air in order to make things more interesting.

'Now then, George,' said he, with a sparkle in his eye, 'I have picked up from Stokes Trecwn and Owen Gelli Fawr that the land agents are pushing for higher rents this year. A very bad idea, I do declare. What, sir, is your opinion?'

After a quick glance in my direction, Squire

Price replied directly to Grandpa. 'There is no option, Isaac. The rents have been fixed for far too long. I am taking the opportunity, at every renewal, to triple my rents so as to bring them in line with the conditions of the marketplace, and to get rid of this nonsense of three or four lives. That is a relic of the past, Isaac, and cannot be supported by any progressive landowner.'

'Indeed? And what has happened to your tenants from Trenewydd and Treffynnon?'

'Rents raised, as was right and proper. They had the chance to stay, but chose not to, and now they are gone.'

'I saw three rabbits in my garden yesterday,' said Fanny.

'And new fellows in their place, George?' said Grandpa.

'Not yet, Isaac, but hopefuls are clamouring at the door, and my attorney expects to sign new tenants at any moment.'

'So you are in the planting season,' said I, 'with fields unploughed and two farmhouses inhabited by bats and mice? If I may say so, Squire, that does not sound like a situation that any progressive landowner would enjoy.'

Having said that, I immediately bit my tongue. But then, I thought, why should I defer to this fellow? Why should I refrain from speaking my mind? It was not my wish to humiliate him, but I wanted to demonstrate that I too am a landowner, and I too have worthy opinions.

The colour rose in the Squire's cheeks, and his eyes narrowed. 'My dear Mistress Martha,' he said, 'these people have a choice, to come in at the market rate, or to stay away. It makes little difference to me. If the farms are not let, I will farm them myself, and take on more labourers to that end.'

'And what do they know about farming, sir? Do they know what stewardship means?'

'Stewardship is a dream for a summer's day, madam. In the real world, there is ploughing and harrowing...'

'I have got a doll with a red cotton dress and a pink bonnet,' said Fanny.

'...and sowing and harvesting. Those things must be done, and they will be done. Don't you worry, Mistress Martha. At Llanychaer we know how to manage an estate.'

'I'm sure you do, sir, but who will do the bird-scaring, and clear the ditches, and plash the hedges and repair the stone walls? Who will tend the cows when they are sick? Who will get up at three in the morning in the middle of a deluge to chase the fox from the chicken house? Only a tenant farmer will do these things, or call in others to do them – for he and his fellows live and die on their land, and water it with their sweat.'

'Beside which,' added Grandpa, 'it stands to reason, George, that a squire cannot organize everything across three hundred acres of land, even if he is a genius. That is why tenancies exist – to spread the load, and to have four or five wise heads involved in the practice of agriculture, instead of one.'

'I like the yellow buns with currants in,' said Fanny, reminding me that I was neglecting my duties as hostess. I jumped to my feet and passed

222

round the currant buns and replenished teacups from my favourite silver teapot. I thought that we might get into deeper and deeper waters if we continued to talk about tenancies, so I decided to change the subject. Before I could open my mouth, Grandma did it for me.

She turned to Mistress Price. 'I was so sad, Susan, to hear the news about your son Iestyn,' she said. 'This has been our first opportunity to offer our condolences, and we do that with all our hearts. We know something about grief here at the Plas, and we know that these are not easy times for you.'

'Thank you, Jane,' said the poor lady, with a tear in her eye and a quiver in her voice. 'I appreciate your concern and your kind words...'

'As indeed do I, madam,' said Squire Price. 'And I recall kind sentiments from you, Mistress Martha, in your letter of recent date. Greatly appreciated, to be sure...' His voice became very throaty, and I observed that he was almost overcome with emotion. He tried not to show it, but he had to take out a handkerchief and dab his eyes with it.

'Four red kites flew over our house this morning,' said Fanny.

'Is that so?' said I, feeling guilty that I had thus far neglected her, and struggling to appreciate that she required attention just as much as her parents. I moved to sit next to her and talked about red kites until her mind hopped off them and onto the new shoes which her father had recently bought for her in Fishguard. But by the time I had expressed an interest in that particular topic she was describing the three slow-worms which she had recently discovered under an old piece of wood in the yard. She was very excitable and noisy, and instinctively I took her hand in an effort to calm her down. To some degree that worked. I glanced up and caught the Squire's eye, and he gave me a little smile that had all the agony of the crucifixion contained within it.

While I did my best to converse with Fanny, Grandpa and Grandma talked to the Squire and his wife about the loss of their son. It was obvious that all four of them felt a need to discuss it, and I picked up small snippets of conversation here and there. Then Mistress Susan started to cough, and glanced across to her husband. He immediately sprang to his feet. 'My dear friends,' he announced, 'I fear that Susan has had enough excitement for one day, and she has missed her afternoon rest. Morgan Medical will never forgive her for disobeying instructions, but she insisted on coming out. Did you not, my dear?'

'Yes indeed, George. I am glad that I did. It is no great pleasure to be stuck in that dusty bedroom all day and every night, watching the shadows of the sun and moon passing across the floor.'

'Come along, Fanny,' said the Squire, motioning to his daughter. 'Time to go.'

And the poor girl stood up, smiled, and gave deep curtsies to all of us, before linking arms with her father. Bessie fetched their cloaks, and Grandpa went to the kitchen, where the Llanychaer coachman was drinking ale with Billy.

'I am so pleased that you were able to join us this afternoon,' said I. 'It was high time, and while we may not agree on everything, sir, that should be no barrier to social intercourse and to gentle manners. I trust that you will agree.'

'Yes indeed, Mistress Martha,' replied the Squire. 'We landowners must stick together, and civility should be on the very top of our list of priorities.'

Before long the coach was outside the front door, and after bows and curtsies and the shaking of hands, the inhabitants of Plas Llanychaer were on their way into the flurries of April rain drifting in from the west.

Afterwards, in assessing the occasion, the old people and I agreed that it had been less stressful than we had feared. Grandpa still does not trust the Squire, and again he warned me that he is quite unscrupulous and capable of almost anything. However, as I sit at my desk late at night, in the flickering light of a pair of candles, I cannot avoid the conclusion that the Price household is a tragic one, and that the Squire has many crosses to bear. His wife is one, his sweet, pathetic daughter is another, and the grief at the loss of a beloved son is a third. On top of that, he has two widowed and estranged daughters who live far away. He may indeed have brutal and bullying tendencies, but he knows what grief can do, and I saw in him touches of humanity, if not warmth, when we talked of his lost son and when I held the fragile hand of his daughter.

16 April 1807

Two pieces of news today. I have a few minutes

to write them down, since it is pouring with rain, and there is no great point in trying to do anything outside. The children are at their afternoon lessons, and Grandma and Grandpa are fast asleep in their respective chairs on either side of the kitchen fire. The house is quiet, apart from Grandpa's snoring and the thundering of the rain upon the slate roof.

Owain visited us yesterday. In truth he could not resist calling, first because he loves me and finds it difficult to keep away, and second because he wanted a report on the tea party with the Prices of Llanychaer. We sat together in the parlour, and afterwards Bessie told me that we sounded, from a distance, like a pair of cooing turtle doves. Well, I do not care. I am very partial to turtle doves and entirely approve of their activities! I told Owain everything about the occasion, and especially about the two wretched Price women. Not knowing the extent of their disabilities, Owain was saddened to hear of them. He was interested in my observation that the man does have some human warmth in his breast, and when I had finished my narrative he told me a little of his own problems with the Squire. I had not realized how serious these were, in spite of intimations from Grandpa Isaac.

'Martha,' he said, solemnly, 'I fear that things may come to a head before long. I have tried to behave diplomatically, and I have appealed to the Court Leet for assistance, but they are powerless because Llanychaer is outside the barony and the Fishguard magistrates are not prepared to intervene.'

'But Squire Fenton is the senior Fishguard magistrate, and he is your friend. Have you asked him for his assistance?'

'I have. He is an amiable old fellow, and I am very fond of him, but he does not like trouble. All he wants is an easy life, with time to wander about studying antiquities. So he is reluctant to intervene in disputes involving other squires. He thinks that they should be gentlemen enough to sort things out for themselves.'

'Very well,' said I. 'What exactly has happened, though?'

'There are a number of issues. His land adjoins my father's land on the south side of Mynydd Melyn, and we have a common boundary on Mynydd Caregog, near Bedd Morris. He has been cutting peat on my part of the mountain, and three times in the last month he has started to enclose the common in the area used by my tenants and labourers for grazing their sheep and cattle in the summer. He has started cutting cart tracks, and he's put three times more animals up there than allowed by the Commoners. He has no Act of Parliament to back him up, yet he seems to think that he will get away with it.'

'But that is outrageous! Surely the Commoners have something to say about it? Are they not supposed to regulate the use of the commons and impose sanctions on those who contravene the rules?'

'In theory, yes. But in practice, no. They are a feeble bunch. Some of them are Price's cronies, and some of them are themselves enclosing land illegally. So I can expect no help from them.'

'So what have you done to fight him?'

'Three times I have sent my tenants and labourers in to destroy the walls and wooden fences that he has put up. Truth be told, they needed no encouragement from me, for their livelihoods are at stake. Three times my men have driven Price's cattle and sheep from his illegal fields to the Newport Pound near Ffordd Bedd Morris, where he has had to pay to get them out again. He is not amused.'

'Surely matters cannot go on like this?'

'Indeed they cannot. I have had two meetings with the Squire, and all I have received is abuse. He says it is no business of mine what he does on the common, and he cannot comprehend why I should be so concerned about the fate of my tenants and labourers, who are the ones losing their traditional rights. He does not understand when I tell him that their interests are the same as my interests, and that it is my duty to look after them...'

'Dear Owain!' I laughed, squeezing his hand. 'You are indeed a man after my own heart. Let us solve the problems of the world together. Alone, we can do nothing, but together we will be invincible! We will fight for justice, lift up the downtrodden, and send dastardly squires packing with their tails between their legs.'

'You may well laugh, Martha. But this is not a frivolous matter. When I met him the other day, he made serious threats against me if I persisted in blocking his enclosure plans. When this weather improves, he will have his men up on the mountain again, and so will I.'

This put a stop to my light-heartedness, and I do not recall too much about the rest of our conversation, for there was a band of fear now tied tight around my heart. I offered the help of my own labourers and tenants, and said that together we could muster a force of about twenty men. He declined, and said that, for the moment at least, he and his confederates could manage. I pray to God that we are not going to have another pitched battle like that which turned our lives upside down in Parc Haidd last year. I cannot fault Owain's actions thus far, and I am sure that in his place I would have done exactly the same, but I am worried. Desperately worried, on his behalf and mine.

The second piece of news is that the Nightwalker has been seen again, today, in broad daylight. Not once, but twice. Both sightings were in the pouring rain, so disproving the theory that ghosts do not like soggy weather for their expeditions into the world of the living. The first encounter was this morning, at about half past ten of the clock. Billy saw the creature when he was chopping turnips at the back of the stable. There it was, dressed all in black as usual, standing stock still on the bank near Ffynnon Brynach, and looking down at the Plas. Billy carried on with his work, transported the chopped turnips into the cowshed on his wheelbarrow, and then came out again. By then the creature had disappeared without trace.

Then this afternoon, just after dinner, with the rain still streaming down out of the black sky, Bessie had to walk to Llannerch to deliver a special herbal cheese which Mrs Owen has made as a present for Owain. On her way home, in the dense woods leading from Llannerch to Penrhiw, she began to feel uncomfortable, and remembered that according to legend that is a place where the Grim Reaper resides. Grandpa tells me that this fearsome manifestation from the spirit world has been seen amongst those trees more than once in the past. Bessie felt as if she was being followed, but was reassured when she turned round to look behind herself on a number of occasions, and saw nothing. But then she got a glimpse through the tangle of trees and branches, and there was the Nightwalker, standing in a clearing, with the water streaming off a wide-brimmed hat and a pitch-black cloak, simply looking down into the Llannerch yard. It had its back to her, and moved not a muscle, but it must have seen her when she had crossed the yard on her way to and from the back door of the house. She was no more than thirty yards from the monster, and was tempted for a moment to throw a stone at it by way of experimentation. But then fear got the better of her, and she thought that she had better not tempt fate. So she hurried home without stopping, to tell me all about her unnerving experience.

I had thought that we were rid of the wretched creature, since it has been more than a month since its last visitation. But now it has returned to haunt us once more, drifting into our lives and out again, giving us no clues as to where it is coming from, or where it is going, and telling us nothing about its purpose. It stands and observes, pointing no finger, wreaking no havoc, making no sound, leaving no trace. That is what is so unnerving. How I wish that it would fly, or scream, or howl, or even moan. But it does nothing. Nothing at all. I think I am getting used to its inactivity in the vicinity of the Plas. But now it has been seen doing nothing in the vicinity of Llannerch, the house inhabited by my beloved Owain. That leaves me with a cold sweat upon my brow, and gives substance to my most terrible fear – that the cold cruel creature dressed in black from head to toe is indeed the Grim Reaper, and that it has come to claim Owain. Dear God, let it not be so.

Giving and Taking

26 April 1807

It is almost midnight. A most remarkable thing has happened, and my astonishment has not been lessened by the passage of nigh on twenty-one hours since my world – not for the first time – was turned upside down.

A foundling has been discovered on the front doorstep of the Plas, and one could never have imagined the chaos which could be carried into the place in the tiny white hands of a small baby. Chaos comes, certainly, with the arrival of every newborn child even after months of expectation and preparation, but this was different.

At about three in the morning, with the whole

house fast asleep, I was woken suddenly by something out of the ordinary. I am a light sleeper, and sometimes even the distant call of an owl will cause me to sit up with a start. At first I knew not what had happened, but then I realized that the dogs were barking. They often bark in the night, usually in anger at the sight or smell of a dog fox, but their barking was now excited but not angry. I was mystified, and decided to investigate. I threw my warm dressing gown over my shoulders, lit a candle from the glowing embers in my bedroom fireplace, and tiptoed to the south-facing landing at the top of the main staircase. I opened the shutters and saw the faint yellow light of a lantern disappearing down the driveway.

My curiosity now turned to apprehension, and I feared that some crime might have been committed. But I decided not to wake the servants until I had cause to do so, and with my heart beating wildly I went downstairs to the kitchen. I unbolted the back door and looked across the yard, which was suddenly bathed in white moonlight with the opening of a split in the blanket of heavy cloud. The dogs had stopped barking, and the world looked as peaceful and as beautiful as it is possible to be on a cold April night. I threw a heavy cloak over my shoulders, slipped my feet into a pair of clogs and went out into the yard. I could hear nothing, smell nothing and see nothing untoward. I went round to the front of the house, and everything appeared to be perfectly normal there as well. Now I was getting cold, and I went back inside to the dark warmth of the kitchen.

I sat in front of the smouldering fire and

pondered. What could have been the purpose of the nocturnal visit by the person with the lantern? Perhaps he or she had come to leave a message, fearing the recognition that would have accompanied a daytime visit? Of course – that must be the answer. I took my candle and looked on the floor inside the kitchen door, half expecting a letter to have been pushed under it. Nothing there. I opened the door again to see if there was anything pinned to the outside. Again, nothing there. Maybe the stranger had gone to the front door. I went along the passage and knelt behind it, and as I did so I heard the faintest of sounds from the other side. For a moment I was terrified. I froze and held my breath. There it was again – a low whimpering sound interspersed with moments of silence. Then I realized that the sounds were being made by a very small baby, awake but not distressed. I reacted instinctively, in a fashion bred into every generation of mothers since the dawn of time. Feverishly I took the front door key down from its hook, slipped it into the keyhole and released the lock. I opened the door gingerly, and it creaked upon its hinges. There on the front door step was a willow basket. And in the basket there was a small baby, wrapped up in a thick Welsh shawl. The little one fixed its eyes on mine, and for me it was love at first sight.

'There now, *bach*, just you come to Mam, and let's go through to the nice warm kitchen,' I whispered. 'It's too cold out here for such a little one as you, is it not?' I picked up the basket with its precious contents, noticing that the child could not have weighed more than eight or nine pounds, and closed the door. Back in the kitchen, I lit half a dozen candles, broke the black crust on the sleeping culm fire and loaded on half a dozen logs. Soon there was a merry blaze on the go, and I thought I had better examine the child. I lifted it out of its cosy shawl and saw that it was wrapped in a clean and sweet-smelling cotton sheet. Placing the infant on the kitchen table, I folded the sheet aside and discovered that the child was a boy, recently cleaned and changed. I wrapped him up again, cradled him in my arms, and sat down in front of the fire. He was still wide awake, quite unafraid, and looking at me. He had brown eyes and fluffy black hair. I hummed a lullaby and rocked him gently while I wondered what to do next.

'Good gracious me, Mistress Martha!' mumbled Bessie, shuffling into the kitchen and rubbing her eyes. 'What on earth are you doing? Where did you get that baby?'

'Oh, my goodness!' said Mrs Owen, following hard on her heels. 'I heard a noise, and thought I had better investigate. Would you care to tell us, Mistress, what is going on? Whose baby is this, and what is it doing here?'

I started to tell the tale of my discovery on the doorstep, but then the little one, disturbed by all the voices and activity around him, started to cry, and the three of us clucked about him like broody hens in the hope of settling him down. But he had no intention of sleeping, and he had a lusty voice, and soon all the other adults in the house were awake and assembled in the kitchen. Luckily the children, who will quite likely sleep through the Last Trumpet, remained oblivious of all the pandemonium, and I thanked the good Lord for his mercy in that respect. I had to relate the circumstances of the child's discovery over and again, as we women all took it in turns to rock him and walk him round the kitchen table. At last he went to sleep in my arms, confirming me in my expectation that there would be a special bond between us.

Luckily the child slept until dawn, as we all sat round the kitchen table and discussed, in a strange gabble of whispers, what our plan of action should be. We estimated that the little fellow was around three weeks old, and on the assumption that he was born on the feast day of old Saint Brynach there was really no discussion as to what else we should call him. He was well nourished and clean, and Grandma confirmed that the sheet and woollen blanket in which he had been wrapped were of such quality that they could not possibly have come from the home of a pauper or a labourer. So was he the child of a disgraced daughter of a small farmer or even of a local squire? We all racked our brains, but could think of no potential mother in the neighbourhood. Questions galore were raised from all sides of the kitchen table. Whoever the mother was, why should she creep up to the Plas at dead of night and abandon her child here, rather than in town where he could be guaranteed a reasonable future, with the cost carried by the parish? And why Plas Ingli, rather than one of the grander houses in the neighbourhood? The others speculated as to whys and wherefores, but I wondered what sort of maternal anguish must have been involved in the very act of abandonment. How could any mother kiss her own baby on the forehead, and place him on a cold doorstep on a black April night, and turn, and walk away leaving him in the arms of strangers? In my wildest imaginings I could not come to terms with this poor woman's pain as she walked away with tears streaming down her cheeks and with bursting breasts, punished for the crime of bringing an innocent new life into the world.

'Martha!' whispered Grandma into my ear. 'I am sorry to break into your reverie, but we have the coming day to work out where little Brynach has come from and who the mother might be, and there is a more immediate problem. He will soon wake up, and he will be hungry. We have to find a wet nurse, and soon.'

'You are quite right, Grandma. But where can we suddenly find such a woman?'

'Well, Liza Philpin from one of the labourers' cottages near Pantry gave birth to a little boy two weeks ago. She is a pleasant girl, busty and wide-hipped, but undernourished like all the other poor people at this time of year. She and her husband Tomos might be prepared for her and her little one to move into the Plas for a few days while we hunt for Brynach's natural mother and decide what to do next.'

'I remember Liza. She helped with the hay harvest two years ago, and I recall that she has a good way with children. Shemi, you spent your childhood not a quarter of a mile from Pantry. Are you on good terms with the Philpins?'

'Of course, Mistress,' replied Shemi. 'Liza and

I played together in the woods when we were little.'

'Good. I would like you to take a message to her as soon as it is light. There is no point in writing, since I doubt if she can read. Explain what has happened. Ask her if she will come immediately to the Plas with her little one and be prepared to stay for a few days while we try to find Brynach's mother. She can feed two just as well as one. She will get a cosy room and a dry bed, and will share our food. I hope to God that she will agree.'

It was now five in the morning, and there was no point in any of us going back to sleep, so we all got dressed and ate an early breakfast. As soon as there was a glimmer of light in the eastern sky Shemi set off for Pantry, carrying with him our prayers that he would return with Liza and a decent milk supply for little Brynach. Our voices woke the little fellow up, and he immediately let us know that he was very hungry. He started to cry, and would not be consoled by the taste of my little finger. I walked him back and forth, and up the stairs and round the house, and it was inevitable that the children would wake, emerge and react with wonderment to the sight of their mother nursing a new crying baby.

'Mam!' scolded Betsi, rubbing her eyes in disbelief. 'You never told us that you were having a new baby. When Sara came, you were very big for weeks and weeks, but this time you were not big at all. How did you manage that?'

'Well, it's not actually my baby at all. His name is Brynach, and he is somebody else's child. We may have to give him back to his mam, if we can

237

find her. But just you get dressed, all of you, and when you sit down to breakfast I will tell you how he came to be here.'

So, with the baby still crying and the children's eyes wide in wonderment, I told them about the events of the night. 'Please, Mam, can we keep him?' pleaded Dewi, jumping up and down and clapping his hands just as he has done since he was less than one year old. 'I want a little brother. Girls are so boring with their dolls and things. Please, please!'

Before I could answer, Billy came in from the yard and announced that Shemi was coming up the driveway with a baby in his arms and Liza Philpin following close behind. The three of them were welcomed like conquering heroes, and within a few minutes Liza was settled in the corner of the kitchen with Brynach at her breast and four young spectators kneeling at her feet as if they were watching some miraculous performance by a travelling conjuror. And miraculous it was, for the milk of the young mother indubitably saved the life of the small baby whom fate had deposited in our midst.

27 April 1807

Last night I fell asleep at my writing desk, having had too much excitement and too little sleep during the preceding twenty-four hours. Now that I am somewhat recovered, I can continue my narrative of the events surrounding the arrival of the foundling baby.

The day was frantic, as may be imagined, for there were a thousand things that needed to be done. When Brynach was fed and cleaned and settled into a cradle, he was very much happier. Then I talked to Liza, who is a sweet girl of nineteen, with a calm nature and a modest demeanour. She was dressed in a rough woollen dress, and had arrived with a flannel cloak over her shoulders and clogs upon her feet. She carried a small bag which proved to contain some rags and small blankets which she used for her own child, whom she called Twm. I asked her if she could stay for a few days, and she confirmed that she was quite happy to do so, and that her husband had given his consent. I was greatly relieved, and told her as much. I knew at once that I would like her, and that we would work well together. I asked her if her milk supply was adequate for two small babies. 'I think so, Mistress,' she replied. 'Twm is very small, and does not have much of an appetite. My mother was a wet nurse once, for little Moses Lloyd, over at Cwmgloyn, and she told me that however much milk is needed, it just comes of its own accord. Mistress, are you all right?'

In truth I was not all right, for the idea of Liza's mother acting as wet nurse for Moses Lloyd, the most evil man to have stalked this fair earth, and then Liza herself feeding the lovely child named after the patron saint of my mountain was too much for me to cope with. I had to sit down, for there were wheels within wheels spinning round inside my head. I felt giddy, and I knew the colour had drained away from my face. Moses Lloyd, nursed by Liza's mother so that he could wreak havoc on the Morgan family before meeting his end at my hands? And Brynach, all sweetness and vulnerability, nursed by Liza ... to what purpose?

And then there was the assumed date of Brynach's birth. The seventh day of April was also the date on which five members of the Morgan family were murdered by Moses Lloyd and incinerated when the old Plas Ingli went up in flames in 1794. Was there some grand design in all this, or was the coincidence just a matter of chance? Perhaps, in a small community where evil and virtue coexist cheek by jowl, innocent folk encounter both and recognize neither?

Liza fetched me a glass of water, and soon I felt better. 'I am sorry, Liza,' I said. 'A sudden turn. It is probably the time of the month. Now then, let us get things organized here. You are an angel of mercy, and deserve to be treated as such. First, some hot soapy water so that you can wash little Twm, and I will not object if you take a bath in the scullery yourself. Sian will help you and show you where everything is. Then some fresh clothes – since we are about the same size I will fetch you one of my dresses with an opening front which makes it easy for feeding infants. You will have Sian's room, and the two babies can have their cots there as well. Sian can share Bessie's room for the time being. Have you eaten breakfast? No? Well, Mrs Owen will organize that for you. We eat modestly but well here, and I trust you have a good appetite!'

'That I do, Mistress Martha. But it is in the manner of things that it is seldom satisfied, although my good man Tomos does his best to get food into my little larder, by fair means or foul...'

Liza's voice cracked, and there was a tear in her eye. I realized that she was indeed close to starvation just at a time when she needed to feed both herself and her child. I could not resist putting my arms about her and giving her a kiss on the cheek. 'Don't you worry, Liza,' I said. 'There will be food for you and for Twm – and for Tomos. You can count on it. Now then, what about that hot soapy water?'

Sian organized everything, helped her to bath and change little Twm, and settled her into our biggest bathtub full of steaming water and frothy soap suds. While she luxuriated like the Queen of Sheba, Sian took her filthy and ragged clothes and put them on the fire.

We discovered, as the day went on, that Brynach was a contented child, very alert and intent upon taking in every one of the strange sights and sounds which now confronted him. The children all wanted to rock his cradle, and almost came to. blows over it, and I had to devise a scheme whereby they took it in turns when he was awake and let him be when he was asleep. Daisy said, 'Oh, Mam, he looks just like you – big brown eyes and fluffy black hair, and little dimples on his cheeks, and a funny nose...'

I laughed. 'Daisy, *cariad*, no doubt you mean well, but I am not sure whether to take that as a compliment or an insult. My hair stopped being fluffy a long time ago, and I hope that you don't find my nose as funny as all that.'

'Well, just a little bit funny. Perhaps he was

brought here by an angel, to make you happy?'

'Well I am very happy already, so long as I have you. Don't I look happy?'

'Sometimes yes, and sometimes no. I think you need another baby, to share with Master Owain when you get married. We need one too. Can we keep Brynach just for ourselves?'

'Maybe. Maybe. But don't count on it, and don't get too fond of him. As I have told you already, if we manage to find his mother he will have to go back to her.'

And it was this very matter that occupied the rest of the day. I decided that I needed to talk to Grandpa about practical matters, and I asked if I might talk to him in the privacy of the office. We sat together by the window and looked out on the bright and blossoming world. 'Grandpa,' I said, 'I need your advice. With little Brynach beneath our roof, not to mention Liza and her own baby, we suddenly have a situation to cope with that is not at all of our own making. I know what my heart and my motherly instincts tell me to do, but what does the law require of us?'

'For a start, as a magistrate I am required to try to find the child's mother. She is probably very young. She has committed an offence by abandoning her baby, and may have committed other offences as well. There is always a chance that the poor girl may suffer from remorse, and may turn up and ask to have her baby back, though in my experience that is unlikely. Then we had better inform the Mayor about what has happened. We must also tell the Overseers of the Poor and the churchwardens of St Mary's church...'

242

'Will they try to take Brynach away from us?'

'Good gracious me, no!' exclaimed Grandpa. 'They will be only too delighted if he stays here. Remember that foundlings and bastard children have to be maintained by the parish if nobody else will take them. The cost is added to the poor rate, and God knows that is high enough already. The child is deposited with some convenient nursing mother in town, who has at least one suckling child of her own and no doubt more than enough of other problems. She is given two shillings a week and some occasional small sums for clothes and blankets if needed, for as long as the child survives...'

'Do you mean that the survival of such children is a matter of some doubt?'

'Of course it is, Martha. You know what conditions are like in labourers' cottages and paupers' hovels. Cold, damp and filthy. Remember that most bastard children are undernourished and neglected almost from the moment of birth. They may be suffering from incurable ailments even before they come to the attention of the parish. Sometimes it is a blessing that they die.' I swallowed hard, and nodded. Grandpa continued. 'The Vestry and the Overseers of the Poor instruct the constables to find the natural mother. The constables search high and low locally, and if they do not succeed messages go to all the neighbouring parishes. This has to be done quickly, for with every day that passes the chances increase that the natural mother will slip through the net. All this costs money.'

'And if somebody knows something, and tells

the constables or the magistrates, what happens then?'

'Then the trouble really begins. The bastard's mother, if she can be found, will be arrested and taken into custody. The child will be removed from its wet nurse and given back to her, whether or not she has the milk to feed it. If her place of residence is in some other parish, she will be transported thither and handed over to the magistrates there. She is then interrogated with a view to finding the name of the father. If, as is usually the case, she is too frightened to co-operate in the matter, in due course she will be charged with bastardy and taken to the county gaol. There she and the baby will stay for two months, or three, or six, or however long it takes for them to repent the error of their ways...'

'Grandpa!' I gasped, burying my head in my hands. 'I am not sure that irony is appropriate in this particular context. The whole situation is utterly appalling, and almost too terrible to con-template. You will recall that I know too much about the inside of our own county gaol – it is a place hardly fit for the incarceration of swine, let alone small babies and terrified mothers.'

'I agree with you, my dear,' said Grandpa. 'But such is the law of the land. Insane to you and me maybe, but accepted and justified by the great majority of those in authority.'

'Very well. But what happens to the mother and child once they are let out?'

'The mother will have to find shelter some-where, probably with her parents or some other relative. There will then be a constant battle

244

between her and the Overseers of the Poor which will last until the child is ten years old and deemed to be capable of work, or maybe old enough to be apprenticed to a local craftsman like Morys Edwards Mason. If the mother is lucky, she will get an allowance of a shilling a week and an occasional load of coal or other help in kind. If she is unlucky, she will have to make frequent requests for Poor Relief to pay for butter, eggs, milk and other foodstuffs for the growing child, and for clothes, blankets and shoes. At regular intervals the Overseers will argue that they should withdraw their support on the grounds that the mother is capable of raising the money she needs through her own efforts. She may try, but that will be at the cost of neglecting the child. A miserable scenario, Martha, as I think you will agree.'

'And through all this mayhem the father of the bastard child runs wild and free, taking no responsibility at all for the spreading of his wild oats?'

'So it has always been, my dear. The woman bears the pain of motherhood in a multitude of ways, and you know only some of them.'

'There is joy too,' said I, 'but only if it is underpinned by some small degree of comfort and security. But you are talking about bastards borne by paupers, Grandpa. Little Brynach's eyes tell me that he was not born in a filthy hovel, and the sheet and blanket in which he was wrapped carry the same message. If he is from a good home, is there not a greater chance that we will find the father?'

Grandpa laughed. 'I doubt that very much, Martha. When it comes to matters of paternity,

245

squires are bred to be skilled in the arts of evasion and denial. Only if she is very brave will a girl who has been misused give the name of the father. If he is a squire or the son of a squire, and chooses to deny the fathering of a bastard, there is very little chance of obtaining an affiliation order against him. If he has no connections with the magistrates, and if there is evidence from other reliable witnesses, then an order may be obtained, and he may be required to put down a recognizance of twenty pounds or more for the upkeep of the child. He may of course admit paternity under cross-examination. I know of three cases where, with the encouragement of the magistrates, a father has agreed to marry the mother of his bastard child as a simple way of avoiding the heavy hand of the law.'

'And have they lived happily ever after?'

'Let us not talk of the mysteries of the marriage bond just now, Martha. We have enough on our plates as it is.' Then he stood up abruptly and smiled. 'Now you know almost as much as I do about these matters. There is a miserable natural mother out there somewhere, but nobody, so far as we know, has been greatly harmed. Little Brynach is warm and safe, and we have done some good in providing Liza and her baby with warmth and safety too, albeit on a temporary basis. Let us hope that this whole episode can be concluded quickly with the discovery of the mother so that we can hand him over and get back to normal within a few days.'

And with an insensitivity which I could hardly credit, he kissed me on the cheek, squeezed my arm, and went off to write notes to the Mayor, the churchwardens, and the clerk to the Overseers of the Poor in order to set in motion a terrible and inevitable train of investigations. He left me sitting by the window, confused to such a degree that I hardly knew myself. Suddenly I felt crushed by yet another burden. Anger swept over me when I realized that the burden was not some personal tragedy or financial disaster, but a small baby with brown eyes. I was furious with Grandpa for the matter-of-fact manner in which he had dissected the options open to us and the requirements of the law. How could he be so crass? How could he accept the idea of handing over little Brynach to some incompetent mother or hateful father or slovenly wet nurse hired by the parish? How could he contemplate, even for a moment, the prospect of that sweet and lovely child living out his life in misery and destitution?

Does nobody in this house but myself realize that this is the place to which destiny has carried Brynach, and so this is where he must stay?

28 April 1807

I spent the whole night wide awake. I had no desire even to get into my welcoming bed. I sat in my warmest dressing gown with a blanket wrapped round my shoulders, sometimes in front of my bedroom fire and sometimes by the window, looking out on a serene landscape bathed in white moonlight. My mind was anything but serene, for it was almost overwhelmed by a deluge of frenzied thoughts. What should I do about Brynach? What would be best for him? What would be best for me, and for the children? And what about Owain, the man whom I love and will shortly marry? I thought about self-indulgence and duty, about emotions and practicalities, and about costs and benefits. I tried to see the problem as a man might see it. But I could not, I could not. And always I came back to my irresistible instinct to take the child in my arms and treat him as my own. I felt a sort of desolation that he was not in a cradle at the foot of my bed, where I could listen to his steady breathing and pick him up and cuddle him if he, or I, needed it. For a mad moment or two I felt a sort of jealousy towards Liza, who had the pleasure of physical contact, the joy of touching and smelling him, the pleasure of feeling his little mouth clamped to her breast. At four in the morning I heard him cry downstairs and was on the point of rushing down to console him, but the crying stopped, and I realized that Liza had picked him up and was feeding him. In a hellish torment, I waited for the dawn.

'Mistress Martha, what is the meaning of this? You look absolutely terrible! And you have not even touched your bed!' I woke with a start as Bessie came storming in at seven o'clock, bearing small coals for the fire and news of the outside world for my edification.

'Oh, Bessie, I am sorry I have been so wicked. But I could not sleep.'

'I can see that, Mistress. But you must get your sleep if you are to find the strength for dealing with urgent matters. You are making a habit of wandering about at night, and I have to say that I do not approve of it.'

'I know it only too well. But my mind has been in a turmoil.'

Bessie stoked up the fire and loaded some coals onto it. She swept the ashes up into a little shovel and tidied up round the fireplace. Then she wiped her hands on her apron, came over to the window, and stood in front of me as I sat in a dishevelled state in my favourite chair. She took my hands in hers.

'I perceive that you want to keep the baby, Mistress.'

I nodded miserably. 'Yes, Bessie, I do,' was all that I could say.

'And you do not know what to do?' I nodded again. 'Well, Mistress,' she continued, 'I dare say it is pretty obvious to everybody in this house. You had love in your eyes as soon as you saw that little fellow, and you spent the latter part of yesterday deep in thought, following your discussion with Master Isaac. It was clear to me what was going on in your head and your heart.'

'Dearest Bessie.' I laughed. 'I must learn to hide my feelings, and to keep my thoughts inside my head instead of spelling them out in large black letters for all to see. But after a night spent on the torturer's rack, I am still none the wiser as to what to do.'

'Torture and enlightenment are not the best of bed-fellows, Mistress. If you seek enlightenment, you need serenity. The first thing you require is a hot soapy bath infused with lavender oil. Then you need a nice clean dress, and some breakfast in your belly. Then I had better wash and put up your hair, since you look as if you have been dragged backwards through a copse of furze bushes.'

She got up and headed for the staircase. 'Give me ten minutes, Mistress,' she said, 'and your bath will be ready for you.'

I smiled and watched her go, and in recognition of the fact that in my dishevelled state I would have frightened the living daylights out of any other person, large or small, I avoided all contact with the world until I was seated at the breakfast table. Billy, who sometimes surprises me with his gallantry, complimented me on my appearance and said that I smelt as fragrant as a field of French lavender. That cheered me up no end, although neither Billy nor I have ever been within a hundred miles of a field of that delightful plant. While we all tucked into our porridge Grandpa Isaac informed us that the Mayor would be calling later in the morning to inspect the baby on behalf of the Overseers of the Poor, and that one Charlie Toms would call on behalf of the churchwardens. After that, he said, a search for the mother of the child would be instigated, and the Mayor would post notices in town offering a reward for information leading to her arrest. I did not comment, although I was tempted to protest about the absurdity of treating a frightened young mother in the same way as a murderer or a highway robber. My four little ones would not settle to their breakfast, since all they wanted to do was rock the two newly arrived small babies in their cradles. I had to admonish them, although in truth I wanted to do exactly the same. Liza, looking as pretty as a picture in one of my old dresses, reported that Brynach was as good as gold and that he had as hearty an appetite as a child of six months. 'Just you take my word for it, Mistress Martha,' she said. 'If he stays here he will surely eat you out of house and home.' I looked at him in his cradle, fast asleep, and thought that he looked like a plump little cherub who has found his perfect place in life.

Later on, when the children were at their lessons and Bessie was putting up my hair, I asked her what I should do. She thought for a while and said: 'In my view, and Sian's, you should do nothing, but let matters take their course. The Mayor and Master Toms will do what has to be done, and Grandpa is surely aware of your wish to keep the child.'

'That was not my impression when I talked to him, Bessie.'

'He has subsequently spoken to Mistress Jane, and he has a better understanding of the ways of women than you might think. He also knows what a dismal fate might await little Brynach should he be removed from this house and given over to the tender mercies of a cruel world. I think that he was trying to prevent you from building your expectations too high, or from falling in love with the little fellow, for fear of what might happen to you if he is taken away.'

'Yes, I see that. Perhaps I have been unfair in my judgement of him.'

'Then, Mistress, there is a second thing. Please try to be clear as to your own welfare as well as

251

Brynach's. It is clearly in his best interests to stay here, where he will be greatly loved. But – dare I say it, Mistress – you have not only the very strong instincts of a mother who wants to protect a small baby, but also the powerful emotions of a woman who has herself conceived a child out of wedlock.'

At this, I froze, and my eyes caught those of Bessie in the mirror we were both facing. I almost reacted with fury, for I thought that my beloved handmaiden was now taking familiarity to extremes, and being both insolent and insulting. But I thought better of it, and controlled my temper. Of course Bessie knew – as everybody in the house knew – that David and I had been forced into marriage by the fact that I was with child, and that I had been suffering from the morning sickness when I arrived as a frightened eighteen-year-old at the Plas back in 1796. Everybody knew. But this was the first time it had been mentioned openly.

I let my shoulders drop, and Bessie's hands, which were in my hair, relaxed too. Our eyes met again in the mirror, and we exchanged smiles.

'Bessie Walter, I should send you packing for insolence and insubordination,' I said. 'But I will not, for I do not know what I should do without you. You are quite right – I was three months gone when I came to the Plas, and I dare say that that experience gives me a certain sympathy for unmarried mothers and children born out of wedlock. I lost my child too, and I know not what that experience has done to me. It almost destroyed me at the time, and perhaps it has given me a certain fierceness and passion for the protection of innocent lives.'

Bessie nodded. 'I am sorry to be so frank, Mistress, but in my simple way of looking at things I think it necessary. We need not dwell on the loss of your first child, for you have had more than enough pain on that account. But with respect to the future, may I make one final suggestion?'

'Please do, Bessie.'

'Well, Mistress, you have a wedding coming up and a new husband to think of. You have already made a marriage settlement. I know nothing of such things, but, if Brynach stays, I dare say it will have to be rewritten. Will you have him baptized, and, if so, in what name? And will he be taken in as your own child, or as a child of the marriage between Master Owain and yourself? There will, I dare say, be gentlemen to consult and documents to sign. But before anything else, Mistress, you must speak to Master Owain. It is more than twenty-four hours since Brynach was deposited on your doorstep, and you have not contacted him. If you are not careful, he will find out about the baby from some other source, and if I were he I would not be amused to have been left out of your deliberations.'

'You are right, as ever, Bessie. Yesterday I was exhausted, and preoccupied with the arrival of Liza and the survival of Brynach. Then I spoke to Grandpa, and spent the rest of the day feeling miserable as well as exhausted. Owain came into my head often, as he does every day, but I am afraid I acted like a coward and feared that his view of the situation might differ from my own. So I did nothing. I fear that I was not thinking straight.'

253

'Mistress, you must trust him above all others. I beg of you, do not delay for another minute. You may fear the loss of Brynach, but you have much greater cause to fear the loss of Master Owain, for it is he who will bring love and security back into your life. You have, I recall, mistrusted him once before, when wicked tongues were doing their mischief before the Glynymel ball. That was careless, Mistress, but to mistrust him again now would be nothing short of criminal.'

'Oh, Bessie!' I exclaimed, leaping up from my chair with half my head tidy and the other half unkempt. 'You see everything. Thank you, my dearest friend. I have been mad to delay for so long. My blue bonnet, if you please, and my walking boots and woollen cloak. I will be out of this house within five minutes, and I promise all the angels of Carningli that in spite of the fact that I was wide awake all night, I will be on the doorstep at Llannerch within the hour.'

And so I was, but not before receiving another slingshot from the cruel hand of fate.

29 April 1807

At last, a peaceful morning after a good night's sleep. It is ten of the clock, and the spring sunshine is streaming through my window. The children are at their lessons, and Liza is by the kitchen fireside, giving Brynach a morning feast. Half an hour since, I bathed him there, and he and I loved every moment of it.

While I can, I must continue my fateful narrative. Yesterday, shortly after ten of the clock on a breezy spring morning, I was on my way to Llannerch. I followed the lane to the Dolrannogs and Penrhiw, but I was in no state to admire the brash golden daffodils and cool yellow primroses that still lined the hedgerows, for I had too much on my mind. I rounded a bend in the lane, and almost walked straight into the Nightwalker. The creature was standing in the lane, facing me, and no more than twenty paces in front of me. I stopped dead in my tracks, overwhelmed by terror. I was so frightened that my recollections of its appearance are sketchy to say the least, but I think that it looked the same as ever, with a tall black wide-brimmed hat on its head, a black muffler round its face, and its whole body swathed in a capacious black cloak. Although I was so close to the figure, I do not recall that I saw its eyes. Perhaps, as a phantom or a demon, it has no eyes, no face, and no body?

For a moment the creature and I stood facing one another. I think I was too terrified to turn and run. Then, with infinite slowness and menace, it started to move towards me, and my fear rose to such a peak that I think I must have fainted. At any rate, some minutes or hours later I regained consciousness and found myself lying in the middle of the filthy track with my bonnet on the ground beside me, mud all over my cloak and dress, and bruises on my elbow and on the back of my head. Next to me, on the ground, there was a small bunch of freshly picked daffodils. What an extraordinary thing! There was no sign of the Nightwalker.

I picked myself up, checked that I was not bleeding from my injuries, and brushed the mud off my clothes as best I could. What should I do now? I felt giddy, and I was still in a state of panic as recollections of the encounter with the creature in black came flooding into my mind. I could have turned and run home, since I was no more than four hundred yards from my front door, but I thought better of it. I could not spend my life fleeing from phantoms, and I had a mission to complete. So I gathered up my skirts, looked about me to make sure that the creature really had disappeared, and hurried on towards Llannerch.

Thomas Tucker was in the yard at Penrhiw, and I waved at him as I went past. I have to say that my mind was in a very unsettled state, for every rustle of the budding branches on the hedgerow trees, every black shadow, every scudding cloud that blotted out the sun, appeared to be filled with menace. But then I realized that the birds were still singing, new lambs were frolicking in the fields, and the spring sun was now high enough in the sky to banish the cold and damp of winter. And I was strangely reassured by the thought of the flowers lying in the muddy lane when I had recovered from my faint. Were they real daffodils, or blooms from the phantom world? I reprimanded myself for not checking, and indeed for not thinking of carrying them with me to Llannerch. But surely they could only have been some sort of gift or gesture from the Nightwalker? Nobody else could have placed them beside me. Was the creature, in some way, trying to communicate a message? Was it apologizing for frightening me? Was it trying to tell me that it wished me no harm?

With these and other questions, and a multitude of inconclusive answers, buzzing about in my mind, I descended through the Llannerch woodlands without thinking of where I was or where I was going. Suddenly I was in the Llannerch yard. I stopped and composed myself, and worked out my strategy. I would not say anything to Owain about the Nightwalker, which would entail the telling of assorted lies. The good Lord in his Heaven would, I thought, probably forgive me.

Mistress Gwilym, Owain's housekeeper, appeared at the open kitchen door. 'Mistress Martha, how good to see you! A very good morning to you!' said she. I returned the greeting as cheerfully as I could. 'Oh, my goodness,' she continued. 'You are in a very muddy state. Not hurt, I hope?'

'No, no. I slipped in the mud on a steep part of the track, and banged my head and bruised my elbow. But I assure you that I am not seriously damaged. Is your master at home?'

'Yes and no. He is up at our top boundary wall with three of the servants, sorting out some problem caused by Squire Price. I think they are demolishing stone walls on the common. But he will drop everything and be back in an instant when he knows you are here. Rhys will go up on the pony and fetch him.' I chose not to argue with her, for in truth I needed to see Owain more than he needed to heave heavy stones about. She sent Rhys off on his mission, and then she sat me down and cleaned me up and tended to my wounds.

When Owain arrived, fifteen minutes later, I

was much more composed, and was enjoying a cup of tea in the convivial company of the Llannerch female servants. His manservant Rhys had already told him of my dishevelled state, and he was greatly concerned. But when I smiled he was reassured, and when we embraced and kissed he had to accept that I was in good working order. He led me into his parlour, and closed the door. We were alone at last, and we embraced and kissed again. And again. I was quite intent upon doing nothing else, but at last he gasped: 'My dear Mistress Morgan! You have quite taken my breath away! And I thank God for it, for I perceive that you still love me in spite of the fact that I probably look and smell like a vagrant who has been sleeping in a hedge for a week. It's very messy work, destroying Squire Price's stone walls.'

'I assure you, Master Laugharne, that your appearance is of no concern to me. What is underneath is all that matters. Come to think of it, I do not exactly look like a summer bouquet, or smell like a rosebud, myself.'

'Now then, Martha, I presume you did not come here just for the pleasure of my embrace or the taste of my lips. Your purpose, if you please.'

'I have come to talk about babies.'

His face registered surprise, and then delight, and then he roared with laughter. 'Well, well, and why not?' He chuckled. 'How many shall we make, and how many boys and girls, and in what order?'

Having thus established that Owain knew nothing at all about the strange arrival of little Brynach, I sat him down, cuddled up next to him, and told him all about it. I spared none of the details, and told him about the arrival of Liza as a wet nurse, and about the procedures which Grandpa Isaac had outlined for me. He listened intently, and asked for clarification where my words were poorly chosen. When I had done, he thought for a long time, the way men do. Then he said: 'Cariad, I think I am learning how to read your heart. You want to keep the child, that much is obvious to me. And why not? Your happiness is paramount to me. But I beg of you, do not fall in love too deeply with him while there is the slightest chance that he will be taken away from you. You bear too many scars upon your heart already. Are you strong enough to face that possibility?'

'Yes, my love. With you beside me, I am sure of it.'

'Very well. I will help you. Tomorrow I have to go to Haverfordwest, but on Friday I will call at the Plas and make the acquaintance of this little rival for your affections. Don't you worry – if his brown eyes are anything like as beautiful as you say they are, and a quarter as beautiful as yours, I shall go weak at the knees and declare myself besotted.'

I gave him no chance to say anything more. My lips sought out his, and I kissed him and would gladly have caressed the morning away. We were brought down from the sunlit heights by a heavy banging on the parlour door. Owain extricated himself from my embrace and called out, 'Come in!'

His man Rhys entered, scattering apologies. 'Very sorry to be bothersome, Master,' he said, 'but there is an urgent message from George on the mountain to say that you are needed. Squire Price is prowling about on the common, and he is not best pleased about our stone-moving operations. He threatens to call in the constables.'

'Oh dear, here we go again,' said Owain, springing to his feet. 'Martha, I fear that I must go.' Then he saw the concern in my eyes, and laughed. 'Don't you worry now. Price will not call in the constables, for the law is on my side. Bluster and bombast are his only weapons. I can deal with him as my father has dealt with him across the valley.'

We walked out to the kitchen. He pulled on his boots and threw a heavy coat over his shoulders. He kissed me once more on the lips, and said, 'I love you.' Then he was gone. A minute later I heard the sound of his horse clattering out of the yard at the gallop.

I was not sure what degree of attention I should give to this business with Squire Price. But the female servants in the Llannerch kitchen told me it was nothing but a minor matter, and I managed to put it out of my mind. Buoyed up by the love of my good man and by the sure knowledge that he and I would deal with the problem of little Brynach together and with a united purpose, I flew up the valley-side track and was home in no time at all. I declare that my feet did not touch the ground between Owain's house and mine, and so elated and distracted was I that I entirely forgot to check whether the Night-walker's bouquet of daffodils still lay where it had been placed on the muddy track.

2 May 1807

There have been developments on many fronts. Yesterday Owain called, as promised, having survived his encounter with Squire Price up on the mountain. He would not talk much about it, but simply said that he and his confederates had sent the wretched fellow packing, and that he hoped that illegal common-land enclosures would now be over and done with.

He came, he said, in order to inspect his new baby. Brynach was on his best behaviour, and I showed him off just as proudly as any new mother might have done. Owain cradled him in his arms, and the little fellow's brown eyes worked their magic. Within a few seconds Owain declared himself to be head over heels in love again, and then he exclaimed: 'Martha! He smiled at me! I am sure he smiled at me! Is that not very advanced for a small baby? He is certainly a genius who will put the world to rights, and he must be given very special attention. Would you not agree?' Of course I agreed, although I knew that Brynach was far too small for smiling, and I hoped that he would reserve his first smile for me.

Owain met Liza, and informed me afterwards that he was well pleased with my choice of wet nurse. She was, he said, tidy and discreet, and he was even more impressed when I reported that in addition to looking after two small babies, she was proving to be most helpful to Mrs Owen in the kitchen and scullery. It was mid-morning, and the house was quiet, so Owain and I took the opportunity of sitting in the parlour with Grandpa and Grandma for a few minutes. Grandpa wanted to report on his discussions with the authorities, and there were decisions to be made. 'Now then,' said the old fellow. 'You need to know the following. The Mayor, Daniel Thomas, has called twice since the arrival of little Brynach. As I suspected, he is only too happy for the child to stay here for the time being, since it relieves him and his fellows of any responsibility. He has put out a search warrant for the mother, and there are notices in town and in Fishguard offering a reward of five pounds for information leading to her arrest. The constables are hard at work, in so far as such a thing is possible. There is no news yet of any positive development. Charlie Toms has been here as well, on behalf of the Vestry, to inspect the child. He says he does not recognize him or see any family likenesses, which is hardly surprising. I called in to see him again yesterday. He has met his colleagues and talked to the clerk to the Overseers of the Poor, and they have decreed that if neither the mother nor the father is found by the end of one month, they will draw up a deed which indemnifies the parish against the future cost of maintaining the foundling until he reaches the age of twenty-one. Almost a week has now passed, and in the absence of any new developments we will meet with Lewis Legal, the Mayor, Master Toms and two justices in order to sign the document on the twenty-seventh day of May. Owain and Martha, a straight question if I may. Are you in total agreement that this is the course of action you wish to follow?'

I looked at Owain, and he looked at me. Then he said: 'Yes, Master Isaac, that is what we both want. We will treat the child as our own and give him all the love that is in our hearts.'

Grandpa nodded and smiled. 'Excellent,' he said. 'I thought as much. Now then, to the matter of the baptism. It should be done before the end of May if possible. I have spoken to Rector Devonald, and he is agreeable. Brynach will not be the first or the last bastard to be baptized in the House of God. The name is yours to choose, but in the register of births the spaces available for the names of the mother and father will be left blank. You have already speculated that the seventh of April was the date of birth. The same date as the Plas Ingli fire. But will the little one be a Morgan or a Laugharne?'

He looked at Owain and me with his penetrating blue eyes, and raised his eyebrows. The two of us spluttered and knew not what to say, so the old gentleman helped us out. 'Although you plan to marry in June, you are still single persons, and I suggest that since young Brynach was deposited by the angels on the Plas Ingli doorstep it is most appropriate that he should be given the name of the Morgan family. There are also implications for the marriage settlement. You, Owain, are an innocent party in all of this, having been caught up in a sequence of events started entirely by others. It would prejudice the rights of any future male children born to you and Martha if Brynach was to be given the Laugharne family name. If he is called Brynach Morgan, he will be treated as one of the children of Martha and David,

263

which makes things much simpler. Lewis Legal can make minor adjustments to the settlement, and when you make your wills you can make further provisions for Brynach if you wish.'

At this stage, I was considerably confused, but Owain was quite on top of everything. 'I agree, Master Isaac,' he said. 'That sounds perfectly equitable. I simply want the best for Martha, and the best for all her children. If Brynach is destined to be counted as one of them, so be it.' I nodded my approval, and squeezed his hand.

'One last thing,' said Grandpa. 'Owain, we need the support of your father and Master Hopkins Legal in this enterprise. Will you arrange that?'

'As good as done. There will be no objections from either of them.'

Then Grandpa jumped up, and our meeting was at an end. 'Good, good. Now then, this estate has been sadly neglected of late. We are behind with planting and rolling, and it is high time that I got my hands dirty again.' He kissed me on the cheek, shook Owain's hand, and rushed outside. Grandma smiled and went out to the kitchen to make some tea.

Owain stayed for long enough to drink his cup of tea and to play hide-and-seek with the children for half an hour. Then he had to go. Before he went through the door he kissed the sleeping Brynach on the forehead and turned to me. 'Martha,' he said, so that only I could hear, 'I have been making plans. May I invite you to a picnic on the day after tomorrow? Just you and me – no children. The weather is set fair, and we have had hardly a drop of rain for ten days or more. Will you agree?'

'*Cariad,* it is the duty of every faithful woman to fall in with the plans of a future husband. I am entranced by the idea.'

'A little peace and quiet on the clifftop near Aberrhigian, with wild flowers around us and seabirds wheeling in the blue sky. Agreed? We have a wedding to plan, and a guest list to arrange, and invitations to write out. I will bring pens, ink and paper, and a little basket with something to eat and drink. I will call at noon, after church. Pray be ready for a stiff walk, and bring with you nothing but your love and a hearty appetite. Till Sunday, then!'

And he held me in his arms, and kissed me, and was gone.

For the rest of the day I went round in a daze, and Bessie had to reprimand me several times for failing to concentrate on various matters in hand. In truth, she was not concentrating too well herself, for she was still recovering from her own lack of sleep on May Eve, when she and Sian spent a good part of the night, with other young ladies of the neighbourhood, in strange activities in and around Cilgwyn church. She would not tell me too much about the occasion when I asked her, but it is common knowledge that when you perambulate the church nine and a half times at midnight, and push a sharp knife into the keyhole of the door, and utter the words 'Here is the knife, where is the sheath?', you will see the spirit of your future husband by peeping inside. Bessie would not tell me whether her enterprise had been successful, but I guessed from her demeanour that it had not. However, when I asked Sian the same question, she blushed very prettily, and there can be no doubt that she now knows the name of her intended. We await developments.

After that the whole house was almost emptied during the afternoon of May Day, when we all went down to the meadow behind Cilgwyn church to celebrate the maypole dancing. The only ones to remain behind were Liza and the two babies, Grandpa and Grandma, and Mrs Owen, these last three all declaring themselves too old and respectable for frivolity and debauchery. We walked down the Gelli lane, and Billy, Shemi and Will took great delight in carrying us ladies, and the children, across the ford at Trefelin, although there were perfectly adequate stepping stones which we could have used. We joined a happy throng along the lane past Penybont, and found that the field was crowded with revellers. It was very hot, and the lower parts of the meadow were aglow with buttercups. Music echoed among the old oak trees, and the many young people of the neighbourhood – gentry and servants alike – joined in the weaving maypole dance, which went on interminably. The children were cross that they were not allowed to join in, but in truth the steps were too complicated for them. They were placated when we opened up our picnic hamper, and we sat on a shady bank surrounded by blue-bells while we ate our crusty bread and butter, scones and cherry conserve, and crystallized fruits. Then I have to admit that I snoozed for a while on my woollen blanket, leaving the servants to chat and laugh with their confederates and the children to play riotous games with all their

266

friends from neighbouring farms and cottages. By dusk I had caught up on most of the local news, and had passed on those pieces of my own news which were fit for public consumption. Everybody wanted to hear the story of little Brynach, for versions of it – mostly very garbled – were already in wide circulation.

Then the children and I walked home, for Sara and Dewi were very tired. We left the manservants, and Bessie and Sian, to continue with the revels, which went on far into the night, with bonfires and more dancing and a good deal else besides.

When we arrived home we were all tired and happy, and I made myself even happier by holding Brynach in my arms as he drifted off to sleep.

3 May 1807

This morning I woke with a start, and was immediately overwhelmed by a feeling of utter desolation. I knew not why, for everything around me was sweetness and light. Bessie was tidying up the fireplace, and humming a little tune to herself. Sunbeams and birdsong were streaming through my opened bedroom window, and the morning air was fresh and fragrant. The children were fooling about in the nursery, as they do on most mornings, while Sian sought to get the four of them washed and dressed. Everything was quiet downstairs.

'Good morning, Mistress!' chirped Bessie. 'I tried not to wake you, for you looked as if you were deeply asleep. However, it is a glorious morning, and it is going to be hot again.'

'Good morning, Bessie,' said I, trying to be civil. 'You are very cheerful, if I may say so. As for myself, I feel terrible.'

'Not to worry, Mistress. I feel terrible, too, when I wake with a start. Just you take your time. I will leave you to wake up properly, and come back in ten minutes with a posy of flowers for your mantelpiece. Then I will bring up your washing water.' And she skipped off across the landing and down the stairs.

Alone, I knew that something unpleasant was going to happen during the day. I had no idea what it might be, no matter how hard I concentrated on the matter. I also knew that I had to walk over the mountain after breakfast to see my beloved friend Joseph Harries. He was in my mind's eye, but I could not work out whether he needed me or I needed him.

Things became clearer half an hour later, while we were all gathered in the kitchen eating our breakfast. Hettie arrived from the Parrog, bearing both a large basket of fresh herrings and news from town. The herrings were welcome but the news was not. She reported that somebody has claimed the reward for finding the mother of little Brynach. When she announced that, I felt that I might faint. All eyes round the table turned towards me, for everybody in the household knows that I am besotted with the little fellow in spite of my best efforts to remain cool and detached. Dewi, of all people, saw the distress in my face, left his chair, and climbed onto my lap in a childish attempt to give me reassurance.

Hettie continued with her story. 'They do say that the Mayor has got a message from a woman in Dinas who says that she knows who the mother is. She says, according to my friends who know, that there have been some Irish vagrants in the parish in recent weeks. Six or seven of them, by all accounts. I saw a couple of them myself. There was a young girl with them who was heavy with child in March. That much I didn't know, for I never saw her. At any rate, they were moved on by the constables to Dinas, where they begged and got into trouble with some of the locals. Then they were moved on by the Dinas constables to Fishguard, and the gossip is that they are still there. The woman who is after the reward says that she saw the Irish in Dinas about a week ago, and that the girl was back to her normal shape and was being carried by the others. Very distressed, she was. The talk is that she was suffering from birthing injuries or from milk fever, or possibly both. There was no new baby with them. This very morning the Mayor swore in three extra constables, and they went off to Fishguard with John Wilson and Evan Evans bearing a warrant for the girl's arrest. She is charged with bastardy and abandoning a baby, and if she has not got on a ship to Ireland the posse will certainly find her. The talk is that they will be back in town with the poor girl in shackles some time this afternoon.'

I buried my head in my hands, feeling so cold and numb that I could not even cry. There was a long silence in the room. Dewi tried to console me, and I held on to him as tightly as a drowning woman might grasp a flimsy piece of floating timber. All of us round the table were shocked by what Hettie had said, for the small child sleeping in the cradle by the fire had woven his spell of magic about all of us, adults and children alike. The silence continued. Hettie was shocked by the impact of her words on the assembled company, for she had clearly failed to appreciate the extent of our corporate emotional attachment to Brynach. She started to apologize for the somewhat brutal and matter-of-fact nature of her report, but Grandpa got up and placed his hand upon her shoulder. 'You must not blame yourself, Hettie,' he said, 'for the nature of the news which you have delivered. I am sure you have reported it faithfully. You were not to know just how fond we all are of that little fellow. It will not be easy for any of us if we have to give him up.'

There was another long silence as family and servants came to a cold realization of what it might mean for Brynach to be returned to a destitute Irish family, and what it might mean for me if he were. They all knew, as I knew myself, that I had allowed emotion and maternal instincts to sweep me along, brushing aside as impudent nonsense all the warnings that I had been given by Grandpa, Owain and almost everybody else. 'Take care, Martha. Take care,' they had all said, over and again, and I had not listened.

Suddenly Grandma piped up. 'Martha, neither you nor the rest of us must give in to despondency. This matter is by no means resolved. Perhaps the Irish family is already halfway to Wexford, in which case the constables will return to Newport today empty-handed. And with no name for the vagrants it will be impossible—'

'Oh,' said Hettie. 'I forgot to tell you. There is a name. The word is that the vagrants were members of the O'Connell family.'

I removed Dewi from my lap, got up from the bench and walked out of the kitchen with all eyes following me. I do not know how I found the strength, but I climbed the stairs, crossed the landing and went into my room, where I closed the door softly behind me. Then I flung myself onto my pillows and wept for a long time. Bessie came in and sat at the foot of the bed. At last I saw her through my tears and grabbed hold of her, and sobbed like a desolate small child for I know not how long. Clinging to her in utter desperation, I wailed, 'Oh, Bessie, what shall I do? What shall I do?' without expecting an answer. When the tears stopped, I looked at her with my red eyes and saw that she had been weeping too.

She knew as well as I did what the news about the O'Connell family meant. For a start, this was the family that came to the Plas every year at harvest time, for whom we have done many favours in the past. If one of their clan had a bastard child to dispose of, there would be every reason for it to be deposited on the doorstep of Plas Ingli, for the place is known to the senior members of the clan as a place of warmth and sensibility. At a past harvest time, we saved the life of a little O'Connell boy who almost severed his leg when he fell on a scythe. One life saved by the Morgans of Plas Ingli, and why not another? In a cruel world, the O'Connells would certainly have no compunction about taking advantage of what-

271

ever kindnesses they could identify. And since the name was known, there would be no difficulty in tracking the family to Ireland. Neither Bessie nor I would be surprised if, in the coming weeks, the constables were to be sent across the water with the express purpose of finding Brynach's mother and bringing her back to Newport. The poor, poor thing. Who would suffer most from this extradition – her, or Brynach, or me?

There was one further thing that Bessie did not know. I am the only person who knows that the man who last year murdered Alban Watkins, our most hated enemy, was an Irishman who called himself Daniel O'Connell. He wrote to me and described for me his actions and his motives, and his letter, which might have been written by a dagger dipped in blood, is still locked inside my desk. Perhaps the lantern which I spied in the darkness of an April night was carried not by a woman, but by Daniel O'Connell? Perhaps the tears that wet my doorstep were those of a father and not a mother?

'Mistress, I think you should go and see Master Harries,' said Bessie, wiping her cheeks. 'He is your friend, and he will know what to do. We are all too close to this matter, and so is Master Owain. You need to talk to somebody with a warm heart and a cool mind.'

'I know it well, Bessie,' I said. 'I knew that I must visit Joseph as soon as I woke up this morning. I had a premonition that bad news was coming. Well, it has come with a vengeance. I think we had better tidy ourselves up, the pair of us. Then I will set off over the mountain.'

'Do you want me to come with you, Mistress?'

I managed a weak smile. 'No, Bessie. I appreciate your concern, but I am all right. You need not worry, for I will not do anything stupid. Nobody has died, and little Brynach is still with us, and the sun is sailing high and bright. There is no reason to grieve for something that has not happened. I will go by myself, and try to banish all my dark thoughts while I walk through the heather. I dare say that the skylarks will cheer me up.'

And so I walked along the mountain crest to Werndew, past Carn Edward and Bedd Morris and over Mynydd Melyn. At least I think I walked that way, for in truth I was too distracted to be aware of anything. I dare say that the sun shone down on me out of a cloudless sky, and it is probable that the skylarks tumbled above me. No doubt the turf was sprinkled with delicate spring flowers, and I dare say that the ravens watched me from the summit of Carningli and then flew high over my head as I walked west and then north.

'Good morning, Martha,' said Joseph as I squeezed through the rose arch into his back garden. 'I have been expecting you.'

He was standing with his back to me, watering his delphiniums. He put his little watering can down, and turned round to face me. As he had expected, I ran into his arms and dissolved into tears. He let me cry for a little while, and then he prised me away from his soggy shirt collar and held my hands in his. 'I perceive, Mistress Morgan, that you have done enough crying for today. I wish that you would learn to cry only when crying is necessary. I am not aware that

273

there is anything to cry about, and in my book self-pity is not a very good excuse.'

'I am sorry, Joseph. But I have been very upset, and I think with good reason. I am, after all, a woman...'

'Never fear, Martha, I had noticed! How could I do otherwise, when you have that wicked red dress on? Now then, just you sit down on that bench while I make some tea. The kettle has been boiling for these past ten minutes, and I have made some griddle cakes specially for you. You must be hungry.'

And he went in through his back door and pottered in his little scullery while I composed myself and smiled wryly at the fact that Joseph Harries, eccentric wizard and student of all things esoteric, had noticed which dress I was wearing when I had hardly noticed it myself. In pondering the thought that he had known perfectly well that I was coming to see him I almost felt guilty that I was ten minutes late.

He came back into the garden bearing a tray with an earthenware teapot, two pretty china cups, and a plate piled high with warm griddle cakes. He sat down on the bench, put down the tray between us, and said, 'Now then, down to work. Tell me, my dear friend, all about the baby.'

'You know about the baby?'

'How could I not? The whole neighbourhood is talking of nothing else.'

So I told Joseph the whole story, and brought him up to date with the appalling news which Hettie had carried with her to the Plas at breakfast time. I articulated my fears as best I could, but as I spoke I realized how self-obsessed I have been over recent days. I admitted as much, and expected further fierce admonishment from my old friend. But he burst out laughing instead, which made me very irritated. He caught my eyes and saw the fire in them.

At last he calmed down and said, 'Martha, I cannot be angry with you, but you must not leap to conclusions all the time. This habit of yours leads to all sorts of unnecessary aggravation. You can well do without it, for you have children to care for and a wedding to plan. Shall we bring the cold eye of reason to bear upon this matter? First, the nature of Brynach's delivery to the Plas. You say that he was in a good wicker basket, and wrapped in a clean cotton sheet and a woollen blanket. A Welsh blanket, locally made?'

'Yes, I am almost certain of it.'

'I will come over to the Plas and examine it. I must clearly make the acquaintance of little Brynach as well. It does not sound to me as if those items would have been available to a group of Irish vagrants. You must have considered the possibility that Brynach is a gentry child, or the son of a moderately well-off young woman?'

'Yes indeed. He was clean and well nourished when I found him, and he is a very contented little fellow. He is perfectly at home at the Plas.'

'And so he should be, since he is well fed and well loved. But that does not necessarily show that he is a child of good breeding. Now, let us move on. The Irish family. I remember them well, and the struggle I had to save the leg of the little fellow called Brendan. One of my most satisfying pieces of surgery. And I also recall your generosity to the family while the little fellow recovered. Would you say, Martha, that the O'Connells are in your debt?'

'Well, yes, I suppose they are.'

'You would do well to remember, my dear friend, that those who are in debt seldom if ever take actions which will compound what they owe. And how would you describe the O'Connell clan?'

'Does it matter what I think of them?'

'It matters a great deal. Take my word for it. Come along then. How would you describe the family?'

I thought for a moment, and wondered whether there was some trap hidden in the question. I could not see one, so I answered honestly. 'Well, very close and very loving. Master and Mistress O'Connell loved their little boy dearly, and so, apparently, did the other relatives. They are all hard workers, very trustworthy. And they are very devout people – good Christians, I would say, fit to put the rest of us to shame.'

'Quite so. That accords precisely with my view of them. Now, do they sound to you, Martha, like the sort of people who would produce a child out of wedlock and then abandon him on some foreign doorstep? Have another griddle cake while you think of your answer, and let me put some more tea into your cup.'

After a while I said, 'Well, Joseph, I have to admit that it is unlikely. But as you and I know only too well, accidents do happen.'

'And what happens in a close family when accidents happen?'

276

'I know. I know. The family takes care of both mother and child. But that is what we might assume for a close family with silver under the bed and food in the pantry. Would it be the same in a vagrant family driven from parish to parish and living day to day on the very edge of starvation?'

To my great surprise Joseph laughed, got up and gave me a kiss on the cheek. 'Dear Martha!' he said. 'Your trouble is that you think far too much. Remember that people hardly ever act out of character. If you have to assume anything at all, assume that they will act in accordance with their beliefs and their code of behaviour. I think that we are getting somewhere. Now then, what does your intuition tell you about little Brynach?'

'It tells me that the Plas is the place where he belongs.'

Joseph nodded. 'And what does your intuition tell you about the O'Connell clan?'

'Why, it tells me nothing at all. I feel a warmth about them, on the grounds that I have already described.'

'Remember, Martha, that you have special powers. You hardly seem to notice them yourself, let alone recognize them as a gift. I urge you to trust your intuition and your instinct. Use your heart more and your head less. If I may say so, you panic too often and place too little trust in the angels which inhabit your mountain. Now then, I am going to make another pot of tea in the scullery. While I do so, close your eyes, and try to think nothing and feel everything.'

I surprised myself by doing as he instructed. When he came back after ten minutes with his steaming teapot he asked me who the mother of little Brynach was. 'I do not know,' I replied without thinking. 'But I do know that it is not one of the Irish vagrants.'

'My feeling entirely, Martha. Now, have another griddle cake and a fresh cup of tea, and I will tell you the truth. The young woman who was almost nine months gone in March, and who is travelling with the Irish vagrants, is Kate O'Connell, lawful wife of Jamie O'Connell. They are both eighteen years old. She went into labour on the twenty-fifth day of April while she and the others were sheltering in a barn near Aberfforest. She had a terrible time of it, and I was called to help. I arrived in time to save her, but I could do nothing for the child. She had appalling birthing injuries, and I repaired them as best I could. Next day Jamie and his father walked into Fishguard with the body of the baby – a little boy – and he was buried by the priest in the Catholic churchyard. I urged the family to stay in the barn so that the young mother could rest and recover. I pleaded with the farmer, Jonas Jones, on their behalf, but some of his neighbours were threatening to burn his barn down if they stayed. He was in an impossible position. He is a good old fellow, and he let them stay for some days. He gave them as much food as he could afford and urged them to move on. Then the Dinas constables arrived and marched the Irish out of the parish and into Fishguard. They had to carry Kate all the way. She is very weak indeed, but I think she will survive. So far as I know, the O'Connells are currently staying in a barn at Glynymel, where

Squire Fenton is looking after them. I had some small part in the arrangements.'

Joseph stopped and looked at me. Then he said: 'Martha, I see that you are crying again. This time I forgive you, for you are crying for others and not for yourself.'

'Oh, Joseph, what a terrible, terrible thing to have happened to those poor people! And to think that since this morning I have hated them, and treated them as my enemies. I am so very ashamed...'

The Wizard of Werndew moved away the tray of crumbs and empty teacups and sat close to me. He put his arm round my shoulder. 'My dear friend,' he said softly, 'things are not always what they seem, as I think you might agree. Shall we try, in the future, not to jump to conclusions?'

We sat together in silence for a while. Then I jumped to my feet. 'Joseph!' I exclaimed. 'I must go to Glynymel this minute, and help those poor people. The Newport constables may be arresting Kate at this very moment, with a view to dragging her in chains back to the lock-up...'

Joseph laughed and held my hand. 'Mistress Morgan, I absolutely forbid it! She is quite safe, and there is nothing you can do that Squire and Mistress Fenton cannot. The O'Connells will tell the constables, when they arrive at Glynymel, about the death of Kate's baby, and Jonas Jones, Squire Fenton and the Fishguard priest will all attest to the truth of what they say. Master Wilson and his posse will be sent packing back to Newport with their tails between their legs. If they want more witness statements, I will give them one tomorrow. There was no bastard child and no abandonment on a doorstep. So far as I know, no crime of any nature has been committed by the Irish, and they may well be able to stay for another month or so until the hay harvest starts. Then they will come to the Plas and ask for work, and if I know you as well as I think I do, you will give them at least one week's employment. All will be as well as can be – you may take my word for it.'

At last I relaxed, and Joseph and I talked of other things – of the children, and Owain, and our forthcoming wedding, and even of the weather. I thought of asking for advice in the matter of the Nightwalker, but decided that it could wait for some other day. I forgave Joseph for his subterfuge in pretending not to know anything about the Irish when he knew about them all the time. I even laughed about his little lesson in the arts of instinct and intuition, and so did he. My spirits rose by the minute, and when at last I walked home across the mountain with the afternoon sun sliding westwards I heard every skylark, spoke to every mountain pony, smelt every delicate spring flower, and observed every subtle colour and texture painted on the canvas of paradise.

4 May 1807

Today has been a day like no other, and I will hold it in my heart until the day that I breathe my last. It started as it intended to continue, with a soaring sun and a cloudless sky. At Sunday break-fast we were all in high spirits, partly because of the weather and partly because I had shared the intelligence about the Irish with the family and servants at supper last evening, on my return from Werndew.

None of us was in the least bit surprised when Hettie came puffing up to the house at eight of the clock with hot news from town. She explained breathlessly that the constables had returned to Newport late yesterday afternoon empty-handed, having met the O'Connell clan at Glynymel and ascertained that one Kate O'Connell had given birth to a baby boy who did not survive. They had taken sworn statements from Squire Fenton and then from an old farmer near Aberfforest who had seen the body, and after all that rushing around they had had to return to Fishguard new town where they had seen the grave. The priest had given them a statement about the burial. So they had returned to Newport in high dudgeon, having failed to earn the few shillings which would have been theirs had they effected an arrest. The interfering old woman in Dinas, who had sent them off on this wild goose chase, had asked for her reward of five pounds and had got a severe reprimand instead. And as for the Irish, although they were vagrants and should have been moved on, the Fishguard constables were not minded to take any action in view of the poor state of health of the miserable young mother who had lost her child. Squire Fenton had apparently given a guarantee that they would make no claim on the parish and would move on at the start of the hay harvest.

Hettie was very disappointed by our minimal

281

reaction to her narrative. So we gave her a bowl of porridge, and explained that Joseph had told most of the story already, and I held little Brynach in my arms at the kitchen table as we talked and laughed, and loved him with a passion born of relief.

We still do not know who the mother and father are, but I suspect that after the fiasco with the Irish the parish authorities will now abandon their search. After all, what will it benefit them to expend time and money on such a futile project, when they know already that I will keep Brynach at the Plas and guarantee his future? However, I would like to know where my beloved new baby has come from, and so would Joseph. He says he will call soon to make Brynach's acquaintance and to set in motion certain investigations, although I asked him yesterday not to make any exciting discoveries until papers are signed and the little one is baptized.

After Hettie had gone back to town bearing butter and eggs for her lodging house, I was left in sole occupation of the Plas. Sian took the children to the woods below Penrhiw for a lesson on spring flowers. Mrs Owen went to Dolrannog Isaf to help with the butter-making. Grandma and Grandpa took the chaise and went off to spend the day with their old friends Squire and Mistress Huws. Shemi spent the day with the dogs in the top fields, supervising the late lambing. Billy sat in the stable repairing harnesses, and Will had the joy of muck-spreading on the fallow fields in the company of the Jenkins boys and two other labourers. Since it is Sunday they will spread only ten cartloads before the day is done. If it had been a Monday I would have expected twenty. Bessie went off to Nevern to see her old mother, and will not be back until tomorrow. Liza took the two small babies for a walk down to her own home at Pantry, with both of them yelling blue murder in their uncomfortable perambulator.

So I dreamt the Sunday morning away, looking at the kitchen clock every five minutes and awaiting the arrival of Owain. I made myself a sweet-smelling bath and then reclined on my bed for an hour or so in my nightgown while I made up my mind which dress to wear and which perfume to use. It was very warm, so I took off my nightgown and lounged naked instead. I wondered if he would love my body as I loved his. I recalled the time when I had watched him floating naked in the Pandy Pools, and I felt my cheeks flame. Then I remembered that he had seen me naked too, just once, on an occasion which I have done my best to forget, for it involved the horrible death of my tormentor John Fenton. Had Owain desired what he saw then? Had he admired the swell of my breasts and the cascade of my loosened hair and the contours of my waist and my thighs? I hoped and prayed that he had, and that he still would. I wondered whether I was still beautiful after bearing four children. He had said often that my beauty was beyond compare, but had he meant it, or were his words simply the honeyed phrases of a man in love? Doubt and anticipation, then apprehension and passion, flowed lazily through my mind and my body. I jumped off the bed and closed my bedroom curtains to shut out the world, and then in the dim light I stood naked in front of my full-length mirror, which had been a present some years ago from David. I think I liked what I saw.

Suddenly I felt guilty at all this unbridled exhibitionism, as indeed I feel somewhat ashamed now in recording my actions in my little book. It was after all a Sunday, and I should have been in church like Owain. I even blushed, and giggled at my own childishness. So I hurriedly put on my nightgown again, and stood at my open window gazing out across the *cwm*. It was an unseasonably hot day for early May, and as the sun swept up towards its zenith even the lambs and the hedge-row birds fell silent. Ten minutes before eleven. Time to get ready. About now Owain would be coming out of the little church at Pontfaen. He would be talking to his parents and to the vicar. Had he, during the prayers and the hymns and the sermon, been thinking of God, or of the sinful world, or of me? Had he been thinking of my body when he should have been asking for forgiveness for his wickedness? Was there any wickedness in him? I doubted it, unless it was wicked to dream of me...

In a hazy state I put on my stays and my silk petticoats and my favourite lime-green walking dress. I knew that it was Owain's favourite too. Twenty-five minutes to twelve. I splashed myself with my most expensive rose perfume, powdered my cheeks and made up my eyes. I brushed my hair, put it up, then thought better of it, and let it down again. I chose a simple silver necklace, and decided on my yellow straw bonnet and my most expensive white shawl. I stood before the mirror and pushed up my bosom as high as I dared. Then, five minutes early, I heard Owain's horse trotting into the yard. Suddenly I was as nervous as a small child. Would our picnic be a dream or a disaster? What would we say? What would we do? I know what I wanted, but I dared not think about it, for I knew that what I wanted was forbidden. And I prayed to the God whose morning service I had failed to attend that both Owain and I would have the strength to wait for just a few more weeks for the moment when we would become one.

'Martha! Are you here, and are you ready?' he shouted up the stairs. I swallowed hard, and set off across the landing to see what good things he had brought with him for the picnic.

5 May 1807

I am afraid that my hand was shaking so severely last night that I was unable to finish my picnic narrative, and, like the lonely widow that I am, I had to climb into bed in order to recover my composure. What a strange creature I am, to be sure! Now a blissfully uneventful day has passed, for which I am eternally grateful. Bats are flitting about outside my bedroom window. The air is still warm, and there is not the slightest stirring of wind. So in a calmer if not dispassionate frame of mind I am able to continue.

I have been thinking for most of the day about what to write. Should I be honest enough to record everything, or should I allow discretion and diplomacy to rule my heart? Then I remembered a book which Grandpa Isaac (of all people) gave to me as a present a few months back – Mistress Wollstonecraft's *Vindication of the Rights of Woman*. I read it with interest, and although I by no means agreed with everything in it it taught me at least to aspire to some sort of independence. I do not want to become a poet or a politician, or to use education as a vehicle for some driving ambition; but I decided long since that I will be nobody's chattel, and I will measure my own independence through freedom of expression. I am no bluestocking, and I will not march about and wave banners as men do. But I will write what is in my heart, for better or for worse, and I will describe beauty and brutality as I find them. I have described too much brutality already, so this is my Testament to Beauty, by which I will remind myself that, a widow with four children, I am still young, and can still see beauty wherever it resides.

Owain and I met halfway up the stairs, and embraced with such vigour that we almost overbalanced and went crashing down. 'Careful, *cariad.*' He laughed. 'This is no time for us to go breaking our necks. If accidents are to happen, we must eat our picnic first.' I laughed too, and we trotted down to the kitchen hand in hand. Then he said: 'Martha, let me look at you.' He stepped back, and we held hands at arms' length. 'May the good Lord in Heaven be praised,' he said, 'for he has made you more beautiful than any woman that ever lived. I knew it before, but it is now confirmed as a matter of scientific fact. Martha Morgan, will you marry me?'

'If you insist on it, Master Laugharne. Pray tell me when it might be convenient for you.'

'How about the fourth day of June? Master Devonald tells me that the church is free on that day, and it so happens that I plan to take a short break on that date from destroying stone walls.'

And so we chatted on like a pair of silly children, although in truth the date was set long since, and the church is booked, and the first reading of the banns will be next Sunday. With Owain's horse settled in the paddock behind the stable, we set off on foot along the track leading to the mountain ridge. Owain carried the picnic hamper strapped to his back, and I carried a bag containing a woollen blanket and a cloak in case the air became cool later in the day. We had a ninety-minute walk ahead of us, for our destination was on the coast closer to Dinas than to Newport. But we looked forward to it, and we were truly filled with the joys of spring, which were manifest all around us. The last of the daffodils had now faded, but alongside the track primroses, dandelions, celandines and buttercups were all in bloom, together with red campion, sorrel, cow parsley, violets and other little flowers whose names were unknown to me. In the last of the hedgerows before we reached the common, there was a veritable blizzard of white mayflower over a distance of fifty yards or more, melted here and there by the warm gold of the winter-flowering furze. The sweet sickly smell hung heavy in the air, for there was not a breath of wind. Then another scent almost swept us away to Heaven, for we passed the highest of the bluebell banks in a place where Grandpa says there used to be a fine oak woodland.

We took a little detour to Ffynnon Brynach, where I anointed myself and then anointed Owain. I have to admit that the anointing was not a particularly religious business, and Owain roared with laughter, and one thing led to another, and we both got very wet. We did not care, for it was too hot anyway, and I thought it not a bad thing that our passions should be cooled by sacred water during the hottest part of the day. We walked on, now on the common, with the battered blue rocks of Carningli towering above us to our right and the dusty green horizons of Presely across the *cwm* to our left. The air was as crystal clear and clean as the waters of Ffynnon Brynach. We were serenaded by the resident skylark choir, which sings come rain or shine. The old black raven and his family watched us silently from the western crag of the mountain. Far over our heads, lifted on quiet winds, we counted four red kites, five buzzards and a pair of kestrels.

We crossed the patch of heather moorland burnt last year, passed the mound of stones which Joseph tells me is a Druid grave, and started to drop down towards the coast. The sea was as placid as one might expect after four windless days, and there were not even any ancient ocean swells sliding in from the west. At last we reached the stone walls of the cultivated land. Owain knew a good path down from the mountain ridge towards the coast road, and he led the way past bramble patches and nettle beds, taking great care that I should damage neither my dress nor myself. Like a true gentleman he helped me over stone stiles and held my hand where the going was rough. When I had the chance, I watched him from behind, admiring his long, strong stride and the slight swagger in his shoulders. He wore dark blue breeches and yellow stockings, and a white collarless shirt which was showing streaks of perspiration. On his feet he wore a pair of well-made walking shoes. His fair hair, which he wears longer than David used to, swept back and forth with every stride, causing him frequently to brush it away from his face. I had not noticed that little mannerism before, but I loved it as I loved every other detail of his appearance and his behaviour.

And as we walked, how we talked! I told him about the latest developments in the hunt for Brynach's family, and about the wild goose chase which led the Newport constables to the innocent and sad O'Connell family. He revealed his sister's latest marital problems, which are causing his parents some heartache. I told him about my discussion with Joseph, taking care to omit those parts of it concerning my special powers, for there are some things best left for another occasion. He relayed a story about an accident which occurred recently at Pandy, where a fellow who disputed the price for the fulling of his woollen cloth was thrown into a pond of urine and almost drowned. I laughed, and then stopped, and then laughed again when I realized that Owain found it funny too. And so on, with easy words, and frequent laughter, and a light and affectionate meeting of minds.

Before I had realized it, we were over the coast road and down in a deep wooded valley – and suddenly we were at the coast: Aberrhigian, where the magic of the countryside is replaced by the magic of the crusted grey cliffs and the salt sea. I had not been to this place before. It was a little cove, cut back into the land for several hundred yards from the outer coastline, with parallel sides clothed with scrubby bushes and then, further inland, with dense oak woodland. There were no houses in sight, and not even any labourers' hovels. The sandy beach was only just visible, for it was almost high water. And above the beach, at the inner end of the bay, there was a pebble bank made of stones of the prettiest colours and the most peculiar of textures. I declared, when I examined them, that they were magic stones, for I had never seen their like before – and Owain said that I was quite correct, for according to the locals they had been carried to this place in silver wheelbarrows from Gwlad y Tylwyth Teg (fairyland) which lies just offshore under the tranquil waters of the bay.

Behind the pebble beach was a grassy bank dissected by a bubbling stream, and a stone's throw away lay a pond fringed with tall bulrushes. The place was as serene as may be imagined. This, I thought, must be our picnic destination, and I said as much. But no, said Owain, he had a little surprise for me along the cliffs which was even closer to paradise. He took my hand and led me up a steep path towards the outer coast, passing mayflower bushes and greening ashes and oaks along the way. We rounded the corner and there before us was a wild and wonderful panorama of turquoise sea and steep craggy cliffs more than a hundred feet high, with one headland after another stretching away into the distance. Newport's Berry Sands and the heavy bulk of Morfa Head basked in the sun on the other side of the bay. There were seabirds near and far, wheeling and screeching over the water, preening themselves on the cliffs, resting in clusters on the water, and sitting on eggs on the narrowest of rock ledges. There were guillemots and gulls, razorbills and cormorants, and as I watched with my mouth agape a falcon flashed past in pursuit of a small dove which had clearly been in the wrong place at the wrong time. And the flowers could not, I thought, have been bettered in the Garden of Eden. Cushions and banks and cascades of colour, and so many fragrances that I could not tell which was which.

I was lost in wonderment, and wanted simply to stand and drink in the beauty of the moment. But Owain said that he was hungry, and led me on. And then after another fifty yards he jumped down a steep slope through a little gap in the flower garden. I followed him tentatively, afraid that we would plunge to our doom in the sea far below. But no – there we were on a little grassy ledge, about ten feet wide and fifteen feet long, which was totally hidden from the outside world. Sixty feet below us was the smooth and silent surface of the sea, and at our backs was a bank of thrift and sea campion overhung by exuberant furze bushes. 'My secret den!' declared Owain with evident satisfaction. We had reached our designated picnic place.

We were both very hot after our long walk.

Owain removed the picnic hamper from his shoulders and flung himself down upon the springy turf. I dropped my bag and did likewise. For a few minutes we lay on our backs with our eyes closed, listening to the seabirds. There was still not a whisper of wind, and there was not even a murmur from the sea where it made contact with the base of the cliffs. I felt sticky and uncomfortable with my stays fastened tightly, and I decided on an impulse to take the wretched things off. 'Owain,' I said, 'these stays may help me to look younger than I am, but they were not made for hot weather or long walks. Will you think me a very loose woman if I take them off?'

'I will not, Mistress Morgan. They seem to me to be uncommonly unpractical things anyway. Besides, I have always wondered what a woman looks like when she is loose.'

'Will you promise not to look while I adjust myself?'

'I promise that I will try to keep my eyes closed.'

So I turned my back on him, loosened the top of my dress, and struggled to undo the bows which kept my stays tight and fast. At last I succeeded, I dare say with considerable mutterings and cursings under my breath, and threw the stays onto the grass in front of me. I laced up my dress again, composed myself, and turned to face Owain. I discovered that he had been lying on his front, with his chin cupped in his hands, watching the whole operation intently. 'I have to say that that was very interesting indeed,' said he nonchalantly. 'I am afraid that it was impossible to keep my eyes closed, since I feared that in the midst of those struggles you might fall over the cliff. By the way, did I ever tell you that I love your back?'

'Owain Laugharne! You have betrayed me!' said I. 'A fellow who cannot keep his eyes closed cannot possibly be counted a gentleman, and deserves to be taught a hard lesson.'

So I leapt upon him, and we rolled in the grass, and we kissed, and we laughed. Our embraces became longer, and our kisses became more intense, and our laughter subsided, to be replaced with sighs. We were in grave danger of being swept away by the freedom and the euphoria of the moment, until we realized almost simultaneously that some self-control was needed. We stopped in the midst of our caresses, and he removed his hand from my breast. 'Martha,' he said, 'I am sorely tempted to continue with this sporting activity and to cause you to miss your dinner. But that would be a pity, since I have here in my little hamper a most sophisticated picnic put together this very morning entirely for your delectation. May I invite you to enjoy it with me?'

'Sir, since you are now determined to be a kind and generous gentleman I will accept your invitation. Besides, the exercise has sharpened my appetite.'

So we untangled ourselves, and I laid out my blanket and cloak on the grass while Owain unpacked his hamper. It was now three of the clock, and with the sinking of the sun there was some shade beneath the furze bushes that overhung our grassy ledge. I lay back with my hands behind my head, and watched him. He took out a little linen cloth, and unfolded it to reveal two delicate china plates. Silver cutlery followed. Then he took out another cloth and with great delicacy removed from it two crystal glasses. I laughed and expressed my amazement that they had survived the journey and all our fooling around. 'Years of practice, Martha,' he said with a wicked gleam in his eye. 'I come here every Sunday with some serving wench or other, just to ply her with Portuguese wine and to have my wicked way with her.'

'Rubbish, sir. I do not believe a word of it. You swore to me that you are a virtuous young man.'

'I swear that to everybody. I dare say that Don Juan did the same.'

And so we continued with this nonsense until all was prepared. Then we sat side by side with our china plates upon our laps, and ate good wheat bread and butter and delicate slivers of smoked salmon, followed by cold cooked potatoes chopped up with chives and slices of ham with mustard. Then we ate gooseberry cream and cold custard from an earthenware pot. And we consumed a most delightful bottle of red wine which he claimed had come from the depths of his father's cellar, and I could well believe it, for it was a world away from the rough tax-free liquid which Will and his confederates collect from Aberrhigian and other hidden coves on moonless nights.

With considerable satisfaction we lay back and looked at the sky, and talked of our forthcoming wedding. Owain said that he had paper and quill pens and a pot of ink in his hamper, and indeed it had been our intention to write out our guest list, but it was too hot and we were not in the right mood. We were probably both a little tipsy. We chatted of this and that, and somehow or other the talk turned to the injuries which Owain had suffered last year at the hands of his torturers. He said that the scars were still raw, and that they sometimes gave him pain. I felt a dagger of concern in my heart. *'Cariad,* I trust that they have healed properly. Will you take your shirt off and show them to me?' He nodded, undid the buttons, pulled the tails from inside his breeches, and dragged the garment off over his head. He sat before me, and I saw again the scars etched across his chest and stomach where he had been cut by John Fenton's knife. Memories came flooding back of the time when he had been stretched out on the kitchen table at the Plas while Joseph fought to save his life. How I loved him then, and how I loved him now! I reached out and touched him, following the scar tissue with my finger. Then I placed the palm of my hand upon the flat of his stomach. 'A little raw in places,' I said, 'but our friend Joseph did a good job. I think you will survive, but only if you receive adequate care and attention from a loving wife.'

He smiled. 'I am working on it,' he said. 'And now I recall that I am not the only one with scars that need healing. Some years ago you were horse-whipped through the streets of Newport. I could not help noticing, when I looked at you a little while ago with my eyes closed, that your back still carries the signs of that terrible episode. Martha, before I marry you, I have to be sure that your back is in good enough condition for carrying the cares of the world. May I see your scars as you have seen mine?'

I hesitated, for I knew where this might lead. But at last I nodded. I sat up and turned my back to him. Then I undid the bows on the front of my dress, slipped it off my shoulders, and let it fall around my waist. Although it was still very hot, I recall that I shivered. For a long time he looked at my back and my old faint scars without saying a word. Then I felt the touch of his skin upon mine – not his fingers, but his lips. He kissed the scars where the constables' whips had bitten into my flesh, and I was instantly healed. The suffering and the ignominy of that miserable day were almost worth it, I thought, just for the pleasure of this moment. Then, his kisses spread away from the scars, onto other parts of my back, and onto my waist, and onto my neck and shoulders. Still I sat with my back to him. Then, as the kisses became less gentle and more prolonged, I felt his hand on my side, and suddenly he was caressing my breast. I felt a flood of passion rising within me, and I could resist no longer. I turned and clasped him to me, with my breasts pressed against his scarred chest. I sought his mouth with mine, and we kissed with a ferocity which surprised me and frightened me. Then his lips moved from my mouth and onto my breasts, and his hand was under my petticoats. My hand was moving too, and he drew in his stomach to allow me to reach down and touch him. He was as hard as an oak post. 'Oh, *cariad*, I love you! How I love you!' I whispered, and his mouth on mine said the same thing, but with infinitely more eloquence.

Simultaneously we decided that breeches, dresses, petticoats and stockings were superfluous, and we disentangled ourselves for a moment. He undid the remaining bows on my dress and removed it, and then he took away my petticoats. His actions were not fevered or frantic, but slow and loving, and I sensed that the process was very sensual from his point of view. I lay on the ground before him, entirely unclothed. Then I sat up and reciprocated, as slowly as I dared, as a wild passion surged within me. I pulled off his stockings and unbuttoned the flap which covered his private parts. I pulled his breeches down and over his ankles, and then removed his undergarment too. That was a difficult process, for there was a considerable obstacle in the way. I laughed, and so did he. Now he too was naked, and he kneeled before me, so aroused that I feared he might hurt himself. It did not occur to me for a moment that he might hurt me. Far from diminishing our passion, the removal of our remaining clothes had brought us almost to the climax of our loving, and so our mouths met again, and I felt for the first time the full press of his body against mine with nothing between us – breasts against chest, stomach against stomach, thighs against thighs, feet entwined. We explored each other with our hands and our lips, and then I heard myself say, 'Owain, my love. I want you now – how I want you!'

'Are you sure, Martha? I want you just as I have desired you since the day I first saw you, but are you sure?'

'Yes, yes! Oh, I love you, *cariad!* Now! Now!'

I rolled onto my back. Then he was on me, and

I recall that he was surprisingly light except for the great hardness pressed to my stomach. I moved my hand in order to guide him, and he kissed my neck and my shoulder with such frenzy that I knew that neither he nor I could delay any further. Momentarily I opened my eyes, and immediately I screamed, for there above me I saw a shadow that became the Nightwalker, looking down at me. I closed my eyes again our of sheer terror.

'No, no, Owain! Please, not now!' I sobbed, as my body went rigid with fear. And to his eternal credit he did not enter me as he could have, but lay on top of me and bore his weight upon his elbows. But he could not contain himself. At once he was filled with remorse, and rolled off me, murmuring, 'Oh, Martha, I am so sorry! I am so ashamed – I should not have persisted, but I am not yet clever enough to control my own passion.'

After a little while I opened my eyes, and saw only the blue sky and the golden furze bush overhead. We lay side by side, on our backs, without speaking, with our hearts racing, gulping in the warm fragrant air of the late afternoon. God only knows what he was thinking, but I thought he surely could not still love me after this. How could I have been so thoughtless as to lead him on and to then deny him the moment for which he had waited since we met? Was that terrible face above me real, or some creature conjured up by my wild imagination? Had the Nightwalker appeared as another warning, or as a mad and cruel joke, or even as some act of retribution for my past misdemeanours? I felt cold, and confused, and betrayed by fate.

'Hold me, Owain,' was all that I could whisper. He rolled towards me and he held me tightly in his arms. We were still as naked as the day we were born. I could not look at him. He gently kissed the top of my head. Then I said, *'Cariad,* I feel terribly cold, even though the air is still warm. Do you mind if I put my clothes back on?'

'By all means, Martha.' He looked utterly desolate, and I thought that he was close to tears. Once again he mumbled, 'I am so ashamed of myself!'

Enough was enough. I forgot about my clothes and sat facing him. I took his hands in mine. 'Owain,' I said, 'I will not hear anything more of that particular sentiment. You talk about shame, but you are a man, and such a man as I have never known. I was yours for the taking, and you could have persisted had you been obsessed with your own needs. But when I asked you to stop, you did so, and that is the kindest and gentlest thing that I have ever experienced. Will you believe that?'

'But we should never have risen to such a peak of passion in the first place. I fear that it was all my fault. I have been quite lacking in responsibility and respect for a lady.'

'No, my love. It was I who was the temptress. As a widow and a mother, I should have known better, and I sit before you covered in shame.'

At last Owain managed a little smile. 'If that is what you look like when you are covered with shame, Martha, please God that I will see more of you dressed in that particular invisible garment.'

'You will, Owain, you will. You will have me, and there will be no shame in it. I promise. We have a whole lifetime ahead of us.'

And I cuddled up alongside him, and we watched the silent sea and listened to the wheeling seabirds. Then he said: 'Martha, why did you all at once become so frightened?'

I had enough presence of mind not to tell him about the Nightwalker, so I said: 'I was suddenly overcome with a strange sort of fear. I know not why, or whence it came.'

'I think I know, *cariad*. We are still a month from our wedding. You have already been with child once out of wedlock, and once is enough. After our wedding, an early child would certainly cause tongues to wag. And if – God forbid – anything should happen to me, and we never do stand before the altar together, a baby in the early spring would destroy your hard-earned reputation for ever. If that were not enough, there is little Brynach to remind you of the folly of men and women who are driven by passion when cool deliberation might be more appropriate. I must have been quite mad to have forgotten that in the heat of the moment.'

'Do you still love me, strange and erratic creature that I am?'

'I do, Martha, with a love that makes me mad.'

'And I will love you until the stars fall out of Heaven. There has truly never been such a man as you, and I want you as my lover and the father of my children, born and unborn, and the light of my life.'

And in such a way we made our vows to each other, and our souls melted together. Consummation, I thought, can wait a little longer, although I will count the days and dream about what I have failed thus far to experience. With the dreaming there will be pain, but I will have to live with it for just four weeks more.

We got up and dressed, and sorted out the debris of our picnic. I packed my cloak and my blanket into my bag, and soon we were on our way home. We stopped at the edge of the brook behind the Aberrhigian pebble bank and washed ourselves. Then I held him in my arms for a long embrace, and kissed him long and hard. 'Thank you, *cariad*,' I said, 'for a day which I will never forget. One particular aspect might have been improved upon, but never fear. The improvement will not be long in coming. And in all other respects everything was quite perfect.'

And we smiled and held hands. We walked up the valley, and onto the mountain, and along the ridge to the beloved house in which he and I will make our home. The swallows were still flying high, and as yet there was no wind to scatter the fragrance of furze and bluebell. We took two hours, for most of the way was uphill, and there was no reason to hurry. When we arrived in the yard the four children tumbled out of the kitchen door to greet us. 'Hello, Mam! Hello, Master Owain!' they warbled. 'Have you had a jolly time? What have you been doing? Where have you been?' We both spent some time answering the first question, but took care to avoid answering the second or the third.

Now, on the day after all of this happened, I am drawn to my lonely feather bed. I have been reading back over what I have written, and I have to record that I am shocked by my own frankness. I am prepared to accept that my words may be seen as evidence of my utter depravity, and even of perversion. What if they are read by my own children? What if they are read by someone outside our family in the years to come? I have thought long and hard about these things, and have decided that by then it will not matter. Owain and I will in any case be long gone.

Whatever happens to me or to him in years to come, the events recorded on the foregoing pages are a faithful record of a beautiful day, during which I learned a great deal about nobility and respect. It is a sort of testament. I will read it over and again as I grow older, when I need to be reminded about the pleasure and the pain of womanhood.

6 May 1807

Today I have had visits from two of my dearest friends, and there are developments to record.

This morning Squire Fenton from Glynymel called in, as promised in a little note which I received yesterday. He wanted to see Brynach, he said, and this gave him a fine excuse to see me as well. We embraced upon the kitchen doorstep, and he complimented me upon my appearance. 'My goodness, Martha!' he exclaimed. 'You are looking particularly radiant, if I may say so. Motherhood appears to suit you well, particularly since you've been spared the difficulties that usually accompany the arrival of a new baby!'

I laughed and replied: 'No, no, my dear sir. Motherhood is as exhausting as ever, I can assure you. But yesterday Owain and I had a most delightful picnic on the cliffs, and I dare say the fresh air and sunshine did me good. And you are looking as sprightly as ever, if I may make so bold. Is Mistress Anne well? And how about young Kate O'Connell in your barn? Is she recovering?'

'Yes indeed. We are all thriving down in the valley. My dear wife is enjoying the weather and the garden. And Kate is getting stronger by the day. She is still depressed by the loss of her baby, of course, but Joseph has visited her again and has given her various herbal essences which appear to have miraculous properties. What we would all do without that fellow, God only knows.'

Never was a truer word spoken, I thought to myself. Then the Squire insisted on taking little Brynach from Liza and cradling him in his arms. 'My goodness, Martha!' he exclaimed again. 'No wonder that you insist on treating this little one as your own! He has your eyes, and your colouring, and your nose, and his high cheekbones are just as pretty as yours. He and Dewi will make fine brothers, and when he is grown up he will no doubt send young ladies into frenzies of passion with his good looks.' And he roared with laughter, which frightened Brynach so much that the little fellow started bawling, and I had to take him in my arms in order to console him.

Later on, over a cup of tea, Master Fenton told me that the Irish will stay in his barn until the first week of June, when they will set off on their harvesting migrations. He said that they were looking forward to visiting the Plas, and asked whether I would have work for them. 'Of course,' said I. 'I will be only too pleased to have them here, after what they have been through. Tell them that I will send a message when Billy judges that the time is right.' Then we talked about Owain and myself, and about our forthcoming nuptials. I took the opportunity of asking him about the dispute on the common between Owain and Squire Price, but he claimed not to know much about it. He confirmed, however, that Price was a lonely and desperate man, his desperation having been compounded recently by the loss of a large sum to a crooked drover who had disappeared without trace after selling his black cattle at Smithfield. I asked him why he and the other senior squires from the Fishguard and Dinas area had not intervened on Owain's behalf to prevent Master Price from enclosing parts of the mountain common, but he said that the law was very difficult to interpret on common lands, and that management was a matter of tradition rather than statute. 'Price has no Act of Parliament to back up his enclosures,' he said, 'but he claims that he is not appropriating land – just building some walls so as to prevent his flocks from mixing with others. It is nonsense, of course, but Price is an unpleasant bullying sort of fellow, and most of the squires will not intervene until their own interests are affected. As for me, I have spoken to him, and he became very abusive. I do not mind having him as an enemy, but I have no sanctions that I can apply against him until such time as he commits a crime and is hauled up before the magistrates. If that happens we have another problem, for he is a magistrate himself, as you know full well.' Then we talked of other things, and Grandpa and Grandma joined us, and so the morning flew by.

Master Fenton went on his way, and we ate our dinner, and later Joseph called in without warning. Wizards are of course excused from the normal conventions of good behaviour. He kissed my cheek, and complimented me on my appearance and my healthy complexion, which made me think that I must picnic more often with Owain on the cliffs. He rushed in to see the baby, and like Squire Fenton he insisted on cradling him in his arms. 'Careful, Joseph,' said I. 'The poor little fellow is being cradled and cuddled by such a multitude of persons that I doubt he will know whether he is coming or going.'

'I share your doubts, Martha. But now he has come, let us hope that he is not going anywhere else. My! How like you he is! Quite extraordinary. This is no pauper's child, that is for sure. And with his colouring and those brown eyes he could hardly be Irish either. Romany, maybe, but somehow I doubt that too.'

He walked round the kitchen for a while, and Brynach went to sleep in his arms. I had noticed such a thing before. When my own children were fretful, or suffering from teething pains, or from the colic, Joseph would always be the one to calm them when David and I had given up in despair. He was, I thought, a sort of universal father. If I could only acquire some of his talents, how would it feel to become a sort of universal mother?

Joseph placed the little one in his cradle and

said: 'Now, Martha, may I see the basket and the sheet and blanket that were delivered to your doorstep with this child?' I fetched them for him to examine. He looked at them and ran his fingers over them for about ten minutes. He even smelt the blanket and sheet. Then he made his pronouncement. 'The sheet is of excellent quality. I have never seen one like it in this area before – it is made of the finest cotton, tightly woven. The basket is local, made by Betty Basged who lives down on the estuary. May I borrow it for a while? Betty uses red willow like this, and always puts this reverse twist on the rim. It still smells fresh, and my assumption that it is recently made is confirmed by the loose weave. Since she started to suffer from the rheumatism she cannot weave as tightly as she could even twelve months ago. The blanket comes from Thomas Weaver on East Street. Only he uses this particular variation on the tapestry design. It might have been bought from him direct, or from his stall at Newport market. If we ask him he might even be able to remember the purchaser. May I borrow it for a while? Yes? Good, good. Both the blanket and the sheet have been pressed into use simply for the delivery of the baby to the Plas. If you smell them, Martha, you will notice that they do not have a baby smell about them. Bedclothes used with very small babies get stained a lot, and have to be washed frequently. The smell is very peculiar, because of the special smell of the rich mother's milk that flows immediately after a birth. That odour is entirely absent. Indeed, I can still smell the lanolin in the woollen blanket.'

I had to laugh at his earnestness and at the fastidious manner of his investigations. 'Dear Joseph!' I exclaimed. 'How I love you! I have looked, and touched, and smelt, and have deduced none of those things. I fear that I still have much to learn.'

'All in good time, Martha. Remember that I have been around a long time, and that I remember little details that others often miss. Now I must go. I have had a premonition that there is somebody in Nevern who needs my assistance. I had better get there as fast as I can. When I arrive I will no doubt discover who the distressed person is, and what is wrong with him.'

'Him? And how do you know that your patient is male rather than female?'

'Oh, I know it all right. I am never wrong on that count. Farewell, my dear friend.' He ran out of the door, taking the basket and the blanket with him, and soon I heard the sound of his white pony galloping out of the yard.

I now had to come to terms with the fact that Joseph might succeed in finding the identity of Brynach's mother. I felt some apprehension about this, but I had no time to descend into misery, because just then young Skiff came trotting into the yard on his new pony. He is a wealthy young man now, following the disposal of his silver cutlery. But he is not so wealthy as to abandon his friendship with me, and he is always willing to place the resources of his spy network at my disposal. 'Good afternoon, Mistress Martha!' said he as he came into the kitchen. 'May I see the new baby?'

'Of course, Skiff. He is over there by the fireplace, fast asleep in his cradle.'

He examined him, carefully, from a safe distance. 'Oh, there's sweet, he is,' he whispered, taking excessive care not to wake him up. 'And Duw Duw, Mistress, he is the exact likeness of you, as they do say down in town.'

Then we sat together at the far end of the kitchen, and Skiff delivered his news. 'Now then, Will tells me that you are trying to find out about the mother of that little one. Some of my boys have picked up on something strange that happened on the Parrog late at night a couple of weeks ago. Not exactly sure of which night it was, indeed, but Daffy is undertaking certain investigations. A coach was heard very late, after midnight, when all good folks were fast asleep in bed. It came and went very quickly, by all accounts, and one of the vagrants sleeping by the lime kilns says he is sure he heard a baby crying. That's all for now, Mistress. Is this helpful to you?'

'Indeed it is, Skiff. It gives us another line of investigation. I am very grateful indeed. Will you call again if you discover anything more?'

'You may count on it, Mistress,' said he. 'I likes a good mystery myself. There is always the possibility of us wealthy people getting bored and lazy if we do not have something to occupy our brains!' And he grinned, and took his leave.

This is interesting. I should really get a message to Joseph right away. On the other hand, I might think better of it and keep this new information just to myself.

7 May 1807

Today little Brynach is, if our calculations are correct, one month old. He has been here for almost a fortnight, and with Liza's loving attention and ample milk supply he is putting on weight and proving to be very contented. I cuddle him whenever I can, and clean him and change his clothes. I almost feel like his natural mother, although that is difficult while Liza is here fulfilling the most important of all the motherly functions. But my momentary animosity towards her has not recurred, and indeed she is the sweetest of girls who is already forming firm friendships with Bessie and Sian. Today she has been away for most of the evening on a visit to her poor lonely husband, for they deserve some time together as man and wife. He does not complain too much about her absence, for she pays him frequent visits, looks plumper and prettier than she ever has, and wears finer clothes. And when she does walk down to Pantry she carries with her eggs, butter, bread and cheese and other good things to supplement his normal diet of oatmeal and buttermilk.

This morning Hattie came up from the Parrog to give us a morning's work in the dairy. She brought with her news that I can still hardly credit. In the privacy of the parlour she told me, in conspiratorial tones, that my friend Patty might know something about Brynach. I was utterly amazed, and said so. 'No, it is true, Mistress. In the middle of the night after the twenty-fifth day of April, a baby was heard crying in Patty and Jake's cottage. My friend Daisy lives only a couple of doors away from Bwthyn Bach, and she swears that it is true. The date is fixed, because the day after was her birthday, and she remembers that date even if she forgets most others. She was very mystified, because she has never heard a baby there before or since. She thought it might be a sign from the spirit world that Patty was, or would soon be, with child. And indeed such may be true. But if I were you, Mistress, I should pay Patty a little visit.'

So this afternoon I walked down to town to buy some ribbons for a new dress I am making for Daisy, and continued to the Parrog. I walked along the sea wall to Bwthyn Bach, and knocked on the door. Patty was inside, because I saw the curtains move in the only window as I approached, but she did not answer. I knocked again and again, but there was still no response. I became concerned, and a little angry. So I lifted the latch, and discovered that the door was unlocked. I poked my head inside. 'Patty!' I called out. 'Are you in there? It is your friend Martha.' I went into the cottage and through to the scullery at the back, and there she was, covered in embarrassment.

She was so flustered that she hardly knew what to say. 'I am so sorry, Mistress Martha,' she mumbled, blushing bright pink. 'I was busy with my vegetables, and I did not hear you.'

I gave her a withering look, for that was a lie, and we both knew it. I came straight to the point. 'Patty, as you may know, a small baby was left on the doorstep of the Plas some two weeks ago. We have called him Brynach. We are all mystified as to where he came from. Now I have it on good authority that a baby was heard crying in your cottage earlier on that same night. Would you care to confirm that?'

'Please, Martha, do not press this matter with me. I do not know what you are talking about.'

'Indeed you do, Patty. I see it in your eyes, and I know you well enough, after all we have been through together, to know when you are lying. Why cannot you tell me the truth?'

'I am not at liberty to do so.'

'But this is quite absurd! I also have information that a carriage came to the Parrog on that same night, without lights, and went rushing off again after the shortest of stops. I have reason to believe that the baby came in that carriage.'

Poor Patty was now in a terrible pickle. I perceived that she was not at liberty to tell me the truth, no matter how hard I pressed her. But I was unwise, and persisted. 'Very well, Patty. The baby was not yours, that much is clear. But how is it that he was carried here at dead of night? Was he stolen? Is he the bastard child of anybody known to us?'

Patty was now close to tears. 'Martha,' she pleaded, 'please accept that I cannot tell you more. I am sworn to secrecy, and will not be party to any betrayal.'

'That is confirmation enough. Has any crime been committed?'

'No, I am sure of it. And nobody has been harmed.'

'Well, Brynach might have been. He could have died of cold if I had not found him on the doorstep within a few minutes of his being abandoned.'

Patty looked even more miserable, if such a thing was possible. 'I am truly sorry about that. That was not very clever.'

'So it was you who left him on the doorstep, and whose light I saw disappearing down the drive?'

'I did not admit that.'

'It sounded to me very much as if you did.'

'Please, please, Martha, if you are my friend, do not press me further. I cannot say another word. I am frightened, and I beg of you not to pursue the matter. It is best that neither you nor I reveal this conversation to anybody.'

Now I became even more concerned, not for myself or for Brynach, but for Patty. 'My dear friend, I love you too much to stand idly by if you are in danger. If you require help, you need only ask for it.'

'No, there is no danger. I am not threatened in any way, and I ask you to accept that. If I become aware of any threat, I promise that I will get a message to you at once. Jake will know first, and you will know second.'

'Dear Patty, you are a mystery to me. But I am reassured to some degree. Forgive me for pressing you so cruelly. Are we still friends?'

'Of course, Martha. Please understand that what has happened arises out of our friendship, and is for your own good.'

So we embraced with as much warmth as we could muster, and I went on my way, deep in thought. I was now as happy as I could be that Brynach was mine and nobody would take him from me. But I was as mystified as a fish in a cloud as to the meaning of the words which Patty

312

had used before we parted.

8 May 1807

I have been mulling over Patty's words, and cannot for the life of me perceive their meaning. How could the delivery of a small baby to my doorstep not be a crime? And how could that act of abandonment be a product of the warm friendship between me and Patty? And for my own good? For Brynach's good, maybe, but for mine?

This morning I was faced with a considerable dilemma. Should I share my discoveries about Patty and the baby with Joseph? He is out there somewhere, I thought, digging around trying to unearth the purchaser of Brynach's wicker basket and woollen blanket. His investigations will probably lead him to Patty, and he might well upset both her and Jake if he knocks on their door and confronts them with the evidence he has in his possession.

Having given this some thought, I penned the following short note to Joseph after breakfast this morning.

Plas Ingli, on the 8th day of May 1807

My dear friend Joseph,
I know that you are pursuing the matter of the blanket and basket which might lead us to the natural mother of little Brynach. Something has happened which causes me to believe that no good will come of it, and that further investigations may well harm the

313

best interests of someone who is a beloved friend to both of us.

You have constantly urged me to trust my intuition, and this now leads me to ask you to cease your enquiries. I assure you that this is a good deal more than a female whim!

You have my assurance that no crime has been committed, and that it is in the best interests of Brynach, myself, the natural mother and all other parties that you let the matter rest.

Please respect my wishes, and at some future time I am sure the occasion will arise when a full explanation may be appropriate.

I hope to see you soon, and we all send affectionate greetings from the Plas.

Your loving friend, Martha

Shemi galloped off straight away to Werndew, and delivered the message personally to Joseph. I was apprehensive as I waited at home, for if I had received a reply from Joseph providing me with further clues I fear I would have been overwhelmed with curiosity and would probably have redoubled my efforts to get at the truth. But, said Shemi on his return, Joseph had simply shrugged his shoulders, and grinned. 'Tell Mistress Martha,' he had said, 'that a lady's request must always be respected. And tell her that she is making progress.'

9 May 1807

I have hardly had a moment to myself over these

last few days, and I have been so preoccupied with establishing the parentage of little Brynach that I have forgotten about other far more threatening matters. The most threatening of all is the matter of the Nightwalker. I am as confused as it is possible to be. The incident on the lane to Llannerch, when I met the creature face to face, was so terrifying that I fainted away. But then I was reassured to some degree by the gift of a bunch of daffodils which indicated – I hope – that it means me no harm. Do phantoms pick daffodils and leave them in muddy lanes alongside prostrate ladies? I doubt it, but I have heard many stories of ghostly beings throwing things, and turning butter churns, and closing doors, and moving heavy objects across floors. So I have to accept that daffodil-picking would be a minor challenge to an experienced ghost.

But is the creature a ghost? If he is a human being, as Grandpa suggested long since, he should have left footprints in the snow during the winter encounters, but he did not. By the same token he should have left footprints in the lane some days since. And I am mortified by my own negligence in not examining the lane in minute detail when I passed that way again on my way home from Llannerch. Joseph would never, with his enquiring mind, have made such an elementary mistake. Had he been in the picture, the mystery would surely by now have been resolved.

And then my terrifying sighting of the creature standing over me at the very moment when Owain and I should have reached the climax of our loving. What did that mean? It had the effect of destroying the moment, but was the Nightwalker real, or simply a figment of my imagination? Was it a warning, a fearsome omen of some disaster soon to overtake me or Owain? I cannot get out of my head the idea that the figure is the Grim Reaper, come to snatch Owain from my grasp.

Tonight, at dusk, with the weather still warmer and calmer than anybody can remember in early May, I think I saw the phantom again, near Ffynnon Brynach, standing as still as a statue and looking down at the house. The light was very dim, and I could not be sure of my sighting, but a cold chill ran through me, and again I experienced the fear that something dreadful was about to happen.

I have been mad to keep this problem to myself, when there are two loving friends – Owain and Joseph – who can give me advice and apply their manly methods to working out what is going on. I am resolved to keep this secret no longer. Tomorrow I will meet Owain, as arranged, to compose our wedding invitations. We should have done it during our picnic on the cliffs, but pens and ink in his hamper had remained untouched. Before we do anything else, however, we will sit down and I will tell him everything I know about the Nightwalker. I will detail all the sightings, and I will outline for him all, or most of, the theories which have been flying round our kitchen table at the Plas.

Then I will walk over the mountain and visit Joseph. I will tell him the same things. I may well find that he knows all about the creature already, for he seems to know more about the spirit world than any other living being. Also, he absorbs

316

news of strange events like a sponge, even though he may not have spoken to anybody about them. Information, both esoteric and mundane, seems to flow like a stream in through the windows of his cottage at Werndew. He will certainly know whether the Nightwalker is evil or benign. And if the Grim Reaper really does exist, Joseph will be the one to confirm it. When he hears my story, he will surely admonish me for not checking very carefully for footprints and other physical signs of the creature's presence, and he will say that I have been a poor student indeed to allow terror to cloud my judgement and prevent proper investigations.

By tomorrow night I will have shared my secret, and I hope that the puzzle of the Nightwalker will have been resolved to my satisfaction. If the creature is a spirit, Joseph will surely exorcise him from the neighbourhood, and we will be rid of him for ever. If the figure is a man, I have no doubt at all that Owain and Joseph will together hunt him down and ensure that he is clapped into a lunatic asylum or otherwise put away. I wish the creature no harm, for it has not thus far harmed me or anybody else, but now would be rid of it, for my peace of mind is disturbed.

10 May 1807

Once again, desolation has swept over me like an irresistible tidal surge. I am now in no doubt at all that the Nightwalker was indeed the Grim Reaper, for he has taken Owain from me.

317

He should have come at two of the clock. I sat in the shade in my flower garden, waiting for him. I had eaten hardly any dinner, for I had experienced a strange sort of expectation. And it was indeed strange, for it was quite unlike the passionate anticipation of some days since, in the prelude to our picnic on the cliffs. I was distracted and short-tempered with the children, but they and the servants probably put it down to the fact that I was counting the minutes until the arrival of the man who owns my heart. They forgave me, for I have acted in such a way before. But in truth I was waiting not for my man, but for something else. Perhaps I was even waiting for his non-arrival. Now, as I look back though my tears, I am afraid, very afraid, of my own power to predict; and in recognizing this, I am even more afraid that my fears and premonitions have somehow influenced the course of events. Could I, through my own doubts, have caused cruel fate to take him away from me?

My hand is shaking, and I can hardly write. But I must try, for the sake of my own sanity and in an attempt to banish the blackness within my soul. Perhaps he will come back to me tomorrow. I must wish it. I must will it. Please God, make it happen, for I need Owain, and I want him more than anything on the surface of this sweet and bitter earth.

By five minutes past the hour I knew that something was wrong. Owain is never late. I waited until half past the hour, refusing to leave my seat beneath the golden blossoms of my laburnum tree. I knew that if I left the garden I would be prowling about the place like a mad thing, spreading alarm and despondency in all directions. At last I could wait no longer, and walked to the house. Luckily the children were not there. Liza was breast-feeding Brynach in the kitchen. 'Liza,' I whispered, 'Master Owain has not come.'

'Mistress Martha, you look as if you have seen a ghost. Please, you must sit down, and stop worrying. Doubtless he has been delayed by some domestic problem, and will be here soon.'

At that point Bessie came in, and saw the state I was in, and sat me down and poured me a drink of water. Then she gave me a good scolding. 'Mistress, you must not allow wild fantasies to sweep you away. Master Owain is, after all, only half an hour late, and that is surely nothing to worry about.'

'Half an hour to you, Bessie, but a century to me. Something terrible has happened to him – I know it. Will you please ask Will to go down to Llannerch and find out where he is?'

And so Will was sent, and while he was away I became so distressed that I had to go up to my room and lie down. At last, with my heart pounding, I heard Will's heavy footsteps returning across the yard. I was at the kitchen door to meet him. 'Well, what is the news?' was all that I could say.

Will frowned, for he is not very good at hiding his feelings. My heart sank even further, before he said a word. 'Mistress, more than a little concerned, they are, down at Llannerch. Master Owain should have been back there for dinner at noon. With the weather still calm and warm, he told them this morning that he was to call and see you after dinner. But before that, he said, he was minded to go out into the bay and see if he could catch some nice fresh mackerel for you. In early this year, they are, so they say...'

'Spare me the details, Will. What else?'

'Well, Mistress, they says that he set off very early, at about six of the clock, on his hunter, as happy as can be.'

'Heading for Cwm-yr-Eglwys, where he keeps his boat and his fishing lines?'

'Quite correct, Mistress. At any rate, they are also worried about the fact that he has not returned, and Mistress Gwilym says that two of the Llannerch men-servants have gone down on their ponies indeed, to see if they can find out what has happened to him.'

'But there is no wind, and the sea is still as flat as a farm pond. Surely nothing untoward can happen, with conditions as they are?'

'My thoughts exactly, Mistress. Very strange indeed, since Master Owain is quite an experienced boatman.'

'We have to find out what has happened ourselves. I want you and Billy to take the two fastest ponies and get down to Cwm-yr-Eglwys as soon as possible. Go over the mountain, for the track is hard and dry just now. God willing, you will find him near the beach, or at least discover some news of him.'

And so they went, and returned late in the evening, by which time I had been reduced to such a state of terror that Bessie had to sit with me at my bedside. She gave me something to calm my nerves and make me drowsy, while Sian and the

320

old people kept the children occupied downstairs and in the nursery. They should have been asleep, but they too were restless and worried. At last, Billy and Will came up the stairs, looking utterly dejected. 'Mistress,' said Billy, 'I fear that the news is not good.' And I heard them out, feeling as I did when news of David's death was delivered to me on a fateful day in February two years ago. At first I was paralysed, and then I wept.

It is past midnight, and I weep still.

Dancing to the Devil's Tune

15 May 1807

Today I walked over to Llannerch. The servants were all there, coping as best they could, five days after the disappearance of their master. Owain's father has been back and forth, trying to organize the affairs of the estate, as has his steward John Bateman, my erstwhile tutor in finance and other weighty matters. When I arrived I found the place to be even gloomier than the Plas, for it is unblessed by the lively chatter of small children and the crying of babies. Mistress Gwilym and I embraced on the kitchen doorstep, and then we both dissolved into tears. She is absolutely devoted to her master, and she needed a female shoulder to weep upon. We have all been trying to put a brave face on things, but tears are never far away, and the smallest incident can bring them flooding up to the surface.

I asked her if I might take away the clothes and the shoes that Owain wore on the occasion of our picnic at Aberrhigian. She probably thought that I was deranged by grief, but she agreed, and we went up to his room together and found his breeches, his undergarment, his stockings and his white shirt in his wardrobe, and then his walking shoes next to the fireplace. I put all of these things into my bag, and as I did so I was almost overcome with emotion as I realized that this was the room in which he had slept and spent his long winter evenings, and thought of me. I looked at his bed and wanted to fling myself upon it, but I managed to control myself, and Mistress Gwilym put her arm round my shoulder and led me gently downstairs.

I emerged into the bright daylight and saw that high wisps of cloud were racing in from the west. Another storm was coming, like that which struck us on the day after he disappeared, wiping out of our minds any hope that we might have nurtured of his survival on the wide acres of Cardigan Bay. I walked home in a daze, wondering why I was so obsessed with his clothes. Was I guilty of some morbid obsession with the things that he had worn next to his skin? Was I involved in some equally morbid attempt to keep alive the memory of our picnic on the cliffs? I knew not, and truly I did not care. But I made a vow that I would keep these things for ever, as a signal of my intent to wait for him, should he by some miracle still be alive. It even entered my mind that when I go to my grave somebody might open my wardrobe, and find Owain's clothes, and say, 'Ah yes, those are the clothes of Master Owain Laugharne, the great love of her life. She kept them as a symbol of the bond between them, and now they are together in the bosom of the Lord.'

After five days of fighting against despair and seeking to maintain hope, I am now forced to recognize that Owain may never return. I must maintain my record of events, in the hope that the process of writing will help me to control my mind and my emotions.

I spent the night after the reporting of Owain's disappearance in a state of turmoil. Bessie asked me if she should stay with me in my room, but I said no, for in truth she could not have helped me. I did not have the courage to extinguish the three candles on my dressing table. I spent part of the night on my bed, seeking to avoid wild speculations, but with my mind rushing hither and thither in trying to assess what might have happened. I was furious with the darkness, for it prevented searches as it prevented discussion. I spent part of the night pacing about in my room, oblivious of the fact that the creaking floorboards might be keeping others awake. Some of it I spent sitting at my window, gazing eastwards into the blackness and longing for the dawn. And with growing horror I realized that the weather was changing. At first there was a mere whisper of a breeze, but then the wind rose and gusted about the dark house and its sheltering trees, and after an hour or two a full gale was assaulting the western gable end of the house. I climbed back into my bed and tried to sleep, but I could not. I got up again and sat at the window, and around four of the clock I saw the first faint glimmer of the dawn far away in the east. But it was a false dawn, for as I watched a heavy band of cloud swept overhead and blotted out the first feeble rays of the rising sun. The world was plunged into blackness again. Then the rain came, first with the gentlest of spatterings upon the slated roof, and then with swirls and flurries, and finally in an unremitting deluge. At last the rays of the sun managed to infiltrate the cloud blanket, and day began to assert itself at the expense of night. But the storm continued, rising in intensity. God help those who are out at sea this morning, I thought. What were the chances of survival for weatherbeaten mariners with strong sails over their heads and sturdy oak timbers beneath their feet, let alone for a fresh-faced landsman in an open twelve-foot rowing boat?

I could not remain in my bedroom for a moment longer, so I went down into the kitchen. It was very dark. I opened the shutters and lit some candles from the fire. Little Twm started to cry in Liza's room, and then stopped as she gave him the breast. I started to work, ensuring that I made enough noise to awaken the rest of the household. That was not very kind of me, but I did not care, for I felt lonely and miserable. I stirred up the fire and carried in some logs from the doorstep. I filled the cauldron with water and swung it over the flames. I moved the furniture about, and swept the floor, and put out the china on the kitchen table in readiness for breakfast. It was still not five of the clock. At last Billy, Shemi and Will appeared, rubbing their eyes, clearing their throats, and stretching their arms. They greeted me with as much good grace as they could muster, spat into the fire, and then pulled on their boots and their oilskins before going out into the storm to deal with the animals. Next Mrs Owen appeared, admonishing me with her eyes for daring to take possession of her kitchen while she had still been fast asleep. Bessie materialized soon afterwards, looking very sleepy, and eventually so did everybody else.

In the chaos of early morning domesticity my mind was distracted from dark thoughts for a little while, but then, as we all sat at breakfast, I had to concentrate on what to do next. Grandpa Isaac was, as ever, a great help. If there is to be any chance at all of finding Owain in this storm, he said, the most important thing is to avoid duplication of effort. So it was that Billy was despatched on horseback within thirty minutes to Pontfaen, to offer help to Squire John Laugharne, who would already be organizing search parties. Shemi went off on the swiftest pony to Werndew, to tell Joseph about Owain's disappearance, if he had not already heard about it. Will went down to town on the black pony, first of all to deliver a message from me to the Mayor in which I pleaded for assistance, and then to ask Skiff and his accomplices if they would turn out in the wild wind and drenching rain to search the cliffs between Fishguard and Cardigan for any trace of Owain, alive or dead. I could not sit at home while all this was going on, and so I said that I would take the chaise down to Cwm-yr-Eglwys to see what else I could discover. Grandpa would not let me go by myself for fear that I might do something stupid, so he came with me, and we both got soaked to the skin.

At Cwm-yr-Eglwys we could hardly see the church or the cliffs through the sheeting rain, but we knocked on a few doors and asked some questions, and discovered nothing new. Then Joseph appeared, and greeted us in a somewhat cursory fashion. There was not a moment to be wasted, he said, and every minute gone was a minute lost. And he went off in the deluge towards the beach, shouting above the wind that he would call in at the Plas later in the day. As for me, I went into the church for a few moments by myself to pray before the altar for the safe delivery of Owain. I fear that I am not blessed with a strong faith, and doubt that my prayers will be heard let alone acted upon, but I thought that in the circumstances I had better clutch at any straw that was within reach.

We went home, got out of sodden clothes and into dry ones, and warmed ourselves by the fire. For the moment we had done all we could. Later in the day Owain's father appeared out of the streaming cloud and rain to inform us that he had posted notices in Fishguard, Newport, Dinas and Cardigan offering a reward of five pounds for information leading to the rescue of Master Owain Laugharne. He was desperately worried, as any father would be, and said that he had sent a message to Carmarthen, to his older son James, asking him to come home immediately to help with investigations. He is a good and loving son with a sharp mind, and practises as an attorney throughout our neighbouring shire. But the Squire admitted that his efforts thus far had revealed next to nothing, and that there was little chance of progress even with a trained legal mind involved.

Shortly after the departure of Master Laugharne, Joseph arrived, and he was grateful for the offer of some dry clothes and a big fire to sit by. We filled him with tea, but he was very uncommunicative. He repeated what we knew already, and added a few details, but he spent the greater part of an hour huddled by the fire with a hot mug of tea clasped in his hands and a frown upon his face. He was so deep in thought that he seemed almost in a trance, and we dared not disturb him. Then he left and went back out into the rain, thanking us for the warmth and the tea and saying that he had certain investigations to make before darkness fell, and that he would be back with us as soon as he might.

Then Will returned, with water seeping from his clothes and pouring out of his boots. He was exhausted, poor fellow, having walked for miles along the cliffs in the teeth of the gale. His mother, our heroic housekeeper, got him into a hot soapy bath which warmed him up, and then he joined us in the kitchen before the fire. He reported that with the help of Skiff and his friends he had assembled thirty men, who had broken into groups and systematically searched the cliffs all the way from Fishguard to St Dogmael's. They had climbed down to every little cove in spite of the appalling weather conditions, and had clearly risked life and limb trying to get at every small beach where a shipwrecked mariner or a body might have been washed ashore. They had found nothing – no Owain, alive or dead, no timbers, no ropes or other items that might provide a clue as to what had happened. I promised that one day I would reward those thirty men for their selfless devotion to a cause that was truly mine and not theirs, and I kissed Will and thanked God for what they had done.

With such a notable lack of progress during this blackest and most terrible of days, the sense of gloom round the dinner table was palpable. We adults knew that there was now little chance for Owain, and the children picked up on the tension and the long silences to become fractious and undisciplined. I could hardly cope with that, but then the two babies responded to the miserable atmosphere by starting to cry, and nothing that Liza or I, or any of the other women, did to console them had the slightest effect. At last I could stand it no longer, and I rushed from the table, up the stairs and into my room, slamming the door behind me. My behaviour was truly no better than that of a temperamental thirteen-year-old, but no young girl could possibly have known the anguish which at that moment was tearing me apart.

25 May 1807

Another ten days have passed, and the unsettled spell has been replaced by warm and sunny weather with a southerly breeze. Grandpa says that the gales and the rain which followed the disappearance of Owain have fattened up the grass, and that the hay harvest will be a little late this year, but good.

Today Joseph called in to bring me up to date. Sian took the children for a walk up on the mountain, and the wizard and I sat in the sun on the grassy bank behind the house. He has spent more than a fortnight on intensive investigations, and says that he has visited almost every house along the coast between Fishguard and Morfa Head, and has spoken to everybody in Cwm-yr-Eglwys and Newport who might have information of value. He has questioned all the Llannerch servants, and many of the local fishermen and mariners. He has done much else besides, but was not very forthcoming as to the details. This is the story, as far as he can piece it together.

Owain left Llannerch on his horse at six in the morning, lightly clad in view of the fact that a glorious day was in prospect, and carrying only a small bag containing his breakfast and a bottle of fruit cordial. He rode over the mountain to Cwm-yr-Eglwys and arrived there at about twenty minutes to seven. He tethered his horse at the back of Ifor Jones's cottage, as he always does when he goes out into the bay. The old man was asleep, but would water and feed the horse as required until his master returned. Owain then fetched his oars, oilskins and warm coat, and his fishing lines and other tackle, from his little shed near the fishermen's cottages. He carried his things down to the slipway near the churchyard, where he keeps his boat above the high water mark. He exchanged greetings with three other early risers, and chatted for a while with Matthew

Huws, a fisherman who was working on his boat on the slipway. He helped Owain to get his boat into the water, and after offering his thanks Owain was away, pulling hard on the oars and gliding off round the corner and out of sight. Matthew says he was in the best of spirits, whistling as he went. He said that he was intent upon rounding Pen Dinas and then heading north for a couple of miles out into the bay, where he reckoned the mackerel would be congregating at a secret spot which he knows from making alignments with certain features on the coast. He left the slipway just before seven. There were two further sightings of him, one when he was rounding the headland, and another – by a servant at Pen Dinas Farm – when he was far out into the bay, still pulling strongly northwards. And that was all. The sea throughout was as flat as a farm pond, and the servant said that there was not another rowing boat or sailing ship in sight. Nor would anything go out from Newport or the Cwm all day, for there was not enough wind to fill a handkerchief, let alone four hundred square feet of canvas sail.

Having related all of this, Joseph suddenly leapt to his feet and said that he had to be off. He came over to me and gave me a little kiss on the cheek. 'Do not despair, Martha,' he said, managing a feeble smile. 'There is always hope. No body has been found on Berry Sands or anywhere else, and that has to be a positive thing. I have asked all of the local fishermen to sail close inshore along the cliffs between Newport and Cemais Head on their journeys in and out of port, and they have done that over and again, examining every cove and crevice in the cliffs. Since no trace of Owain or his boat has been found after those two westerly gales, we have to maintain the hope that he has drifted away elsewhere or been picked up by some passing vessel.'

'I hope you are right, dear Joseph, for I have to admit that my faith in his safe return is rapidly diminishing.'

'I shall do what I can to restore that faith. Now then, with a very hot day in prospect, and another to follow, I have a certain experiment to conduct. I shall call in with a further report as soon as I have a positive outcome.'

And off he went on his white pony, not towards Werndew, as I expected, but towards Newport. I was mystified by his words and by his direction of travel, for I knew that he normally conducts all his experiments in the quiet and mysterious confines of his own cottage.

27 May 1807

Today has been one of those days on which I have been assaulted over and again by happenings which have sapped all energy and emotion out of me. Indeed, I have been battered to such an extent that I could hardly climb the stairs to my room at bedtime.

It started after breakfast, as soon as Sian had taken the children off to town to play with some of their friends. I was still in the room when Billy and Grandma Jane became involved in a heated exchange. Since Owain's disappearance we have all tried to avoid speculation, seeking instead to accept the facts of the matter and maintain the belief that Owain might walk in through the door at any moment. But confidence in such a miracle is waning day by day, and the moment had to come when talk about his fate would come bubbling to the surface.

Billy reported that it is widely held in town that Owain has been taken by the fairies, for it is known that Gwlad y Tylwyth Teg lies beneath the surface of Cardigan Bay and can be seen twenty fathoms down when the sea is placid and the sun is high. Indeed, said he with authority in his voice, so green and beautiful is this magical kingdom that sailors who have been becalmed above it have been tempted to dive down in order to enjoy its delights. Down and down they go into the depths, he said. Most of them drown and sooner or later float back to the surface. But some are never seen again, and they are the lucky ones who will live beneath the sea with the fairies for ever. 'Rubbish!' said Grandma. 'Stuff and nonsense, put about by people with primitive minds. Rector Devonald will have none of it, and neither will I, for it is an established fact that one cannot breathe beneath the sea.' Then Bessie chipped in, saying that those who go to live with the fairies do not disappear for ever. On the contrary they always return after fifty years, still looking as young as the day on which they departed, and quite unaware that they have been away. Will thought that Owain had been stolen by pirates or smugglers, and Grandpa argued that that was impossible, since there was not enough wind on the sea to propel even a toy boat with a little paper sail. On balance, he inclines to the idea that Owain has been taken by a sea monster, for it is known that such creatures, longer than a twenty-ton ketch, lurk in Cardigan Bay. Shemi speculated that his boat had disintegrated and that he had plunged to the sea bed entangled in ropes and fishing lines. And Mrs Owen thought that on a placid sea and beneath a burning sun Owain had become delirious and disoriented, and that he had rowed on northwards until he died, far away from the sight of land.

So the talk continued, round and round, and I slipped outside and sat in the garden, for I could take no more of it. For me, what mattered was not the practical details of his death or disappearance, but the reasons for it. Why, oh why, had he gone out into the bay, away from me and out of my life? Was it really so that he could catch me some mackerel for my supper? I could not believe it, and searched in my heart for some deeper cause. I came up with questions, but no answers. Had he suddenly realized that he did not love me? Had he pondered deeply on the fact that marriage to me would bring with it domesticity and responsibility, and had he decided to flee rather than to enter into such a contract? I have heard of other young men who have taken fright at the very idea of a settled life with wife and children. Had he set out into the wastes of the ocean with the deliberate idea of taking his own life? Could he really have been so miserable? Was he still, in spite of my soothing words, so ashamed about what happened at the climax of our loving on the cliffs at Aberrhigian that he could not live with himself, or with me? And was his disappearance all my fault? Had I been too intense in my loving of him, and too passionate and too jealous of his love? Had I – quite literally – frightened him out of his wits by so openly demonstrating that I needed him and wanted him?

Questions, questions, and no answers. Then I set off upon a train of thought that was even more frightening. Could I have caused his death through my own special powers? I know that on the morning of his disappearance I felt a strange sort of apprehension, and I recorded in my little book at the time that I felt that I was waiting for his non-arrival. Without knowing it, could I have placed some sort of curse upon him? Then there is the matter of the Nightwalker. Over and again, this devilish creature has appeared and warned me that Owain has been marked for its special attention. I have tried to dismiss such morbid thoughts from my head – and to what purpose? I have deluded myself, and my family, into the belief that all will be well, and I have led Owain on, and seen him sink to his death beneath the green waters of the bay.

'Mistress Martha, your visitors have arrived.' So said Bessie, dragging me temporarily from the gloomy shadows. I had quite forgotten that today was the day for the hearing which would make Brynach legally my child. 'Oh, my goodness!' I exclaimed, leaping to my feet and rushing towards the house. 'Please apologize to them, Bessie, and tell them that I have been dealing with other pressing business relating to the disappearance of Owain. Tell them that I will be with them in five minutes.' And indeed I was. The five gentlemen whom I should have been expecting were very forgiving, and I found them in the kitchen making gurgling noises at little Brynach, who had each and every one of them under his spell. I curtsied, and they stood up and bowed, and we chatted for a while until Bessie served us with tea and griddle cakes. Then we settled down round the kitchen table to deal with the business of the day. In the deputation there were five gentlemen: Master Daniel Thomas, who is the Mayor of Newport, Master Charlie Toms representing the church-wardens and the Overseers of the Poor, Squire Ellis Prosser of Frongoch and Squire John Bowen of Llwyngwair representing the magistrates, and finally Master George Lewis Legal representing me and the Plas Ingli estate. Grandpa Isaac also sat in on the discussion, because I could not have done without him. Master Toms agreed to act as clerk.

Squire Prosser, as senior magistrate, took charge of the proceedings, and moved things along with admirable despatch. First of all he established the facts surrounding the discovery of the small baby on the doorstep of the Plas on the morning of 26 April. I was required to give a statement on oath, and evidence was also taken from Grandpa Isaac, Mrs Owen and Liza. Brynach had to be duly identified, on oath, as the very child who had been discovered in the basket. Then the Squire sought to satisfy himself that genuine efforts had been made to discover the identity of the child's mother. The Mayor, in response, described his futile efforts in this regard, and had to admit to involvement in the fiasco which led to the pursuit of the O'Connell clan and to the false accusations of bastardy against the poor grieving mother in their midst.

'No reports of women recently pregnant and now apparently childless, either near or far?' asked the Squire.

'Nothing at all, Squire,' said Charlie Toms. 'All those who were heavily with child in the months of February and March have been visited and duly accounted for.'

'And do we have any other clues as to the provenance of the child?'

'Only one, Squire. I heard yesterday that Widow Susanna Warlow, the daughter of Price Llany-chaer, was seen two months back in Dinas, heavy with child. I asked the Squire about it, and he almost bit my head off. He said it was none of my business. Anyway, Mistress Susanna lives near Llandeilo and so any child of hers, bastard or not, is the Price family's problem and not ours.'

'Well,' said Master Prosser, 'the baby is here and Mistress Susanna is presumably fifty miles away, and therein lies our particular problem.'

I was greatly surprised by this turn of events, but there was no time to think about the implications. I had to report on what I knew, so I said: 'I have reason to believe that the baby was carried to Newport at dead of night in a carriage, which then immediately left. We have no clues as to the ownership of the vehicle, and we know not where it came from. Could it possibly have come from Llandeilo?'

'Maybe, and maybe not. But we cannot go

chasing about all over Wales in pursuit of strange carriages and wild rumours. I am minded to proceed. I doubt that there is anything more that we could have done or that we can do in the future. Now then, Master Mayor and Master Toms, may we take it that neither the borough nor the parish wishes to take on the responsibility for raising and maintaining this child?'

'I speak for both of us, and for our colleagues among the Overseers of the Poor,' said the Mayor, 'when I say that we have no resources for taking on this responsibility without a substantial increase in the poor rate. We are looking after four bastard children already.'

'Very well. We have an offer from Mistress Martha Morgan of Plas Ingli to look after this child, whom she calls Brynach, and to raise him as her own. Correct, Mistress Martha?'

'Yes, I am willing so to do.'

'And is there any objection to the acceptance of this offer?'

The Squire looked round the table, and four heads were shaken. But Master Toms, all smiles previously, and behaving now like a coiled adder among the pebbles, said, 'Excuse me for mentioning this, Master Prosser, but I have to say that it would be most unusual for a single woman, or indeed a widow with four children of her own, to take on the responsibility of looking after a bastard and a foundling. It is well established that a child needs a father. Bearing in mind the best interests of baby Brynach, one has to ask whether the resources of this family are adequate to take on the responsibility of a fifth child...'

Master Lewis leapt to his feet, which was just as well, for I was blushing like a guilty child, and I was also dumbstruck. 'Sir, I object to that remark!' he exploded. 'The credentials of this family are beyond reproach. Do you see signs of deprivation and squalor around you? Have you heard tales of Mistress Morgan's young family running amok or collapsing through starvation? I can tell you that in my experience I have seldom encountered a more disciplined and loving family. Take care, sir, lest Mistress Morgan should be minded to withdraw her generous offer!'

'Indeed, indeed,' and 'Quite so, point taken,' and 'Well spoken, sir!' said three other gentlemen round the table. Master Toms was covered with embarrassment, and proceeded to make matters worse.

'I do not doubt for a moment the wonderful abilities of Mistress Martha as a mother,' said he, 'but I am aware of the difficulties she has faced since the loss of her dear husband two years since. Further, on the matter of her betrothal to Master Owain Laugharne, we are all aware that problems have arisen because of his disappearance. In the midst of her natural sadness, I merely ask whether she will be able to summon up the resources of energy and time that will be required to raise a further small baby. I ask this, of course, on the baby's behalf.'

This time I did not need Master Lewis. I stood up and faced him, and spoke through clenched teeth. 'Master Toms, I do not know you, and I do not know anything about your abilities as a father. But those remarks were cruel indeed, and I had

338

hoped that all of us round this table might have had the good grace to steer clear of the very sad circumstances which have afflicted me in my private life. You appear to think that I am some feeble woman who spends her time in the trivial pursuit of pleasure, and is liable to subside into self-pity whenever adversity arises. Well sir, I run an estate, and I run it as well as any gentleman. I also give time and energy, in abundance, to my young family, and I am greatly blessed to have Master Isaac Morgan and Mistress Jane Morgan to help me in all manner of things. Let me, sir, be the judge of the state of my mind, and what I can cope with. Now, gentlemen, do you wish me to withdraw my offer?'

I sat down, shaking like a leaf, and hoping that none of the gentlemen whom I had addressed knew just how fragile my emotional state actually was. With some relief I saw that Master Toms had slid so low in his chair that he was almost under the kitchen table. I closed my eyes, and heard the other gentlemen of the deputation thumping the table in approval. The crisis had passed.

'Thank you, Master Toms, and thank you, Mistress Martha, for those remarks,' said Squire Prosser. 'I think that there is nothing more to be said? No? Good, good. So, to the final formalities. Master Lewis, you have two copies of the document?'

'Yes indeed, Squire. The details have already been agreed with the Mayor, the churchwardens, and the Overseers of the Poor. Mistress Morgan has agreed to indemnify the parish against any costs associated with the child, whom she names

Brynach Morgan, at least until he reaches the age of twenty-one. In effect, this means that the little one will become a member of her family. If in due course the real mother is found, that will be a matter for my client to resolve with my help. She has asked me to adjust her will, and she assures me that Brynach will also be mentioned by name in any future family deeds and marriage settlements. The parish has every reason to be well pleased with the generosity of these arrangements.'

Lewis Legal then placed two copies of the document on the table, and all those present placed their signatures upon them. Master Lewis dabbed them with a piece of blotting paper, affixed a seal, and the deal was done. There was much shaking of hands, and back-slapping, and laughter, and I was gratified when Master Toms took me to one side and apologized for the insensitivity of his remarks, which had, he said, not come out of his mouth quite as he had intended. I managed to raise a smile, and told him that all was forgotten already and so we parted the best of friends.

Then the gentlemen were gone. Master Lewis will keep one copy of the document among our family papers, and the Mayor will keep the other. And little Brynach, the bright and mysterious light of my life, is mine. Tomorrow he will be baptized, and his address will be given as Plas Ingli in Newport parish.

I took a little while to recover from the intensity and emotional ups and downs of the meeting, but with an ample dinner in my stomach I managed to face the afternoon with something approaching good humour. The children came back from their walk on the mountain full of tales of butterflies and buzzards, spring lambs and skylarks, and strange patterns on the rocks. Their wide-eyed innocence, and their rosy complexions and boundless energy reminded me that my life is full of treasures, regardless of what I may have lost, and so I thought that a celebration was in order. Tonight, for supper, said I, we would have a little party with some specially good things, and I instructed Mrs Owen accordingly. I told the children that following the visit of certain gentlemen this morning little Brynach was now officially their brother, and that caused them to laugh and yell with delight, and to dance about and clap their hands. I had to laugh too, and we all embraced in a chaotic jumble of arms and legs. Brynach had to be incorporated into the celebrations, of course, and he was cuddled by all and sundry with a great deal of accompanying noise. It was all too much for him, for he dissolved into tears, and it was my pleasure to take him outside into the yard and nurse him until he quietened down and went to sleep in my arms.

As I walked round the yard and hummed lullabies to my new son, my mind returned to the speculation that he might be the bastard child of Squire Price's daughter Susanna. Surely two and two added together to make twenty? I determined that one day I would make investigations, but that in the meantime I would look to the future. I would keep Brynach, and hold to the belief that Owain was still alive. I would learn to bend to the breeze like the tall grasses of summer rather than allowing myself to be tipped over and uprooted like some grand tree in shallow soil.

Fine thoughts and excellent intentions. And then there was a thundering of hooves on the driveway, and the black hearse belonging to Master Davy Death clattered into the yard. Master Davy himself was driving, and in the back was a huddled figure in a blanket flanked by my disreputable friends Skiff and Halfpint. Both of them were soaking wet. 'Mistress Martha!' shouted Master Davy, hauling on the reins. 'Your assistance, if you please! We have the Wizard here beneath this blanket, and he is barely alive. He almost drowned a hundred yards out from the Parrog quay, and indeed would have been lost had it not been for the prompt attentions of these two excellent fellows.'

'Oh, my God!' I exclaimed in horror. 'Quickly, get him into the house!'

And Skiff and Halfpint carried him at the trot, still wrapped in his blanket, into the kitchen. I handed over Brynach to Liza, who had come outside to see what all the commotion was about, and ran in with them. Joseph was unwrapped, wet and blue, but mercifully still alive and shivering. We cleared the kitchen table and placed him on it, face down. He was violently sick, and I dare say got a good deal of sea water out of his system. He groaned, and opened his eyes, and said, 'Ah, Mistress Martha, how good to see you! You look remarkably beautiful today, if I may say so.' And then he groaned and closed his eyes again.

We stripped all his clothes off, and paid no attention to his protests. We have all seen naked gentlemen before, as I reminded him. Then we dressed him in some of Grandpa's warmest clothes, and placed him in a chair before the fire with a big mug of hot tea in his hands. Skiff and Halfpint changed out of their soggy clothes in the scullery and put on breeches, flannel shirts and stockings belonging to Billy and Shemi. They too were given hot tea and placed in front of the fire to thaw out. Davy Death, as the only dry member of the invasion party, stayed long enough to be sure that all three of his charges were going to survive, and then he excused himself and drove the hearse back into town with our thanks ringing in his ears.

We all crowded round the three steaming men and tried to find out what had happened. Joseph told the story. 'I am afraid that this was an episode for which I take full responsibility. I was in a little rowing boat, leaky but generally seaworthy, just offshore, down on the Parrog. I was conducting an experiment of the utmost importance, as I may explain privately to Mistress Martha later on. For the moment, suffice to say that the experiment was entirely successful, and as a result of it the boat sank with such speed that I could not get back to the shore. It took a bare six minutes. I was in the water, and I fear that I was sinking rather rapidly. Luckily my cries were heard by Skiff and Halfpint, who were sitting on the sea wall drinking cider and watching my experiment. They leapt into the sea, swam out to me and managed to get me back to the shore.'

'But why should that have been necessary, Joseph?' I asked. 'Surely you are a good swimmer?'

'No, Martha. I cannot swim at all. I have a strong dislike of salty water, and I have never had

343

any reason to get acquainted with it.'

'So what were you doing out in the estuary in a leaky old boat? That sounds to me as if you were asking for trouble, and got it.'

At this point Skiff intervened. 'Two days he has been at it, Mistress Martha, with one trial after another, and the old boat so badly messed about that it was bound to sink sooner or later. Me and Halfpint thought we'd better keep an eye on Master Harries, knowing he was no swimmer. Very entertaining, it was.'

'Some people have no respect for science,' said Joseph. 'But none the less I am truly grateful to these fine fellows. One day I shall repay them for their courage, and they will be truly blessed. Now then, I am hungry, and so are my friends. I smell roast beef in the top oven and apple cake in the bottom one. That means that a feast is in prospect, unless I am very much mistaken. Is there sufficient for three extra mouths?'

I laughed, partly out of sheer relief that Joseph was still very much alive, and partly because his acute powers of observation had clearly not been affected by his recent life-threatening experience. 'Of course, Master Harries,' said I. 'There is always sufficient on our table for unexpected guests. And you are quite right. Tonight we have a special feast to celebrate the fact that little Brynach is now officially my son, all the paperwork having been completed today.'

And Joseph shouted, 'Wonderful! Wonderful!' and leapt to his feet and embraced me, and Skiff and Halfpint insisted on doing the same. So we laid the table, and brought out the feast. Grandpa produced some bottles of excellent red wine from somewhere, and we all enjoyed a boisterous and good-humoured evening. Now and then my thoughts strayed to Owain, and I longed for him to be here with us; but I fought against melancholy and tried to remember my recent resolution not to despair. The children were allowed to stay up later than normal, and Joseph found the energy from somewhere to tell them a long and wonderful fairy story at bedtime. Then we adults continued to chat and laugh in the candlelit kitchen. At dusk Skiff and Halfpint took their leave, again with our thanks ringing in their ears, and walked back into town. I insisted that Joseph should stay for the night, for I was afraid that after his experience he might catch a chill. We made up a bed for him in the parlour.

At last the servants and the old people took themselves off to their beds, and I was left alone with Joseph in the kitchen. 'Now then, Joseph,' I said. 'I want to know all about this experiment which almost cost you your life. Tell me, if you please.'

He was flushed as a result of drinking rather too many glasses of restorative red wine, and took a minute or two to adjust his mood. 'Very well, Martha, I will tell you. But before I start, remember that we have as yet no evidence that Owain is dead. Will you promise me to hold that fact in your heart, and to remember that what I am about to tell you does not change it?' I nodded, and he continued. 'For these past two days of hot weather, I have been experimenting with the use of candle grease and pitch in the sinking of small boats. You will perceive that this is connected to the probable sinking of Owain's rowing boat out in the bay. You will remember that on the morning after his disappearance was reported, I rushed past you at the Cwm in a somewhat uncivilized fashion. It was pouring with rain, and I was desperately concerned that the streams of water on the slipway might remove whatever signs there might have been of sabotage. I knew not for what I was looking, but I felt sure that I would find something. Having ascertained from one of the fishermen where Owain kept his boat, I went to the spot and crawled about on my stomach, sniffing and straining my eyes in the deluge for anything out of the ordinary. The locals probably thought I was mad. However, I found something. Several extensive patches of congealed tallow or candle grease mixed with sawdust, some ash and small coals, and significant traces of pitch. I scraped up some samples with my knife and put them in my pocket. What might one deduce, Martha, from these discoveries?'

'Not much, I dare say. Presumably that Owain has at some time mended his boat? Sawdust means that planks have been cut and shaped and possibly replaced. Pitch is used all the time on small boats, and has to be heated up over a fire. As for the candle grease, I cannot be sure...'

'You have identified the crucial item, Martha. Why on earth should there be candle grease on the slipway? There are two possible answers – either somebody was working on Owain's boat in the dark, and was in need of illumination, or the grease was used for some other, nefarious purpose. When I got home, I examined my samples very carefully under my biggest and strongest magnifying glass. I discovered that the pitch was clean and glassy and therefore very new. Old pitch on a heavily used slipway gets softened and hardened over and again, and grit and muck are incorporated into it. And the candle grease was full of sawdust, almost as if the two substances had been deliberately mixed together in a pot. This was not just the product of some dripping candles used to illuminate a nocturnal boat-repairing task. I immediately began to suspect sabotage, Martha, but I needed further information. I spent several days at Cwm-yr-Eglwys, aware of the fact that others were taking care of the searches for Owain along the cliffs and further afield.'

'And what did you find?'

'Exactly what I suspected. On the night before Owain went out into the bay, lights were seen down on the slipway, and some of the locals smelled boiling pitch. At least half a dozen boats are kept there, and each of the fishermen thought that one of their colleagues was working late. Or, at least, that is what they tell me. Some of them know something, but I have not yet got to the bottom of it.'

I was increasingly appalled by this narrative, for I could see where it was leading. 'But how could anybody have known that Owain would be going out into the bay very early next morning?'

'Because he had widely advertised the fact himself. He spent part of the previous evening in the Sailor's Safety talking to the Cwm fishermen. He was overheard talking of his intention to spend a quiet morning on the sea, catching mackerel for his beloved Martha.'

Touched as I was by the evidence of his devotion to me, I still could not see how any saboteurs could have damaged his boat in such a way as to be invisible to the boat owner. I expressed this sentiment to Joseph.

'It was fiendishly clever, Martha, and it could only have been done by men who were experienced boat builders. I had a suspicion as to what they had done, but I needed to experiment in order to prove it. This very afternoon my experiment in the estuary proved the correctness of my hypothesis. The person or persons who did this late at night knew that the morrow would be hot. That is the key to the whole thing. Working in the light of candle lanterns, they cut out at least two planks from the bottom of Owain's boat. They got a brazier going on the slipway. Then they made a mixture of tallow and sawdust, and fixed the planks back in again, dripping the mixture in to seal the joins. As we all know, tallow has a distinctive smell, and it had to be disguised. They also had to hide the evidence of their carpentry. So when the wax had set – a few minutes is enough in the cool of the night – they rubbed dirt onto the joins and the planks, and painted on some pitch as well. Then they probably threw dust and dirt on again, making their handiwork all but invisible. The pitch smell would have persisted to the morning, but the slipway smells of pitch all the time, and they hoped – correctly – that Owain, a man in love and dreaming of other things, would not examine his boat minutely

348

before pushing it into the water and rowing off into the bay.'

'Oh, Joseph, this is truly appalling. So what happened to Owain's boat out in the bay?'

'In the cool of the morning he rowed for maybe an hour or more, and maybe did some fishing. Then, when the sun was high, the pitch did another job for which it was selected. Pitch is black, and black things attract heat. Gradually the surface of the boat got hotter, and slowly the tallow holding the planks in place was melted. When it was sufficiently soft, the pressure of the water on the boat's hull would have caused the planks to spring up, allowing the water to come pouring in. It would have been impossible to fix them back in place, and the boat might well have gone down in a couple of minutes.'

Now I buried my head in my hands, with all my resolutions of stoic acceptance overtaken by events. I wanted to cry but could not. Joseph came and sat with me, and put his arm round me as a father consoles a miserable small child.

'Joseph, are you certain of all this?'

'As certain as a man can be. I demonstrated all of it with my foolish experiment.'

'Attempted murder, if not actual murder?'

'I fear so.'

'And whom do you suspect? Owain is greatly loved in the community, and has hardly any enemies.'

'Well, the fellows who did the work were probably hired for the task. And who would make it worth their while to take the risk? Only a wealthy squire or a merchant of some standing. The man

I suspect is Squire Price of Llanychaer.'

I remember little more of our conversation. In truth I was so shocked that I could take no more, and talk of motives and other things will have to wait until the morrow. I asked Joseph to forgive me, and said that I must go to my room and try to sleep on it. He said good-night, and looked concerned, and kissed me on the cheek before settling on his temporary bed in the parlour. I extinguished the candles in the kitchen, damped down the fire, and then struggled up the stairs to my room, too giddy to stand without support and too tired to sleep.

28 May 1807

I sat at my dressing table, recording the events of yesterday, until the early hours. This helped me, to some degree, to come to terms with Joseph's discovery, and at last I did settle into a fitful sleep. I awoke with a start at eight of the clock, and realized that the activities of the day were in full swing, with children's voices in the nursery, two crying babies downstairs in the kitchen, and cattle, dogs and geese sounding excited outside. I thought of reprimanding Bessie for allowing me to sleep in for so long, but thought better of it when I realized that she must have looked in and decided that I needed sleep more than an early breakfast. And so I went downstairs in my dressing gown and discovered Joseph at the breakfast table, tucking into a considerable bowl of oats with creamy milk and dried apple rings.

'Good morning, Martha,' he said, full of good cheer. 'Under protest, I am being forced by the wonderful Mrs Owen to consume a large breakfast. While she had me at her mercy yesterday, on this very table, she realized that my ribs are too prominent and my stomach is too flat, and she is taking remedial measures.'

I greeted Joseph with as much good cheer as I could muster, and ate a good breakfast myself. He said that he needed to get back to the Parrog to collect his pony and to recompense the owner of the rowing boat which he destroyed in his scientific experiment, but before he went off I managed to sit with him for a few minutes in the parlour. I needed to make absolutely sure that I had not misunderstood him last night, when I had been very tired and more than a little confused. 'So you are utterly convinced, Joseph,' I asked, 'that somebody, probably Squire Price, paid some fellows to sabotage Owain's boat in the full expectation that he would be killed?'

'Yes, Martha, I said it last night and I say it again.'

'But do you have evidence to support such a claim and to encourage Owain's father to take out an indictment against Master Price?'

'Not enough as yet. But just you wait and see. I think I know the two fishermen who did the work on the slipway, but it may be more difficult to connect them to the Squire. I need a few more days.'

'But why should the Squire wish Owain dead? I cannot conceive of any circumstances which would lead a man to wish to take another's life.'

'It may be difficult to comprehend for you and

me, Martha. But some people are consumed by hate, or jealousy, or even by a sort of fury against those who have found happiness when they themselves have nothing but pain. I think that Squire Price is such a man. I also think that resentment and rage against Owain – who possessed good looks, a modest fortune, and the love of Mistress Martha Morgan – was more important in his mind than the piffling dispute up on the common. We shall see. I will get to the bottom of it, you may be sure.'

'Oh, I do hope so, Joseph. I fear that today I will think of nothing but the fact that the two great loves of my life have both been murdered in cold blood. It seems to me already, in the clear light of this new day, that somehow I am doomed, and that those good men who give me their love are also doomed, to die young...'

'Stuff and nonsense, Martha! You just pull yourself together! Remember that in the case of Owain, murderous intent has not necessarily led to his death. He may still be alive, and we all have to believe that, unless strong evidence is found to the contrary.'

And so my dear friend and I embraced, and he set off on his walk to Newport. He would not accept my offer of a ride in the chaise, and said that after all the salty water that had entered his lungs yesterday, some fresh air blowing off Carningli was just what he needed.

Once Joseph was gone, I had little time for further analysis or self-pity for we had a baptism to attend. I had my morning wash, and Bessie put my hair up, and I put on my demure church dress, which could be guaranteed not to offend the sensibilities of Rector Devonald. Liza got little Brynach fed and cleaned, and then we dressed him in the same baptismal garment that has been worn by the other four children, one after another. We were due at the church at twelve noon, and we all went there in a little procession of chaises, *gambos* and trotting ponies. Although Brynach was fast asleep at the time, I wanted him to have a proper baptism witnessed by all the adults and children of Plas Ingli. I did not contemplate for a moment the normal procedure for bastard children, involving just the Rector and two witnesses, since that would have marked him for life as a child apart. The ceremony involved all of the Plas servants as witnesses and me as the surrogate mother. It was short and somewhat chaotic, since Sara could not be prevailed upon to behave herself and had to be taken out in tears by Sian. Brynach had the holy water sprinkled on him, which I thought amusing, for it is the selfsame sacred water from Ffynnon Brynach with which we wash his bottom several times a day. He was named Brynach Owain Morgan, and some prayers were said for him, and that was that. The register of births was filled in, with gaps left where the names of the father and mother should have been, and three of us witnessed the entry.

When we got home we had a late dinner, and I am ashamed to say that after that, with the weather still warmer than it normally is during the corn harvest, I went to bed and slept for four hours. Afterwards I felt guilty and admitted as much to Bessie, but she replied cheekily that guilt was unnecessary, since she had greatly enjoyed the silence.

30 May 1807

Tonight I have had an altercation with Bessie and Grandma Jane, and I feel very much put upon. It arose out of the last two days of domestic activity on my part, when I have tried to occupy myself creatively around the house and in the garden with a view to banishing thoughts of Owain and his fate from my mind. I was aware, as soon as Joseph left the house a couple of days since, that I would think of nothing else but that Owain had probably been murdered. I knew that I was in danger of sliding into such a miserable mood that I might not be able to climb out of it again. Action and involvement were the antidotes to self-pity and apathy, I thought, and so I set to with a vengeance, helping with the cleaning and the nursing of Brynach, playing with the children, ordering things in the kitchen, rearranging the furniture in the parlour, and even rolling my sleeves up and washing out the dairy. I assumed that my beloved family and servants would be delighted to welcome me into the working world of Plas Ingli, and little did I expect the response that came my way after supper.

I should have read the signs. I recall that yesterday Liza was not best pleased when I sought to give Brynach a warm soapy bath in mid-afternoon, and there was a frisson of discontent from Mrs Owen when I dictated a menu for the evening meal when she had already organized something quite different. I thought that to be no bad thing, for Mrs Owen needs a firm hand sometimes. Bessie was, I recall, not amused this morning when I refused to put on the dress she had put out for me and insisted on examining the full contents of my wardrobe before putting on a dress that was too delicate for working and too light for a day of blustering wind and rain. Sian walked out of the nursery when I came in and read out a long story for the children, and I thought she had simply gone to answer a call of nature. And, now that I come to think of it, there have been three or four occasions when I have found the servants chatting furtively together and stopping as soon as I approached. My sensitivity to the needs of others appears to have entirely deserted me, and it was probably inevitable that I would have to face up to the consequences sooner rather than later. Thank God it was sooner, for had it been later I should have had a real disaster to cope with.

So it was that after supper, as we all sat in the kitchen, Grandma Jane said to me softly, 'Martha, my dear, may I have a quiet word with you in the parlour?'

'Of course, Grandma,' said I, in all innocence. And I got up and led the way, and we sat down in our comfortable chairs by the window. I was surprised when Bessie then came in, without knocking, and joined us. 'Excuse me, Bessie,' I said, 'but Mistress Jane and I need a few moments to talk in private. Would you please–'

'No, Martha. I asked her to join us here, and you need to hear what she has to say.'

I was mystified, but not for long, for Grandma Jane does not waste time in getting to the point. Before Bessie had shut the door and sat down, she said: 'Martha, I have to tell you that I have been gravely concerned about your behaviour recently. As have Isaac and the servants. Do you know what I am talking about?'

'Not really. I've tried to be helpful and involved around the place, in an attempt to keep my mind off Master Owain. Surely that is better for everybody than having me shut in my room feeling miserable, or wandering about in a daze?'

'Well, yes and no. Of course we want you to be fit and well, and we all realize that you have had great difficulty in coming to terms with this latest news, but...'

'Grandma, do you know what it is like to have a beloved man taken away from you, but to have no body to grieve over?' As I said this, I felt a flush upon my face, and I immediately knew that I had made a serious misjudgement.

Grandma fixed her sharp eyes upon me and breathed deeply. After a long pause, during which I felt an urge to sink through the floor and disappear, she said: 'Actually, Martha, I do. My son William, David's father, died when the old Plas burnt down in 1794, taking his wife and children too. His body was never found, having been reduced to ashes. And my grandson Griffith, David's brother, was lost at sea. His body was never recovered. I think I know more than a little of the emotions which have swept over you in recent days.'

'Oh, Grandma, please forgive me,' I replied, feeling like a small child. 'That was a cruel and

356

thoughtless thing to say, and I am truly sorry.'

'Apology accepted, Martha.' Grandma smiled. 'The matter is forgotten. Now, let us move on. Over to you, Bessie.'

My beloved handmaiden looked embarrassed for a moment. Then she swallowed hard, and said, 'Mistress, I have been asked by the other servants to raise this matter with you. It is not that we want you out of the place, or that we resent your interest in our daily tasks, but please be aware that your dabbling in many things of late has caused difficulties.'

'Difficulties? Whatever do you mean?'

'Well, Sian was in tears in my room last night, and Mrs Owen almost refused to make supper this evening, and as for me, I am at my wit's end, for everything I do is wrong, and you are constantly nagging me and for ever changing your mind. I do not know any longer what you want, or what I can do to make you happy.'

'Bessie! I can hardly believe what I am hearing! Do we have some sort of revolution beneath our roof?'

'Hardly, Mistress. We all love you too much for that. But I must also tell you that Liza is threatening to leave.'

'But she cannot do that! Brynach must have the breast for at least two more months, and the process of weaning must be handled very carefully.'

'Indeed she *can* do it, Martha,' said Grandma. 'She is here entirely of her own free will. You do not pay her any wages, and it follows that you have no hold over her.'

Now I buried my head in my hands, for I felt

crushed, and knew not what to do. 'Bessie, tell me the worst,' I whispered. 'What have I done wrong, and what must I do to make amends?'

'Well, Mistress, as for Liza, I will say this. She is here as a wet nurse, and you have entrusted her with feeding, cleaning and caring for little Brynach while he is too small for grown-up foods. She knows that you want to be his mother and that it is difficult for you to see her fulfilling that role. It is difficult for Liza too though, for she has to try to stop herself from becoming too attached to him, in the knowledge that he will soon be snatched away. Thus far you have shown admirable restraint in your dealings with Brynach and with her. But these last two days your restraint has entirely disappeared, and you have become almost obsessed with the little fellow, picking him up and nursing him when he should have been asleep, demanding that he should be fed when he was not hungry, cleaning him when there was no need. You have, probably without knowing it, nagged Liza and criticized her and questioned her judgement, to the extent that the poor girl knows not whether she is coming or going. Such has been the disruption in the routines established by Liza that Brynach is now very unsettled, and is giving Liza very little chance to sleep or to look after her own child. She says that she will pack her bags and leave tomorrow if you do not withdraw your attentions and entrust her once again with doing her job.'

'Oh, my God! Is this really how I have been behaving?'

'It is, Martha,' said Grandma Jane. 'Bessie has represented the situation most accurately.'

'And what have I been doing to the other servants?'

'Similar interference, criticism and unthinking comments which have undermined their positions in the household, and indeed their self-respect.'

I was frozen in my seat for several minutes, while Bessie and Grandma Jane sat and looked at me without saying a further word. Then I said: 'Dear Bessie and dear Grandma, I thank you for your concern and your love. I must learn my lesson, even if it is a hard one. Please leave me alone for five minutes, and then I want to see each of my servants, and Liza, one after the other, before we all go to bed.'

And so I have eaten humble pie. It tasted less bitter than I might have feared. One by one I have talked to Bessie, Mrs Owen, Sian and Liza, and I have given them my apologies and exchanged conciliatory embraces. There have been tears, and there has been laughter, for I am learning gradually to laugh at my own idiocy. I have also spoken to Billy, Shemi and Will and have obtained honest assessments from them as to the desirable extent of my involvement in matters about which they know a good deal more than I. I pray that I have now got my relations with my staff back onto an even keel, and that they will all still be here when I wake up in the morning.

31 May 1807

The news which I have been dreading has finally reached the Plas. This afternoon Skiff came up to the house on his pony. He did not greet us with his usual good cheer, but said immediately: 'Mistress Martha, a serious development there has been, in the matter of Master Owain's disappearance. I am afraid that the news is not good.' And before I had a chance to take in his words and prepare myself for the worst, he handed me a small bottle with a cork in it.

'This bottle was found yesterday on the beach near St Dogmael's,' he said. 'A fellow found it when he was out collecting driftwood. He thinks it had just come in on the high tide after all the westerly winds we have been having. He passes the same way every day, and swears that the bottle wasn't there the day before. Are you all right, Mistress?'

'I think so, Skiff.' I swallowed hard and said: 'From Owain?'

'Yes, Mistress.' He put his hand into his pocket and produced a tattered piece of paper, folded tightly. He handed it to me. 'This was in the bottle. It had to be read, for there was no other way of knowing who it was from, or who it was intended for. It could have come from a desert island on the other side of the world. The fellow on the beach knows how to read, and he worked out at once that it was for you, since he had met my fellows when they were searching the cliffs and bays the day after Master Owain went missing. He brought it to me in Newport this morning, thinking it was a matter of urgency.'

I nodded, for in truth I could say nothing. I sat down at the kitchen table, unfolded the piece of paper, and held it in my shaking hands. It was sticky, for the bottle into which it had been stuffed had contained Owain's fruit cordial. The writing was unmistakably his, although it was rushed and hardly legible. This is what it said:

My beloved Martha,
The end is near. I am not a good swimmer and I am very far from land. I fear that somebody has wished me harm. Three planks have sprung up from the bottom of the boat and I cannot fix them back.
I love you for ever.
Owain

That was all. I sat transfixed, with the eyes of the other inhabitants of the kitchen upon me. Confirmation, if any were needed, of Joseph's speculations as to the sabotage of Owain's boat. Confirmation, if any were needed, that he is dead. I pushed the letter across the table for the others to read, and went out of the kitchen, along the passage and up the stairs in a daze. I held myself together until I reached the sanctuary of my own room, and then I wept as I had needed to weep for days. I flung myself onto the bed and wept with a sort of wild rage. I hammered my pillow with my fists, and paced about the room, virtually blinded by the curtain of tears, and knocked over the chair at the side of my bed. God knows what the family and servants must have thought, for my grief was by no means that of a silent and stoical saint, and must have been heard by everybody in the house. And then, magically, Bessie was at my side, and offered herself without a word as a beloved friend, and I

361

clung to her and wept until I was spent. She knew, bless her, that after the tensions and difficulties of last evening I might have felt abandoned even by my own family and servants. And she knew instinctively that this was not one of those occasions when I needed to be alone.

When at last I went downstairs again, holding Bessie's hand, two hours had passed. Betsi, Daisy, Dewi and Sara were all waiting in the kitchen for me, concern writ large across their lovely and innocent faces. I know not whether that was serendipity or good planning on somebody's part. But we all embraced, for we all needed loving physical contact.

'Are you all right, Mam?' said Betsi.

'I think so, *cariad*,' said I, just managing a smile. 'As you will know, I have had rather bad news about Master Owain. I needed to cry, and I am sorry if I upset the rest of you in the process.'

'Don't you worry, Mam,' said Daisy, cuddling up close. 'We are all here to look after you. Do you know that we love you?'

That almost brought the tears back again, but I struggled to control myself, and held all four of them as close as a mother hen with four fluffy chicks. And I thanked God for reminding me that even in the darkest hour of the night, love stands guard as a silent protector, and that a bright dawn will surely come.

1 June 1807

I have come to some sort of acceptance of my

circumstances. I cannot grieve properly, for I still have no body to grieve over, but I have to move forward for the sake of the five small children whom I love. They have suffered from this miserable episode far more than I have been prepared to admit, and as they need healing I have to make amends. I have neglected them sorely since Owain's disappearance, and been a poor mother indeed, brushing aside their small gestures of affection and failing to respond to their mute requests for attention. When they have shown me their works of art or their little poems, I have nodded and given them empty words of encouragement and appreciation, and have proceeded to busy myself with other things. When there have been tears and tantrums, I have left Sian to cope with them, and when Sara and Dewi have needed cuddles I have given admonishments instead. Brynach has, I think, not suffered too much at my hands – at least not until these last two or three days – for all he needs is a full belly, a clean napkin and a warm cot, but the other four need a great deal more from me than I have given them. To her eternal credit, Sian was very honest with me when we talked the other evening, and she has reminded me of the difference between her duties and my responsibilities.

So this morning I put everything else out of my mind and gave myself to the children. Sian and I discussed what to do before breakfast, and we rediscovered the joy of working together as nursemaid and mother. The weather was breezy but dry, with scudding clouds and long sunny spells, and as the shadows marched across the landscape there was enchantment in the air. Enchantment, I thought, has been something sorely missing from my life of late. Sian and the four children and I sat round the kitchen table and discussed how we should spend the morning. I dropped the word 'kite' into our discussion, and so it was decided that we should make kites, and climb to the top of the mountain, and have a kite-flying competition, and then celebrate the whole occasion with a most wonderful picnic. We banished Mrs Owen from the kitchen and took over the table with our manufactory. Soon there was a dreadful mess, with pieces of brown paper, sticks, lengths of string, coloured crayons and pots of glue much in evidence. Grandpa gave considerable assistance to Dewi in the making of a most magnificent creation which was taller than the little fellow himself. Daisy was not much interested in the matter of handicrafts, so Billy and Shemi helped out while she and Sian prepared the picnic in the scullery.

By eleven of the clock all was ready, and off we went up the mountain, whooping and yelling like the hordes of Genghis Khan. The children carried their own kites and balls of string, and Sian and I carried the picnic and blankets to sit upon. On the way up we stopped for a drink at Ffynnon Brynach, and I anointed myself as I always do. Then on we went through the unfurling bracken and the spiky furze bushes until we were up among the old blue rocks. Betsi led the way for at the age of nine she is already getting used to the mountain and its network of tracks. Sara needed to be carried here and there, but

Dewi struggled on manfully without any help. We all reached the top without mishap, and it was nothing short of a miracle that the kites also reached the top without falling to pieces.

Up there the westerly wind was more like a hurricane than a breeze, but it was a warm wind, and we revelled in it. We all stood on the topmost rock, and spread our arms wide and let the wind tear at our clothes and tug at our hair. We all pretended to be angels, and we shouted at the world below to see whether anybody could hear us. Then we all fell down onto the grassy patch in the lee of the summit in a jumble of arms and legs and laughed hysterically. I looked up at the sky as I lay on my back with Dewi and Daisy on top of me, and saw the old raven wheeling high overhead with his wing feathers fluttering in the high wind. Then Betsi, who is becoming quite a bossy big sister, decided that it was time for the competition. So we got ourselves organized, and one after the other the kites with their wonderful patterns and drawings were launched into the atmosphere, and flew. Not only did they fly, but they all flew away for one reason or another. Sara let go her line, and Dewi's line snapped in the middle. Daisy's line got snagged against a sharp rock and frayed and broke, and Betsi had omitted to tie a decent knot on hers. So one by one the kites swooped in the sky and then fell to earth and got smashed to pieces on the crags and boulders. Such is the fate of all man-made things sent up into the air. We truly did not mind, for we had known what would happen to the wondrous contraptions. We clapped hands and cheered for every kite that crashed to earth.

Then it was time to judge the winner. 'Mam! Mam! Tell us who won!' they all yelled. Dewi was so excited that he clapped his chubby hands and jumped up and down, as is his wont.

'Now then, this is a very difficult matter,' said I, with a severe frown upon my face. 'I do declare that Dewi's kite was the biggest, and was therefore a worthy winner. But I also have to declare that Betsi's was the most beautiful kite I have ever seen, and that it should win even the most severe of contests. Then again, the kite which flew best was certainly Sara's. And I have to admit that when it comes to crashes, I have never seen anything so spectacular as that involving Daisy's kite. So after due consideration I declare that your kites were all equally wonderful, and that you are all winners of this great contest! Three cheers for all of you!' So we cheered, and laughed, and groaned, and yelled and clapped our hands together.

We gathered up those bits of kite which we could find. Then we spread our blankets on the grassy patch out of the wind, and laid out our picnic. The sun beamed down upon us, and the clouds passed us by. It was hilarious and utterly chaotic, and I was undoubtedly the one who enjoyed it most. When we had finished, we lay on our backs and looked at the sky, and had another competition, counting birds. Betsi won, for she is the one who concentrates best, and she counted twenty-one seagulls, two buzzards, five ravens, one red kite, sixteen swallows and twelve house martins, making fifty-seven birds in all. She probably counted some of them more than once as they swooped and drifted over our heads, but I was in no mood to be pedantic. Then Dewi and Sara cuddled up to me and snoozed off for a while, and Daisy and Betsi cuddled up to Sian. I watched them from the other side of the grassy patch, and felt no sense of resentment that the two older children had grown very close – without my noticing – to my happy nursemaid who has been a surrogate mother for far too long. I caught Sian's eye, and smiled at her, and she smiled back.

It was time to go, and we gathered up our plates, mugs, pots and cutlery, together with the remains of the picnic, and packed everything back into the hamper. Betsi said: 'Let's take the western track home!' and went bounding off, and we had to obey instructions. I let Sian and the other little ones go first, and before I left the summit I stood for one last time on the topmost crag and looked out over Newport Bay. There were five ships in sight, their masts tilted and their sails filled with the fresh wind from the Atlantic Ocean. Cloud shadows and white-crested waves raced eastward across the emerald salt sea. This, I thought, was a scene of such beauty that it always took my breath away, but today it brought a lump to my throat, for somewhere beneath those scudding waves lay the body of Owain Laugharne and the heart of Martha Morgan.

'Come on, Mam! You will get left behind!' said a little voice carried on the wind. So I turned and followed Sian and the four children, leaving behind on the mountain an assortment of breadcrumbs, apple cores, currants and pieces of carrot. And I carried away with me a picnic hamper, memories, and more memories.

2 June 1807

This morning Joseph called again. Before I had a chance to tell him anything, he said: 'Martha, I perceive that you have further news. Will you tell me about it?' So I did, and gave him Owain's note and the little corked bottle which had carried it to the shore at St Dogmael's. He examined the note carefully, commenting on the fact that it was written in wax crayon on a page torn from a little notebook. He nodded. 'You knew, Martha, that he carried his notebook with him at all times, largely so that he could write poems about you?'

I was staggered by this revelation, and said so.

'Well, it is true. He told me that he was planning to present the poems to you on the occasion of your wedding. I fear, my dear, that they will now be on the bottom of the sea.'

'Joseph, that does little to console me.'

'I know, Martha. I am sorry. But remember that he may still be alive. You must never give up hope. And I find it hard to come to terms with the fact that my speculations about sabotage were apparently well founded. I take no satisfaction from that, and indeed I have been harbouring some faint hope that my ideas were all poppycock.' Then he sniffed at the neck of the small bottle. 'Raspberry cordial,' he said. 'Owain's favourite. The authenticity of this note is established beyond doubt.'

He invited me to sit at his side on the bench by

368

the kitchen table, and put his arm round my shoulder. 'Now then,' he said. 'I have further news too. My investigations about the men who interfered with Owain's boat have led me to two Newport men named Maldwyn Biggs and Freddy Cobb. Thugs and petty thieves, both of them. The latter is a wayward cousin of Morgan Cobb who lives near Patty and Jake on the Parrog. Both of these fellows spent a good deal of time in the Sailor's Safety at Pwllgwaelod in the later part of April and the early part of May. They were drinking in the corner when Owain announced his plans for a fishing trip on the evening prior to his disappearance. They are quite capable of murder, both of them. Morgan Cobb tells me that they have been used frequently by Squire Price when he requires dirty work to be done, and the three of them have been seen together quite frequently in recent months. Biggs knows very little about anything, but Cobb worked for a time in Master Havard's shipyard, and he knows more than enough about boat-building to have worked out how to sabotage Owain's boat. Even more interesting, they have not been seen in the Sailor's Safety, or in the Cwm, since the ninth day of May. They have every reason to lie low, but they have been spending freely in the taverns of Newport of late. There is speculation that they have come upon unexpected riches, but in my view they have simply been paid what was promised.'

'Have you spoken to them?'

'Yes, I have. In the Black Lion, yesterday evening. It was not a very pleasant conversation, and I was lucky that Skiff and his friends got me out of there before I sustained structural damage.'

'So they deny any knowledge of the incident, and any involvement?'

'Of course. But I will persist. My ultimate sanction is to place a curse upon them, but I prefer not to resort to such tactics. Neither do I have any irrefutable connection with Squire Price, even though I am now even more convinced that he is the man behind this whole miserable affair.'

Just then there was a clatter of hooves in the yard, and when I looked outside I was utterly amazed to see my parents climbing down from the Brawdy coach. I said, 'Excuse me, Joseph, but my parents have appeared quite out of the blue. May we continue our conversation some other time?' He smiled and nodded, and we both went out into the yard.

There were loving embraces all round, and I ushered Mother and Father into the parlour. They were delighted to see me, of course, and were more than happy to renew their acquaintance with Joseph. Then I called the children down from the nursery with the words: 'Come, children. Grandpa George and Grandma Betsi have come from Brawdy to see us!'

They came rushing down the stairs and abandoned all decorum as they kissed and cuddled the grandparents they see all too seldom. Then Dewi took his grandfather's hand and said 'Grandpa, come and see our new baby brother!' and no sooner had the puzzlement registered on his face than my dear mother said at the other end of the room, 'And tell me, Martha, how is Owain? I trust that he is well?'

I was almost overcome by the realization that they knew nothing about the disappearance of my beloved man, or the fact that I had taken delivery of a foundling, and had made him a member of my family. I had thought once or twice of writing to them, but had never got round to it on the grounds that they were travelling somewhere in England, in London or Oxford or Bath, and had left me no addresses. I should have discovered their whereabouts, and written to them, but with so much going on around me my good intentions had somehow never been translated into actions. Joseph, who was standing nearby, immediately perceived that I had some explaining to do, and decided that he had better leave us to it. He lifted his eyebrows, shrugged his shoulders, and gave me a kiss on the cheek, and then he went.

My parents were covered in confusion by the excited chatter of the children concerning the arrival of little Brynach and the loss of my husband-to-be, so at last I asked Sian to take the little ones into the garden so that Mother and Father and I could be alone. We settled into the parlour, and Bessie delivered tea and currant cake. And so to it. We talked for the rest of the afternoon, and since there was still much to relate, I persuaded them to stay the night. We ate supper at the kitchen table, and then we retired to the parlour and talked again as the summer evening faded away. I told them everything – or almost everything, for I was still not minded to share my fears about the Nightwalker with anybody, least of all my parents. They questioned me endlessly, and at last I was greatly relieved when they gave me their blessing in the matter of little Brynach. They both took him in their arms, and of course fell in love with him immediately. They were shocked and horrified when I spoke about Owain's disappearance, but I stopped short of telling them about Joseph's researches and our suspicions that this was a murder rather than a terrible accident, and that Squire Price of Llanychaer might be implicated. It was a blessed relief to unburden myself thus to my dear parents, who asked over and again whether I needed any help, or whether there was anything they might do, or any legal or financial arrangements they might make on my behalf. 'No, dearest Mother and Father,' I said. 'I have good friends around me, and I have to learn to cope with the joys and pains of life without running to you all the time. You have done more than enough for this particular wayward daughter since she went away from Brawdy ten years since, in the very same carriage that brought you here today.'

And the conversation having turned to wayward daughters, I had to ask them for news of Elen. They both brightened up immediately, bringing balm to my troubled breast. 'Ah yes,' said Mother. 'I had quite forgotten about Elen in the welter of news that you have delivered to us. Yes indeed. News of Elen. Was that not why we came here in the first place, George?'

'It was indeed, Betsi. And delighted I am, Martha, to deliver some good news for a change.'

'Did you manage to see her in Bath, then?'

'Yes, we did. Her circumstances were somewhat reduced, which saddened us a little, but I have to say that she appeared to be in good health, and has put on a little weight since we saw her last.'

'That was all to my liking,' said Mother, 'for last time we saw her she was far too thin to catch herself a decent husband.'

'At any rate,' said Father, 'we turned up at her latest residence a few days ago, as arranged in advance, on our way home from Oxford. We travelled with her in our coach from Bath to Bristol, where we saw her onto a ship bound for the United States of America! Exciting, don't you think? We paid her fare, as we had promised, and waved her a very tearful farewell as the ship pulled away from the quayside. But our sadness at her departure was more than compensated for by the eagerness in her eyes and by her anticipation of a new life across the sea.'

At this news, I was rendered speechless, and I dare say that my jaw dropped in a most unladylike fashion. Mother laughed. 'Why do you look so surprised, Martha?' she asked. 'There are great opportunities in that new land. Many young people travel out there nowadays to make their fortunes. And, by all accounts, many of them succeed.'

'But Elen of all people!' I exclaimed. 'Of all of us in this family, she is the one who likes adventure the least and home comforts the most. I can hardly see her rolling westwards on a wagon and grappling with dastardly outlaws and Red Indians.'

'I'm sure that's not in her mind.' Father laughed. 'She told us that she plans to settle in New York, which has all the makings of a great city. She has various contacts already, and it is her intention to obtain employment as a musician or a music teacher. Such people as she will be in great demand.'

'Oh, Father,' I sighed. 'I hope that you are right, and that she will be happy. Will we never see her again?'

'I am sure we will,' said Mother. 'She promised that as soon as she is rich and famous, and happily settled with a husband and family, they will all come back to visit us. Of course she will keep her word. And of course she will write to all of us.'

I knew in my heart that Elen would never again visit Wales, and that filled me with an unutterable sadness. But I was still puzzled. 'I cannot for the life of me understand what is in her mind,' I mused. 'The letters which she wrote to Catrin and me some months back were strange indeed, and suggested to us that she was suffering from some great tragedy, or even that her mind was deranged. Did you manage to find out what that was all about?'

'She was not very forthcoming,' said Father, 'and she does not enter into confidences very easily, even with her own parents. It was always thus, as you may recall, Martha.'

Mother sighed, and said: 'As her mother, I think I know her well enough to say that there was an affair of the heart in the spring. She was very hurt by it, and was so upset that she even left her employment and moved to new lodgings. Perhaps she was seeking to get away from some young gentleman of her acquaintance, and perhaps her old lodgings carried so many unhappy memories that she could not bear to be there for a moment longer. Strange indeed are the workings of a woman's mind.'

'Very true, very true,' said Father, putting his hands together in a gesture of prayer and looking towards Heaven.

Now I had to laugh. The mystery of Elen's misery was by no means satisfactorily explained, but at least it appeared that she was now happy and excited, and I had to take pleasure from that.

'Oh, I almost forgot the letter,' said Father, fishing into his pocket and pulling out a tidily sealed envelope with my name upon it. He handed it to me, and I read it out loud.

Bath, on the 22nd day of May 1807

My dearest sister Martha,

I am writing this on a quiet summer's evening looking out onto the sunlit streets of Bath. My mood is transformed since I wrote my last letter, which in retrospect must have appeared very strange to you and Owain. By the time you read this I will be halfway across the ocean to America. I pray to God that the crossing will be smooth, as indeed it should be at this time of year.

I will soon meet Mother and Father, and they will take me to my ship at Bristol. What an adventure I shall have! Forgive me for not informing you more fully of my plans and of the circumstances which led me to formulate them – one day, when we meet again, I will tell you everything. I had hoped to come to Pembrokeshire to say farewell to dear Morys, and Catrin and yourself, but I fear that I should have been quite overcome with emotion, and I could not do it.

Be content, dearest sister, that I am well and thrilled by the prospect of my new life in a new land. I send you and Owain and the little ones all my love and kisses, and I will think of you often.

Pray for me, if you will. I will write again as soon as I can.

Your loving sister, Elen

As I finished I had a lump in my throat, for the realization came to me that she knew nothing about either the arrival of little Brynach or the tragic loss of Owain. I felt impotent and frustrated, and even angry, for I still had no address to write to, and no way of contacting her. I expressed these sentiments to my parents, but they calmed me down by saying that she would certainly send an address as soon as she had one, and that our correspondence might thereafter be more frequent than that which we maintained between Bath and Plas Ingli. 'These modern vessels simply fly across the water,' said Mother, 'and letters can be carried from writer to reader in a matter of just a few weeks.' What could I do but smile?

By now it was late at night, and my parents and I were hardly capable of keeping our eyes open, let alone maintaining polite conversation. So we all went off to bed somewhat better informed than we had been, but with our heads still full of questions.

4 June 1807

Yesterday my parents set off early, for they

wished to visit Catrin and James in Castlebythe and then Morys and Nansi in Haverfordwest before travelling home to Brawdy. They all needed to know the news about Elen, and indeed my adventurous sister had written letters to them too that had to be delivered.

I have been pondering on the wording and contents of her message, and think that it was almost too carefully crafted to convey the tidings that all was well, and that she was as happy as may be with her voyage to America. I still think that behind her words there lies some great sadness, and that she wept as she wrote. The difference between this letter and the last one is that this time she kept the tears off the paper. But I must not be churlish, and I must try to rejoice in her adventure, if that is what she wishes us to do. Endless speculation on my part will do no good at all, and I must try to accept that a chapter in her life, and mine, is now closed.

Today should have been the day of my wedding. My mind has drifted back, over and again, to what might have been – the church ceremony, my clothes and his, the smiles on the faces of the guests, the wedding breakfast, and the unbridled joy of the children at the acquisition of a new father. There would have been happiness and fulfilment for me and for him, a perfect consummation of the love which we both took for granted. And as I thought of that, my mind returned over and again to the fact that I had rejected him at the last moment during our picnic on the cliffs. If only I had not done that. If only I had not caused him to suffer when he might have given me the greatest gift that love can give, and I might have accepted his gift. If only I had seized that moment of ultimate joy.

Inevitably, my mind turned to the Nightwalker. Was the creature really there, sneering at us from above that golden furze bush, or was it simply a terrible figment of my imagination? The figure does exist in some shape or form, for others have seen it and been frightened. I am still uncertain whether it is the Grim Reaper or simply some sad phantom sent to haunt us – but whatever it is, I blame it for taking Owain from me, and one day I hope to get answers to the questions which I ask myself endlessly about it. And perhaps I will even get revenge, if such a thing is possible in the world of spirits.

To happier things. While I have been obsessed with the disappearance of my love, something else has been happening beneath my nose – a blossoming affection between Shemi and Sian. I cannot be certain of it, but there are little signs. He spends more time dreaming these days than working, and she too has been distracted. In the evenings, when we sit together, servants and family, in the kitchen, they appear to migrate together as if governed by some mysterious force which has recently begun to operate. Once or twice I have discovered them canoodling in corners, and the canoodling has clearly been of a different sort from that which operates in the barn or in the hayloft at the festive times of the year. I wish them well, for they are both good young people, and they deserve each other. I will watch developments with interest. Pray God that the growth of their love is smoother and steadier than mine.

15 June 1807

The story of the Nightwalker has entered a new phase, for the wretched creature has been seen not just by my own family and servants but by others who are helping with the harvest, and the news is now all round the town.

This year the hay harvest is smaller than in recent years, for I have put more fields down to barley and oats and I am planning to keep fewer animals over the coming winter. But the harvest is bountiful in spite of the long dry spell early in May, and I have taken on fifteen labourers, including the seven members of the O'Connell clan. They came here three days ago, having already worked on the harvest in the Letterston area. It was a pleasure to welcome them back, and I was reassured to see that Kate, the young woman falsely accused of producing a bastard child, has recovered her good health and her countenance remarkably well. Another demonstration of the healing skills of Joseph Harries.

Yesterday the seven men working with scythes beneath a white-hot sun were in Parc Haidd, and the others, who were turning and raking the sweet and beautiful hay, were occupied in Parc Bach. Late in the day, before the dew began to fall, I called all the workers in for supper, and as they were walking back towards the Plas three of the O'Connells saw the Nightwalker standing close to Ffynnon Brynach. They were very fright-

379

ened, for although they are very devout and religious people they also have a great understanding of the world of spirits, and they declared at once that they had seen a ghost.

When they got back to the Plas, they could talk of nothing else, although they respected my wishes not to mention the strange figure in black in the presence of the children. Then, when the children were in bed, Billy and Seamus O'Connell went out into the moonlit yard for a smoke, and again saw the Nightwalker standing on the bank behind the house. It was there for a minute or two before disappearing. Seamus was very frightened, but Billy less so, since he has come to view the creature as quite harmless. He decided that he would do some investigating, so he ran into the house to fetch a candle lantern, and then approached the spot where the creature had been standing. He examined the grass and the ground with great care, but found nothing, and concluded that the creature was indeed a phantom rather than a man. In my own mind, I am not so sure about the diagnosis this time, for the ground is presently dry and as hard as a bone, and even the heaviest and clumsiest of our harvesters could have walked across it without leaving a trace.

For better or for worse, the news of these sightings was immediately transferred to the labourers who had come up from town to help us, and when they returned to their cottages and to the Newport inns after supper it was inevitable that they should spread the news far and wide. So the town now knows not only about these sightings but about others too, since servants' tongues are also loosened by ale and the conviviality of hay-making suppers.

28 June 1807

At last the hay harvest is complete, and the sheep are dipped and shorn. One big hayrick has been built in the rickyard on the new ventilated stone base which Billy and Will made last winter. The haylofts above the cowshed and the stable are filled, and the warm fragrant hay is now the children's favourite playground. The house is quiet, since today the three menservants and Bessie and Sian are at Gelli, helping with Caradoc Williams's hay harvest in reciprocation for help given to us by his wife Bethan and himself. The children have gone too, to help with the hayfield picnic. They will not be very helpful, but they will have fun.

I like this time of year, between the hay harvest and the corn harvest, for the sun is high and the shadows are cool, and the animals are drowsy in spite of the pestilential attentions of swarms of flies. The birds are singing less, and a benign quietness has settled across the landscape. And I have decided today to take Joseph into my confidence in the matter of the Nightwalker. I have waited far too long for this, but in truth I have been reluctant to draw my dear friend into too many of my dilemmas and mysteries, for he has patients to heal and sick animals to visit all over the north of the county. It would have been an abuse of our friendship if I had demanded any more of his time and attention than he has already freely given. He has worked unceasingly to find out precisely what happened to Owain and why, and he has been sucked into the business of little Brynach too.

At any rate, today I decided that the time was right, and I invited him to tea. I baked some currant buns myself, and made a nice pot of Dai Canton's latest blend, and when he arrived we went and sat in the shade of the orchard. He looked tired, and I told him so. 'You are probably right, Martha,' said he. 'This business about Owain is proving very difficult. I know that Squire Price is behind it, but I cannot find the crucial piece of evidence which will confirm it. Very frustrating indeed.' But then he brightened up and added: 'However, we must not give in to doom and gloom. And what better way to relax than to accept an invitation to tea from my favourite lady, the Mistress of Plas Ingli?'

'My favourite guest is always welcome, I can assure you. But I dare to hope, Master Harries, that you do not relax too much, for I wish to talk to you about something.'

'About the Nightwalker?'

'Joseph! How dare you? You always seem to anticipate what I am about to do or say, and that is very bad for a woman's self-esteem. Surprise is the greatest weapon in a woman's armoury, and you have rendered that weapon redundant.'

With due deliberation Joseph put some black-currant conserve on his scone and munched at it. He smacked his lips, and then took a gulp of tea. Finally he grinned in such an infectious way that I could not resist grinning too. 'Perfectly obvious,

Martha,' he said. 'You have talked to me about everything else, but not about the Nightwalker. I have known about him for some little time. But now, since the whole town knows about him too, I thought it inevitable that you would wish to take me into your confidence.'

And so we talked about the Nightwalker. I told him about my sightings of the creature back in the time of the winter snows, and of the sightings by my family and servants. I told him of our failed attempts to find its tracks in the snow and in other locations, and of our conviction that we were therefore dealing not with a man but with a denizen of the spirit world. I told him about the apparent coincidence of the sightings of the creature with one terrible event after another: first the executions in Haverfordwest, then the fearsome storm which led to the sinking of the *Pole Star* and many other vessels, and finally the series of sightings culminating in the disappearance of Owain. I said that I was quite convinced that the black and ominous creature was far more interested in Plas Ingli than in any other location. I wondered whether the phantom appeared to me more frequently than to others because of my love for Owain, who was singled out for its sinister attention. Or maybe I was its ultimate quarry, and the monster was just playing with me, increasing my apprehension and my terror bit by bit until the time came to drag me down to Hell?

At this point Joseph intervened. 'Martha!' He laughed. 'Stop, if you please! Seldom have I heard such wild speculations tumbling out in such quantity. Now then, shall we take one thing at a time? First, the matter of the coincidence of sightings with one disaster after another. Are you sure about that, or do these coincidences simply exist inside your head?'

'Well, I have not examined the dates in detail, but I am convinced that it is not simply a matter of random events.'

'Maybe. Maybe. But perhaps it is the Nightwalker's misfortune to have been in the wrong place at the wrong time.'

'Poor thing!' I snapped. 'Do you now want me to feel sorry for it, this creature who has heaped such misfortune upon my head? If he is a man or a benign spirit watching over me, why does he lurk about in dark places, and appear and disappear without warning, instead of knocking on my door and giving me a cheery greeting?'

'I quite accept that that is a problem, Martha. I am mystified myself, and I have to admit to being confused by the information currently to hand.'

'You seem to have looked into this matter in some detail already, Joseph. Where has your information come from?'

'I never reveal my sources, Martha. Suffice to say that I know a good deal, but not enough. Over the coming days I will give the matter my undivided attention, and will hope to get to the bottom of it. But one further thought – are you quite sure that all of your sightings were real?'

'Whatever do you mean, Joseph?'

'Well, I have observed in the past, when dealing with one world or another, that when people are obsessed with a particular phenomenon they are sometimes able to conjure up images of it from inside their own heads. That may happen even if they do not want it to happen. In the cold light of day, my dear friend, might some of your sightings have been of this kind?'

I thought for a long time, and realized that my sighting on the cliffs, when Owain and I were reaching the peak of our loving, might have been more a matter of wild fantasy than reality. 'Yes, one sighting at least might have been the product of a fevered imagination, and of some fear inside my own mind. But if you do not mind, I will not talk about it.'

'I will not press you, Martha. But one last question. Most of your concerns about the Night-walker appear to have come from inside your head. Do you feel, in your heart of hearts, that he means to harm you?'

Again I thought for a long time, and had to admit that my intuition did not lead me to think that I was personally threatened. I even told Joseph of the creature's peace offering of a bunch of daffodils when I had fainted in the lane near Dolrannog Uchaf, and I told him that it had caused me some difficulty.

In that disconcerting way of his, Joseph roared with laughter, and slapped his knees. 'Difficulty! What difficulty?' he chortled. 'Not even the vilest of phantoms or the meanest of spirits would present a deadly enemy with a bunch of flowers. Take my word for it, Martha. You may be reassured that he means you no harm, and that he may even be seeking to protect your interests.'

'I hope you are right, Joseph. And can I ask you one last question? Do you think, in your heart of hearts, that the Nightwalker is a man or a phantom?'

'I am not sure. I have several theories, but am not yet in a position to place them in any sort of order. I know that you think he is the Grim Reaper, and I suspect that you also think him to be the ghost of Matthew Lloyd, or Alban Watkins, or another of your dead enemies–'

'Quite correct.'

'–but his behaviour does not appear very ghostly to me. Neither does it appear to fit into the usual pattern of behaviour of human beings. I currently incline to the view that he may be a harmless and very unhappy spirit, or a demon conjured up by some other witch or wizard. Never fear. I have my contacts in the spirit world, and I will consult them. I will get to the bottom of it, and if he is supernatural you will soon be rid of him.'

So our interview was at an end. Joseph swept the crumbs from his breeches, and licked his lips, and said that I must compliment Mrs Owen on the quality of her blackcurrant conserve. He gave me a long embrace which I found very pleasurable. Then he jumped onto his white pony and was gone, by all accounts to heal a lame bullock near Brynberian.

1 July 1807

Suddenly things have started to move, and it could be that the mystery of the Nightwalker will soon be solved. There are certain frightening developments, not here at the Plas, but down in town.

Today is a Wednesday, and we were surprised when Hettie came up to the Plas on a morning which she normally reserves for domestic matters in her lodging house. She huffed and she puffed, and she was in such a fluster that we had to sit her down and give her a cup of hot cordial before she could find the right words to describe what had happened. Things are still very confused, and what she relayed was mostly hearsay, but this is the essence of it.

Patty, my dear friend recently married to Jake Nicholas, has been seen twice down on the Parrog in the company of the Nightwalker. The first sighting, a few days since, was but a fleeting one by a shipyard worker who was on his way home after a few drinks at the Black Lion. He recognized Patty but did not recognize the figure in a black cloak and a wide-brimmed black hat to whom she was talking in an animated fashion. They were some distance away from him, and the black-robed figure slipped away into the bushes as he approached. Then yesterday there was a much more serious happening. An old lady called Mistress Willey almost bumped into Patty and the Nightwalker around dusk. They were in deep conversation on the estuary path, very close to the spot at which Alban Watkins's rotting corpse had been found last year. The old lady, who had previously heard the rumours of the Night-walker, was so shocked that she collapsed. She says that the Nightwalker 'flew away', and Patty had to get help from some of her neighbours to carry the old lady home. When she came to, she had hysterics, and Havard Medical had to be called to give her some sedation. She is so old, and is still so shocked, that there is a fear that she might die.

When I had heard Hettie out, I could hardly believe her story. Patty, of all people, involved with the Nightwalker? Had she not got herself into trouble enough over the business of little Brynach? And here she was again, attracting attention in a most unfortunate way when she should have been concentrating on building a quiet and respectable life with her new husband. My problem with this strange creature of the night was now affecting others, and this caused me great concern. I thought I had better try to get to the bottom of it, so I offered to walk back into town with Hettie.

An hour later I knocked on the front door of Bwthyn Bach. It looked, to all intents and purposes, like a perfectly ordinary day, with a flock of gulls wheeling and screaming overhead in celebration of the fact that mackerel were being cleaned in front of some of the fishermen's cottages. Jake poked his head round the door. He looked very apprehensive, and did not invite me in. 'Oh! Mistress Martha!' he said. 'It is good to see you. We were almost expecting you.'

'Good morning, Jake. I heard about that unfortunate episode last evening. May I speak to Patty?'

'She is very upset, Mistress, and does not want to talk to anybody just now. She is also suffering from the morning sickness – you knew, I think, that she is with child?'

'Oh, Jake, I am so pleased for you both! I did not know it. But if Patty is two or three months gone, the last thing she wants is troublesome gossip and old ladies dying of shock. She needs peace and quiet now more than ever.'

'I know it, Mistress. Will you come with me to the sea wall, where we can talk for a few minutes?'

So we wandered along to the high wall, and sat there with our feet dangling over the water. It was high tide. There were three vessels bobbing about at anchor, and there was a good deal of activity around the warehouses. Half a dozen gulls sat nearby and looked at us, anticipating breadcrumbs, but were sorely disappointed.

'I am seriously worried about Patty,' said Jake. 'She has secrets from me, and I cannot understand it, since she swore when we married that we would share everything.'

'This business about the Nightwalker, Jake. Do you know what is going on?'

'I fear I do not, Mistress. All I know is that she has had various meetings with him ... or it. She will tell me nothing, other than to say that one day all will be revealed. And she promises me, on pain of death, that there is nothing untoward going on, and that she is utterly faithful to me and to her marriage vows.'

'And why on earth should that particular protestation be necessary, Jake?'

'Because of the rumours that are flying around, Mistress.' The poor man sounded utterly distraught, and there was a break in his voice. He looked over his shoulder, as if to seek assurance that nobody was overhearing our conversation. Then he swallowed hard, and continued. 'This very morning I have spoken to my friend Osian, and he tells me that they say that Patty is a witch, and that the Nightwalker is the Devil, and that he and she are in communion.'

'But that is patently absurd, and involves putting two and two together and making two hundred!'

'I know it, and you know it, Mistress Martha, but the fisherfolk who live on the Parrog are simple people, and rumours have a habit of spreading and enlarging themselves. And if you think that rumour is bad enough, it gets worse, for people are now saying that in the past Patty has been impregnated by the Devil, and has borne his demon child.'

Now I moaned and buried my head in my hands, for I could see ahead of me a trail which would lead straight from Patty to little Brynach, the sweet and innocent baby who was now mine, and safe beneath the roof of Plas Ingli. I hoped and prayed that I would be the only one to make the connection, and I reassured myself with the recollection that several bastard children are born in Newport every year. I hoped that in the public mind dates and memories would be confused. Jake continued: 'They say that on various occasions the sounds of a baby crying have been heard in our cottage, and that the baby has now been sacrificed in some Satanic ritual. How else, they ask, can the baby have been heard but never seen? And how else, they reason, can Patty have given birth without ever having the appearance of a woman seven or eight months gone?'

'And what do you think, Jake?'

'Stuff and nonsense, Mistress. I love Patty dearly, and will trust her to the ends of the earth. But it is not easy for her, or for me since she will not tell me the truth. I am away on fishing trips sometimes for days on end, and there are many nights when Patty is alone in the cottage. The neighbours know that, and it is easy for them to assume that those are the nights during which she practises her witchcraft and fornicates with the Nightwalker.'

I thought for a long time.' Oh, what a tangled web!' I said at last. 'Of course I believe you, Jake, and I would trust Patty with my life just as you would. It is vital that we now seek to influence the course of events. How is Mistress Willey this morning? I trust that she will not die?'

'I think she is somewhat recovered.'

'Good. Her testimony might be vital. I understand that she saw the Nightwalker fly away through the air following their surprise encounter?'

'So she says. But she was hysterical when she said it, so I suppose we can take it with a pinch of salt.'

'Has anybody made the connection with the death of Alban Watkins? I gather that the place where the unfortunate encounter occurred was very close to the spot where his body was found.'

'That is correct, Mistress.'

'Very well, Jake. Let us forget for the moment what the truth of the matter may be. I think it would suit your purpose, and mine, and Patty's, if we put it about that she was being threatened by the ghost of Alban Watkins, and has been threatened by him before, and is entirely innocent of any misdemeanour. We have to get rid of these allegations of witchcraft, for they are very dangerous. Will you seek Patty's co-operation in holding to this story?'

Jake thought, and then nodded. He could now see a glimmer of light in the darkness which had previously threatened to overwhelm him. 'I will do it, Mistress Martha,' he said. 'I hope Patty will agree, and that we can put the word about before we are overtaken by events.'

So he went his way, and I went mine. I pray that his enterprise will be successful, and that Patty will come through this episode unscathed. But in truth I am desperately worried about her and about what may happen next.

2 July 1807

Things are spiralling out of control, as I feared that they might. This afternoon, having fulfilled my promise to myself and the children to spend some hours with them singing rhymes and enjoying other activities, I was filled with a sense of dread that all was not well with Patty and Jake. As soon as I could get away, I rode over the mountain to Joseph's cottage, in the conviction that he was needed more than I. Luckily, he was at home, and I urged him to come with me to the Parrog. Of course he agreed. He fetched a few things from inside the cottage, and saddled his pony with haste. We rode down the Werndew lane to the coast road, and continued eastward to Newport. As we rode side by side, I told him almost everything about my conversation with Jake, without revealing the link between Patty and baby Brynach. To my great relief, he agreed to the stratagem of blaming the ghost of Alban Watkins for almost everything, and also agreed that he would do all in his power to dispel the rumour that Patty is a witch.

But when we got to the Parrog it was too late. There was a wild mob outside Bwthyn Bach, led by some of the more disreputable characters from town. Joseph, who knows all of them well, immediately identified for me Maldwyn Biggs and Freddy Cobb, as well as some of the members of the Nonconformist movement who have recently been swept along by religious fervour. Thugs and good Christian gentlemen together, I thought – strange bedfellows indeed. But they were united in their hatred of witchcraft, and in their conviction that any trace of it must be purged from the community. They had all picked up on the idiotic rumours carried on the sea breeze, and without thinking they had assumed them to be true. So now they were shouting and waving their fists, and throwing stones at the cottage. The windows were already broken. When we arrived some of the men were approaching the house with lighted braziers, and it was clearly their intention to burn the place down. I was horrified, and reined back my horse, but Joseph spurred his pony on and rode into the middle of the mob.

The rioters were taken aback by his arrival, and as they paused in their enterprise he took advantage of the situation. He held up his hand for silence, and secured it, reminding me that while the Devil is feared, and witches are loathed, wizards are respected. And Joseph Harries is

393

respected more than most. 'I urge you, brothers, to stay your hand!' he shouted. 'Are you prepared to do murder? There are innocent people in that house!'

'No, they are gone,' shouted somebody in the crowd. 'They went some minutes since, by the back door. We saw them go, and good riddance to them!'

The crowd cheered and roared, and urged Joseph to get out of the way. He got off his horse and stood before the front door. Somebody threw a stone at him, and it hit him on the head. He put his hand up instinctively, but there was a trickle of blood. He looked dazed, but stood his ground. 'Why do you direct your fury at this house?' he shouted.

'Because it is inhabited by the Devil!' they shouted back.

'Where is your evidence?'

'It is well known!'

'Where is your evidence?' shouted Joseph again.

And so this exchange went on, getting nowhere. At last the mob became quieter, and I perceived that people began to feel some concern at the injury done to Joseph. You do not injure a wizard and expect to get away without punishment. The braziers were thrown into the sea. Joseph, always the showman, refused to wipe the blood from his face, and he let it stream down his nose onto his chin and his white shirt collar. The red stain spread across his chest. 'I urge you, gentlemen, to control your emotions and think,' he called. 'If you are in pursuit of the Nightwalker, why do you look here? Have any of you seen him in this cottage?'

There was silence. 'No? Very well, where was he last seen?'

'Along the estuary path.'

'Quite so. At exactly the spot where Alban Watkins was murdered last year. I have had dealings with devils and spirits, and I have even looked into the face of Satan. The Nightwalker is not Satan – you may take my word for it. We have here a manifestation of the spirit of Alban Watkins. I have seen his ghost here before, unknown to any of you. Now he has chosen to terrorize Patty, and she is overwhelmed with fear. And what do you do about it? You hound her and her husband out of their house, and set about burning it down. One injustice after another! Are you all entirely mad? Do you have no respect for the process of rational thought, or for the law?'

'Well, if you are so sure, Master Harries, why do you not send the ghost of Alban Watkins packing, back to the world of miserable spirits?'

'I could do that tonight, but the devout persons among you may not approve of my methods. Would you settle for a proper exorcism, conducted in the proper way by Rector Devonald?'

There was a low hum of conversation as the leaders of the mob consulted with their fellows. Then Freddy Cobb took on the role of spokesman, and said: 'All right. We will agree to that. And will you promise us, on pain of death, that the Nightwalker will never be seen on the Parrog again?'

'You have my word for it,' said Joseph. Then he gave a sharp gasp, followed by a long-drawn-out moan, and slid down into a crumpled heap on the

395

doorstep of Bwthyn Bach. I was at the back of the crowd, still on my horse. But now I jumped to the ground and ran forward, screaming.

'Joseph! Joseph! Oh, my God, what have they done?'

Simultaneously there was another scream, and Hettie, who had appeared with miraculous timing, shouted: 'Murder! Murder! They have killed Joseph Harries of Werndew! Oh, he is dead! He is dead!' And she waded through the crowd like a Roman gladiator, scattering Baptists and thugs in all directions. The crowd melted away in an instant, and within a minute the only people on the doorstep were Joseph, me and Hettie, and one or two passers-by who had the instincts of the Good Samaritan. 'Carry him to my house this instant!' said Hettie. 'I will see what can be done for him.'

His limp body was carried along the sea wall to Hettie's lodging house. We put him down for a moment, and since we were not sure whether he was alive or dead I put my ear next to his mouth to see if I could sense any trace of a living breath. Unseen by anybody else, he kissed my ear! I reeled back, and only just managed to control my surprise. 'I think I can trace faint signs of life,' I said, and so we carried him into Hettie's house and placed him on the kitchen table so that he could be worked on. He moaned, and opened his eyes, and looked into mine. Then he smiled and apparently lapsed into unconsciousness again. The old fox, I thought. Truly, this is carrying theatricals too far. But that was just the start of it, for when the Good Samaritans had gone, and Hettie had gone rushing off to fetch Havard

396

Medical, I was left all alone with Joseph. For a minute I carried on wiping away the blood from his neck and his face, but I could find no trace of an injury. 'Joseph, this is outrageous!' I whispered fiercely in his ear. 'This is all a piece of play-acting, is it not?'

He nodded faintly, without opening his eyes.

'But all that blood?'

'The oldest trick in the book, Martha. Sometimes, when I am going into dangerous situations, I take with me a little piece of pig's intestine filled with blood. Usually it is my own blood, got from a prick in the finger. Did you notice that when the stone apparently hit my head, I reeled back and slapped my hand to the "injury"? The piece of intestine burst, and – abracadabra – blood everywhere. Very effective.'

'Joseph, you are a charlatan!'

'Of course, Martha, and I am proud of it. I am a liar too, but I think you will agree that occasionally untruths are necessary in the pursuit of justice.' Then he became serious. 'Martha,' he said, opening his eyes at last. 'Hettie may come back at any moment. I will have to explain to her and Havard Medical my miraculous powers of recovery from a serious flesh wound. I will manage it, for I am after all a wizard. I have done my part, and now you must do yours. First, go down on your knees and pray to that God of yours. I hope that he owes you some good turn or other. Pray that the Nightwalker will never again be seen on the Parrog. If he is, I fear for my life as well as Patty's. Then pray that Rector Devonald is here rather than in Carmarthenshire. If he is not here, we have a problem. Go to the Rectory and insist that he comes to the Parrog tomorrow at noon in order to conduct an exorcism. We have to get rid of the spirit of Alban Watkins, even if it is already absent.'

Then we heard the voices of Hettie and Havard Medical approaching the house. 'Go now!' he said urgently. 'I shall stay here tonight in order to recuperate from my terrible injuries. Hettie makes the most delicious moist strawberry cake, and it has wonderful healing powers. I am minded to enjoy a little pampering from an excellent lady, for I have that privilege all too seldom.' And so he started to groan and writhe about on the table, and I only just managed to suppress a wicked smile as I passed Hettie and Master Havard in the passage.

I prayed as I walked to the Rectory, and I thank God for answering my entreaties. Master Devonald does not like exorcisms, and said so, but I said that more than one life depended on it, and that there was a serious chance of civil disorder should he not accede to my request. I had to use a number of basic female persuasion techniques, including tears. At last, after a great deal of hard work on my part, he agreed. Tomorrow he will turn up on the estuary path and get rid of the evil spirit of Alban Watkins, even if it never was there in the first place.

5 July 1807

The exorcism has been done, and a great success

it was too. Rector Devonald quite enjoyed himself, for he had the undivided attention of half of Newport and most of the Parrog. He could hardly find the space for his ceremonials, such was the crush. But he strode round and round, and there was a great deal of swinging of incense, and ringing of his handbell, and he insisted on the candles too, even though it was a bright and sunny day. He chanted various things in Latin, and read extracts from the Bible, and then he banished the spirit of Alban Watkins from the place, and enjoined it never to return.

The crowd stood in awe, and clapped when he was finished. Joseph and I, standing at the back of the crowd, joined in the applause, for in truth we were quite impressed with the solemnity and theatricality of the occasion. 'Utterly meaningless,' mumbled Joseph, 'but he enjoyed it, and so did the crowd.' I thanked Master Devonald for his intervention in this miserable business, and noted with interest that he appeared exhausted. Joseph, in contrast, was as sprightly as a spring lamb, and greatly enjoyed the many greetings and enquiries after his health, some of them from the very people whom he had confronted just the day before.

After their terrible experience at the hands of the mob, Patty and Jake were missing for the rest of that day, and for the whole of the next, and so missed the exorcism. We were gravely worried on their behalf, but then yesterday they appeared at the Plas, looking frightened and tired. We took them in at once, and Bessie gave them her room and moved into the office. I had already decided that I would not press Patty at all on the matter of the Nightwalker, and indeed I did not. But the first thing I did was to ask after her health, and that of her baby. I lost my first child at about the same time in my childbearing, and I would not wish that experience on my worst enemy, let alone one of my dearest friends. 'I am all right, Martha,' she said. 'I still feel very ill, but Jake has been an angel and he has protected me with a gentle hand through all this business. I will not lose my baby, whatever the Parrog mob tries to do to me.' We packed the pair of them off to bed, and they slept for fifteen hours while we endeavoured to keep the house quiet.

Now they have gone back to their cottage, and we trust that all will be well. One or two of the locals are still muttering, but for most of them the episode has been brought to a satisfactory conclusion. Today Billy and Will have been down at Bwthyn Bach, helping with the repairing of windows and the removal of splintered glass, which was all over the furniture and the floor. Hettie has also been a pillar of strength, and with other Parrog women she has been in and out, helping with gifts of food and other things to replace the odds and ends which were so damaged by glass and stones that they had to be thrown away.

With things quieter on that particular battle-front, I have taken the opportunity to visit Pont-faen and Castlebythe to talk to Owain's parents and his sister Mary Jane about his disappearance. I have been very careful in my choice of words, for I want to keep the theory of murder or attempted murder hidden away for the time being. It is now almost two months since my beloved man disappeared, and Squire and Mistress Laugharne seemed to understand, during our conversation, that I am trying for my children's sake to maintain the illusion of normality. But my friend Mary Jane was much more difficult, and appeared to expect me to go into hiding so as to demonstrate to the world the grief from which I was suffering. I asked her not to doubt my grief, but to accept that with a young family, and as mistress of an estate, it was not really an option to shut myself away. She has been more affected by the loss of her brother than even I could have anticipated. We parted on frosty terms, and I fear that I will have to work hard to restore the loving friendship which we have both so valued in the past. I left with her words ringing in my ears: 'Martha, how could you even think of other things, when we do not know the truth about Owain? You are still betrothed to him, and he may still be alive...'

Hunting for the Devil

1 August 1807

My confusion is compounded, for the Nightwalker has apparently decided to shift his attentions from Newport to the neighbouring parish of Nevern. Not satisfied with terrorizing Plas Ingli and Llannerch, and then the Parrog, he has now appeared at Cwmgloyn, the home of my dead enemies Moses and Matthew Lloyd.

The details are very uncertain, but today Billy delivered a rumour from town that the creature has been seen on the Cwmgloyn estate. He says that the servants are too frightened to talk, and he seems to think that they have been sworn to secrecy. Perhaps the creature is terrorizing Meredith Lloyd, the new squire, in the same way that he terrorized me, and maybe the squire is trying to discover the truth about him before wild rumours turn into mass hysteria as we saw on the Parrog? If that is his hope, he is probably too late, for according to Billy the word in Nevern and Felindre Farchog is that the Devil is paying one of his periodic visits. People are already very frightened, which amuses Billy since he is quite convinced that the Nightwalker is as harmless as a newborn child. But the locals think that the Devil has had a pact with Cwmgloyn over many generations, and that he treats the place as his second home. Look how evil old Squire Lloyd was, they say. One feud after another, brutal with his own children, and finally raving mad. And look at his sons! Moses Lloyd, as mean-spirited and vengeful a person as ever walked this earth, responsible for all manner of wickedness during his time in the community, and now disappeared without trace. Probably taken down to Hell, like Don Juan. And his brother Matthew, not much better, as sly and devious as any man can be, involved in the murder of Master David Morgan of Plas Ingli, and in February strung up on the gallows at the county gaol. It stands to reason that Cwmgloyn is just a staging post on the road to Hell...

When I heard about all this, I might have been pleased that the Nightwalker had finally decided to leave me alone. But I know how the minds of local people work, and I was now desperately worried on behalf of Meredith Lloyd and his family. Meredith is a decent and kind man who is doing his best to undo some of the damage done to the family name by his father and brothers. He has a sweet and sensitive wife, and two children who are both under ten years old. God knows what will happen to them if the smouldering rumours are ignited. I determined that I would call in tomorrow morning, and I sent Will down with a message to announce my intention.

Two hours later Will returned with a brief message from the Squire which was cool but not unfriendly. I perceived from his words that Meredith was not particularly keen for me to visit, but that he realized that a refusal would do more harm than good. What was of greater interest to me was the information gleaned by Will from the servants, while their master was away reading my note and drafting a reply. They reminded Will that Meredith had buried the body of his brother Matthew, after his execution, in the rose garden near Plas Cwmgloyn, under conditions of some secrecy. The Vicar of Bayvil had attended the burial, but only under protest. The grave is now marked with a simple wooden cross, with no name on it. According to the servants the Nightwalker has been seen dimly at night, standing near the grave. So they think that he is simply the ghost of Matthew Lloyd, who is by no means as much of a threat to them as the Devil might be.

On the other hand the lonely cottage on the estate which was used by Matthew and his family, and has stood empty for about a year, has become a focal point for speculation since one of the farm workers saw a light in the window and smoke coming from the chimney around midnight last Thursday. This, apparently, had been reported to the Squire, and he had simply said, 'Huh! Vagrants again, or Irish harvesters. Leave it to me – I will have them out of there in no time at all.' He has forbidden any of the estate workers to go near the cottage – not that they are minded to do so anyway, for it stands amid gloomy trees and has long had a reputation for being haunted.

This is all very mysterious, and also intriguing. I look forward to discovering what it is all about when I visit Cwmgloyn on the morrow. I have waited far too long for a visit anyway, having promised myself back in February that I must call on Meredith and seek to establish friendly relations between our two ancient families.

3 August 1807

I have been to Cwmgloyn, and have come home again having strengthened family ties, but having learned little more about the Nightwalker.

Before I went, Grandpa warned me that I would find the place dark and sombre, as indeed I did. As Billy drove me along the driveway in the light chaise, it was a bright day with scudding clouds and a fresh wind from the west. But the first glimpse of the house was somewhat forbidding, for it is squat and square with little architectural merit. There is a rose garden in front and a walled garden behind, and most of the farm buildings are out of sight. But there were too many trees for my liking, and the tall beeches and oaks looked so heavy and dusty and their shadows were so dense, that I longed for the open freshness of Plas Ingli. There was a strange silence about the place too, which I found disconcerting. Billy felt it too. We exchanged glances, but said nothing.

I knocked on the ancient oak door, and I was invited inside, warmly enough, by a pretty serving maid. Billy went round to the back to get some water for the horse and to encourage the house-keeper to give him a quart of ale. The house was very gloomy inside, with dark wood-panelled passages and large rooms with small windows. It was a place which kept many secrets, I thought, and which did its best to keep out the light. But then I was surprised when the servant led me right through the house to a bright conservatory at the eastern end, and there I met Mistress Jane Lloyd. She was resting on the sofa with her foot bandaged up, and explained that she had recently suffered a fall in the garden. I expressed my con-cern, and my good wishes for a speedy recovery. She apologized for the fact that her husband had not met me at the front door, but explained that he had had to rush out to deal with some estate business and would be back very shortly. I said that I was not at all offended, and the two of us sat down with a glass of fruit cordial and con-versed very amiably indeed. She proved to be a polite, cultured and charming lady, and I regretted the fact that while we have met fleetingly once or twice, we have never had an opportunity to talk properly. Mistress Jane expressed her concern about the disappearance of Owain with obvious sincerity, and complimented me for taking on the foundling child whom I had named Brynach. We studiously avoided any talk of Moses, or of Matthew, or of the Nightwalker.

Then the Squire returned, giving me advance warning through the urgent booted footsteps which echoed around the long downstairs passage. 'I am so sorry, Mistress Martha!' he said, after acknowledging my curtsy with a deep bow. 'Unforgivable, to be away at the predicted time of arrival of a welcome guest. But I had to attend to something urgently at the far end of the estate. You know how these things go. All sorted out, I am glad to say. You have a glass of cordial? Good, good. Some more refreshments are on the way. Excellent. So, this is delightful, is it not?'

He chatted with such speed, and with such nervous energy, that I knew perfectly well that the 'something' was not sorted out at all. But I was not going to make an issue of it, and assured him that Mistress Jane and I had enjoyed having the chance to get to know each other a little better. She graciously agreed with me, and so we spoke of this and that while cups of tea and light cakes were served. While we talked I tried to work out from his demeanour just what the pressing matter could be. He is handsome, tall and lean like his late brothers, with brown eyes and dark hair. He has an open and guileless face, and from his fresh complexion I guessed that his eyes have seen a good deal more of the weather than those squires who spend their time in coffee taverns and gambling rooms. The creases on his face were the product of smiles rather than frowns and scowls, and that gave me confidence that he was, as I had hoped, an honest man. He is kind too, and he is in love with his wife. I was greatly impressed with the sweet attention which he bestowed upon Mistress Jane, who was obviously in some pain because of her foot injury. But he also behaved nervously, and at times I observed that he was not singing from the same sheet of music as Jane and myself. Women's talk and male boredom? I thought not.

When I judged the moment to be right, I raised the matter of Matthew's burial. 'Master Meredith,' I said, 'I wish to say something that I should have said six months ago. The time was not appropriate then, and many things have happened subsequently which have diverted me from my course. But I must express my personal admiration for the love which you showed to your brother Matthew by attending the county gaol on the day of his execution and then bringing his body back here to Cwmgloyn for a Christian burial. That was a truly noble thing to have done, and it was the act of a gentleman. There are few that I can think of who would have done the same in such circumstances...'

I felt my voice breaking as I completed these words, but my emotion was as nothing as compared with his, for tears welled up in his eyes, and he had to turn away while he dabbed at them with his kerchief. After a while he turned to face me, and came across to me and kissed my hand.

His voice was thick with emotion, and tears still filled his eyes. 'Thank you, Martha,' he said. 'You are the first person to have said such a thing to me concerning an event which almost cost me my sanity. It is deeply appreciated. And I value your remarks all the more because they have come from the lips of the one person living who knows the full extent of my brother's wickedness, and has suffered terribly because of it.'

Now I too was almost overcome with emotion, for I realized that in his innocence he knew only a part of the story. He knew that sitting before him was the woman who had brought Matthew to justice, but he did not know that that same woman – Martha Morgan of Plas Ingli – had killed his other brother Moses in a fearful conflict in the cave on Carningli some years before. It was better, I thought, that he should believe Moses to be alive somewhere, just as I hold to the belief that Owain still lives.

At last, when both Meredith and I had regained our equilibrium, we were able to turn the conversation to other things. We did not exactly chortle with glee, for neither the Lloyds nor myself were in the mood for it. But we got on well enough, and talked more of Owain and Brynach. Then I swallowed hard and took another risk. 'Meredith,' I said, 'may I ask you a question about certain recent events?' I did not wait for a reply, but continued immediately. 'I have heard reports, and I pray God that they are untrue, that a phantom creature called the Nightwalker has been sighted around the Cwmgloyn estate. I have an interest in this, for I have been visited by this same creature

408

for six months or more, and I have enough experience of it to have become certain of its malign intent. I do not wish misfortune upon any family, least of all yours after all that you have suffered in the past. So please be kind enough to tell me – are these reports well founded?'

Master and Mistress Lloyd exchanged glances. Then she said, in order to give him time to think: 'Yes, we are aware of the rumours, and we have come to the conclusion ourselves that this creature, if he exists, may be the same one who has been spotted on the mountain and on the Parrog.'

'Thank you Jane,' said I. 'But I fear that you have not satisfied my curiosity.'

Then Meredith joined in. 'Yes, some of our labourers have told us that they have seen a figure dressed in black at Cwmgloyn, and they have been uncertain as to whether they have been looking at man or ghost.'

'Come now, Meredith. I dared to hope that you would be honest with me. I hear the rumours that the figure is neither man or ghost, but the Devil himself.'

'I think we may take that as superstitious nonsense, Martha.'

'Do you know it to be nonsense?'

'Yes, I do.'

'Very well,' said I, feeling, and probably sounding, like a learned attorney in a court case, 'where is your evidence for saying that?'

'I am sorry, Martha, but I cannot say more until I have got to the bottom of things myself.'

'So you have more information but cannot divulge it?'

'I did not say that.' Meredith looked thoroughly miserable and not a little agitated, so I changed tack.

'I am sorry to press you, Meredith. But I only wanted to help in case you are threatened in some way. Have you seen the Nightwalker yourself?'

'I have, but I do not wish to discuss it.'

I turned to Jane and asked her the same question. She simply nodded, and I began to get the clear impression that these good people were frightened almost out of their wits and had agreed, either between themselves or with the Nightwalker, upon a code of silence.

I tried one last line of attack. 'I have also heard mention of the cottage which was once used by Matthew and his wife and child at the far end of the estate. A rumour has reached my ears that it is haunted, and that the Devil resides there.'

'I can assure you, Martha, that that is perfectly untrue.'

'Untrue it may be, but if your labourers and people round about believe that it is true, you have a dangerous situation on your hands, as we discovered when a certain cottage down on the Parrog was attacked by a mob just a month ago.'

'I am aware of that danger, Martha, and I am doing my best to prevent anything untoward from happening.'

It was now clear that any further pressure on my part would cause my hosts to feel very uncomfortable indeed, and so I desisted. I rose to my feet and said that I really must be going, and that I had already taken up far more of their time than I had intended. I thanked them warmly for their hospitality. They graciously bade me farewell, and I invited them to visit me at the Plas at any time that might be convenient to them. The Squire saw me to the door, and five minutes later Billy and I were trotting away in the chaise down into the Nevern valley. I was glad that I had called, but felt great frustration at my lack of progress in my investigations of the Nightwalker. Billy, apparently without any effort at all, had found out far more in the Cwmgloyn kitchen. 'Strange goings-on in this place, Mistress,' he said.

'Oh, indeed?'

'Yes indeed. Very strange goings-on.'

'Well, come on then, Billy, before I have to clamp the thumbscrews onto you.'

'They say, Mistress, that last night the Nightwalker appeared in the moonlight, in the rose garden near to Master Matthew's grave. He was seen quite clearly from the house, by at least five people. Mistress Jane went rushing outside before the Squire could stop her, saying that she was going to frighten him away, she was. Then across the face of the moon went a big black cloud, and when the cloud had passed the Nightwalker was gone and, Duw Duw, there was the Mistress on the ground, with a bad injury to her foot. She says that she tripped on the edge of the path, but the servants swear that she was struck down by the Nightwalker.'

'Oh, dear. This gets more and more serious.'

'And that is not all, Mistress. This very day, shortly before we arrived, the Squire was called out in the middle of a mad panic. A couple of Irish vagrants came upon Matthew's old cottage and decided to settle in there for a day or two. Up to no good, probably. They pushed the door in, and got the fright of their lives they did, for there, with his back to them, was this huge figure in black, with the smell of sulphur in the air. The Devil himself, they thought, and they was so scared that they ran without stopping till they bumped into some harvesters, and they went and fetched the Squire. Funny old business, Mistress, don't you think?'

15 August 1807

I have been too busy with the corn harvest of late to think of anything else, but now I have to report that events at Cwmgloyn have culminated in a way that I feared and almost expected.

This morning, at eight of the clock, as our harvesters were turning up for a day's work in Parc Glas, Abraham Jenkins Brithdir came with news of terrible events at Cwmgloyn. He said that yesterday a rumour started circulating among the harvesters hired by Squire Lloyd that the Nightwalker had been seen again at the hovel once inhabited by Matthew. They probably had too much ale for dinner, and they probably had too much for supper too, since Cwmgloyn is renowned as a place where liquid refreshment is available in abundance. Whatever the reason, it so happened that by evening time the harvesters were talking of nothing else but the Nightwalker, and they had become quite convinced that he really was the Devil in their midst. Some of them went off home, and as evening turned to night the wild speculations started to run out of control. Abraham himself was at the Trewern Arms in Nevern, and he said that with nobody to contradict the rumours, and harvesting money being spent freely on rough cider and ale, common sense had departed via the back door by ten of the clock. He went home at about midnight, and he said that by then passions were so inflamed that he feared for the safety of the Lloyd family and the big house, let alone the rough hovel at the far end of the estate. He suspected that a mob was about to start marching towards Cwmgloyn, and some of the wilder Nevern men were already preparing torches.

'But Abraham, why would Nevern men feel so concerned about Cwmgloyn?' I asked. 'And why would they feel moved to attack a miserable hovel in the woods?'

'Remember, Mistress Martha, that people have long memories,' replied Abraham. 'Most of the men who drink at the Trewern Arms have worked at Cwmgloyn at some time or other. They know the land well, as do those whose only visits have been on poaching expeditions. The old squire was mean-spirited and vindictive, and many men suffered at his hands. Some others were sorely used at various times by Moses Lloyd and Matthew Lloyd. As of yesterday, there were many old scores which had not yet been settled. They know that Meredith is a good man and an honourable squire, but he has not yet had time to heal ancient wounds. Then there is the cottage. For years, ever since Moses lived in it, it has been hated by the

413

locals and even by the farm servants. It is in a dark and shady place, with tall trees in front of it and a steep bank behind. It is the sort of place around which spooky stories circulate, and since being lived in by the two most evil members of the Lloyd clan it has been inhabited, so they say, by rats, bats and ghosts. It is very easy to move from that to the view that the Devil is in residence, and the episode a while back involving the two Irish vagrants was of some assistance in that regard...'

'You mean that lots of the locals knew about that?'

'It was the talk of the whole community for days afterwards, Mistress. There are two things that the Irish enjoy – one is drinking and the other is talking.'

'So, Abraham, pray tell us the worst.'

'I heard it this morning on the road, when I set out for the Plas. That boy Benny from the Pantry cottages was coming home, the worse for wear. He was there, and he saw it all. He says that a mob set off from the Trewern with torches blazing, yelling blue murder and saying they were going to get rid of the Devil from Cwmgloyn. Very ambitious of them, I thought, since Rector Devonald and his ilk have not yet managed that, even with all their Biblical quotations and holy words. At any rate, they went through Felindre Farchog and up the hill, picking up more people all the way, and proceeded to the big house. Some of the wild men wanted to burn that down, but the Squire and the servants pleaded with them and told them that the Devil was not there. So the cottage became the target. Off they marched along the farm track

414

towards the woods, joined by some of the travelling labourers who had been sleeping in the barn. When they reached the hovel there was a great cheer. The two little windows were smashed and torches were thrown inside. More torches were thrown onto the roof, and soon the whole place was an inferno. The men cheered and danced, and then a great ball of fire went up in the air. 'There he goes, back to Hell!' they shouted. And they cheered and danced around the burning building until there was virtually nothing left of it. It was not very big in the first place. Some people swore that they could smell sulphur, which confirmed that the Devil had been in residence. Well satisfied with their night's work, some of the men staggered home in the dark, and others slept in hedges until the dawn came. And that is all I know.'

There was a long silence. I was appalled, and so were the other listeners round the kitchen table. I hoped that no human being had been inside the cottage when it was burnt down, and I thanked God in his Heaven that we had managed to control the news of the Nightwalker's visits to the Plas. If we had not succeeded in that, the flames might have curled into the night sky here rather than at Cwmgloyn...

We could not spend the whole morning talking about mob violence, devils and ghosts, and I set the harvesters to work. I knew that further news would reach us before the day was out, and so it did. It was carried to the Plas by my friend Skiff, who has used his ill-gotten gains from the sinking of the *Pole Star* to set himself up in business as a wagoner. He now has five horses and two heavy

415

wagons, one of which is ideal for the carting of barley. He comes up each afternoon at about three of the clock to move the harvest that is dried and gathered into the barn. So he turned up today, a little late, with further news of the burning at Cwmgloyn. He was disappointed to hear that we knew all about it already, but revealed that during the day, with the remnants of the cottage somewhat cooler, some of the servants had raked through the debris and confirmed that there were no human remains there. A good many people, said Skiff, were greatly relieved by that particular piece of news. And why? Because the Squire had insisted on the search, on the grounds that if there had been bones, the Coroner would have become involved, and the mob would then have been liable to arrest for murder. The Squire was furious about the riot, said Skiff, because his wife and children had been terrified almost out of their wits, but he was not minded to take out indictments against the leaders for riotous assembly and other crimes, and thought it best to let the matter rest.

I thought that Master Lloyd might well be pleased that the cottage – and whatever was within it – was now but a pile of rubble. I am sure it will never be rebuilt. I will endeavour to visit Cwmgloyn again before too long – but first, we have five more fields to harvest, and ricks to build, and a barn to fill before the weather breaks.

25 September 1807

Sian and Shemi are in love. It is perfectly obvious

416

to all of us, and indeed they are such a cooing pair of turtle doves that it must be apparent to the rest of the world too. I have had to remind them on a number of occasions that there is work to be done, and to their credit they do try, but whenever one of them catches sight of the other horse harnesses are strapped up the wrong way, the words of nursery rhymes are forgotten, and conversations with other people fade away into thin air. Such is love, and I cannot frown upon it, for I behaved exactly that way myself.

Today Shemi came to me, looking a good deal younger than his twenty-five years, and asked for a private meeting. I agreed, and we went into the parlour together. We sat down, and I asked him what he wished to discuss, although it was perfectly obvious. He looked very bashful, and hesitated. 'Come along, Shemi,' said I, in my most motherly voice. 'I assume you want to talk about Sian.'

'How did you know that, Mistress?' said he, genuinely surprised.

'Let us put it down to a woman's intuition. Well?'

'I have to say, Mistress, that I am very fond of her.'

'Yes, I had noticed.'

He swallowed hard, and then blurted out what was on his mind. 'I should like to do some courting in bed, Mistress, and Sian is agreeable, and Bessie says she is happy to sleep on the sofa in the parlour now and then so as to give us some peace, if you are agreeable.'

'How often, Shemi?'

'Once a week, Mistress, if you will allow it.'

I pretended to give the matter considerable thought. But in truth there was no reason to discourage them. They, like all other servants, have virtually no free time, and they are hardly ever away from the Plas and the company of other servants. And here they have the additional blessings of a milk nurse, two small babies, and four lively children to cope with. If Shemi was intent upon getting under Sian's skirt, and she was agreeable, he could have done it long since in the hayloft. Bundling is frowned upon by the Nonconformists, and by many others in town, but I am fully aware that it is widely practised in the country and that it is the only means whereby two young people in love can talk and cuddle in complete privacy. The only cost to me would be two very sleepy young people, and not much work, on the days after the nights before.

'Very well, Shemi,' said I. 'I will allow it, but I want you to promise me one thing. Breeches on, and buttoned up, all night?'

'I promise, Mistress.'

'And remember that if you get Sian in the family way, you will both be out of here in an instant. Her father Caradoc is, as you might have noticed, a hard man, and I would not fancy your chances of survival should a little accident happen. Your passions will be high. Can you control yourself?'

'Yes, Mistress. And Sian will not allow any nonsense either. She is a good girl, and that is one of the reasons why I am quite attached to her.'

I could not resist a smile, and Shemi smiled

too, with relief as much as anything. I sent him off to do some work, although I will not get much value out of my ten pence today.

That was the good news. Now for the bad. The strange and winding trail left by the Nightwalker appears to be leading me towards my good friend the Wizard of Werndew. I would not have believed it a month ago, but now I am coming to the view that anything is possible, and that I may be unwise to trust even my nearest and dearest.

Since my last conversation with Joseph about the Nightwalker, back in June, and since his promise that he would shortly get to the bottom of the matter, I have heard nothing new from him. That is not entirely surprising, since he leads a fuller life than I do, but he has not delivered on his promise, and that does cause me some concern. We have not communicated since the events at Cwmgloyn, although he must have been made aware of them and has no doubt given them some thought. If anybody knows who or what was in the cottage that was burnt down, he does.

I have been alerted over the last few days by comments in the kitchen about Joseph that surprised me. Normally, when he comes into the conversation, people talk of his latest cure, or of some recent mystery he has solved, or of his increasingly eccentric and outrageous behaviour, but always there is affection and admiration in the voices of those who speak. But now I sensed something different, and I decided at dinner today that I would ask the servants about it. At first they were reluctant to comment, knowing of my close relationship with the Wizard of Werndew, but then it came out, bit by bit, that accusations are being levelled against him of a kind which could be very damaging. In short, he is being accused of being in league with the Devil. When I heard this first, from Will, I laughed and said: 'Come now, Will, wizards are accused all the time of being in league with the Devil. That is why churchmen dislike them so intensely, and why people like Joseph and old Aby Biddle near Haverfordwest are both feared and respected.'

'No, Mistress,' said Will. 'I am aware of all the stories about strange contacts with the spirit world. Master Harries doesn't deny them himself, and seems to enjoy them indeed. But this is different. He has not been alone in his house recently.'

'Is that so strange? He might have an old aunt from far away, come to visit for a few days.'

Billy laughed. 'If only, Mistress!' said he. 'An old aunt in a black cloak and a wide-brimmed hat?'

'You don't mean...?'

'Yes indeed, Mistress. The Nightwalker has been seen around his cottage of late – just faint glimpses now and then, but enough to leave the locals in no doubt.'

'Oh, my goodness! This could be very serious if it is true. Perhaps the creature, having been frightened away from the Plas, and then the Parrog, and lately Cwmgloyn, has realized that Joseph is on its trail and has decided to terrorize him instead. Perhaps it is challenging Joseph or taunting him. I fear that there will be a mighty conflict between them, and between the forces of good and evil–'

'Excuse me, Mistress,' interrupted Billy. 'The goings-on appear to be a good deal cosier than that, if I may say so. Bessie has heard say that the monster is actually living in Joseph's cottage. Is that not correct, Bessie?'

'Indeed it is,' said Bessie. 'My cousin Dolly, who lives in Dinas, says that Master Harries is refusing to allow any visits to his cottage just now. Normally he holds open house, and poor suffering people are welcome to visit him at any time of day or night. And Dolly says that she has infallible information that it is the Nightwalker who is there, and that the creature is indeed the Devil.'

Billy and the other servants round the table all nodded and murmured in agreement, and it became clear to me that I was the only one involved in the conversation who was not in possession of this infallible information. So, with an expression of incredulity, I asked for it.

Shemi was the one who volunteered the facts of the matter. 'I found out about this soon after Bessie did, from a fellow from Dinas who was in the Black Lion the other evening. He said, and swore on the Bible that it was true, that two fellows from the village crept up to the cottage as part of a wager, to find out the truth. It was on that night when we had horrid weather, with pouring rain and a strong wind off the sea. Soaking wet they got, but they thought there was less chance of being spotted by the Wizard. They got there safely and peeped in through the window. And there they saw the most terrible thing. Joseph Harries, kneeling in front of the Devil himself!

The Devil was clad all in black, and they saw his face – so horrible, it was, that they could not find words to describe it. And they ran! Like mad things, so scared that they dared not look back or stop for a second. They was in such a panic when they got back to the village that they was shaking all over. Three stiff whiskies they needed to calm them down, and they do say that the fellows are even now nearly out of their minds, suffering from nightmares and palpitations and the like.'

'Well, Mistress,' said Bessie. 'What do you make of that?'

I sat there white-faced, not knowing quite what to think. Was this all hearsay and rumour, or was the story accurately reported? This was the first time, after sightings galore, that anybody had obtained a glimpse of the creature's face – and it was assumed immediately to be the face of the Devil!

'I cannot make head nor tail of it,' I said at last. 'I would be foolish to deny what those fellows from Dinas are reported as having seen. There are for sure more things in Heaven and Earth and Hell than we may be aware of. The only way of resolving the matter is to confront Joseph directly, face to face. I will do so tomorrow.'

And I will. Billy wants to come with me to protect me from a potentially very dangerous encounter, but I shall go alone. I plan to walk over the mountain and arrive at Werndew quite unannounced. I will not be deceived by Joseph. I have shared all my secrets (or, at least, most of them) with him, and I count him as my oldest and dearest male friend. But as I have been honest with him, I expect honesty in return.

26 September 1807

It saddens me to record this in my little book, but I have had a most unpleasant encounter with Joseph. I walked over to Werndew in mid-morning, with a fresh wind in my face and a few squally showers from the west to dampen my spirits. As I walked, I felt apprehensive, for I knew not what I was walking into. I began to regret my failure to accept Billy's offer of company, and in my mind's eye I saw devils, ghosts, demons and goblins swirling about me, whereas in reality I suppose I was looking at nothing more threatening than wisps of low cloud.

I arrived at Werndew with my heart beating wildly, which distressed me because Joseph's cottage has always before been a haven of calm in my sea of troubles. I brushed aside the late flowering roses over the doorframe, and knocked on the door. Joseph was clearly inside, for I heard a good deal of shuffling about and moving of furniture. But was he alone? If he was not, I thought, I would soon enough find out, for he has no back door, and there are only two rooms inside, which are easily examined. And the windows are so small that the Devil himself could not climb out through them. They also have fixed glass, so even a mouse would have to smash a pane to get in or out. I could smell smoke from the fire, but could I also smell sulphur?

'Oh, Martha, it's you!' said Joseph, poking his head round the door in a way that I had never observed before. He was hiding something, and he did not want me to come inside.

'Good day, Joseph. Are you going to let me in? It is wet and miserable out here on the doorstep.'

'Very well, Martha. Just wait a moment while I get the door open.' There was no warmth in his voice. He moved away a heavy chest so that the door would open properly, and let me in.

The scene which confronted me was intriguing, to say the least. He had had company, and there were several unwashed plates, bowls and mugs on the table together with used knives and forks and some crusts of bread and other food remains. Joseph was not the most fastidious person in the world when it came to keeping his house in order, but the place was a good deal more chaotic than usual. Also on the table was his big book – always referred to by the locals as his 'Magic Book' – and assorted pots and jars, piles of chopped herbs, and a large pestle and mortar. There were some strange scents that I did not recognize, and a smell of sulphur.

'Joseph!' said I, in my most maternal voice. 'This place becomes more of a pigsty every time I visit. You must get yourself a wife! And I suppose your back room is just as bad?' Before he could stop me I opened the door to his bedroom and looked inside. There was nobody there, but the bed was unmade, and there were blankets and clothes scattered everywhere.

'So, Martha,' he said, without smiling, 'having satisfied yourself that the place is a filthy mess, and that I have had company, I suppose you want me to confirm certain rumours which you have picked up on?'

'Correct, Joseph. You are the dearest of my friends, and I want to protect you from rumours, but before I can do that I must know the truth.'

'The truth about what?'

'Come now. You know as well as I, since you have ears everywhere, that you are reputed to have the Devil in residence just now. It is also said that he wears a black cloak and a wide-brimmed black hat.'

'You should not believe everything you hear, Martha.'

'Nor do I, Joseph. I try to disbelieve as much as possible, as you have taught me. It is my ambition to be a good pupil. But will you deny the rumours?'

'I will certainly deny that the Devil has been in residence at Werndew.'

'Well, that is a start. But what about the Night-walker? Has the creature been here?'

'That is something I am not at liberty to divulge,' said Joseph, with a flush upon his cheeks, 'for reasons that will become clearer in the fullness of time.'

'Really, Joseph! It is a sad thing when two old friends cannot be honest with each other.'

'Honesty in a friendship works both ways, Martha. Will you tell me, with your hand on your heart, that you have never had any secrets from me?'

'That is unfair of you, Joseph. You know that there are some things that are so close to my heart, or so terrifying to recall, that I have never shared them with anybody – not even David.'

'And have I ever pressed you to reveal them to me?' said he, with a perfectly level voice.

'No, Joseph. You have always respected my wishes when it comes to private matters, and I thank you for it.'

'We all have things that we choose to keep to ourselves. Please, my dear Martha, trust me when I say that I do not wish to discuss the matter of my recent visitor with anybody. Not even with a dear friend like yourself.'

Now, to my eternal shame, I found his cool rationality quite unbearable, and I could not bear the thought of his keeping a secret from me which was so clearly related to my own well-being. Raising my voice, and I suppose getting very red in the face, I said; 'Joseph, you are quite insufferable! Do you not realize that we are talking here about the Nightwalker, a cruel and menacing creature who has made my life a misery for the greater part of a year? I have the right to know what is going on!'

Joseph made me more irate still by remaining quite cool and collected. 'Let me be the judge of that, Martha,' he said quietly. 'I have rights too, including the right to silence when it may be appropriate. You may take it from me that I have never, since the day we met, done anything to harm you, nor would I allow any other to do so. Please trust me as a friend.'

'Friend! A fine friend indeed is a man who hides in his house some vile creature who has spread nothing but misery at the Plas, and at Llannerch, and on the Parrog, and even at Cwm-gloyn. I cannot stand this ridiculous conversation

426

for a moment longer!' And I swept up my bonnet from the table, lifted my skirts, and stamped out through the door, remembering to slam it behind me.

I stopped fifteen yards up the lane, expecting Joseph to open the door and call me back, but he did not, and that made me even angrier. I was in a fury all the way home, going over our conversation and trying to make sense of it. How dared he! How dared the wretched fellow withhold essential information from me which might help not only those of us who live at the Plas but others as well? Did he not realize that this creature has brought utter misery to me and my family, to Jake and Patty, to Meredith and Jane Lloyd, and probably to a multitude of others as well, unknown to me? Had the Nightwalker not caused one disaster after another? Had he – or it – not been responsible for the disappearance, and probably the death, of my beloved Owain? The detestable creature lurked with ominous intent in the shadows, pointing the bloody finger of fate, orchestrating and influencing the behaviour of others.

Ninety minutes later I stormed in through the kitchen door of the Plas, to find that dinner was over and done with, which made my mood even blacker. The only person there was Mrs Owen. 'Well well,' said she, looking up from her dish-washing operations. 'Very sorry we are, Mistress, but we have eaten dinner already. The children were hungry, and with you being so late, we imagined that you might be taking a bite to eat with Master Harries.'

'He did not invite me, and even if he had, I

would not have accepted.'

'Oh, sorry to hear it, I am,' said she, in that insolent way of hers. 'Do not fear, Mistress, for we have some cold potatoes and meats left. That should suffice.'

I went noisily up the stairs and into my room, slamming the door. I spent the rest of the day in a state of high dudgeon, and I never did eat any dinner.

27 September 1807

I have spent the day irritated with the world and with myself. As usual, the person who helped me to come back to some sort of accord with the rest of the household was my beloved Bessie.

I admit to being somewhat morose at breakfast, for I had not slept well. Sian read the signs and reckoned that the children would be better off out of my way, and since it was a mellow damp morning with a hazy sun she took them off hunting for mushrooms. Bessie said that my long walk in the rain yesterday had not done my hair any good, and so she insisted on giving it a wash. As she dried it, she said: 'I hope you are not going to make a habit of missing your meals, Mistress. You need to keep your strength up, since you will have to look after young Brynach all by yourself quite soon.'

'I know, Bessie. I was in a very bad mood yesterday when I came back from Werndew. And I thought Mrs Owen very insolent as well, so I decided that she could give her cold potatoes and meat to the pigs instead.' As soon as I had said that I realized how absurd it sounded. To Bessie it must have sounded like something straight from the mouth of a petulant little girl, and she could not resist a snigger behind my back. At last I had to laugh too, and said: 'Oh, very well, Bessie. I know that sounded silly. And I know Mrs Owen did put a plate of good things out for me, and I should indeed have thanked her for it. I will apologize to her as soon as my hair is done.'

Bessie carried on with her towelling, and then said: 'Difficult time with Master Harries yesterday, Mistress?'

'Yes, Bessie. As you know, I had to find out about this Nightwalker business—'

'You mean you chose to find out about it, Mistress. Other people might not have bothered, or have assumed that it was none of their business.'

'It was self-evident that it was my business.'

'Was it? Surely the creature has not visited you for a good while, so far as I am aware. He seems to have gone off and bothered other people instead. Surely it is now their business rather than yours?'

'But I have to get to the bottom of it, Bessie, on their behalf.'

'Is that not just a little presumptuous of you, Mistress? Do these people want you to be rushing about like an avenging angel in pursuit of the Devil?'

'I have not actually asked them, but I am sure that they would be grateful to me if I could send the creature packing.'

Bessie said not another word on the subject, and as she brushed my hair and put it up she talked of the weather and the apple harvest, and the children. Then she skipped off down the stairs, humming a merry tune, and left me to stew in my own juice. Of course I was furious with her, but I became more and more angry with myself. I went downstairs and apologized to Mrs Owen for my attack of bad manners yesterday, and gave her as warm an embrace as her large bosom would allow. Then I sat at the open window in my dressing room and looked out at the world – the calm and beautiful world of the early autumn, with leaves starting to turn colour, and the white light of summer moving gradually towards red. I realized that I had been forgetting to look for beauty, and had become obsessed with looking for ugliness and evil. Was it really my business to hunt for the Nightwalker? Had he really done me harm? In truth my only close contact with him had resulted in a gift of a bunch of daffodils!

Suddenly I realized that if I could just let him be, he would probably disappear out of my life for ever. Still a mystery, to be sure, but only one of many, and the appearance of baby Brynach, the secrecy surrounding Susanna Warlow, Owain's tragic disappearance, and the puzzle of Elen's sadness are all surely of much greater import. People of goodwill must surely learn to live with mysteries, and resist the temptation to try to solve all of them. I fear that I am an incorrigible busybody, and that I have more learning to do than most.

On thinking about it, I concluded that my behaviour yesterday towards Joseph had been utterly reprehensible. Why should I have pressed him as I did? He had behaved exactly as a gentleman should. Why had I not accepted his assurance, as a friend above all friends, that he would never do me harm or allow any other person or creature to harm me? I have been going about in a daze, suspecting almost everybody of conspiring against me and failing to trust even those who love me.

I will now close my book for the evening, and write Joseph a letter of abject apology. It will be a difficult task. I hope that he will accept it with a gracious heart, for I have lost too many good men already in my life, and I have no wish to lose another.

For Better, For Worse

7 April 1808

Winter has come and gone, and in the realization that I have neglected my little book for six months or more, I am moved to settle down and write again. In reading through my last entry I am reminded of my arrogant and intemperate behaviour towards Joseph during the confrontation at Werndew, and I am happy to report that when he received my apology my dear friend immediately jumped onto his white pony and invited himself to tea and cakes at the Plas. I would happily have paid him whatever peace offering he might have required, but he is a man of modest tastes. And so we resumed our easy and loving friendship as if nothing had happened. He did not volunteer any information about the Nightwalker or the Devil, and I did not press him.

Speaking of such things, we have had no sightings of the Nightwalker over the whole of the winter season, and we have heard no reports of sightings anywhere else. Perhaps the creature really has taken fright and fled to some new territory, or perhaps he has simply retreated back into the world of spirits. I pray that we will never meet again.

Today has been one of those curious days. This morning Grandpa Isaac, Grandma Jane and myself walked down to Cilgwyn church to visit the family enclosure where David and other members of his family are buried. We do it every year on the seventh day of April, on the anniversary of the 1794 fire in which David's parents died, as did their three small children Thomas, George and Rose. Five members of one family perished in one appalling tragedy; but only I know that they died not because of the smoke and flames, but at the hand of the insane murderer Moses Lloyd. I will never tell anybody the facts of the matter – not even Joseph Harries. So we placed daffodils and other spring flowers on the lid of the tomb and stayed there for a while, praying and holding hands. Then we walked home through the spring lanes with the sun on our backs, reminiscing about the good times and trying to forget the misfortunes.

Then, because this is Saint Brynach's Day and little Brynach's first birthday, we had a small celebration. It was rather sedate, for small babies tend to be frightened by too much noise and frivolity, but I declare that he enjoyed being the centre of attention and receiving little gifts from all and sundry. Liza, her husband Tomos and her little boy Twm were Brynach's special guests. Mother and baby left here about a month ago to return to the cottage at Pantry, but I invited the three of them to the Plas for afternoon tea, and it was delightful to see them again. When Liza went, we were truly sad to see her go, for she had proved a wonderful wet nurse – clean and competent, and utterly patient and calm with two little boys fighting for her attention and her milk supply. She wept when she left, for truly she had grown very fond of Brynach, as he had of her. And she liked it at the Plas, with a warm dry room to herself, good food in abundance, and tidy clothes which she would never have been able to afford herself. I think that she has put on at least a stone in weight since she arrived, and she looks a good deal better for it. She comes up to the Plas frequently, and I have promised that I will consider her for a position when Twm is a little bigger and more independent. But for the time being she has to settle back into a life of relative squalor and poverty, surviving as best she can on the few pennies which Tomos brings back in exchange for his labour at assorted farms including Llystyn and Brithdir. There is a huge contrast between what she has experienced here and what she has now returned to, but I will forget neither her nor her family.

As for the celebration, the four older children enjoyed it the most, as I knew they would. With

Twm crawling around the parlour at high speed and Brynach toddling somewhat precariously, the three girls were thoroughly attentive, rolling balls for them, putting up and knocking down skittles, and encouraging the babies to take an interest in various soft cuddly toys including a beautiful fluffy lamb made out of a sheepskin by Shemi for Brynach. Dewi, who is now five, cannot wait for Brynach to be big enough to join him in boyish games. As far as he is concerned, the family is dominated by females, and that is a terrible thing. My golden boy is less chubby-cheeked than he was, but he still has his mop of golden curls, and in the years to come he and Brynach will make an interesting pair, one blond and frivolous, and the other dark and moody. That is my prediction – I wonder whether it will come to pass?

On a more serious note, it is now almost a year since Owain disappeared. Throughout the autumn and winter Skiff and his friends, and assorted local fishermen from Parrog and the Cwm, have kept a careful watch on the coast for debris or anything else that might provide a link to Owain, but to no avail. Twice we have been alerted by reports of bodies washed ashore, but on checking one of them was identified as a lost fisherman from Fishguard and the other was a young fellow from St Dogmael's, swept overboard from a merchant vessel around New Year.

On a number of occasions over the winter, with the Nightwalker business out of the way, I have asked Joseph whether he has made progress on the matter of the murder – or attempted murder – of my dear missing man. He says that he has tried, but is frustrated by the fact that the information he now needs is locked inside the heads of three men, namely Squire Price, Freddy Cobb and Maldwyn Biggs. He asked me last month whether he should proceed to place curses on the two thugs who undertook the carpentry work on Owain's boat, and assured me that that would certainly loosen their tongues, but I was not ready for such drastic measures since my head was full of children's birthday parties at the time. I asked Joseph to give me time to reflect. And when I did, and opened myself to my intuition, I had a strong feeling that things would resolve themselves without pressure from either me or Joseph. I knew that justice would be done, and that all that was needed was time.

When I told Joseph this the other day, he laughed and said: 'Excellent, Martha! Of course I will respect your female intuition in the matter. It relieves me of a good deal of bother as well. If truth be told, I am tired just now because of other things requiring my attention, and as I get older I find that my enthusiasm sometimes races far ahead of my energy resources. Like you, I must learn to think more and rush about less.'

'Do you mind, Master Harries?' I said with ferocity in my voice but a twinkle in my eye. 'I will have you know that I am just entering the prime of life. Rushing about suits me very well indeed. You are not that ancient yourself. The only reason why you run out of energy now and again, if I may say so, is that you do not eat enough or sleep enough. What you need, Joseph, as I repeatedly tell you, is a tidy wife. I assure you that you would be instantly transformed.'

'Nobody will have me, Martha, for I am too set in my sordid bachelor ways.'

'Well then, make a love potion and slip it into some sweet lady's drink when she is not looking. That should do the trick.'

Joseph grinned and shook his head. 'Not allowed by the rules in my Big Book,' he said. 'But then again, I suppose, if the urgency should be great enough, and if the lady should be sweet enough, rules can always be broken...'

And before he could finish, little Dewi, my golden-haired hero, came bounding in and insisted that Joseph should run into the garden with him in order to examine, with the greatest possible urgency, his collection of interesting pebbles.

10 April 1808

Daisy has had her seventh birthday today, reminding me how badly organized my children's dates of birth are. Betsi and Sara have birthdays only three days apart in March, and Daisy and Brynach only three days apart in April. I dare say that when I am old and grey, these approximate coincidences will help me to remember dates so as to avoid embarrassment. At any rate, we had a lovely time, in spite of the fact that it was pouring with rain, resulting in our eating the birthday tea and playing silly games indoors. Daisy had invited five of her special friends from neighbouring farms – little ladies, all of them, far more interested in clothes and bonnets than I was at that age. Such is the modern world. Daisy wanted yet another dress as a present from me, which means that she now has two winter dresses and two summer dresses in her wardrobe. She is growing so quickly just now that she will have grown out of them in a few months' time, but I am not too concerned since Sara is coming along behind, and the money spent on Daisy will certainly not be wasted.

I was relieved, when the time came for the visiting little girls to go home, that everything had passed peacefully. Dewi has developed a distinct liking for provoking Daisy through word and deed, and he has realized that she is much less phlegmatic than Betsi and Sara. He knows just how to precipitate a tantrum or a session of weeping and wailing from his over-sensitive sister, and occasionally the two of them come to blows. When that happens Dewi usually comes off worst, since Daisy is still the bigger and stronger of the two, but it will not be long before Dewi holds the upper hand, for he too is growing fast and he has a boy's strength and stubbornness. This is not to say that the children have a miserable time of it. Far from it. When trouble does occur Betsi usually sorts things out. She is ten years old now, and loves her role as big sister. She consoles the little ones when they are hurt or sad, and has all the qualities of a peacemaker. I am ashamed to say that she also acts as a 'little mother' at times, dealing with situations that should actually fall to me. I have had to plead guilty to the charge of neglect at times, especially in the spring of last year, when I was so preoccupied with the disappearance of Owain and the appearance of Brynach that I was a very bad mother indeed. Since my confrontation with Grandma and Bessie on that occasion I have tried to give my little angels the attention they deserve – and they, and I, are happier because of it.

Over the past winter I have made a considerable effort to concentrate on family and estate matters, having left far too much of the former to Sian and far too much of the latter to Grandpa Isaac. He is the sort of man who quietly gets on with things, and he has been here for so long that he makes instinctive decisions on ploughing and harrowing, sowing and harvesting all the time without realizing that they are decisions. I have a profound admiration for the way in which he organizes Billy, Shemi and Will. But he is certainly beginning to creak at the joints, and his memory is not as good as it was. He will soon be seventy years old, and he deserves more time with his newspaper in front of the fire, and with his old confederates in the back room of the Royal Oak. So I have put more time into decisions myself, always making sure that I listen first to his considered advice.

As for Sian, she and Shemi have obviously not discovered anything too disagreeable about each other over the winter. They have not bundled every week, because ailments and other things have intervened, and over Christmas, New Year and *Hen Galan* there was so much going on in the house that Bessie could not evacuate her place in the room she shared with Sian. But when Liza and her baby moved out in March Bessie got her own room back, making both her and Sian very happy. But I will not have bundling more than once a week, for I would then have two servants permanently incapable of doing a decent day's work. The happy couple have set a date for their wedding, in June, and they have already spoken to Rector Devonald about it. This pleases me, for it allows me to solve several problems at once.

The first problem is that Sian has reached the limit of what she can teach the children. She is intelligent, and she can read and write, but her own education was limited, and she plays neither piano nor harp. It has been clear to me for some time that Betsi and Daisy need to be challenged to a greater extent than Sian can manage. So they need a tutor, and I am minded to employ young Lisbeth Prosser from Frongoch whenever it may be convenient. She has been to meet the children already, and they all found it agreeable. I like her, for she is very cultured, and is a clever pianist. She is quite strict enough to deal with both Daisy and Dewi. She will have no trouble at all with Betsi, who is mature beyond her years, or with little Sara, who is only three, but intelligent enough to educate herself if I was minded to turn the nursery into a library. Sian is happy to move on, for she is already broody, and wants nothing more than to start her own family. One of the labourers' cottages near Gelli has fallen vacant following the death of old Mistress Johns, and I will give that cottage to Sian and Shemi as soon as they are married. Shemi will continue to work at the Plas, and I will give Sian the job of dairy-maid, for three days a week. Lisbeth will occupy Sian's room at the Plas, and when Shemi moves out I will give Billy a room of his own. It will all work out for the best.

I am also starting to make plans, inside my head, to cover for the ageing of Grandma Jane and Mrs Owen. These two good women are slowing down mentally and physically, and they are no longer able to contribute to the running of the household and the estate as they were ten years ago. In any case, they give far more unpaid labour than I have any right to expect. I will soon need more hands to do the work which they currently do without any complaint. And I am worried about Mrs Owen, for her moods are more changeable than they were, and she has suffered from a variety of ailments over the winter. She is still not sixty years old, but when the time is right I will encourage her to enjoy her old age in peace. I will find a cottage for her if she does not wish to move in with one of her grown-up children. Bessie is wonderfully competent in all manner of things, and I may well promote her to the position of housekeeper. I will sorely miss her as my personal maid, but she will after all still be beneath the same roof, and she will no doubt still feel empowered to admonish and advise me when necessary. Then I will employ Liza as my housemaid, if she can avoid becoming pregnant again, and if she is happy to walk between her cottage and the Plas every day.

Plans, plans and more plans. There is much to be said for planning things, but I am only too aware that plans need to be accompanied by prayers. Things seem to happen in my life, with fateful regularity, which push plans into the background and cause me to devote all of my energy to the simple matter of survival.

440

11 April 1808

I realized, quite suddenly, when I woke up this morning, that I had not been to my cave for a very long time. And I felt guilty about it. That was quite absurd, of course, since a cave is nothing more than a hole in a mountain; but then I conjectured that this was not just any cave, but the sanctuary where Saint Brynach had found peace and communed with his angels, and the place where I had fought many of my demons. As I thought further on the matter, I realized that my feeling of guilt might well have related to the fact that all my visits in the past have been at times of crisis. Would it not be the action of a mature and sensible woman to visit her cave at a time of peace, perhaps as old Brynach had done? A visit would mark it not just as a sanctuary, but as a cathedral where I could celebrate love, and talk to my angels, and forget for a while about fighting my demons. Joseph, I thought, would approve, but of course I will never tell him, since the existence of the cave is one of my few secrets that he is not privy to.

And so, for no particular reason, I told everybody at breakfast that I was minded to take a nice walk on the mountain, all by myself. The children were furious with me, and all wanted to come, but I would have none of it, and Grandma Jane intervened by saying, 'Come now, children. Your mother is with you all the time, as well as being busy with the household and the estate. Can she not have a little bit of time to herself, to recover from all the noise and bustle? She will be a much nicer person as a result of it!' And she gave me an angelic smile, to which I responded with a scowl. But then we all laughed, and I was given the permission of the household.

Off I went, with my oldest walking boots on my feet and my most ragged dress covering the fact that I was wearing no stays. I hate them, especially when I am climbing mountains, puffing and panting and perspiring. I used to care about the etiquette of such things, but no longer. I wandered up to Ffynnon Brynach at a leisurely pace, anointed myself and then pressed on, enjoying the freedom and the wide sky and the cool crisp air of the April morning. It was going to be hot, I thought, and indeed so it turned out. I wandered northwards, then westwards, then northwards again, following one sheep track after another and gaining altitude all the time. I sat down frequently on convenient boulders, turning my back on the mountain and letting my eyes wander across the *cwm* to the crags of Carnedd Meibion Owen and the far, hazy summits of Mynydd Presely. One day, I thought, when I have time, I will walk that mountain and test whether its serenity is superior to that of Carningli. I doubted it, for there is no place on this planet which is as beautiful and has such a capacity to calm and heal the troubled soul. A cuckoo called in Gelli Wood. The first of the year, I thought, and early too.

I had no wish for other eyes to follow me as I approached the cave, so I climbed over the eastern summit, and down the other side, and then up again from the north. There was just a gentle breeze, and only a few fluffy clouds drifting in from the west, making lazy shadows on the sea surface. When I saw the sea, and the wide blue horizon, I thought of Owain, but I was determined not to dwell on my miseries or my mysteries, and I turned my thoughts to other things which brought me joy. I thought of my children, and my new baby Brynach, and my times of bliss with David and Owain. I thought of my female friends – including Mary Jane, Ellie and Patty – who had given me companionship and support at times of crisis. I thought of my own family and David's, and of their strengths and foibles and frailties. And I thought of my own dear servants, sometimes cheerful and sometimes sad, and none of them perfect, but perfect servants would probably be insufferably dull. How I loved them all! And in loving them, I realized that I could never have survived my turbulent past without them. And what of the future?

The future, I thought, I would leave till I was inside the cave. And so I did. Five minutes later I abandoned the summit and dropped down between the bluestone crags that I knew so well. The old raven sat on one of his favourite watching places – he has five – and watched me in silence. His mate wheeled overhead, seeing off a buzzard which had strayed into their territory. I squeezed between boulders and discovered a new rock-fall that caused me to go on hands and knees along a part of the grassy passageway leading to the cave entrance. Then I had arrived, pressing between the guardian stones, brushing aside the leafless branches of the rowan tree, and settling into the cool darkness inside. Here, inside the beating heart of the mountain, I was in my cathedral. An orchestra of wind instruments and strings, fern fronds and dry grasses murmured gentle songs of worship, and the light of heaven filtered through the stained glass cracks at the eastern end of the nave. I sat on my mossy bed near the altar, and waited for the choir to sing a benediction.

At first my mind was buzzing, as it does all too often, but then the quietness and sanctity of the place began to penetrate my soul, and a sort of calm washed over me. In my quietness, I thought, in a lazy sort of way, of Joseph's words of wisdom. On more than one occasion he had encouraged me to empty my head and listen to my heart, to analyse less and trust my intuition more. So I did. Time passed.

What did I feel? Apprehension, fear, mistrust, suspicion? None of those, but an overwhelming instinct that all would be well. All would be well, and none would be harmed.

At last, I was dragged from my reverie by the faint sound of the Plas Ingli dinner bell echoing round the *cwm* and bouncing off the bluestone crags of the mountain. I knew it was our bell, because the dinner bells belonging to Penrhiw and Brithdir sound so different.

I thanked the angels of the mountain for their beneficence, and crawled out into the bright, brash daylight. Twenty minutes later I sat down at the dinner table. Sara came and sat on my lap. 'Hello, Mam,' she said. 'I have been drawing angels on my blackboard, with long dresses and big wings. Have you ever seen an angel?'

'Oh yes,' said I, looking very wise. 'I see them all the time.'

25 April 1808

In pursuit of my resolution to abandon misery and live a life which is positive and creative, I have done something which satisfies me a great deal even though it may cause Rector Devonald and the Mayor some concern. For better or for worse, I have held a *twmpath* at the Plas.

I had been thinking of it for some time, as a means of celebrating the end of winter. Easter was late this year, and our usual family celebrations on top of Carningli at dawn on Easter Day had to be abandoned because it was blowing a gale and sheeting with rain. So I thought that a little jollification in compensation for that disappointment might be in order. In addition, as of three days ago, I owed a great deal of thanks to a good many people. I had still not made recompense to the thirty fellows gathered together by Skiff for that mad hunt in wind and rain along ten miles of cliffs for traces of Owain's boat, or even of my man himself, the day after he disappeared. Almost a year had passed, and I was ashamed of my failure to act on my promise of repayment. Then there were others who had helped in various ways to protect my interests, on such matters as the finding of little Brynach, and the assorted alarms and excursions involving the late and unlamented Nightwalker. Yes, a celebration was in order. Besides, the barley threshing was done last month and there was plenty of room in the barn, with a wide and smooth threshing floor just perfect for dancing...

It is a strange thing that when most of the circumstances are right for something to happen, serendipity takes over and other things fall into place. So it was that on the day after Easter Monday, I went down to town and became involved in a little awkwardness. There, on the street near Master Price's shop, was a group of Irish musicians fiddling and banging and tootling away on their instruments with such gusto that I found myself almost skipping and dancing down the street instead of walking sedately as a fine lady should. Other people were similarly entranced, and there were happy smiles on many faces. I put a few pennies into the hat that was on the ground, as did other people, and enjoyed their music for ten minutes or so. Then who should come along but Constable Wilson, looking very weary and embarrassed, holding a piece of paper in his hand. He went up to the leader of the players, forced all of them to stop in mid-jig, and announced dolefully that they were breaking the law. He said that his letter was a complaint from 'various respectable persons of this town' on the grounds that the Irish were obstructing the public highway, begging and being a public nuisance. Besides, he said, it was obvious that they were vagrants, and that it was his duty to move them on to the next parish. He said that if they did not immediately go, he would obtain a warrant for their arrest and take them into custody. I did not fancy the Constable's chances in that particular enterprise, since the leader of the musicians was a good twelve inches taller than him, and built like a champion shire horse. The others looked as if they were well used to taking care of themselves too.

The crowd started to jeer and hurl abuse at Master Wilson, for in truth people do not get a great deal of light entertainment in Newport, and I suddenly felt that they were looking to me to sort the situation out. So without thinking I stepped up to the unhappy man, took the sheet of paper from his hand, and tore it up into small pieces. The crowd cheered, and the Irish musicians grinned. 'That is what I think of your complaint, Constable,' said I. 'It is utterly unfounded. Are these people causing an obstruction?'

'No! No!' shouted the crowd.

'And are they a public nuisance?'

'Not at all!' shouted the crowd, which grew bigger by the minute.

'And as for begging, it seems to me that they are earning a more honest living than many whom I could mention in this town. Those who put pennies into the hat on the ground are simply rewarding musical skill. Would we not all agree?'

'Yes! Yes!' everyone shouted.

'And they are certainly not vagrants, rogues or vagabonds, for they are here at my invitation, to play at a *twmpath* at the Plas. So I will be pleased, Master Wilson, if you will simply leave them in peace.' The musicians were surprised by this statement, as indeed I was myself. Everybody

447

was happy. Master Wilson had no wish to deal with the Irish anyway, and went away with a smile on his face. The crowd was happy, since the musicians carried on playing, and I was happy since I went away with a promise from them that they would turn up at the Plas on Friday and entertain us in exchange for a pound, a good meal and unlimited ale.

The *twmpath* has come and gone, and a splendid affair it was too. I invited Skiff and all his friends, and they brought with them quite a few of the girls from Newport and the Parrog. The Plas Ingli servants invited various relatives, whom we see far too seldom, and then there were the tenant farmers and labourers and their families from the estate, and many of those who help out with our hay and corn harvests and other matters. Joseph came, sporting a tall wide-brimmed black hat and a yellow waistcoat and blue breeches, and when I told him how disgusting he looked he was very pleased. Patty and Jake came with their baby girl, who is now two months old.

At the beginning of the evening, I announced some ground rules, and Grandpa Isaac and Billy helped me to enforce them. The first was that there should be no unprotected candles or rush-lights in the barn, but only candle lanterns. The second rule was that there would be no food (we were almost eaten down to the bare wood of the pantry shelves over the Christmas and New Year season) except for a good dinner for the musicians. The third rule was that we would only provide two barrels of ale, but that others were welcome to bring their own ankers and flagons if they wished. And the last rule was that there should be no fighting or fornication, since there were quite a few children present. The word was put about, and indeed I was thoroughly delighted that those present tried hard to respect my wishes.

And so we sang and danced. The Irish musicians were rough fellows, and they had no knowledge of Welsh and not much of English, but they truly had magic in their fingers and in their lungs. The children danced with the adults, weaving long patterns, ducking and bobbing, hopping and skipping and tripping over themselves and getting under other people's feet. They screamed and giggled, and had a wonderful time. Even Mrs Owen and Grandma Jane danced, the latter with such nimble footwork that I was lost in admiration. I asked her how she had acquired such skill. 'Ah,' she sighed, with a dreamy look on her face. 'When I was a young lass we danced often, and we learnt twenty or more of the old Welsh country dances. We learnt a good deal about life too, at one *twmpath* after another. And then I became respectable, and had to move among the gentry, and they danced these silly dances with delicate steps and subtle gestures and virtually no contact between man and woman. Very frustrating!' And Grandpa reminded us that he used to know the steps of a good many dances too, Irish and Welsh, before the Nonconformists started on their self-ordained task of making Wales miserable.

When, at about ten of the clock, the children were almost asleep on their feet, I escorted them across the yard and got them all safely tucked up in bed. Indeed, Sara did not even have the energy left to climb the stairs, so I carried her up and undressed her, and before she was even settled between the sheets she was already fast asleep. Grandpa and Grandma were overcome with tiredness at about the same time, and they agreed to stay in the house with the little ones. The rest of us kept going for as long as our legs would carry us. Other guests wandered off home with their families around midnight. I stayed up until about two of the clock, and then said goodnight to everybody who was capable of listening, and took my leave. As I drifted off to sleep, contented and exhausted, the sound of fiddles and drums and tin whistles drifted across the yard.

We all woke late. I felt somewhat the worse for wear, since I do not normally drink large quantities of rough ale, but I went to the window overlooking the yard and checked that the barn still stood. Indeed it did, much to my relief. As I looked out on the world, assorted persons – male and female – emerged into the daylight, decorated with bits of straw, and staggered off down the lane towards Newport. The musicians, who had required more ale than everybody else to fuel their energetic thumping and puffing and fiddling, slept until noon in the hay at the far end of the barn. Then they went on their way, a pound better off, in the general direction of Brynberian. I am not sure that that was where they wished to go, but the destination was immaterial. From my point of view, the event was a great success, with a good many debts repaid in appropriate fashion. So far as I can gather, there were no altercations, and no injuries. On the matter of fornication, I am less certain.

30 April 1808

According to the news from town, the Plas Ingli *twmpath* is being talked about as one of the jolliest occasions for many a year. I have greatly increased the number of people to whom I can refer as friends among the poorer classes, even though there are many in town who do not approve at all of such contacts between gentry and labourers. News has reached my ears that Rector Devonald is already grumbling about my connivance in debauchery and fornication, and apparently Squire Price of Llanychaer was yesterday so disgusted when he heard that the Morgans of Plas Ingli (including the children, God bless my soul!) had been dancing Irish jigs in the company of Skiff Abraham and other disreputable characters that he required a couple of stiff whiskies to calm him down.

But I have by no means abandoned my social contacts with the gentry families of the area. I have been out and about to a considerable extent of late, to musical evenings at Puncheston and Castlebythe, to a ladies' artistic afternoon at Glynymel in the company of Mistress Anne Fenton and others, and to three tea parties in Newport. My harp has been well used. Though thoughts of Owain are never far from my mind, life must continue and I must maintain and even extend my circle of friends. I am flattered that a number of gentlemen, some of them very silly fellows indeed, are showing more than a little interest in me; but I have told myself that I will never fall in love again, and if any should ask me I will tell them as much. But if they wish to pay court to me, I will not discourage them, for some innocent entertainment is to be had from playing off one gentleman against another. I have not been jolly enough in the past. The role of Merry Widow appeals to me, and I will seek to combine it with the role of Perfect Mother, if the two are not entirely incompatible.

The biggest social event of the year thus far was the wedding of my friend Ellie Bowen of Llwyngwair with Walter Phillips of Ambleston Hall. It took place just three days since, with the wedding itself in St Mary's church in Newport and the other celebrations (which were considerable) held at Llwyngwair itself. There was an additional wedding ceremony in the church chapel in Newport, which is used by the Methodists and within which the Bowen family participates not only in Sunday worship but also in week-night prayer meetings. They are a devout family indeed, and I wish I could match their discipline and holiness. Because of the attention which Squire John Bowen and his wife pay to the principles of moderation and self-control, there was little in the way of alcoholic refreshment at the wedding breakfast, but in all other respects the affair was very grand indeed. The Bowen family is one of the greatest gentry families in the county, and so all of the big families had to be invited, including the Phillipses of Picton Castle, the Owens of Orielton, and the Vaughans of Jordanston. Many of them came, and that caused a good deal of bother in matters of precedence both in the church and at the feast. As a minor player in the great game of social climbing, I watched with interest and amusement, and spent most of my time on the outside looking in.

The biggest guests of all were the Cawdors of Stackpole, and when they arrived at Llwyngwair prior to the church procession the amount of bowing and scraping was wondrous to behold. Lord Cawdor and his lady wife climbed down from the selfsame coach which he had placed at my disposal some years since, following my false imprisonment and release from Haverfordwest gaol. I doubted whether he would recognize me as the widow of Master David Morgan of Plas Ingli, the man who had saved him and his army from the French invader in 1797, but indeed he did. During the ball following the wedding he spotted me across the room, and walked over to greet me. I got up from my chair and curtsied, and he gave a deep and elegant bow. 'Mistress Morgan!' said he, in that boyish voice of his. 'What a pleasure to see you again! I trust that you and your family are well?'

'Yes, thank you, sir. The little ones are thriving, but I am not sure that you know about my husband...?'

'Of course I know. A very bad business indeed. I followed events with great interest, and was appalled. But I was gratified to see that through your own efforts, and through the skills of the Wizard of Werndew, you brought those responsible to justice, and that they paid the ultimate price. You are managing the estate in a satisfactory fashion?'

'To the best of my ability, sir. And we have been spared from some of the financial disasters that have afflicted some of the good families in our neighbourhood.'

'Excellent. Excellent. I have heard many compliments about the Plas. A well managed and pleasant little estate, by all accounts. And are you happy, Mistress Martha? You deserve to be, and a beautiful lady such as yourself deserves a good husband.'

At this I blushed, for fine gentlemen do not normally fling out such outrageous compliments when there are a hundred pairs of ears tuned in to their every word. 'I thank you, sir, for your kind words. But I have to admit to being less content than I might have been, for Master Owain Laugharne, to whom I was betrothed, disappeared at sea almost a year ago.'

'Yes, I remember hearing news of that. Another very bad business indeed. Squire Laugharne's boy, from Pontfaen, and farming Llannerch, was he not?'

'Correct, my lord. You say "was", but I prefer to use the present tense, for I retain the hope that he may still be alive.'

'Quite so. I apologize – the remark was insensitive. Keep up hope, Mistress Martha, and be sure to let me know if there is any matter on which I might be able to offer assistance in the future. And now, please forgive me, but I must give my attention to our host, who is waiting for me.'

And he kissed my hand, and bowed deeply, and strode away with his entourage in his wake. I had to sit down again, for I was hot and bothered, and quaking at the knees. There is something unutterably magnificent about a fine gentleman, I thought. Maybe it is a matter of confidence, and Lord Cawdor is certainly confident, but there is also a sensibility and a capacity for demonstrating concern for others that can only come from good breeding. He is also most attractive, even though he is past his prime. And his clothes – a perfectly fitted red jacket, well-made blue breeches, and–

'My goodness, Martha, that was an encounter for which most of the ladies here today would have given their right arms!' said Ellie, the beautiful and unblushing bride, suddenly appearing at my side. 'Carefully observed by the cream of the Pembrokeshire gentry, the most powerful gentleman in West Wales has demonstrated that you and he are on very friendly terms, and that he has the greatest respect for you and the Plas. And his offer of assistance – why, it was almost an offer of patronage!'

'Come, come, Ellie. I would not go so far. But his attention was flattering, I have to admit.'

'And with good reason, Martha. You look especially elegant and radiant today. Mark my words – you will not miss a dance this evening, and every eligible bachelor in Pembrokeshire will be instantly head over heels in love with you!'

And off she went, to talk to more of her guests. As she promised, I did not sit out a dance, and by two in the morning my feet were beginning to suffer. I was also losing my voice, for a succession of gentlemen, some of them from very elegant and ancient families, had indeed vied for my attention. I played along, and enjoyed myself enormously, although in retrospect my flirtatious behaviour occasionally strayed very slightly beyond the bounds of what was deemed acceptable.

Then Ellie, Mary Jane and I found ourselves alone in the conservatory, reminding all three of us of an occasion more than ten years ago when we had confided in each other and talked of the murky history of the late Moses Lloyd. Then we had shed tears. This time things were altogether more cheerful, although the absence of Owain cast a shadow over each one of us. We talked of Ellie's new husband Walter, with whom she is obviously very much in love, and she was pleased to inform us that this was by no means a marriage of convenience arranged by ambitious fathers. And we talked of other things, including Mary Jane's little boy William and my five beloved angels. Then the conversation turned to gentlemen, and we laughed at the recollection that on the occasion of our last meeting beneath the palm fronds I had been the chaperone and they had been the eligible and eager young ladies. Now they were both respectable married women and I was the one who was eligible, if not exactly eager.

'Well now,' said Mary Jane. 'There is always young Frederick Campbell of Stackpole, the son and heir of the very grand Lord Cawdor. Since the father obviously has a soft spot for the Mistress of Plas Ingli, something might be arranged.'

'Never!' I laughed. 'He is but a child, and even when he comes of age and needs a wife, the least he will have will be an heiress worth ten thousand a year! In any case, Stackpole Court is by all accounts a dreary place, with not a single mountain in sight. No, unless Owain returns I am determined never to marry again, and to become a dowdy old widow involved in charitable works and embroidery.'

Ellie and Mary Jane both giggled at this. 'I cannot see it, Martha,' said Ellie. 'If anybody needs a man, it is you, and it is our duty as your oldest friends to find one for you. What of the young fellows who pursued you with such enthusiasm after David died?'

'Those who had looks, manners and fortunes have all gone, and those who are still unmarried are not worth talking about.'

'Ah, yes,' sighed Mary Jane. 'We can all speculate on what might have been. If Dafydd had not come along when he did, there was always William Owen from Stone Hall, or young Iestyn Price from Llanychaer...'

'Now there was a gentleman,' said Ellie. 'I had a brief dalliance with him once. Dead now, and with a father from Hell, but you should have met him, Martha.'

'Indeed I did,' I replied, 'more than once, when we were young. He was twenty-three, and I must have been about sixteen. He was very dashing, and danced divinely. A very forward and romantic young man, as I recall. Once, when he had had too much to drink, he swore that one day I would carry his child, for which impudence I slapped his face. Then David came along, and I was bottom over bosom in love, and that was the

457

end of my youthful liaison with Master Price. Later on he went off to join the army, and I never saw him again.'

'And then there is Master Ceredig ap Tomos from New Moat. How many dances did you give him this evening, Martha? Three? Four? No matter. The man is madly in love with you – no doubt about it. He has that look in his eyes of a sheepdog puppy waiting for commands. Give him any orders, Martha, and I know he will follow them to the letter.'

I squealed with horror, for the idea of marrying Master ap Tomos was so preposterous that I had not even thought about it. 'Oh, he is polite enough,' I laughed, 'and knows his dances a great deal better than some of the other gentlemen who have stepped on my feet this evening, but he has little to talk about besides sheep and the management of common lands. I should die of boredom if I were to spend more than half an hour in his company without a break.'

And so we chatted on, and at last it was time to go home and leave Ellie to the tender loving attentions of her new husband. To his credit, he came and more or less dragged her away from her confidantes, with the look of a man impatient for action. He knew, as we did, that on his wedding night a man has to do his duty.

25 June 1808

Today we have had a visit from Madam Bevan's Circulating School, with Master John Jeremy on

458

fine form with his teaching of reading, writing and other essential skills. We did not see him this last winter, because the poor fellow was in bed with a chill on the chest when he should have come. Over sixty pupils were disappointed then, but in the summer he organizes visits at short notice, whenever the weather is too inclement for the harvest. So it happened that yesterday, with pouring rain and the weather experts promising the same for today, Master Jeremy asked if he might use the barn for a teaching session. Of course I agreed, and the word was passed round to all the farms and cottages in Cilgwyn. More than forty people turned up, of all ages from five to eighty, and I gave all of the Plas Ingli servants the opportunity to join in. Even my disreputable friend Skiff turned up, for a wagoner needs more than just basic intelligence if he is to turn himself from an enthusiastic journeyman into a success-ful businessman. After ten years or more of occasional lessons on long winter evenings from Master Jeremy, and from Grandpa, Grandma and myself, all of our servants can now read and write, but I am keen to push them further along the road of knowledge, and they are all showing admirable talents. Shemi has an extraordinary knowledge of, and love for, all wild things, and reads every book he can find on the subject. Indeed, he now teaches Master Jeremy which flower is which, and which little brown bird nests where. Will is becoming a considerable mathe-matical expert, and Bessie adores learning about the history of our island race. As for the little ones, Daisy is beginning to recognize the letters of the alphabet, and Betsi, who tires of reading the Welsh Bible, is starting to speak, read and write English. I am very proud of all of them.

The session in the barn, for four hours in the morning and four hours in the afternoon, was as chaotic as ever. But Master Jeremy is an efficient teacher, and he divided his pupils up into groups according to ability rather than age, and the concentration and commitment of all and sundry was commendable. The special thing about the Circulating School is that all who attend the sessions here, there and everywhere across the parishes of Newport and Nevern are interested in what they are doing, and have to pay for their learning as well. They all turn up with five pennies in their pockets and little bundles of food for their dinner in the middle of the day. Master Jeremy provides the books and the slates and chalk, and I provide other things like pictures, newspapers, bottles and measuring rules. The teaching is done by Master Jeremy himself for the most part, but also by Grandpa Isaac (who is a good teacher, but somewhat lacking in patience), Abraham Jenkins from Brithdir, and myself. Today I loved every minute of it, but I was sad to think that this would be the last time that we would act as host for the Circulating School. The reason is that Madam Bevan's bequest, made in order to set up permanent schools in West Wales, has finally been released by the courts in London after some family dispute, and the money can now be spent. A site for a proper school has been found close to the castle in Newport, and next year, if all goes according to plan, Master Jeremy will have his own classrooms to work in, his own cottage, and over one hundred and fifty pupils to keep him occupied. There will even be facilities for training new teachers. Newport will thus enter the modern and enlightened world of learning after decades of backwardness. One can only rejoice.

But there is something else that gives me no cause at all for rejoicing. Before he left today at the end of the teaching session, Master Jeremy took me to one side and said: 'Mistress Martha, did I not hear something about that creature in black haunting the Plas some months back?'

'Why yes, Master Jeremy. It bothered us for a while, and then moved on to pastures new. We did not advertise its presence very widely, but since then, as you know, it has caused some trouble on the Parrog and at Cwmgloyn. Now the phantom has disappeared. Why do you ask about it?'

'Because, Mistress, it has not disappeared at all. I was in Trecwn giving lessons the other day, and heard the news. The Nightwalker, as they call the monster, has now moved its attentions to Llanychaer, and Squire Price is not amused.'

'Are you quite sure of this?' said I, feeling a wave of apprehension sweeping over me.

'Quite sure,' said the teacher. 'Just you wait and see. There will be developments.'

12 July 1808

Master Jeremy was quite correct. I have not been directly involved in any of the latest developments, but over the last week or so news has filtered through of further sightings of the Nightwalker around Llanychaer. By all accounts the creature has done nothing untoward, but has simply appeared now and again, mostly at dusk, frightening the life out of Mistress Price and her daughter Fanny. Neither of them is in robust health, and God knows what the sightings will have done to their nerves. Squire Price, who appears in normal circumstances to be close to an apoplectic fit, was yesterday, so they say, in a state of great agitation. An agitated squire with a liking for alcohol is a dangerous thing indeed.

So it proved, for this morning three squires rode into the yard. I knew when they came galloping along the driveway that one of them was Squire Price, for his magnificent black stallion can be recognized from a distance of half a mile. It so happens that Joseph was with me at the time, and the two of us were enjoying a peaceful cup of tea in the shade of the garden. We went into the yard to greet them, and they dismounted in a flurry of dust. With Squire Price were Squire Owen of Gelli Fawr and Squire Williams of Langton, a gentleman who very seldom penetrates this far east.

'Good morning, Mistress Martha! Greetings, Master Harries!' said Master Price. 'We come on urgent business, so forgive us for turning up without warning.'

'No forgiveness is needed, gentlemen,' said I, giving them a curtsy. 'You are always welcome. Pray join us in the garden, where it is cool. Billy will take care of the horses, and my housemaid

462

will fetch us some more tea. Just give me a moment.'

I went off to call Billy and to ask Bessie to make some more tea, and then returned to the garden. I found the four men deep in conversation about the Nightwalker. The squires obviously had no wish to exclude Joseph from our discussions, and that intrigued me, for Joseph and Squire Owen are not the best of friends. 'Mistress Martha, we come to seek your help,' said Squire Williams, a slim and elegant man in his late sixties. 'Master Philip and myself have agreed to help Master George to rid himself of a great scourge.'

'Oh, and what might that be?' I asked, knowing perfectly well what was to follow.

'The creature whom they call the Nightwalker,' said Philip Owen. 'Having spread great alarm in the Newport and Nevern area, he has now turned his attentions further west, and is terrorizing the Llanychaer estate. People are in a state of near panic, and we must get rid of him before public order is compromised. You have, I think, some knowledge of the creature?'

'Well, we have had sightings here,' said I with due caution, for I was not sure where this was leading.

Joseph picked up on my apprehension. 'Has the creature done some harm?' he asked. 'If it is harmless, might it not be best to leave well alone? It might then simply go away quietly, as it has elsewhere.'

'He has done no direct harm, it has to be said,' muttered Master Price, 'unless we count the damage done to my wife's nerves. But I am not so much worried about physical matters as about the tendency among the common people to see devils and demons where they may not exist. Look what almost happened on the Parrog, and what did happen to that cottage on the Cwmgloyn estate.'

'We have come to the view that if civil order is to be maintained, the creature must be hunted down,' said Squire Owen. 'Then he will be arrested and brought to justice.'

'And how, sir, will you hunt down a phantom or a demon, if that is what we are dealing with?' asked Joseph.

'It is our considered view,' said Squire Price, 'that the creature is not a denizen of the spirit world, but a man with flesh and blood like you and me.'

'And what has led you to that conclusion?' I asked.

'Our conclusion is based partly on the fact that he flies about from one place to another,' said the Squire. 'It is an established fact that ghosts haunt one place and one place only. Besides, if he had been the Devil he would certainly have done some dire harm by now, or dragged somebody down to the fires of Hell. In our view he is a common criminal or a vagrant, looking for opportunities to do mischief.'

'But you cannot arrest him, sir, without some evidence of a crime,' said I, intrigued by the fact that I was acting in effect as a defending attorney for the creature whom I had sworn to bring to justice.

'That is why we have come, Mistress Morgan,' said Squire Williams. 'We three are justices, and we have the right to issue a warrant for the arrest of a suspected criminal. But we need a complaint or an indictment first, preferably from somebody who has suffered at his hands. We think that you would fit the bill, since we are reliably informed that you have a long history of encounters.'

'But I cannot say, with my hand on my heart, that the creature has done me harm or even threatened harm.'

'But it is common knowledge in town, Mistress Martha, that you have been greatly exercised by the mystery surrounding this dark figure, and have beseeched others for help in being rid of him.'

'That is true. But if the creature is a man, the worst that we can say about him is that maybe he is a vagrant—'

'Precisely! And vagrancy is a crime, and criminals must be arrested! How many times have you seen this particular vagrant?'

I thought for a while, and answered: 'Maybe five or six times. And others have seen him on our estate maybe three or four times.'

'Excellent!' said Squire Price, jumping to his feet. 'And will you repeat that statement in court, if required?'

'Yes, I suppose so, if you do find that the Night-walker is a man, and bring him face to face before the justices.'

'That is all we need,' said Master Williams, also jumping to his feet. 'The creature is clearly an incorrigible rogue. When we catch him we will order a good whipping, and then we will give him two years with hard labour. We will issue an arrest warrant immediately. We will also put out notices increasing the price on the creature's head to fifty pounds. Tomorrow we will raise a posse of at least sixty men, and hunt him down. I can guarantee the involvement of at least two hundred hunting dogs. We will scour every inch of the Llanychaer estate, and every inch of the common. We will find him, you may be assured.'

And so Master Owen leapt to his feet as well. The three gentlemen then bowed, and thanked us for the tea and for our assistance, and called for their horses. Then they galloped off out of the yard, intending like Don Quixote to go tilting at windmills. Joseph and I shrugged our shoulders, and wondered what the consequences of this insane and precipitate action might be.

16 July 1808

For the last three days groups of horsemen have been riding about on the common like wild things, hunting for an invisible enemy. Twenty of them galloped around the mountain, and some even managed to get onto the summit with their horses, but they made so much noise that any fugitive worth his salt would have just huddled down behind a convenient boulder and evaded them without even raising a sweat. By all accounts there were indeed sixty horsemen altogether, each paid a shilling a day with another shilling paid for the use of their horses.

Several of the local squires joined in, and lent their hunting hounds to the cause, and both gentlemen and dogs ran about barking and howling over many square miles of countryside, to no purpose whatsoever. I do not think I want to hear another hunting horn as long as I live.

Another large band of men, numbering at least forty, has worked its way on foot along Cwm Gwaun, scouring the woodlands and searching through every derelict and unoccupied building, interviewing all the peasants and farm workers discovered upon their way, and generally making a fearful amount of noise.

Most of the locals, attracted by the prospect of earning fifty pounds, have been hunting through all the nooks and crannies of Newport, Parrog, Dinas and other places. They have turned up a few vagrants sleeping rough, and encouraged those poor people to move on to the next parish, but otherwise they have found no trace of the Nightwalker or his clothes. I am not surprised, since if the creature is a man, he would surely have heard the pandemonium and walked in the night to some peaceful place like Fishguard or Puncheston.

Now things have returned to normal, and the three squires have succeeded in spending in excess of twenty pounds which might otherwise have been spent on something sensible. They claim that their crusade was a 'resounding success', for while no villain has been apprehended and no clue found as to either the identity or the location of the Nightwalker, they are sure that they have driven him away. They may well be right, and indeed I hope that I never see the creature again. But I have to admit to feeling some guilt about my part in the enterprise, and, though it surprises me to say it, if the Nightwalker is indeed nothing more threatening than a vagrant, how sad it will be if he has been chased out of the community by huntsmen and hounds and men with bludgeons.

I noticed the dismay on Joseph's face when the squires first announced their intentions, and I was intrigued by his reaction at the time. Now, having had three days to reflect on it, I almost feel sorry for the Nightwalker myself.

★ ★ ★

Editor's note: There are only occasional diary entries for the period between 17 July 1808 and 6 April 1817. Most of these relate to estate and family matters, children's illnesses and education, and the weather. In 1810, 1814 and 1815 Martha made long visits to the Lake District and to Yorkshire to visit distant relatives, and there are records of a number of shorter social visits to London and Oxford. There are also many references to 'lessons' with the wizard Joseph Harries. Since these entries do nothing to advance this story, they are omitted from the present text.

There are some long gaps between entries, and it seems that these gaps coincide with intermittent periods of ill-health, which might now be recognized as depression. Indeed, the impression of such a condition also pervades the subsequent section of the diary, written in the spring and early summer of 1817.

PART TWO: 1817–1818

A Matter of Trust

6 April 1817

How long is it since I have sought solace in this diary of mine? I had almost forgotten about the creature in black, but now he is about to enter my life again. I know this because last night I had a nightmare in which he stalked me through the woods of Tycanol and across the bleak moorlands of Mynydd Caregog before finally trapping me on the summit of Carningli. He was fully clothed, but I was quite naked, and bruised and bleeding from the chase. Among the blue crags of the summit I collapsed, exhausted, and crawled to the grassy hollow visited on hundreds of occasions in the past by me and the children. I knew that I was at his mercy. He approached me, and in my dream I smelt sulphur and heard his rasping breaths. His cloak was wrapped tightly about him. His muffler hid his face, and as ever he wore a wide-brimmed black hat on his head. He came to within a few feet of me as I lay on the grassy patch, petrified with fear. I tried to cover my nakedness with my hands, but still he came on. I held up my hand towards him, as if to fend him off. Then I saw his hand reach out towards mine, and I knew that if our fingers touched I would be inexorably dragged down to Hell...

I woke with a start, and sat bolt upright in my

471

bed, with my heart beating wildly and perspiration dripping from my brow. Relief flooded over me as I adjusted to my familiar surroundings. It was still so early in the morning that the only illumination came from a faint dawn lightening the eastern sky. The house was still quiet. I collapsed back onto my pillow and pulled my sheets up to my chin. I lay there for a long time, with my eyes wide open, torn between seeking to banish those terrible images from my brain and attempting to decipher them. Was it the intention of the creature to ravish me, or simply to drag me into the depths? Was he really hunting for me, or for some other member of my beloved family? Of one thing I was quite certain, after my years of study with the Wizard of Werndew, and that was that this was no ordinary dream but a premonition of events to come. And then I realized that tomorrow is Brynach's tenth birthday, and that he, rather than I, was the object of the Nightwalker's attention.

What was I to do? Tomorrow we will have a picnic at Carn Edward, since that is Brynach's favourite place and we always have a picnic there, come rain or shine, on his special day. It is already planned, and he and the other children are looking forward to it as ever. Should I search for some feeble excuse, and cancel the occasion? But then I remembered Joseph's wise words during one of my lessons. 'Martha,' he had said, 'premonitions must be heeded and used for the settling of your mind. Be prepared for something, but do not assume that you know what that something might be. Do not change your plans, for fate cannot be diverted. And do not spread your concerns to your nearest and dearest, for there is nothing more cruel than the destruction of other people's innocence.'

I mulled over these words for some considerable time as I stared at the dark ceiling, and I knew that Joseph was right. There would be no point at all in abandoning our family plans, and nothing to be gained by spreading alarm and despondency. Times are difficult enough as it is. We will proceed as if nothing had happened, and I will conceal the apprehension which now grips my heart. But I have now determined to resume my intermittent record of happenings at the Plas.

Whatever may happen to me or, if my instinct is right, to Brynach, I know that I will not have to face my trials and tribulations alone. Betsi is now nineteen years old, as cool and beautiful as may be imagined, and she, more than any other beneath this roof, is the one who lifts me when I am low and curbs my wild excesses. She is a clever pianist, and is far better informed about the outside world than I. She is truly my best friend, and I am wonderfully proud of her both as a daughter and as a calming influence upon the family. Would that I could have been half as sensible and half as sensitive when I was her age and newly arrived at the Plas!

Daisy is another matter entirely, almost seventeen years of age and desperate to be twenty-one. I love her dearly, but she has always been a difficult child, and my relationship with her has often been on a knife edge. On one day we will share love and laughter, and on the next I will be trying to cope with tears and tantrums. Sometimes the tears and tantrums are mine rather than hers, and it may be that we are too close temperamentally ever to share the sort of relationship which I have with Betsi. But dear Daisy is as pretty as a picture, and she has many admirable qualities which are recognized by me and by a host of male admirers.

And the younger ones? I still think of them as my babies, but they are little no longer. Dewi is fourteen, rosy-cheeked and good-looking, and still recognizable from a mile away because of his tousled golden hair. He is as cheeky as ever, and has the insufferable optimism and excessive energy which goes with youth. I become quite exhausted just by watching him for ten minutes. He still provokes Daisy when he can, and he is still very close to Sara, but of course he spends most of his time in the company of Brynach, wandering far and wide across the estate and further afield doing whatever boys do. I want him to go to Eton in the autumn, but I have to confess to grave concern because he will not take his studies seriously and will not show a proper interest in the estate. I keep reminding him that he is the next Squire of Plas Ingli, and that there are many things to learn in preparation for the day when he will assume responsibility for land, tenants and servants; but he laughs and says, 'All in good time, Mam!' and returns to his frivolous pursuits.

Sara is twelve, also golden-haired, and so calm and studious and methodical that I can hardly credit that she is my daughter. I am waiting for some ill-humour to make an appearance, but I doubt if it ever will; she is the easiest of children to manage, and in truth she generally amuses herself. When she does take part in some youthful escapade, it generally turns out not to have been of her own making, but to have been dreamt up by one of the boys. She is, I fear, a little too naive for her own good, but with two fierce guards alongside her she breezes through life unaffected by the disasters which afflict poor Daisy almost on a daily basis. Truly I love them all, and have cherished these past years of learning to nurture them. One day I might even become a good parent, by which time it will be too late, for my fluffy chicks will by then all have flown away from the nest.

And Brynach? Little no longer, and ten tomorrow. He is already taller than Sara, and with his dark complexion, brown eyes and black hair he looks much more like me than any of the other children do. He was a difficult child when he was little, and that is perhaps not surprising, since he spent the first year of his life not knowing who his mother was. Of course he still does not know who she is, and neither do I. He was nursed, and washed, and cleaned and cuddled by a multitude of adults and children. Liza Philpin was the one who gave him the breast, and I was the one who gave him motherly love once he started on cow's milk and normal food, but until he was five he was very unsettled, and for a time he was a naughty and selfish little boy. Looking back on it, that was probably my fault, for I lavished too much of my attention on him and accommodated his every whim, causing resentment among the other children. Daisy was especially difficult, and on several occasions tried to harm him. But now we all adore him. He knows that he was a foundling, for in a household such as ours secrets are impossible to keep. Indeed, I have explained to him how he came to be found on the doorstep, and he accepts the story with grace and humour in spite of occasional silly comments from the other children when they are involved in juvenile quarrels.

As far as the rest of the household is concerned, there are changes to report. Grandpa Isaac is now seventy-seven years old, as lean and weather-beaten as an old oak post, but he has suffered from many ailments over the past few years, and he jokes that he is kept alive by Joseph's magic potions. He may well be right, for he consumes prodigious quantities of them alongside equal measures of ale. His mind is as sharp as ever, but rheumatism has made movement very difficult, and, much to his irritation, he cannot any longer help out around the farm. But I consult him all the time on estate matters, and I am still learning from him. Grandma Jane, who was such a sharp and perceptive presence around the house, and has rescued me from myself and from my enemies on innumerable occasions, is now a sad frail figure who spends most of her time sitting in her settle by the *simnai fawr*. She has lost weight, although I thought she had none to lose. Her mind is now very slow, and she is very forgetful. She does not even remember the names of the children or the servants, and repeats herself end-lessly, but she enjoys her reminiscences of days gone by, and her memories of her own childhood back in the middle of the last century are quite astonishing. She sleeps for much of the time, but when she is awake she is very calm and un-demanding, and she receives love and respect in abundance from all the other Plas Ingli adults, and indeed from the children. She has a very special relationship with Brynach, who sits at her feet and listens, entranced, to her tales of high-waymen and smugglers and drovers.

Sad to say, the household now has to survive without the redoubtable Mrs Owen. In the year 1812 she became very ill and could not continue with her duties. I offered her the chance of staying on at the Plas, but she knew that she would be a burden, and went to live with one of her daughters in Newport. She died in 1814, which caused all of us – and especially Grandma – great distress, for she had been a beloved and faithful servant for more than forty-five years. Bessie took over as housekeeper, and has proved competent in every respect. She does not rule the house with the same rod of iron as was wielded by her predecessor, but she is very strong-willed, and she keeps me and everybody else in proper order. Billy and Will are still here, older and not necessarily wiser. Shemi and Sian married in 1808, and I gave them a cottage on the estate. Shemi works here every day, but Sian now has her hands full with three small children. And there have been other changes too. Liza, who was Brynach's wet nurse, is now here as my housemaid. She has two children of her own, and still lives at Pantry, but she walks up to the Plas every morning at six and walks home every evening at eight. Very often the children come with her, and help with bird-scaring and stone clearance. For four years I employed young Lisbeth Prosser from Frongoch as a tutor for the children, but then she left to get married, and I employed Alexander Williams from Langton in her place. He is a studious young fellow, but Billy and Will are grateful to have another man around the place as a counterbalance to what they see as a burden of emotional females.

And so our little world is reorganized, refreshed and renewed. We are all older and a good deal more practised in the ways of the world, but I dare to hope that we have the corporate strength to deflect the poisoned spear which cruel fate will shortly fling in our direction. I know that it will come, and I wonder if it will come tomorrow.

7 April 1817

Though events have unfolded more or less as I anticipated, I fear that I can take no credit for my reaction to events.

We woke early to find that the day was a strange one, with a hazy sun and with mist swirling around the Plas. At breakfast the children were in high spirits, and would talk of nothing else but their birthday picnic at the rocks of Carn Edward. I tried to discourage them, saying that it was cold and damp, and that a picnic surrounded by sea mist had every prospect of being a miserable affair, but they would have none of it. Brynach, whose special day it was, said, 'Oh, Mam! Don't you be so dismal! The air will warm up and the sun will soon melt the mist away. We will have a wonderful time, and I want to sit on top of that high pinnacle of rock and eat my feast like a king on the topmost battlement of his castle. We must go!' So what could I do in the face of such enthusiasm, especially when he was supported by his older brother and sisters?

In mid-morning I left Bessie and the young people to the task of preparing the picnic, and Betsi, Grandpa and I took the chaise and travelled down to Cilgwyn church, on our yearly pilgrimage to the family enclosure where we hold our annual remembrance of the Plas Ingli fire. In the past we have always walked, but this year Grandpa's joints were too stiff for such exercise and he wanted to drive instead. Grandma stayed at home, for she has a chill at the moment, and in any case her appreciation of such occasions has diminished as her confusion has increased. When we got there we tidied up the enclosure, placed posies of prim-roses and other spring flowers on the graves of David and the others, and stood with our arms round each other for some minutes of silent con-templation. The mist drifted about us, and there was an eerie silence. With every slight stirring of the air, cascades of water droplets splashed down from the trees at the edge of the churchyard.

When we got home the picnic was ready, and there were three wicker baskets full of good things on the kitchen table. 'Come on, Mam!' said Sara, her eyes shining. 'We have got hard-boiled eggs, and smoked sewin, and ham, and sorrel leaves, and currants, and fresh bread and butter, and–'

'Wait, Sara!' I replied with a laugh. 'Don't give

all your culinary secrets away! I thought the contents of the picnic were supposed to be a surprise for Betsi and me?'

'Oh yes, Mam, so they are.'

And with Sara being scolded by the others for her indiscretion, and laughter and bustle on all sides, we got ourselves ready and set off. The five children and I wrapped up well, since the mist was reluctant to clear and the air was still cool and damp. We could just make out a hazy sun above the invisible *cwm*. As we walked, we could sometimes see for fifty yards and sometimes for no more than ten, but there was no chance of our going astray since we had all walked this way a multitude of times before, and the mountain track was easy to follow.

When we arrived at the rocks we settled down on the big woollen blanket which Sara had carried with her. As the sun reached its zenith it became warmer, and we enjoyed our feast in bright conditions. With Betsi and Daisy in charge, there was little for me to do, and so I ate and drank well, and then lay back and closed my eyes, listening idly to the chatter of the two boys and Sara. The moorland behind us was still enveloped in drifting banks of mist, and down below Cwm Gwaun was still so heavily shrouded that it was quite invisible. Daisy and Betsi lay on their backs and started to chat about the latest young gentlemen who had taken their fancies. The other three became bored, and decided that they would explore every nook and cranny on the carn, searching for birds' eggs and other treasures. They rushed about, whooping and yelling

480

like savages in a jungle, and climbed up all the rock faces they could find.

Then Brynach climbed up onto the topmost pinnacle of rock, which was quite an achievement for a ten-year-old, and stood there on one leg, yelling 'I'm the king of the castle! Get down you dirty rascal!' at the top of his voice. The others had to watch him, probably fearing that he would fall down and break his neck, but on a sudden impulse I looked in the opposite direction, northwards towards the mist-shrouded common. The mist thinned and drifted away for an instant, and I saw him. The Nightwalker, standing stock still as ever, just watching us. It was ten years since I had last seen him, but he was quite unchanged, with his long black cloak wrapped tightly round him, a heavy black muffler covering his face, and a wide-brimmed black hat upon his head. My reaction was the same as it had always been on our previous encounters. I froze, stiff with terror. I turned and looked at the others, no doubt with wild wide eyes, but they were preoccupied with Brynach's antics, and Betsi was telling him to come down off that pinnacle before he hurt himself. I turned again and looked at the common, but the mist had drifted back once more and the creature had disappeared.

'Mother!' said Daisy, placing her hand on mine. 'Are you all right? You are shivering, and you look as if you have seen a ghost!'

I stood up, and in truth, in spite of the hazy sunshine, I felt as cold as when I had hidden in the dairy on the occasion of my first encounter with the Nightwalker all those years ago. 'Suddenly, I feel very unwell,' I lied. 'I fear that I have eaten something that has not agreed with me. Brynach, come down off that rock at once! Come, children, we must get all our things back into our baskets and get down off this mountain at once!'

'Oh, Mam!' objected Sara. 'Do we have to? We are having such fun, and I want to climb up on that tall rock when Brynach jumps down–'

'Sara! I will not have you talking to me like that. You heard what I said. I am not well, and I insist that we go home immediately.'

To their credit Betsi and Daisy realized that something was wrong, and they supported me by getting to their feet and packing up the remains of the picnic. I was very much afraid that if the mist drifted away again we would all see the Night-walker standing on the common a hundred yards away, and that was something I did not want. So, albeit with a good deal of grumbling from the younger ones, we were soon on our way back to the Plas. As we walked downhill towards the safety of that beloved place, I could not resist looking over my shoulder at intervals to see if we were being followed. Luckily the blanket of mist remained in place, but still I dreaded that one of the young people – most likely Brynach – would be snatched away from the rest of us. So I insisted on holding his hand all the way home, making him greatly irritated.

When I arrived back at the Plas I maintained my pretence of feeling ill, and retired to my room. I wanted to lie on my bed and work out what to do next, but then there was a knock on my door and Betsi came in. 'Now then, Mother,' said she, bold as brass, 'what is all this about?'

'I told you, Betsi, that I felt suddenly ill, and I have to say that I am still not fully recovered.'

'Nonsense, Mother. I do not believe that for a moment. You are not very good at play-acting. You saw something on the mountain, did you not? You were suddenly petrified, and had to flee. Would you like to tell me what it was that frightened you so much?'

'I am not at liberty to say.'

'Come, come, Mother. I beg you not to have secrets from me. Did you see your famous Nightwalker through the mist?'

I was flabbergasted when I heard this from the lips of my own daughter, and my astonishment must have shown on my face, for she laughed and came and sat down on the bed beside me. She put her arm round my shoulder. 'Your face is an open book, Mother,' she said, smiling that angelic smile of hers. 'So it was the Nightwalker, come back to haunt you.'

'How did you know about him? I thought that he was my secret.'

'Secret indeed! Daisy, Dewi and I have known about him for years, although we have not talked about him in the presence of Sara and Brynach. How could we not have heard about him? I remember that when I was nine or ten there was a time when the servants talked of little else.'

'But they were sworn to secrecy, Betsi. I was determined that you children should not be frightened by the encounters that we all had, and by the dark speculations in which we all indulged at the time.'

Betsi laughed again. 'Dear Mother! Small children have big ears. We knew what he looked like, and how he behaved. The servants, and Great-grandma and Great-grandpa, were very discreet, but we could not help overhearing snippets of conversations, and when we played with other children from the *cwm* and from town we heard all about the famous exorcism on the Parrog when the Rector tried to get rid of the creature in black, and about the burning of the cottage at Cwmgloyn where he was supposed to have lived. We even heard from some children in Dinas that he lived in Master Harries's cottage for a while. You might not have realized it, but the Nightwalker is very much a feature of our local folklore. We are actually quite fond of him.'

'Betsi! How can you say that? The Nightwalker is an evil creature, and I am still not sure whether he is ghost, Devil or man.'

'So where is your evidence that he is evil?'

'It is perfectly obvious to everybody. Over and again he has been a harbinger of doom. He appeared before Owain was taken away from me, and before the Sahara storm of 1807, and before Aunt Elen fled to America, and before Patty and Jake were attacked on the Parrog...'

'Mother, how many times were the links between his appearances and such events caused not by the Nightwalker himself but by the primitive imaginings of those who saw or heard about him?'

'I will not accept that, Betsi. I know far more about him than you do, and I ask you to accept my judgement in the matter.'

Betsi sighed and rolled her eyes in that irritat-

484

ing way of hers. 'I can see that I am not going to get very far along that particular route,' she said. 'But can we please dispose of the primitive idea that he is either a ghost or the Devil himself?'

'That is not as easy as you might think, *cariad*. If the creature is a man, why should he lie low for eight or nine years, and then appear again suddenly out of the mist? There is no logic in it. And remember that he comes and goes without leaving footprints or other traces. Pray tell me how a man could manage such a trick.'

'That is a difficulty, Mother, I will concede that. But I am still not inclined to believe in devils and demons flying about the place, and I prefer to think that the creature is a man. I am sure that is Master Harries's view too, for I spoke to him on this subject some months back. In my mind the Nightwalker is some lost soul carrying with him a dark and terrible secret. Perhaps, Mother, he is really begging for help? Now wouldn't that be wonderfully romantic?'

Our conversation was at an end. I got up and embraced my lovely and sensible daughter. She has not lessened my apprehensions about the creature, but I am greatly relieved that whatever happens in the future, and whatever flights of fancy I may indulge in, I can turn to Betsi as well as Joseph for reassurance and for assistance in the matter of coming back down to earth.

20 April 1817

A week ago we were saddened by the news that

Mistress Susan Price of Llanychaer had died. She had been poorly for many years, and indeed confined to her bed for the last five, and death must have come as a merciful release for both her and her husband. He was apparently distraught when she passed away, and he must have been very fond of her in spite of the fact that he never showed her, in my presence at least, any great affection. But brash and bullying fellows may sometimes have tenderness hidden deep within their breasts.

Two days since I went with Grandpa Isaac to the *gwylnos* at the big house on the hillside above Cwm Gwaun, to pay our last respects before the open coffin. Mistress Susan, poor thing, looked a good deal more serene in death than she had in life, although there was little left of her but skin and bones. I wanted to go, for I liked Mistress Susan and I felt that she liked me, although we met socially on only a few occasions. Squire Price welcomed us cordially enough, but there was no sign of Fanny, and when I asked after her health the Squire said that she had taken her mother's death very hard and would not see anybody. We stayed for some refreshments, and I was struck by the fact that those attending the coffin were neighbours and servants rather than relatives. Grandpa Isaac told me that there was now virtually nothing left of the Price family apart from Susanna and Mary, the two estranged and widowed daughters living far away, and a couple of very ancient maiden aunts and two male cousins who were too infirm to travel. What a sad thing, I thought, for an ancient and respected family to simply fade away, unloved and almost unnoticed by the world.

Yesterday we travelled again to Plas Llanychaer for the funeral, which was not very well attended. That might have been because it was a day of strong wind and streaming rain, when all sensible people should have been sitting indoors before their kitchen fires. Perhaps there were thirty people in the procession from the house to the church, and it was a blessing that the burial took place at the little church of St David in Llanllawer, only a few hundred yards along the road. If the funeral had taken place in the Llanychaer parish church, down in the valley, we would all have been soaked to the skin on the walk downhill and exhausted by the walk back up again afterwards. Squire Price and Fanny followed the hearse. There were a few other members of the gentry, but most of those present were servants, tenants and labourers from the Llanychaer estate.

The funeral service in the church was unremarkable, but as we entered the church I glanced up at the bank above the holy well, and there I saw the Nightwalker again. He was only just visible through the deluge, standing stock still, with water cascading off his black hat and cloak. I thought that he looked almost pathetic. Inside, during the prayers and hymns and psalms, I could not concentrate on the matter in hand, and felt very guilty about it, but my mind was fixed upon the creature in black. Afterwards, as we attended the burial in the bleak and rainswept graveyard, I was moved to look away at the moment of interment, when everybody else had their eyes fixed upon the open grave. My eyes wandered again to the bank near the holy well, and he was still there. He had not moved an inch, and I thought he might as well have been made of stone. The rain still streamed off him, and his hat looked as if it was in danger of being torn from his head by the raging wind. His cloak flapped wildly about him and he looked more like a bedraggled raven than a fearsome denizen of the spirit world. Then he sneezed! It was a very strange sneeze, stifled and nasal and only just audible above the sound of the raging wind and the driving rain, but I was sure it was a sneeze, for there was an almost simultaneous and certainly involuntary movement of his body.

I think I was the only one who saw and heard him, and now, more than twenty-four hours after the event, I am still bemused. I do not think that devils, demons and ghosts sneeze, so I am now increasingly tending to the belief that the Night-walker is a man. Perhaps Betsi is right, and he is nothing more threatening than a lost soul with a dark secret. Perhaps he does indeed need our help, and is pleading for it? But if that is the case, why does he not knock on the door of Plas Ingli, and ask to see me, and tell me precisely what it is that he wants?

23 April 1817

In trying to keep my thoughts off the Night-walker, it occurs to me that I must report on other happenings which have thus far gone unrecorded, before they slip entirely out of my memory. Both of Owain's parents are dead. Squire John Laugharne died in 1810 of a chill that went onto his lungs, and his wife Olwen passed away two years ago. It was a great sadness to me, and to Mary Jane, that they both died without the matter of Owain's disappearance having been resolved. I think, towards the ends of their lives, that they accepted that he was dead, but the burden of hope and fear was a heavy one indeed, and because they were never able to grieve for Owain properly they became sad and almost reclusive in their declining years. Mary Jane and I know exactly how they felt, but with the advantage of youth we have learned to cope with loss and uncertainty somewhat better. On the death of Squire Laugharne, Owain's older brother James took over the running of the Pontfaen estate, and then made a good marriage, better late than never, with one of the Vaughan daughters of Jordanston. He decided to retain Llannerch out of respect for Owain's memory, and says that if his brother has not returned at the end of twenty years, he will dispose of it. In the meantime, it is farmed by a tenant, one William Morgan. As for Mary Jane, she is as happy as may be at Trecwn, with a kind husband and two boys, little Samuel having been born in 1811, seven years after his big brother William. And younger sister Liza, Mistress Allen of Cresselly, is childless but contented, although she sometimes misses the mountains and the wild moors of her birthplace.

And my own family? My father George is not well, but still manages the Brawdy estate with panache. He has given up his magistrate's duties, but he still appears, whenever I meet him, to know everything that goes on in Pembrokeshire. Mother is hale and hearty, and comes to see us at the Plas whenever she can. Morys, my wise and discreet older brother, still ministers to the Baptists in Haverfordwest, as he has done for the past twenty years. We see him and his dear wife Nansi, and their three children, all too seldom, but it is a good thing to have a friendly place in the county town where we can enjoy good fellowship and hospitality when we have to be there for shopping expeditions or on business matters. Sister Catrin and her husband James and their two children are struggling at Castlebythe, for it is a bleak and difficult estate to manage, but they retain their good humour and their optimism to a remarkable degree. And it is a pleasure to report that sister Elen is happy. I am still convinced that we will never see her again, but she does write from America now and then, and she is married, with two children. She now styles herself Madame Elen Bradshaw, Private Music Tutor to Young Ladies of Good Breeding, which I must say sounds more than a little pretentious, but in a new land I dare say that services and skills have to be sold with confidence, and I am happy that she is happy. I have written to her occasionally, and have always been delighted by her interest in the fortunes of my growing family. She keeps urging me, in her epistles, to remarry, and I keep telling her that I am not ready for it, and that I will only take another husband if my heart dictates it.

Then there are my other friends. Ellie is settled at Ambleston, and has three beautiful children, but I am not sure that she is contented or fulfilled. Her husband Walter is a man who is short on refinement, and he has a cruel streak which manifests itself occasionally. On more than one occasion I have had Ellie here in tears, and have been able to do little other than offer a shoulder for her to weep on. A gentlewoman trapped in a difficult marriage is no better than a prisoner in a dungeon, and I thank God that in my life, although I have been in the latter situation, I have never been in the former. But her experience does make me cautious and more than a little afraid of what can happen in a marriage when love and mutual concern die, and a shaky structure is held up only by the crumbling foundations of respectability and duty.

My old friend Joseph is now in his fifty-eighth year, and is beginning to creak at the joints, but he is as slim and active as ever, and I enjoy his company and his wisdom whenever I can. For the last eight years I have walked over to his cottage at least once a month, where he seeks to instruct me in some of his esoteric knowledge. I fear that I am not a very good student, but I have learnt a good deal, and he says that there will be times in my life, and his, when I will be grateful for the access he has given me to his Big Book and for the hours we have spent in picking herbs and mixing potions.

Patty and Jake have four children, and the fishing business is thriving now that vast herring shoals are coming into the bay every year. As their family has grown, they have moved out of Bwthyn Bach and into a larger cottage further along the Parrog sea wall. Jake has three fishing smacks and is thinking of building a fourth. Skiff Abraham, once upon a time the wildest fellow in town, is now older and a good deal wiser. He is married and settled down, and has five wagons and twenty horses. Recently he bought Hubert Harry's warehouse near the lime kilns, and he threatens to become the most successful merchant in town. He certainly has a head for figures, and he and I do a good deal of business together. But his accumulating wealth is still something of a mystery, and I suspect that as long as there are smugglers on this coast, Skiff will continue to become wealthier. He will never be caught carrying a tax-free anker himself, but he knows everybody in the trade and probably controls almost everything that happens on wild moonless nights between Fishguard and Cardigan. I have more than a sneaking admiration for him, especially since he says that he abhors violence. He has told me more than once that he learnt a great lesson from the battle of Parc Haidd, all those years ago, when I defeated ten of my treasure-hunting enemies in one fell swoop without lifting a finger in aggression against any of them. 'Brains and quick wits is what wins battles, Mistress,' he said last time we talked business. 'Those who kill and maim are only storing up trouble, and will get their come-uppance as sure as kippers is herrings.'

I trust that I can relearn the lesson that Skiff learnt from me, and keep cool and calm in the midst of my own troubles. Most of all, I must seek to rid myself of the aggression which pounds away in my heart whenever my mind turns to the creature in black, be he man or phantom.

27 April 1817

No matter how much I try to drag myself away from this destructive obsession with the Night-walker, I cannot do it, and once again my tendency towards introspection has landed me in trouble with my nearest and dearest.

Two days since, on thinking back over my sighting of the black creature on the occasion of Brynach's picnic, I became preoccupied with the idea that he has some designs not upon me or even Brynach, but upon Betsi or Daisy, who are now both very beautiful young women. Daisy is just sixteen but looks far older, with a fine complexion, a full bosom and a narrow waist. When she walks, she swings her hips like a madame, and in the presence of gentlemen she uses her eyes to create mayhem in a manner which makes me blush when I think of it. She has, I fear, grown up far too early. She clearly does not know the meaning of modesty, and for this I have to take most of the blame. If nothing else, Daisy knows how to look after herself, and Betsi is the more vulnerable of the two.

My oldest daughter has spent too much time helping me, covering for my inadequacies and taking the role of 'little mother' when I have been ill. She does not realize herself just how beautiful she is, with her fine high cheekbones, her sparkling eyes and her delicate lips. She is taller than me and has a smaller bosom than Daisy, but while she may not look voluptuous, she moves with a lithe grace which causes heads to turn whenever she walks down Market Street. If she was not destined to become a country squire's wife she could become a London hostess, and would entrance gentlemen and fine ladies in equal measure. She is the one I worry about, especially since she is now the same age as I was when I was almost defiled by that demon Moses Lloyd in my cave on Carningli. Briefly, I thought that the Nightwalker might be his ghost, come to claim not me but Betsi, the most beautiful member of the next generation of the Morgans of Plas Ingli. A fantastical idea maybe, and yet...

Then it occurred to me that the Nightwalker must have been standing on the misty moorland of Mynydd Caregog before we arrived for our picnic at Carn Edward. Did he stand there all the time, waiting, on the off chance that we might turn up? No, he must have known that we were coming. That means that somebody must have told him. There must be a spy at the Plas, passing messages to the Nightwalker about our movements. The more I thought on this matter, the more convinced I became. But who could it be? Neither of the old people, I was sure, and I could also rule out the children. Neither the tenants nor the labourers would know about our family outings in any detail. That left the servants. A cold chill swept over me when I realized that one of my own dear, trusted servants, to whom I have often referred as 'my angels', had been involved in an act of betrayal. Perhaps that betrayal was nothing new. Perhaps it stretched back to the earliest encounters with the Nightwalker, and in recalling them I was struck by the extent to which he appeared to have anticipated my movements around the estate and back and forth between the Plas and Llannerch.

Who could it be? Should I confront the servants one by one, and see if I could extract from one of them some sort of confession? I thought better of it, since that would make me appear paranoid and would send waves of disquiet sweeping through our peaceful household. Those waves would be quite likely to wash one or more of the servants away from the Plas and its mad mistress, and would almost certainly harm the children as well. No, I had to work it out for myself. So I lay on my bed and closed my eyes, and pondered for a very long time. Thought got me nowhere, and so I started again. I tried to empty my head of wild buzzing thoughts, and I allowed intuition to take over. And within a few minutes it came to me. The traitor was Bessie, the one of whom I would least have expected it – my beloved friend and confidante, the sweet handmaiden who had rescued me from myself and from others on countless occasions, the one in whom I had always placed my trust and from whom I had over and again sought wise counsel. And now my betrayer.

At first I could not cope with this terrible knowledge. I stood up and walked across my bedroom and turned the keys in both of the doors that allowed access. I did not want to be disturbed. I sat bolt upright at my writing desk, gazing out over the sunlit *cwm*. But the sun's rays could not reach my soul. Would that they could have done, for it was encased in ice. I felt cold and sick. I wrapped a blanket round my shoulders, and continued to sit there at the window, with my eyes open but seeing nothing, and my ears blocked against the whispering of the wind and the songs of the birds. I shivered and wept, feeling once again utterly alone in the world. I had never encountered betrayal in my own house before, and I had not the faintest idea how to handle the situation.

It was still mid-afternoon, and I had to endure the rest of the day without alarming the rest of the household. Somehow I managed it, and succeeded in fending off various comments about my black mood and my red eyes by explaining that it was all down to feminine troubles. When she heard that, Liza raised her eyebrows, for she knew perfectly well that it was not my bleeding time at all. But my eyes met hers, and she said nothing. I knew that I would have to confront Bessie, and that the encounter would be distressing for both of us. But I wanted to sleep on it, and I wanted to be quite specific in the allegations that I would make. I did not sleep much, but I did remember details of Bessie's behaviour that convinced my head, as well as my heart, that she would be found guilty as charged.

This morning, after breakfast, I settled in my room, and then asked Liza to send Bessie up and to ensure that we were not disturbed. Even before the poor dear woman arrived, I was shaking with apprehension. My throat was dry, and my palms were moist with perspiration. Bessie came breezing in, and closed the door behind her. 'Well, Mistress?' she said cheerfully, but even as she spoke she saw my face and my posture and knew that there was trouble in store. I asked her to sit down, and she pulled up a chair and sat just a few feet in front of me.

'Bessie, you have been my dearest and most trusted friend ever since I arrived at the Plas as a frightened and pregnant young woman all those years ago. Have you valued our friendship as I have?'

'Why yes, Mistress,' she replied, with puzzlement in her face. 'It has been the greatest blessing of my life, and it has been a privilege to serve you and to share in your bad times and your good times. You must know it yourself.'

'I thought I knew it, Bessie. I have shared secrets with you, and trusted you with things which I have never told to another man or woman.'

'I am aware of that, and I thank God for it. But I know you well enough, Mistress, from your words and your demeanour, to know that there is no warmth in you today. What it is that you wish to say to me?'

I would normally have smiled at this impertinence, but today I could not. In response to a direct question, I made a direct accusation. 'Bessie, I have reason to think that you have betrayed my trust, not once or twice, but on many occasions in the past.'

'Mistress! That is a most unkind thing to say,' she spluttered, with her pretty eyes registering anger and distress in equal measure. 'I would never, never betray you. I love you and your family far too much for that.'

'So you say, and so you have said before. But I ask you now: have you been in direct communication with the creature whom we call the Nightwalker?'

At this, poor Bessie was struck dumb. The

colour rose in her cheeks, and she averted her eyes from mine. Her guilt was so obvious that it could have been read by a small child.

'Will you reply, Bessie?'

She shook her head, and I saw that she was close to tears. I was close to tears myself, but I managed to control myself since I had more to say.

'Very well. I will take your silence as affirmation. It has become obvious to me that somebody from within this household has been informing the Nightwalker about my movements and those of the children. This miserable business came to a head on the occasion of Brynach's tenth birthday, when I discovered that the creature was waiting for us – forewarned – on the moorland near Carn Edward. I wondered who could have told him about our picnic. Then I remembered that we had made our plans for it on the previous morning at breakfast, in the company of you and the other servants. I also remembered that in the afternoon you asked if you might take a walk towards Dinas, to fetch some special cheeses from a friend of yours. I happily gave you permission and thought no more of it. The cheeses probably never existed. But you were away for a long time, Bessie. You arrived back late in the afternoon, splashed with mud and very tired. You must have walked a great way. Would you like to tell me where you went?'

'I cannot say, Mistress. I fear that I am sworn to secrecy.'

'Secrecy, indeed! I thought, Bessie, that there were no secrets between us!'

'Please accept, Mistress, that this one is a

necessity. Please also accept that there is no harm in it, either to yourself or to anybody else, and that my silence is required for your own protection.'

At this, I slammed my hand down on my dressing table in exasperation. Had I not heard this before? I was sure that I could recall almost identical words being used by Patty when I confronted her about the Nightwalker, and by Joseph when he and I had our unpleasant contretemps all those years ago. Always these confrontations, these secrets, involved the creature in black. Did he have some strange power over all of my friends? Was there no-one whom I could trust? I could not understand it, and it made me furious.

'Bessie, I find your attitude quite insufferable! First Patty, then Joseph, and now you, all under the control of this vile creature! I can see that I will get nothing more out of you, for he has corrupted your soul and drained virtue out of you. But will you do me the honour of one straight answer if I ask you an oblique question?'

'If I can give it without breaking a confidence, Mistress.'

'Very well. I have come to the conclusion, quite independently, that the Nightwalker is a man. Will you care to confirm that?'

Bessie thought for a moment, and then nodded, confirming both his humanity and her knowledge of him. She realized immediately that she had been tricked, and tears welled up in her eyes. 'Oh, Mistress Martha!' she pleaded. 'Pray do not press me any further. I cannot lie to you, and you are being more cruel than you may realize in thinking ill of me. Please, Mistress, I swear before God that I would never do anything that might harm you or any other of the blessed folk who dwell beneath this roof.' And at last she could control herself no longer. She got to her feet and stood before me, weeping like a small child who had lost a favourite toy. She had lost the trust of her mistress, and I realized that that is a terrible thing for a servant to experience. I did not know what to do, so I went up to her and took her in my arms, and I wept too.

Then she tore herself away, still with tears streaming down her cheeks, and said, 'I am sorry, Mistress, but I must go. I have the supper to attend to, and the potatoes are not yet peeled.' And she opened the door and ran down the stairs to the kitchen, leaving me feeling not at all like a champion of virtue but like a vindictive and mean-spirited wretch.

28 April 1817

I took a long time to recover from my discussion with Bessie, as indeed did she. The evening was a difficult one, with Bessie red-eyed and miserable, going through the motions of preparing and serving supper and me doing my best to pretend that nothing had happened. But it must have been obvious to all that there was a great coolness between us, and after supper both Grandpa and Betsi took me to one side as we sat in the parlour and insisted that I explain what was going on. I could see no point in being evasive about our discussion, so I told them everything. Immediately they took Bessie's side, and although they were no more in possession of the truth than I was, they admonished me for even daring to think ill of the dear sweet woman who had served me with compassion, sensitivity and discretion for twenty years or more. I protested that there must be something underhand going on, and that Bessie's refusal to answer my questions directly was an admission of guilt, but Betsi became angry with me, and gave me a little lecture on loyalty and trust.

'Mother,' she said, 'you expect loyalty from your servants, and reward it generously, but why will you not give loyalty to them? The bonds of mutual respect will simply fall apart if you do not give Bessie and the other servants the trust which they so richly deserve. Have you become so preoccupied with the Nightwalker that you have forgotten what the word "trust" actually means? I beg of you to call Bessie up to your room without further delay, and to apologize to her without reservation for your behaviour. There is absolutely no indication that she has done anything wrong, and you must believe her when she says that she would never dream of harming you or any of the rest of us.' I was shocked that Grandpa seemed in agreement with her, but I could not fight them both. I did not have the strength in me to maintain a conflict with the two most intelligent people beneath my roof.

So it was that, suitably chastened, I went up to my room and called Bessie in. I did apologize, and I promised to suspect her no further and to press her no further as to her actions or her motives. With considerable relief she accepted my apology, and we embraced, and held hands for a moment, and parted. I went back down to the parlour, shaking like a leaf, and nodded to Betsi. 'I have done as you asked,' I said, 'and I trust that all will be well again between Bessie and myself.' Betsi smiled, and came and sat next to me, and put her arm round my shoulder.

What a strange thing it is, I thought, that in a growing and maturing relationship between a mother and a daughter, there comes a point at which roles are reversed, and the young instruct the old in the art of living.

20 May 1817

There has been more sad news from Llanychaer. Fanny, the sweet and simple daughter of Squire Price, has taken her own life. It happened some days ago, and there is no doubt about what happened because she left a note before hanging herself from a beam in the barn. According to the servants, they were afraid that she might do something foolish, because she has been in a very erratic state since her mother's death, and she could not be helped even by calming potions made for her by the Wizard of Werndew. There was no proper funeral, and she was buried without much ceremony somewhere in the garden.

Thus has the tragedy of the Price family been compounded. Squire Price is now all alone in the house, attended by just a few servants. His wife and two sons are dead, and now poor Fanny has gone and his remaining daughters are remote. The Squire is in very low spirits, and I would not wish his particular concoction of miseries to be fed to even the worst of my enemies. I wrote him a little note when I heard the news about Fanny, although in truth it was difficult to find words to express my sympathy. What can anyone say in such singularly tragic circumstances? But he wrote back this very morning, thanking me for my concern and my condolences, and saying that my insights and expressions of support had brought him great comfort.

That is but one of the difficult matters with which I am having to cope at the present time. I have also drawn further conclusions concerning Bessie's involvement with the Nightwalker. I will not discuss the matter with her, nor will I make any further accusations of disloyalty, for I have made her a promise and I will stick to it. I will not even discuss this matter with Betsi, for my fierce daughter will probably wag her finger at me and subject me to further admonishment. So I will keep it to myself, and ponder on it.

It refers to something that happened a while ago, and I had forgotten about until the other day. But back in March there was an occurrence at the Plas which I hardly noticed at the time because I was preoccupied with organizing the last of the barley threshing. Bessie received a letter. Now that I come to think of it, that was a very strange thing in itself, for Bessie is not a great sender or receiver of correspondence. It was a letter from Swansea, a place of great manufacturing industry in Glamorgan, about sixty miles away from here.

When she read it she was sitting at the kitchen table, and she turned as white as a shroud. She started shaking, and had to go and lie down in her own room for a while. Liza went with her, and she soon recovered. But she would not divulge to anybody either the source of the letter or its contents. I was puzzled at the time, but then she said that the letter had carried some distressing family news, and so I thought no more about it. I also recall that at the end of March Bessie went out on several occasions without explaining where she was going, or why. Billy joked that she had suddenly taken to long and healthy walks in the countryside, and Will gave a broad wink and said that Dai Canton had better watch out for his interests, implying that a new man had entered Bessie's affections. I was intrigued at the time, but not concerned, for my servants have a right to some little privacy in their lives. But now that I look back on it, I wonder whether Bessie herself has some dark secret, and whether she is being blackmailed by somebody. Perhaps some dastardly fellow has her under his control. Could it be connected in some way with the creature in black? Or is it all to do with some ancient affair of the heart? Even more intriguing, could the Nightwalker be a rejected lover of Bessie's from years gone by, and could it be that he has been directing his attentions throughout not at me or my children but at my dear handmaiden? She is still very attractive, and is only a couple of years older than me, and she has retained the ability to cause male hearts to flutter. Now that could be a wonderfully romantic thing, especially if it results, in due course, in some dramatic unmasking of the creature in black to reveal a handsome nobleman, followed by a declaration of undying love and a request for Bessie's hand in marriage! This may all be too fanciful by half, but it is intriguing none the less.

A third matter of concern involves my dear friend Joseph, whom I have not seen recently. Two days since, I decided that it would be pleasant to invite him to join us for supper, for we all enjoy his company and I thought I might have the opportunity to discuss with him my latest sightings of the Nightwalker. He knows more about the creature than he has ever been prepared to admit, and I find that more than a little irritating. Also, I recalled that on the day before Brynach's birthday Bessie had walked over to Dinas. I still suspect that when she was there she met the Nightwalker. Could the rendezvous have occurred at Joseph's cottage? That would be interesting to know. So I sent Shemi over to Werndew on the chestnut pony to deliver my invitation note and receive a reply. When he returned Shemi was very agitated, and asked if he might see me alone. 'Why yes, Shemi,' said I. 'Just you come into the parlour, and we can talk without interruption.'

'Very strange it was, Mistress,' said Shemi. 'When I arrived at the wizard's cottage there was smoke coming out of the chimney, and his pony was in the paddock, so I knew that he was at home. But the door was closed, in spite of the hot weather. It was locked too. I knocked and knocked, and at last Joseph came to the door. Put his head round it, he did, but he did not look at

505

all pleased to see me. He greeted me warmly enough, but without any welcome in his smile. I asked if I might come inside, but he said "Excuse me, Shemi, for not being hospitable today, but I have a patient in my back room who is suffering from a most foul and infectious disease, and I am dreadfully afraid that it will spread to others." Quite understood, said I, but I have a message from my mistress who will appreciate a reply. Master Harries took the letter and went inside to read it, excusing himself for shutting the door again in my face. So I hung about for a while outside, and eventually he opened the door again and peeped around it...'

'Yes? And do you have a note from him?'

'No, Mistress. He did not write anything in reply. He said I must thank you for your kind invitation. But then he said that he is unable to accept just now in view of the serious condition of his patient within, and for fear of spreading this noxious disease himself. He said that he hoped for a speedy recovery by the poor person, and said that he would call in at the Plas in a few days when his patient had gone back home.'

'Very strange, Shemi,' said I. 'That reminds me, somewhat too forcefully, of a visit which I made to Werndew myself about ten years ago. I wonder who his patient is? Man or woman? Did you notice anything which might provide us with a clue?'

Shemi frowned and thought for a moment. 'Well yes, Mistress, now that you mention it. I did notice when Master Harries opened the door that there was a smell of sulphur in the air. And some coughing and snuffling from within. And

506

then when I was getting back on the pony to come home, I was sure I heard somebody sneezing in the back room. Very strange sneezes they were – sort of nasal and stifled.'

Good Times, Bad Times

21 June 1817

Midsummer, but it certainly does not feel like it. On the day after I wrote the last entry in my little book, it started to rain, and we have had rain and wind on every single day since then. Most of the hay is flattened, and I fear that the harvest will be lost, not just here at the Plas but throughout Pembrokeshire. That spells starvation, for with no fodder in haylofts and rickyards animals will die if they are not sold. And who will buy them if no merchants or breeders have fodder of their own? Prices will plummet. At the end of the summer there will be a glut of skinny sick animals passed over to the drovers, and they will try to get them alive to South Wales or to Smithfield, where they will have to compete with the drovers from Ceredigion and Cornwall who will also have too many miserable animals on their hands. Thank God that we had a light winter, and that our animals were outside a good deal, with the result that we still have one hayrick left from last year.

The rain and the wind and low cloud have made everybody miserable, but I have had so much to do in keeping the household going that I have had no time to be miserable myself, and indeed Betsi told me off this very morning for being so cheerful. I have been making great efforts to forget about the creature in black, and I am pleased to report that there have been no more sightings of him. Be he phantom or man, it has not been very good weather for wandering about on the common and frightening innocent people, so he has no doubt been tucked up somewhere nice and cosy. If he was at Joseph's house a month ago, he is certainly not there any longer, as I have observed for myself on two recent visits. My good friend has also been to see me once or twice, as jovial as can be, and both he and I have maintained our good relations by studiously avoiding any mention of the Nightwalker.

The bad weather has resulted in a much more varied midsummer social life than usual, and both Betsi and Daisy have been to visit various grand houses as guests. Daisy has so many invitations that I have to ration her acceptances, and I remind her frequently that acceptances create indebtedness and that debts have to be repaid. I foresee hard times ahead, and I am not prepared to contemplate streams of young gentlemen and young ladies and their chaperones descending upon us and requiring hospitality during the hungry months. Betsi is easier to satisfy, and I perceive that her main priority in life is to meet young Ioan Rhys of Cenarth as frequently as possible. He is a lively and good-looking fellow who is heir to an estate somewhat smaller than Plas Ingli, and if love should flower and marriage follow, the financial settlement will be but a modest one. Of course I would like her to marry up, but I married down, for love, and if she wants to do the same I will not object.

As for me, I try to remind myself that I am not as old as all that, and I have been greatly flattered by gentlemen's attentions during the past three weeks. In particular, my good friend Ceredig ap Tomos of New Moat has called to see me on several occasions, and I have accepted one invitation to visit him. Betsi went with me to his estate up in the mountains, and she assures me that the fellow is madly in love with me. I do not see that myself, but when I think of it I have to admit that his attentions have not wavered over ten years or more, and that he is nothing if not persistent. He is far too polite, of course, to declare his love openly. I am thankful for that, because it means I can enjoy his friendship and his hospitality without feeling greatly obliged to him, and can avoid the necessity to make decisions.

Today, in the pouring rain, I went up to my cave. I felt trapped by the four walls of the house and by the noise and bustle within it, and I needed to feel the wind in my hair and the driving rain upon my cheeks. I borrowed Billy's oilskins and must have looked a strange sight indeed as I set out to conquer the elements, but I was not in the least concerned about my appearance. I knew that I would get very wet, and indeed I did, but the wind was in the south, and there was warmth in the air. I battled my way up the mountain, and although I was lost in the cloud for most of my ascent, I was not really lost at all, for I knew every inch of the way. I had not been to my cave in pouring rain before, but it was a joyous experience, for it was surprisingly dry. Creeping inside, I made my way to my bed of plucked moss against the innermost wall, and there I sat, listening to the drips that came from various cracks and crevices in the roof and to the thundering deluge outside. I sat and dreamt, and my mind drifted to Owain, as it has often done, year after year. I knew that I still loved him, and wondered whether, against all the odds and against all the missiles fired at him by a cruel world, he might still be alive. Somewhere. Maybe, maybe. Ceredig, kind gentleman that he was, could never be a substitute for my beloved poet and gentle lover, brave beyond belief and sometimes as impulsive as a small child. Owain Laugharne was by no means perfect, but even with his imperfections I thought him quite perfect for me. Oh, that his eyes should still sparkle, and that his lungs should still breathe the good air. Oh, that he might be out there somewhere, with his heart still filled with love for me. Oh, that I might feel his lips upon mine and feel his arms folded around me.

Warmed by passion and by a strange sort of optimism which defied all logic, I wandered back down to the Plas, soaked to the skin and looking like a soggy sheepdog. Bessie gave me a reproving look, but I felt as happy as a small child who has just succeeded in making her parents very angry.

26 July 1817

The bad weather has continued, and the hay harvest is lost. The grasses and herbs in all of the hay meadows have been flattened by the wind and rain, and where there should be warm dry fields close-shaved by the harvesters' scythes there are pools of muddy water and matted vegetation. Even if the sun comes out tomorrow it is too late, for seed is set and there is no standing grass left to cut. If we try to harvest flattened grass we will have scything accidents, and in any case we will get only mud and woody stalks for our pains. There is nothing for it but to put the cattle into the hayfields in the hope that they can get some goodness into their stomachs, but within a few days they will turn the meadows into quagmires. The sheep are still on the mountain, looking thoroughly miserable and bedraggled, and we are seeing an outbreak of foot rot and other ailments about which Billy and Shemi are greatly concerned. Before long we will see deaths among the older animals, and, as I predicted, market prices are dropping sharply.

The animals are not the only ones who are suffering. The poor labourers and their wives and older children all depend upon the hay harvest for earning their first shillings of the year, and this year they have been sitting at home waiting for the rain to stop. I have been to visit some of them, and their leaky and ill-constructed hovels are streaming with water. Their packed-earth floors have been converted to muddy morasses, and their blankets, clothes and other fabrics are all damp in spite of their best efforts to keep fires going in their hearths. The typical hovel does not even have a proper chimney, and as the smoke filters out through the thatch, so the rain filters in, creating an atmosphere inside which is damp, smoky and putrid. Almost all of the poor people are suffering from chills and more severe ailments, some of which are very catching, and Havard Medical and Joseph Harries have hardly a moment to themselves as they rush hither and thither. I have tried to help too, since I have learnt a great deal from Joseph about ailments and how to treat them, but I have seen five old people and six children die in the last month in Cilgwyn alone, and God alone knows how many deaths will have been caused by the weather across the whole of West Wales.

Another problem arises out of the presence of several hundred travelling Irish harvesters in the area. They always arrive in early June, and follow the harvest from one estate to another, moving inland to the higher parts of mid-Wales in July, and then returning to Pembrokeshire in August to help with the corn harvest. This year there are even more vagrants in the area than in the old days, since many thousands of English and Welsh soldiers have returned from the wars with the French and are hunting for work. They are rough fellows, most of them, thrown from the blood and heroism of Waterloo straight into vagrancy and destitution. Their presence causes problems with the Irish, and there have been some ugly confrontations in the Newport inns. All of these labourers and their families, of whatever nationality, have been sitting around in barns, and crude shelters in the woods, waiting for the rain to stop. Now, after two months of looking for work and money, starvation is setting in, and petty thieving is on the increase. There has been a good deal of poaching from the River Nevern, and nearly all of the estates in the area have suffered from thefts of chickens, turnips, cabbages, geese and even sheep. Billy says that four of our older ewes have disappeared off the mountain, and he is sure that they have been stolen. I have been relatively lucky in that the members of the O'Connell family, who help with the Plas Ingli harvests, are perfectly honest, but they have been stuck in my barn for seven weeks and are very miserable indeed. I have tried to give them jobs in the pouring rain, mending walls and clearing ditches and plashing hedges, and I have paid them at half the harvesting rate, but I cannot afford to pay them or feed them any longer, and I have asked them to leave the barn tomorrow and move on. God knows where the unfortunate things will go, but I simply cannot afford to run down my cash resources any further.

In the midst of all this misery, I have worked hard to keep family and servants occupied and happy, although it has not been easy. We have maintained our social contacts, and just now Betsi and Daisy are in Haverfordwest staying with their cousins at the Bethesda manse. Dewi spends most of his time down on the Parrog, helping out in the shipyards and dreaming of the sea. As for me, the most notable occurrence has been the visit of Squire Price this very afternoon. He gave me advance warning, and arrived on

513

time, having ridden alone on his black stallion through the rain. He was very wet when he arrived, and I admonished him for placing his health at risk in such weather when he might just as well have come in his coach. He laughed that off, and said that he was not greatly concerned about his health, and that anyway he enjoyed a fast gallop through the wild wet wind.

He was in surprisingly buoyant humour, given the recent loss of his wife and daughter. He was not exactly jovial, but neither did he give the appearance of being a broken man, and I was pleased to find that he spoke quite freely about Mistress Susan and poor Fanny. Both he and I know something about grief, and this meant that there was a real understanding between us. I cannot say that I like the fellow, but his behaviour was less bombastic than it used to be, and I sensed that he was very lonely. That was understandable, since he is now all alone with his few servants in that enormous bleak house of his. There was more than a little awkwardness in our conversation, but then I was greatly surprised when he suddenly made an effusive apology for his past antagonism towards the Plas Ingli estate and towards me personally. He asked me for forgiveness, and for an assurance of future friendship between our two families and estates, and indeed I was happy to give such an assurance since he does not appear at present to be doing anything that might threaten me. However, I cannot forget that he is almost certainly the man who planned and paid for the sabotage of Owain's boat and presumably wished him dead.

Was this overture of friendship an admission of guilt, and a crude attempt to make amends?

The Squire suddenly asked to meet the children, and was greatly disappointed when I said that Betsi and Daisy were away. But Dewi, Sara and Brynach were at home, and they came into the parlour and behaved just as two young gentlemen and a lady should. They were very respectful, and the Squire showed great interest in their lessons and accomplishments. To my surprise, he made a special fuss of Brynach, who did not want to be made a fuss of. Finally, slightly embarrassed by his rebuttal, the old fellow had a quick chat with Grandpa Isaac and Grandma Jane before taking his leave. He wrapped up well in his capacious oilskins, and Billy brought his horse to the back door. Then he was off into the rain, with his big horse snorting and prancing and telling his master quite forcefully that the ferocious wind was not to his liking.

When the Squire had gone, I sat in the kitchen and consulted Bessie and Grandpa. I told them that I was puzzled by the Squire's sudden desire to make friends, and admitted that I did not trust him. I said that I had had too many encounters with elderly squires in the past, and that it was probably better for the estate if I had nothing to do with them. 'I have learnt to be very cautious,' said I. 'And I know from experience that when a spiteful squire suddenly makes overtures of friendship, he usually wants something. I suspect that that is what is happening here, but I cannot for the life of me work out what it is that he wants.'

'Come, come, Martha,' said Grandpa. 'George Price is a sad old man, and he has no family to speak of, and few enough friends. He needs friendship and social intercourse just as we all do, and maybe he sees the Plas as a place filled with life and love, and youthful energy. He probably finds that very attractive, and wants to come here occasionally to sniff the air and listen to the babble. Who knows what importance it might have for him in awakening happy memories and banishing recent sad ones? Give him the benefit of the doubt, Martha.'

'I agree, Mistress,' said Bessie. 'He is very lonely, of that there can be no doubt. He was a brutal fellow once, but people can change, and I perceive that the tragedies that have afflicted him have made him a gentler, kinder person. Have you not altered? Have I not, Mistress, as the years have slipped by?'

I laughed, and said: 'I see that I am overruled as usual in this revolutionary household. Very well. I must endeavour not to be vindictive myself, and to seek out goodness where in the past I might have searched for evil. I will try hard as it might be, and in spite of the misery brought on by this accursed rain, to be a friend of the Squire.'

But then, in the back of my mind, I recalled a mention long ago of the advanced pregnancy of the Squire's widowed daughter Susanna, around the time of Brynach's birth. I had never investigated that rumour properly, but could it be that Squire Price is Brynach's grandfather? And could that be the real explanation for his interest in the child? Father Time may yet reveal the truth.

1 September 1817

We had a few breaks in the weather during the month of August, but they came too late to save the corn harvest. We have lost three fields of barley, two of oats and one of wheat, with almost nothing left standing. The grain is spilled, there is mildew everywhere, and the beaten-down ears of corn are sprouting on the ground. This year there will be virtually no brewing, and there will be nothing to sell. The only field which we managed to harvest was Parc Haidd, which is very sandy and well drained. But the barley we were able to get into the barn is wet, and may not even suffice for our own needs over the winter. Grandpa and Billy are very worried that it may overheat, and I fear that I will have to employ my servants in moving it about in the barn in order to get air into it. I will probably also have to thresh before Christmas, and that goes against all the traditions of the Plas. Thank God that we have two acres of potatoes and will have a modest crop, whereas others have lost everything from the blight. We will survive somehow or other, but those who have no sandy fields are in desperate trouble.

A strange thing happened today, and I know not what to make of it. It was market day in Newport, and I wanted to dispose of six heifers and six bullocks for whatever price I could get. Billy drove the animals down on a morning of blustery wind and showers, and Will drove the light coach with Betsi, Bessie and me inside it. We all had different things to do. I spent most of my time trying to sell the animals, and in the end I disposed of them to a cattle merchant from Puncheston who will in turn pass them over to one of the drovers. I wanted cash in hand, and got it, but in truth two pounds a head meant that I was selling at a loss. Having done my deal, I drifted off to find the others. Betsi was in Master Price Very Nice's shop looking at some of the latest fashions from London, and I left her there with a gentle reminder that now was not an appropriate time to be looking at expensive clothes, let alone buying them, Master Price overheard me, and gave me a stern look. So I absented myself, and went in search of Bessie.

I happened upon her outside the Royal Oak, engaged in a deep and animated conversation with my friend Patty and none other than Squire Price. At first they did not see me, and I observed from a distance that they were talking on perfectly familiar terms, with much gesturing and even occasional laughter. But they were not speaking very loudly, and I could not make out what they were talking about. Then they saw me, and all three were covered in embarrassment. Bessie and Patty blushed, and then looked as if they were trapped upon a sinking ship. I was too close for them to take evasive action, so they could not melt away into the crowd, and Squire Price attempted to rescue them although in truth he was as discomfited as they were. 'Why, Mistress Martha!' he exclaimed, giving a deep bow. 'A very good day to you! Today I am truly blessed by chance encounters with beautiful ladies. We have been discussing this appalling weather, but I have been pleased to hear from Mistress Nicholas that the rain has not affected the mackerel, and that they have swum into her dear husband's nets in considerable numbers.' I curtsied and greeted all three of them, and talked about fish in order to make the Squire happy. But the conversation was very peculiar, with Bessie, Patty and the Squire all thinking more about what not to say than about what to say next. At last the Squire decided to absent himself on the grounds that he needed to buy a couple of good yearling rams, and knew where they might be found. He removed his hat and bowed with a flourish, and off he went. When he had gone, I looked Bessie and Patty in the eye asking them, without speaking, what that had all been about, but they declined to answer, and talked of other things. I did not press them, for I am resolved to be less inquisitive than I was, and to leave placid waters undisturbed.

We went our separate ways, for we all had other things to do. Purely by chance, I wandered back up to Market Street, where the sheep and cattle are always sold, and from a distance I spied Squire Price deep in conversation with none other than Meredith Lloyd Cwmgloyn. Their discussion was animated, but they spoke very softly, with frequent looks over their shoulders to ensure that nobody overheard what was passing between them. Then they shook hands, and Squire Price walked off to the yard of the Llwyngwair Arms. He collected his black stallion, which was tethered there, and a minute later I saw him riding off along East Street, heading for home. I walked up the street, and almost bumped into Meredith, who was looking at a rather scrawny sow which one of the Dinas tenant farmers was trying to sell. We talked of children and other things, and then I said: 'I hear that you had a couple of yearling rams for sale. Have they gone, and did you get a sensible price?'

'Yearling rams?' Meredith laughed. 'Wherever did you get that idea, Martha? I sold all my surplus stock in June, and having lost twenty ewes and five rams to this miserable weather I should be buying rather than selling just now. No, I can assure you that you have been misinformed.'

1 December 1817

I will not indulge in a catalogue of our woes, but I have to record that the harvest failures and the damage done to livestock and to farming activities generally have brought the estate to a low ebb. Market prices which were once stable and predictable have been so erratic that the only people making money have been the middlemen. Skiff Abraham is the only one I have dealt with on a regular basis, since he and I have an understanding and neither of us wishes to exploit the other. But generally I have tried to buy and sell by direct trades with other squires or tenant farmers. Hay cannot now be bought for love or money, and the prices of barley, wheat and oats dropped sharply in August and September because the quality of the harvest was so miserable, and then went shooting upwards in

November when everybody wanted to buy and nobody wanted to sell. Animal prices have been similarly erratic, but generally they are lower than anybody can remember as nobody has the feed to keep beasts alive over the winter. I have sent forty sheep and twenty cattle off to Birmingham with Ifan Dafis Drover and have broken a rule of a lifetime by allowing him to pay me on his return. He would not pay me cash in hand, because he says that conditions are so bad across the Welsh mountains that he cannot guarantee the survival of any of the animals in his care. And he knows not whether the prices at the other end of his route will be sky high or rock bottom. So I have to wait until the New Year for his reappearance, with not the faintest idea of how much money he will be carrying home in his bag for me. I trust him, for he is an honest fellow, but we are dealing with matters beyond his control.

While our returns from the land have fallen, there has been a terrible reduction in garden and wild supplies also. The potato crop was modest, but there were virtually no apples, pears or cherries to pick this year, and the usual hedgerow harvest of blackberries, bilberries, damsons and elderberries failed to materialize. The field mushrooms were so rotten and maggoty that we could collect hardly any. The hens and ducks have almost stopped laying. Milk supplies have dropped sharply, and that means we will have problems through the winter with butter and cheese. I am sorely tempted to sell four of our working horses since they have to be fed regardless and give us no produce in return, but nobody wants to buy horses just now and I will have to keep them for better or worse. Bessie has already started to put the household on hard rations, and there will be no high living at Plas Ingli this winter. I am putting the word about that there will be no Christmas feasting for tenants and labourers this year since there is so little on the pantry shelves that Bessie will be hard put to it to feed those of us who live beneath this roof, let alone a multitude of starving people from the cottages and hovels dotted about on the estate. I know that disease will be rife in the coming months, and that people will die, but what can I do?

I will not lay off any of my servants, although on rainy and windy days when the yard and the fields are streaming with liquid mud there is virtually nothing they can do outside, and it might appear that they are all under-employed. But here I am driven by sentiment rather than economics. They have truly been my guardian angels over the years, and I will not betray them. I will keep all of them on, and they will stay fed and clothed and warm. But they know that my cash reserves have almost run out, and I have therefore had to reduce their wages.

Grandpa Isaac sat with me in the office three days since, and we looked at the estate accounts in great detail. We were appalled at what we discovered, and we asked Lewis Legal to call in and give us the benefit of his advice. He appeared out of the driving rain this morning, and found a household that was not very cheerful. He was not very cheerful himself, and reported that five substantial estates in the neighbourhood have become insolvent during the last fortnight. They were all carrying large debts, unlike the Plas, and the prospects for the future of all the local estates are dismal indeed. Master Lewis looked at our figures, shook his head and said 'Oh dear, oh dear' in a manner that appeared to presage the end of the world. Then he said: 'Mistress Martha, my advice is that you should get married as soon as may be convenient.'

'Whatever do you mean, Master Lewis?' I asked.

'I mean that the estate is only just solvent, and cannot stand any further reductions in farm prices. You have no big debts, but next year you will be hard pressed to collect your rents from Penrhiw and the other farms either in cash or in kind. The tenants are all in desperate trouble, and even if you evict all of them you will be no better off. You have five growing children to clothe and feed. Indeed, they are hardly children any longer, but young people with hearty appetites, a passion for good clothes and a need for education. You want to send Dewi to Eton, and then maybe Brynach as well. Betsi and Daisy will require allowances, and when Betsi marries you will have to make a marriage settlement...'

'Enough, enough, Master Lewis. I know all of this, and am considerably worried about it. But getting married will not solve anything, for every other estate in West Wales has similar problems to those of the Plas.'

'But Master Ceredig ap Tomos of New Moat? As I understand it, he has demonstrated a great affection for you over the years. He has a sizeable estate, well run and in good order, with no encumbrances, and no children to educate or feed. And I know, for I look after his affairs, that his tenants pay their rents on time, and in cash.'

'But New Moat is a terrible place. It rains there all the time.'

'The same can be said, I think, of Plas Ingli.'

At this I managed to smile. 'In that you are correct, at least for this miserable year of 1817,' I said. 'But next year will be different. I will not marry Master ap Tomos, kind gentleman as he is, because I do not love him. In any case I am still betrothed to Master Owain Laugharne.'

'Very convenient, Martha,' said Master Lewis with a sigh. He stood up and prepared to leave. 'But remember what I say. You need more cash if you are not to go to the wall within three months. You will soon have people banging on your door and demanding monies. How will you pay your tithes, your county rates and the poor rate? Mark my words, the latter will go up next month; there are so many paupers and vagrants to be fed and clothed that the churchwardens are in despair. I know it, for I spoke to Charlie Toms and Daniel Thomas yesterday. I happen to know that Master Ceredig has cash reserves, and I am trying to be helpful.'

'I appreciate your kindness in that regard, Master Lewis,' said I, as he bowed and kissed my hand. 'I will think on what you say.'

When he had gone, I went up to my room and sat there for a long time, looking out of the window at a desolate landscape washed by sheets of rain and partly obscured by drifting low cloud. I should have been overwhelmed by despair, but in truth I was not, and when I allowed free rein to my intuition I knew that there would soon be sadness, but that all would at last be well. Should I dig up the Plas Ingli treasure? Should I marry Ceredig? No, and no again. My instinct told me that times were hard, and might get harder, but that I could cope.

21 December 1817

The shortest day of the year, and tomorrow the days will start to lengthen. Christmas and New Year will be miserable indeed, with good cheer and fine food in short supply, but at last the rain has stopped, and we have a cold dry spell of weather. Grandpa says that the weather pattern was similar in the famine year of 1768, when after six months of almost unbroken rain the following winter was mild and dry and the next harvest was the heaviest he has ever known.

The sadness which I predicted has come, for three days after the last entry in my little book I received a message to say that my dear father George had died quietly in his sleep at Brawdy. He had not been ill, and my mother was greatly shocked, but we all gained some consolation from the fact that he never suffered, and was not, in his declining years, confined to a sickbed. When I got the news I left Betsi in charge of the Plas and travelled over to Brawdy with Dewi and Daisy in the coach. We stayed there with Mother until the funeral was over and done with, and we were blessed by the fact that Catrin and Nansi also moved in. The *gwylnos* was a busy affair, with last respects paid by several hundred people. I judged that Dewi was old enough to take a turn in guarding the coffin, and he did this with his cousins John and Edward. Morys came and arranged the funeral with the Rector of Brawdy. And a big funeral it was, with over two hundred walking behind the hearse on a calm and warm December day. Mother was of course distraught, and we all wept, but the grieving was not as dramatic and intense as it might have been, for Father was a good age and his death was as good as these things *can* be.

Then, in the sorting out of the Brawdy estate, a very considerable benefit came my way. When we sat down with Phillips Legal from Haverfordwest to hear the contents of Father's will, I was surprised to find that I was to receive a substantial inheritance. Morys inherits the estate, of course, although Mother will remain in residence until her death. And much to my surprise, Morys says that he will abandon his ministry and move back to Brawdy as soon as may be arranged. He has ministered to his flock for nigh on twenty years, and he is reluctant to leave it, but he feels that it is now his duty to take over Father's role. And he will be a wise and benign squire, of that I have no doubt, in spite of the fact that at present he knows next to nothing about farming or estate management. I will help him, and so will Catrin and James, and in any case the estate has an excellent steward who has been there for twelve years.

Catrin, Elen and I receive five thousand pounds each, to be paid immediately after the legal affairs have all been sorted out. Elen, in America, will no doubt be thrilled when she receives a communication from Master Phillips, but Catrin and I were almost speechless when we heard the news. 'Five thousand each!' I gasped. 'Are you sure there is not some mistake, Master Phillips?'

'I can assure you, Mistress Martha, that all is in order,' replied the attorney. 'Your father was a man with foresight. He has been putting away cash for many years when others might have purchased land. I have it in gold sovereigns and paper money in my safe. He assumed that it is the way of the world that money would be used more and more, and he reasoned that his daughters would need it in considerable quantities.'

'I am ashamed to admit that he was quite correct in that regard,' said I. 'I have resisted this obsession with money as hard as I could, but I also have to confess that it will be very welcome at the moment.'

So it was that this very morning Phillips Legal came over from Haverfordwest with a sturdy leather bag containing five thousand pounds. Lewis Legal accompanied him, and I had to sign various bits of paper to make everything official. Then off Master Phillips went to Castlebythe, to deliver another windfall to Catrin and James. When he had gone, I sat down with Master Lewis and Grandpa Isaac and made a list of all our debts. I gave my legal friend all the money he needed, and instructed him to pay them off. I also restored the wages of my servants to former levels, and paid them a sovereign each in recompense for past hardships. That left almost four thousand pounds in the leather bag. I decided to set aside a thousand as a protection against future catastrophes, and to keep five hundred in order to replenish our larder and see us through the winter. I then asked Master Lewis what I should do with the residue.

'Buy more land, Martha,' said he. 'Your father made very wise provision for you and your sisters, but money under the bed does not appreciate. Nobody is in the market for land at the moment, not even the big squires like Lord Cawdor or the Owens or Phillipses. The harvest failures and continuous rain have hit all of them hard. I happen to know that if you put in offers of £1,280 for Fachongle Isaf, and £1,100 for Llystyn, you will get them.'

'I had no idea they were for sale, Master Lewis.'

'Everything is for sale, Martha, if price and time are both right.'

I turned to Grandpa Isaac. 'What shall I do, Grandpa?' I asked.

'Buy, Martha,' he said without hesitation. 'This period of low land values is an aberration. With all these soldiers and sailors returning from the wars against the French, I predict that there will soon be thousands more mouths to feed in this area, and a great demand for land. The value of farms, especially fertile ones like Llystyn, will go shooting upwards. It pains me to say this, but insist on cash payments of rent from now on. And remember that you can always sell land if things should become tight, or if you need to raise money for marriage settlements.'

'Very well,' I replied. 'Gentlemen, I respect your judgement, and I will follow your advice. Buy Llystyn and Fachongle Isaf, if you please, Master Lewis, and try for both of them at a starting price of one thousand pounds. We might be lucky, especially if we offer cash on the nail. And finally, my dear friends, may I please now have your permission not to get married?'

'In the circumstances, yes,' said Grandpa. Master Lewis smiled and concurred, then went on his way, carrying my leather bag over his shoulder.

12 July 1818

More than six months have passed. And I thank God for the fact that the new hay harvest is safely gathered in and that the barley harvest looks like being a good one. We will survive, but some estates have collapsed already and others are still in grave danger. The winter was neither as hard as I feared, nor as benign as Grandpa Isaac predicted, but there were three cold and snowy spells, and the Grim Reaper has been stalking about with a cruel sneer on his face. Starvation was already a fact of life in the neighbourhood before Christmas, and matters deteriorated steadily in the first three months of the New Year. I have counted twenty-seven deaths in our small community alone, mostly of elderly people and small babies, but including a number of previously fit and healthy labourers and their wives and children. There have been food riots, protests against the game laws, and major disputes over the payment of tithes. Six distraint sales have taken place in and around Newport, and each of them was accompanied by ugly scenes in which the Rector and the constables were subjected to a torrent of stones and abuse. Indeed the Rector has become so unpopular in Newport that he has decided to absent himself more or less permanently, and nobody has seen him since Christmas. Curate Maggs, poor fellow, has had to cope as best he can with a diminishing and increasingly critical congregation. I have made a number of contributions for the relief of the poor, and I have helped Joseph whenever I can in his ministrations to the sick, but even if I were to spend all of my cash reserves on food and clothing for the needy I could not divert the Grim Reaper from his chosen route. However, I think that at last he has gone on his way, discouraged by the improved weather and the prospect of a fruitful late summer and autumn.

While the world beyond the Plas has been in a state of upheaval, I have had quite enough to cope with beneath my own roof. My greatest problem has been Daisy, who is now seventeen. Of course I love her dearly, but of late she has been rebellious and impertinent, and I have had many flaring disputes with her. She seems to me to be quite uninterested in improving herself, and her tutor, young Alexander Williams, can do nothing with her. She will not study her music or her literature, and although she is perfectly fluent in Welsh she increasingly pretends, in the presence of others, that English is her preferred language and that Welsh culture has nothing to offer but leeks, flannel skirts and tall moleskin hats. She appears only to be interested in young men and parties, and I am currently fighting to prevent her from rushing off to Tenby for the summer season. She says that it is the only place where civilized company is to be found, and that she is bored at the Plas. Betsi, as her best friend and confidante, pleads with her to contain her wild excesses, and I told her some days since that I would not contemplate an expedition to the south coast without a chaperone. So she made it her mission to try to arrange a suitable lady, and came back to me with a triumphant smile, announcing that she could stay with Mistress Olwen Owen, who is the great-aunt of the Squire of Gelli Fawr. I replied that I would have nothing to do with the Owens of Gelli Fawr, for they are silly people who live beyond their means. In any case, I told her, I would give her no allowance for a stay in Tenby. And back she came, yesterday, with the information that she could now stay with Mistress Dilly Huws, who is a cousin of the old Squire of Bayvil and has a splendid town house overlooking the North Beach. What is more, she declared with victory in her voice, Mistress Huws insisted that she should travel thither in her carriage, which she would send for her, and that if the finances of the Plas are as tight as they appear to be she would be only too pleased to have Daisy to stay as her special guest, at no cost at all. Naturally enough, I gritted my teeth and glared at her, and said: 'Daisy, how could you? How could you betray me and our family by spreading such malicious rumours for your own ends? That settles it. I absolutely forbid you to go to Tenby. Now go to your room and consider how best you may recover the goodwill of your mother!' And off she stormed in a torrent of tears, slamming every door between kitchen and bedroom. At such times, when I am red hot with fury and frustration, I long to have a man at my side who can impose discipline and bring a cool detachment to situations created and exacerbated by female emotions. If only Owain were here! Perhaps even Ceredig could play the role of hard-hearted father in a perfectly satisfactory fashion.

But I will not be worn down by Daisy, for I have other loyalties too. At least Sara and Brynach are diligent with their lessons, and are growing up to be delightful young people. Dewi will go to Eton in September, whether he likes it or not. He is a perfectly intelligent and charming young fellow, and he has all the qualities to make an excellent Squire of Plas Ingli. But he insists that he wants to go to sea, and that he has no interest in the classics or in mathematics or in mastering French. I hope that Eton will convince him of the virtues of learning. In order to satisfy his maritime leanings, I agreed last month to take a majority share in the sloop *Lucy* due to be launched in August from Master Havard's shipyard on the estuary. He can be a merchant and a shipowner if he pleases, but I will not allow him to be a sailor. He has begged over and again to be allowed to join the crew of the vessel on its maiden voyage, but he is too young, and no son and heir to the Plas Ingli estate will ever go to sea again. That happened once before, when David's elder brother Griffith went to sea at the age of nineteen, and was pushed overboard by a fellow sailor at the behest of Moses Lloyd Cwmgloyn. Furthermore, Grandpa Isaac, who was the one who allowed Griffith to go to sea in the first place, has been racked by guilt ever since. He has never talked about it, but I know it none the less.

And Betsi? My dear, beautiful, desirable oldest daughter was betrothed to Ioan Rhys of Cenarth last month, with my blessing and the blessings of Grandma and Grandpa. The marriage settlement is already agreed, and I am well pleased with it. The wedding will be at the end of August in St Mary's church in Newport, and I will ensure that it is a grand affair. I will be distraught to see Betsi leave home, and without her I am sure I will find it harder to be a sensible parent and a wise guardian of the estate. But her happiness is paramount, and it is apparent that she is very much in love with this fine strong young gentleman. I have met him on many occasions, and he has been a great support to us over the long winter and spring. I could not wish for a finer son-in-law or a better father for my first grandchildren. The prospect, which now confronts me, of becoming a grandmother at the age of forty-one is something which delights and terrifies me at the same time. How I long to cuddle a little grandson in my arms, and to tell him long and magical stories! Betsi's firstborn will be a son, as will her second child. I do not understand how I know these things, but there is not a shadow of doubt in my mind or my heart. Joy indeed, but alongside the joy is the anxiety that accompanies the passing of time. Time passes. Inexorably, with every rolling wave on the sands of Traeth Mawr, with every bursting bud and every falling leaf...

★ ★ ★

Editor's note: There are no diary entries for the period between 12 July 1818 and 6 April 1822, apart from one brief note relating to a fortnight spent in Cardiff, and another mentioning a week in Haverfordwest. There is effectively a gap of almost four years in Martha's record of events relevant to this story.

PART THREE: 1822

Destiny and Duty

6 April 1822

I have had a premonition unlike any other, and I know now that my last encounter with the Nightwalker is imminent.

As before, my sense of foreboding coincides with the approach of Brynach's birthday. Tomorrow he will be fifteen years old, and as usual we will take a picnic on Carn Edward. I suspect that it will be the last time we follow this particular tradition, for young gentlemen are generally not very keen on picnics with their old mothers. But since Brynach is currently home from school to celebrate Easter he agreed to it, so long as he could invite various friends including young Anne Edwards of Trefach. Mention of that young lady's name brings a sparkle to his eye and a blush to his cheek, and since she is his first love it is just as well, when they are together, for me to keep a maternal eye on the proceedings.

When I went down to the kitchen this morning Sara and Brynach were already sitting at the table, tucking into their toasted barley bread and butter. Sara immediately picked up on my troubled mood, and asked me what was wrong. 'Oh, I did not sleep very well, *cariad*,' I replied, 'for I had a troublesome dream. I will probably recover as the day goes on.'

'Oh, Mother! You and your dreams and pre-monitions! You are always the same when Brynach's birthday draws near, prowling about all day long, with a countenance like thunder...'

'Sara, whatever do you mean?'

Brynach laughed and replied for her. 'Come now, Mother. It is a family tradition that you love going up to Carn Edward on my birthday, but that you are terrified before we go and greatly relieved when we arrive home again afterwards. We joke about it every year.'

'And of course nothing terrible ever happens,' said Sara. 'The worst thing that ever happened was some years ago, when we had that picnic in the fog, and you suddenly insisted that we should pack everything up and come home for no reason whatsoever.'

Now I had to laugh too, and in truth I did feel more than a little foolish. I had not realized how observant my children were. So I said, 'You are quite right, both of you. But one day you will realize for yourselves that mothers do have wild and terrible fantasies about things that might happen to their children. It is one of the afflictions of parenthood. But let us be positive. The weather will be wonderful tomorrow, and I suspect that up among the rocks we will all be seeking the shade. Betsi and Ioan and little Benjamin will be with us in mid-morning, and so will your friends. Cousins John and Mark will arrive this afternoon, bearing news of Castlebythe. I want Bessie and Liza to join us as well. We will be a veritable multitude!'

As I spoke, I caught Bessie's eye, for I recalled my confrontation with her following the occasion of Brynach's tenth birthday picnic. She read my mind, and gave me the slightest of smiles, and carried some dishes out to the scullery. I wished that I could be equally clever at reading her mind, and discerning what she did yesterday and what she will do tomorrow. Then I caught the eyes of Billy, Shemi and Will, and realized that they had been listening to the breakfast table conversation as well. They looked as innocent as bewhiskered newborn babes, all three of them, and I knew that something was afoot.

7 April 1822

The occasion which filled me with dread has come and gone, and I am relieved to report that nothing untoward happened. The day dawned calm and bright, and throughout daylight hours we were blessed by unbroken sunshine and the gentlest of southerly breezes. In mid-morning Sara and Brynach and I visited the family enclosure in Cilgwyn churchyard and paid our respects at the graves of my beloved David, Grandpa Isaac and Grandma Jane. While we were away, the young men from Castlebythe helped with the picnic-making, and when we arrived back at the doorstep of the Plas everything was ready. Anne Edwards had arrived, looking as pretty and fresh as the first spring buttercup, and there were three other friends from Newport. Betsi, Ioan and their lovely little boy Benjamin - my first grandson – were also there, and for a while there was a pandemonium of laughter, greetings and embraces. We three residents changed out of our sombre clothes into lighter and brighter garments, and away we all went up the mountain track. The strong young men carried the picnic hampers. On the way, I insisted on anointing myself at Ffynnon Brynach in spite of the frivolous and flippant comments from the young people. I laughed with them, of course, but if truth be told I was a little irritated by their lack of respect for my traditions.

The picnic was a perfectly happy affair, enlivened by the cheerful conversation of the five cousins and by music and dancing. What gave me most pleasure was the spirited fiddling and tootling by Brynach. I was quite taken aback by his new skills on the violin and the tin whistle. I knew that he had some musical talent, but since he has been in Haverfordwest he has had some lessons with a young and sprightly music teacher who clearly knows more about Irish jigs than about the stately works of Masters Handel and Mozart. Sara was thoroughly delighted, as were my nephews John and Mark, and dear Betsi and Ioan, while Anne, of course, was utterly entranced. I watched her, and saw young love in her eyes. I was not at all surprised, by that, for Brynach, with his dark complexion, his brown eyes and his black hair, and his lean and lively body, has every girl in the *cwm* chasing after him. For all I know, every girl in Haverfordwest may be chasing after him as well, when he is in residence at the grammar school.

After our picnic I wanted to rest and listen to the happy laughter and chatter of the next generation, and the one after that, but they would have none of it, and wanted me to dance. So we all made merry on the dusty grass, with Brynach providing the music and Betsi teaching the steps. We spun and whirled, and made intricate patterns, and got thoroughly confused, and tripped over each other, and sometimes fell into hysterical heaps of humanity on the ground. 'Mother,' said Brynach after a while, with a cheeky grin on his face, 'your dancing does you credit. You do very well for an old lady.' So I chased him and caught him, and boxed his ears for his insolence, and was rewarded with gales of laughter and three cheers from everybody else. After that I really did have to lie down, and while the rest of them carried on dancing little Benjamin crawled over to join me, and he and I searched for beetles and ants in the grass. At last he was overcome with exhaustion, and so I sat up and took him onto my lap, and he fell asleep in my arms.

In the midst of all the jollification, as I sat with my back against a rock, nursing the new love of my life, I could not resist glancing up onto the moorland at intervals, and to west and east, and down the rocky slope towards the *cwm*. I still had a gnawing concern that the Nightwalker might materialize out of nowhere and transform hilarity into horror. But all I saw were sheep, and the occasional mountain pony, and ravens and buzzards overhead. My blessed friend Bessie noticed my restlessness, and came over and sat next to me. She put her arm round my shoulder and whispered: 'Do not worry, Mistress Martha. He will not come. You can take my word for it. You will never see him again.'

541

'Dear Bessie,' said I, 'you are getting too clever by half at reading my mind. But may I ask how you know these things?'

'You may ask, Mistress, but I will not reply.' And she kissed me on the cheek, and went off to tidy up the debris of the picnic with Liza. She left me reassured, but also irritated. Not for the first time, I feel that I am the only one at the Plas who does not know what is really going on.

8 April 1822

There is a postscript to the picnic. I was so tired last evening, after all that prancing about on the mountain, that I forgot to mention the strange activities of the menservants. Soon after breakfast yesterday, before we three remaining members of the Morgan family made our way to the churchyard, Billy, Shemi and Will nodded at each other and got to their feet together. 'Mistress Martha,' said Billy, 'we were up early, and have done our chores. We are missing four lambing ewes, we are, and we think they might have lambed up on the mountain. If it is all right with you, Mistress, we are minded to go and find them since the weather is so auspicious just now.'

'By all means, Billy,' said I. 'Off you go. The weather may well be inauspicious by tomorrow.'

We did not see them all day, and they returned to the Plas at dusk, just in time for supper. Their clothes were even more filthy than usual, and they looked dog-tired. They had clearly walked a long way. 'Did you find the sheep?' I asked.

'Indeed no, Mistress,' said Shemi. 'But there's a funny thing for you. When we got back, there they were, with the rest of the flock, and with six new little lambs. They must have found their own way home while we was away.'

'Now pull the other leg,' said I. 'Come on, Shemi. What were you three really doing today?'

'I am sorry, Mistress, but I cannot speak of it. Shall we say that we were simply protecting your interests?'

14 April 1822

Brynach has gone back to school in the county town, John and Mark have gone home, and suddenly this place filled with youthful energy has been transformed into something quiet and sombre. I am not sure that I like it this way. Sara and I are left all alone with the servants, and I fear that at such times I am prone to introspection. I am driven even further towards dark thoughts by the realization that almost everybody in the Plas seems to share some secret from which I am excluded. Sara claims to know nothing about it, and I tend to believe her. But Bessie, Billy, Will, Shemi and even Liza know something, and no matter how much I press them they will not divulge what is going on. It has something to do with the Nightwalker, of that I am certain, but my attempts to extract information leave them all smiling at me beatifically while I shake with impotent rage.

Joseph came today for tea, and I sat with him and complained about the secrecy and evasiveness of my servants. I said that I was minded to dismiss the whole lot of them on the grounds that they were conspiring against me, but Joseph slapped his knees and chortled with glee. 'Martha Morgan, you are quite priceless!' he spluttered. 'You will of course do nothing of the sort. How, on earth or in heaven, would you replace such a cloud of angels? Quite impossible. You have made excellent progress, my dear friend, in curbing your tendency to interfere and to insist on knowing everything. Do you not remember what I have told you over and again during our years of friendship? Trust them, Martha. Trust them all. If ever you are threatened again, by forces inside or outside your household, your intuition will warn you. I am quite certain of that. Do you feel threatened?'

'Well, no, but–'

'So there we are. Excellent! Now might I have another slice of that incomparable *bara brith?* That Bessie of yours is a miracle-worker when it comes to baking. If I was ten years younger, I would steal her from you and marry her myself.'

Joseph would not say another word about secrets or about the Nightwalker, and insisted on talking instead about traditional baking recipes. I thought it very insensitive of him, and said as much. He was quite unmoved, and that does not really surprise me since he, like my friends Patty and Meredith, and probably like most of the neighbourhood, is part of the plot.

While I am in the mood for it, I must record that in the four years which have elapsed since my entry of 12 July 1818, I have experienced a good deal more sadness than happiness. Some of the misfortunes were of my own making, and in spite of long conversations with Joseph and Bessie I am still trying to come to terms with the consequences of my mistakes.

In the year 1819 the sloop *Lucy* was finally made seaworthy after long delays over sails and ropes, and during sea trials in Cardigan Bay it proved to be a fine and beautiful vessel. I accepted it, and paid the residue of my majority share. I took Jake's advice on the skills of the Parrog sailing fraternity, and appointed Willy Ifans as Master. He chose three local men as his crew, and we organized a cargo of wool, barley and slates from the Aberrhigian sea quarry to go across to Cork and the other southern Irish ports. He said he would have no difficulty in disposing of everything on board, and would spend the earnings on linen cloth, butter, cheeses, and other farm products which were cheap on the other side of St George's Channel. There would be healthy profits for me and the other shareholders. Then Dewi started to bother me with endless requests to be allowed to join the vessel on its maiden trading voyage. I refused absolutely, on the grounds that he was due to go to Eton in three weeks' time. But he kept at me, and said that the *Lucy* would be back in plenty of time for him to set off for college. Besides, he said, if he was to be a competent manager of the estate in the years to come, and a sensible ship-owner, he needed to learn about sailing, trading, cargo stowage and such like. He sensed that I was weakening in my resolve, and faithfully promised that he would work with all possible diligence at Eton and Oxford if he could learn how to be a seafaring merchant by joining occasional short voyages between times. So against my better judgement I let him go to Cork. The voyage was a great success, and brought me a tidy profit. Captain Ifans reported that Dewi was a natural seaman and a dependable colleague, and said that he could join the crew on any future voyage if he so wished.

So Dewi went to Eton, and came home for Christmas and New Year. Immediately after New Year the *Lucy* was in port, and Captain Ifans planned a short trading voyage to Wexford. He would be away for no longer than a week. Dewi begged to be allowed to go too, since he had some days to spare before returning to college, and I agreed. Off he went, sixteen years old and full of the joys of youth. I never saw my sweet golden-haired boy alive again. On the return voyage the ship was overtaken by a fearsome northerly storm and was driven onto the Bishops and Clerks to the west of St David's. I knew immediately that something terrible had happened, and was not surprised when the news came that it had been lost with all hands. Five men dead, including my bright and loving child who had brought me endless joy. His blessed body was washed up a week later on the beach at Whitesands, desecrated almost out of recognition. They found the bodies of Captain Ifans and one other crew member as well, but the others were never recovered. Billy and Will went with the light carriage all the way to St David's and brought the three bodies home, wrapped in canvas bags.

Even now, more than two years after, I cannot

bear to describe the funeral or the days that pre-
ceded and succeeded it. In truth I can hardly recall
any of the details, and even now, as I write on a
calm and warm April evening, I find that my hand
is shaking and my heart gripped by a cold fear.
The loss of a beloved husband or an old parent is
hard enough for even the bravest soul to cope
with, and God knows that I have coped with grief
less bravely than most. But the loss of an innocent
child is something different, something darker and
infinitely more terrifying. Dewi, who came from
my own body, whom I nursed and loved with an
intensity I still cannot describe, died because of
my stupidity. I cannot forgive myself. It was all my
fault. In my black moments, when guilt and grief
join forces in assaulting me, I feel a physical pain
in the very pit of my stomach, as if my womb has
been torn out of me. Not even the kind and gentle
words of Joseph and Bessie and my other friends
can reduce the agony of my affliction.

I fear that I am too upset to continue.

15 April 1822

Last night, not for the first time, I cried myself to
sleep like a small baby. Today I am calmer, and
Liza, who knows all about hardship and loss, has
encouraged me to keep on writing about the year
1820. She says that it will help me, and I hope
that she is right.

After Dewi's death I tried to struggle out of my
melancholia, and indeed Sara and Brynach did all
that they could to cheer me up. But it was not easy

for me or for them, for I felt isolated and abandoned. My sister Catrin and my friends Mary Jane and Ellie were occupied with their own domestic affairs, and even Joseph was not able to call in as often as I would have liked. So things came to a head with Daisy, who was nineteen at the time. Perhaps I was too absorbed by my own grief, and maybe I neglected her needs as a growing young woman. But relations between us worsened dramatically, and she became so fickle and flirtatious that local tongues began to wag. In spite of Sara's attempts to calm both of us down, and to act as an intermediary, we had furious arguments about clothes, and lessons, and which parties she could attend, and even about hair styles and shoes. In retrospect, it was all silly and even childish, on my part as well as hers. But in May, after endless pleading from my erratic daughter, I agreed to let her go to London to train as an actress. I thought that she was probably old enough to look after herself, and that the discipline of training might be good for her. I obtained assurances from Bella Simpkins, a remote relative of mine, that she could stay with her in Hampstead under conditions of close supervision. But I fear that Bella proved not to be a very good chaperone, and as early as June I began to receive messages from Daisy which suggested that she was living well beyond her means, with parties, balls, and visits to coffee houses featuring strongly. There was no mention of acting or training. At first she asked for her allowance to be increased, and when I refused she started to send unpaid bills to the Plas, marked for my attention. At first I paid them, for they were trifling amounts, but then they became larger, for exotic dresses and bonnets, and for necklaces and bangles made of gold and precious stones. I refused to pay these, and I wrote to Daisy and demanded that she should come home immediately. At about the same time I picked up rumours, from other local families who have relatives in London, that Daisy had been seen regularly in the company of the new king's disreputable confederates. In August Daisy did return home, but we had a truly terrible argument and she swept off to London again, taking all her possessions with her. Her parting words, which are carved onto my heart, were these: 'Mother, I do not need your money and I do not need the Plas. I am better off in London, and I have patrons who will look after me. Farewell. I have a life to live, and you will never see me again.' Since then, all of my desperate and loving letters have gone unanswered, but early in October news came from a friend to say that my daughter was with child, and that a Scottish duke was the probable father.

Before I had come to terms with that heart-churning news, another tragedy followed. My beloved Grandpa Isaac suffered a seizure and died after a few days in his sickbed. He was eighty years old. At the end he could not speak, and I am not sure that he recognized me or anybody else, and I suppose that his passing was preferable to a long period of agony or of wasting away. Joseph came, but could do nothing for him. I was at his bedside with Sara when he stopped breathing, and afterwards I was far more distressed than I had been at the death of my own father. Grandpa had given me love and respect, which I had willingly reciprocated. He and I had shared a great deal, and he more than any other person had taught me how to work with servants, tenants and labourers, and how to look after the affairs of the estate. When I had finished with weeping, I knew that I would find it hard to manage without the old man, and so it has proved.

Grandma Jane reacted not at all to the death of her husband, and although she attended the funeral she did not weep. She continued for several months to behave as if Grandpa was still alive, but she stopped eating properly, and we all think that she decided it was time to die. She lasted for some months, growing weaker and weaker, and then died in her sleep in the month of February in 1821, at the age of seventy-nine. With her, our grief was more constrained, for her death was a matter of choice, and nobody was surprised by it. But she had been a woman of strong character and infinite wisdom, and in looking back at my time in Plas Ingli I was reminded forcefully of the unconditional love which she had given me from the day of my arrival. Cool and constrained she might have been, but I had loved her as if I had been one of her own children, and I recalled one occasion after another when she had rescued me from impending disaster or had offered me wise counsel and even admonishment as appropriate. The settle by the side of the *simnai fawr* looks empty indeed without her, and with her passing the quality of my own life has been greatly diminished.

10 May 1822

Since the day of Brynach's birthday I have been overwhelmed by waves of despair, and I cannot explain why. The Maytime weather is as bright and cheerful as can be, and the hedgerows are aglow with bluebells, primroses, buttercups and red campion. When I wake every morning the dawn chorus echoes round the misty *cwm*, as it has done in May from the dawn of time. The estate is doing well, and we have recovered from the horrors of the past. I should be content, but I am not.

The house is too quiet. Oh, for the sound of a crying baby, or even the noise of small children squabbling in the nursery or rushing back and forth along the passages. Sara is the only one left at the Plas, seventeen years old and growing more beautiful with every day that passes, but not at all interested in young gentlemen and balls and social evenings. She says that it is her duty to help me, and I tell her that indeed it is not, for her main duty is to herself and to the securing of her future happiness. She is studious to a fault, and although she has not had a regular tutor since Master Alexander Williams left to get married, she is now a very accomplished young lady who sings delightfully, converses freely in three languages, and even understands Dimetian Welsh. If I would let her, she could read my diaries. But her health is a concern to me, and she catches chills with alarming frequency. Joseph has examined her, and thinks that there may be something amiss with her blood, but his tonics have only a limited effect. I love to have her here with me, and indeed she is a great support and a practical help with estate accounts and other matters, but I feel to blame that she stays close to me not because she is afraid of the company of her peers, but simply because I am lonely.

And I have to admit that I am still stretched on a rack of guilt because of what has happened to Dewi and Daisy. Over and again my servants and my friends have reiterated that I am not responsible for the death of my son or the loss of my daughter, but they are both gone, and I know that if I had been stronger and more insistent upon discipline they might both still be beneath this roof, sharing in the joys and the tribulations of this blessed place. I say 'blessed' but it might just as well be cursed, for it is afflicted by silence and gloom. In my mind, I can accept that Dewi's death might have been a matter of chance, and that realization does something to lessen my pain. But Daisy's transformation from sweet innocent child to loose woman had nothing to do with chance. That was down to me, and I am certain that my erratic temperament when she was young, and especially my neglect of her when Brynach arrived at the Plas, did more to damage her than poverty or starvation might have done. My misery following the disappearance of Owain must also have been accompanied by neglect. I know now that I asked Sian to do too much while I did too little myself.

Some weeks ago I consulted Joseph about this, and he said: 'Martha, my dear friend, you cannot take upon yourself the responsibility for the virtues and the vices of your children. They are made as they are, in a fashion that is utterly mysterious. Yes, they are blessed or cursed by the manner of their upbringing, but parents can only be true to themselves, and parents and children alike are afflicted by misfortune and blessed by sunshine. The children lost their father when they were very young, and maybe that affected Daisy more than it affected the others. But that is speculation, Martha, and hindsight is a wonderful thing. You must not blame yourself for anything. Let go, and move forward.'

I have thought of Joseph's words over and again, and they do bring me comfort. But while I struggle to come to terms with the business of banishing guilt and being a good parent, I am also beleaguered by the business of running the estate. It is now vast, and even with the help of Lewis Legal and Sara, and occasional timely interventions from Joseph, I fear that I am only just coping. I miss the friendship and wise counsel of Squire Fenton too, for that dear man died suddenly about six months ago, leaving us all very shocked. Since the acquisition of Llystyn and Fachongle Isaf there are seven tenanted farms to look after, in addition to the farming activities of the Plas itself, and I am getting worn down by the responsibility. I am no less competent than any other squire in North Pembrokeshire in what I do, and indeed I am a good deal wiser than many of them, for I try to move forward and keep abreast of new developments. In that, I have been greatly helped in the past by my old tutor John Bateman, but he too died suddenly in November of last year, and I sorely miss his company and his advice. Stock-breeding, and buying and selling, and trying new machines and new crop varieties use up both time and energy, and I have to admit in the pages of my private book that I am feeling tired. Unutterably tired.

12 May 1822

Today was my forty-fourth birthday. Sara took the initiative and insisted that I should do nothing about it at all. Without telling me, she invited Catrin, Ellie and Mary Jane, and even sister-in-law Nansi from Brawdy. And they all came, without their husbands! My mother should have come too, but she was confined to bed with a swollen foot and she sent her love, accompanied by a large bouquet of flowers and some delicious crystallized fruit. Sara said that she felt I needed female company, and indeed I did. We sat outside in the garden, four female guests and four female residents of the Plas, laughing and chattering to such an extent that my misery was entirely banished. Billy told me afterwards that he came to the garden to ask me something, but that he was so overwhelmed by the sight of eight beautiful women gathered together beneath the mayflower tree that he entirely forgot what was in his mind, and had to go away again.

We had a wonderful time, and in truth I came to realize that I was not lonely at all when such friends as these were on hand to give me their support and their love. Inevitably, the talk centred on families and estates, and I realized that I was not the only one in difficulty. Ellie, trapped in an unhappy marriage to a cruel husband, has a heavy cross to bear, and Mary Jane's second son Samuel is proving to be virtually uncontrollable. Bessie has just lost her mother and her brother in quick succession, and now has not a single surviving relative. And Liza's son Twm, who shared the breast with Brynach, died only a month ago in a horrid accident in the woods at Pengelli while he was felling trees for his master. Good women, all four of them, and they deserve all the support I can give them. But today they all wanted to talk about me, and it was clear to me that Sara had informed all of them about my melancholic state of mind. I obtained a very clear message that in spite of all the help they could give me, the only real solution to my problems was marriage. To be precise, marriage to Ceredig ap Tomos. I protested that I did not love him, but they rebutted that feeble excuse by saying that love was no guarantee of a happy marriage. Had not Ellie married for love, and had not that love turned sour? I protested that New Moat was a horrible place, too high in the mountains and always lost in the cloud. Rubbish, said Ellie, and reminded me that it is very close to Ambleston, and that she could well do with me as a new neighbour. I said that Ceredig was too old and too polite, but they rounded on me by saying that he was in truth only a few years older than me, and that a polite gentleman was infinitely preferable to an oaf or a philanderer.

Then Joseph turned up, as he has a habit of doing, uninvited but none the less welcomed with open arms by all eight of us women. What with all the kisses and embraces, he thought he was in heaven, and as I stood back for a moment and rejoiced in his pleasure, it struck me that all of us have been helped by Joseph at various times in our lives, and that each of us holds him in special affection. A good man indeed, who owns a part of my heart. When he had recovered from his reception, he presented me with a posy of birthday flowers and a little green bottle containing a lavender-scented lotion. The latter, he said, would preserve my youth and prevent a single wrinkle from appearing on my face or my body until I reached the age of eighty-five. 'Nonsense, Master Harries,' I laughed. 'You are already too late with this magical mixture, for I am already a battered old crone. What I need is not your skin lotion, but your love potion.' So we chatted on, as frivolously as may be, which provided great cheer. But in the midst of all the light-hearted banter I was left with the clear impression that Joseph agreed with my fearsome army of friends that I should marry Ceredig without delay.

When they had all gone, I went for a long walk on the mountain in order to settle my mind and my heart and to commune with Saint Brynach and his angels. I talked to the old raven and his family. Through their looks they all said that life was slipping by, and that I should marry Ceredig. So I was getting unanimous advice from all sides. I rebelled against that advice for a while, and thought, 'Why should I do this just because others tell me I must? Should I not simply follow my heart?' But then I thought of the future of

Sara and Brynach, and the estate, and of generations as yet unborn, and I knew that marriage to Ceredig would bring security and prosperity to all of them. I knew that with every passing day my options were being closed off one by one, and that the imperative towards marriage was getting stronger and stronger. I sighed, and said to Saint Brynach, 'Very well, you wise old fellow. I will do it, if you insist.'

As I entered the yard on my return from the mountain, as if decreed by the writer of some frothy theatrical entertainment, a rider came thundering up the driveway and stopped in a cloud of dust. A young fellow dismounted, and I recognized him as James, Ceredig's stable lad. 'Good day to you, James,' said I. 'What brings you to the Plas today?'

'Message from Master ap Tomos, Mistress Martha. He says it is your birthday today, and he is not often wrong in these matters.'

'Quite correct, James. How kind of him to remember.'

'This is for you, Mistress.' And he handed me a little parcel wrapped in patterned paper and tied up with a red bow. Then he reached into his bag and took out a single red rosebud, and handed that to me too. 'From the Master's greenhouse. Smell it, Mistress! It is truly wonderful. Shall I wait for a reply?'

I swallowed hard, and said: 'Yes please, James. Tether your horse and come into the kitchen. Bessie will give you a pint of ale.'

I went upstairs to my room, feeling weak at the knees. I sat down on the bed, and with shaking fingers I untied the ribbon and removed the paper. I found a delicate wooden box, and when I opened the lid there was a quite beautiful gold ring, with gold of three different colours woven together. It was obviously very old and well worn. I tried it on, and it was a little tight, but it fitted on the same finger as I used for the ring given to me by Master and Mistress Fenton all those years ago. Very fitting that the two rings should be together, I thought, and smiled at my little private joke. Also within the box was a piece of fine paper, tightly folded. I flattened it out, and read the message which was tidily inscribed upon it. This is what it said:

New Moat, on the 12th day of May 1822

My dearest Martha,
I send you this ring and red rose as tokens of my affection, and with my best wishes for a very happy birthday. I know that my felicitations are echoed by my servants at New Moat, who are – as I am sure you are aware – very fond of you.
The ring belonged to my mother and to her mother, and I want you to have it as a birthday present. Please accept it without condition. I wish you to have it whatever may happen between us, in remembrance of the happiness which you have given to me since we first met.
I know that I am cursed by shyness and a certain reserve, and I do not find it easy to express myself when I am with you, but that is because I am overwhelmed by your beauty and by the vitality and compassion which you display in everything you do. I love you,

Martha, with every fibre of my being. There – I have said it in writing! It is now my earnest desire to pluck up even more courage, and say it to your face. I cannot be sure that you love me, and I am certain that I do not deserve you, but I dare to hope that love can grow, and that we can fashion a contented future together. I swear before God that there is nobody on this sweet earth who is more devoted to you than I.

May I call and see you on the afternoon of 25th May at two of the clock? Please do not refuse me this honour, or it will break my heart.

Your loving friend, Ceredig

I sat on the bed for a long time, shaking like a leaf. Then Sara popped her head round the door, saying nothing but looking at me questioningly. I patted the bed beside me, and she came and joined me. 'Read this letter,' I said, 'and tell me what I should do.'

So she read it, and squealed with delight. 'Oh, Mother,' she sighed. 'How romantic! Master Ceredig loves you dearly – that is plain for all to see. I suppose that this is not exactly a proposal of marriage, but it is as close as maybe. And the ring?' I showed it to her, on the third finger of my right hand, and she gasped. 'It is quite, quite beautiful. It must be worth a fortune, and it must have great sentimental value for the Squire. He does not want it back, Mother, and you must of course accept it.'

'Yes, Sara, I know that.'

'And he will come here in a fortnight's time, and go down on bended knee, and ask with due courtesy for your hand in marriage. You will accept him, will you not?'

'Yes, I will. I think that the time is now right.'

So I wrote a brief note in reply to Master Ceredig, thanking him for his kind and affectionate words and for the ring and the rose. I accepted all of them with gratitude, and said that I would treasure the ring until my dying day. I wrote that I was greatly touched by his generosity and by the realization of his love, and extended a warm welcome to him on the afternoon proposed. I showed my note to Sara and asked her whether it was too cool or too overfamiliar, and she said that it was just polite enough to be acceptable, since gentlemen should never be given too much encouragement in matters of the heart. So off the letter went to New Moat, accompanied by a posy of bluebells picked from the bank in front of the house.

I am now set upon a course which I trust I will not have cause to regret. If I cannot give love, at least I can accept it with good grace. And if I cannot look forward to a life of passion, a life of companionship, contentment and comfort will have to do.

25 May 1822

Ceredig has come and gone, and I am betrothed to be married. I have spent the last two weeks in a turmoil, talking endlessly to Sara, Bessie and Liza and pondering so laboriously myself that I have lost many a night's sleep. But they all believe that marriage to Ceredig will enhance my happiness, and that is an argument I can accept, since they all appear to know me better than I know myself. As for me, I feel sure that marriage will be settling for Sara and Brynach, and beneficial for the estate.

Ceredig arrived this afternoon, on time, riding on a fine chestnut hunter. It was a blustery day with black clouds dragging showers in from the west, and he was well wrapped up against the weather. But I thought he looked handsome enough on his horse and off it. He greeted me with a deep bow, and kissed my hand. Billy took his horse and I led him into the kitchen, where he greeted Sara, Liza and Bessie with obvious affection. We made small talk for a while, and then I led him through to the parlour for our private audience.

I turned round to face him, and realized that he was actually quite a desirable fellow, if truth be told. He is of medium height and stocky build, but he is not at all overweight, and it is clear that his sporting pursuits keep him in the best of health. He has kind blue eyes and tousled dark hair, and the complexion of a man who spends time out on his estate. I like that, and I like most of the things that I have discovered about him. He is an excellent dancer, as I know from experience, and an accomplished musician. I have also heard him sing, in a deep bass voice. He hates the frivolity of the card tables and the social gatherings and parties of Haverfordwest just as I do, but he is acutely aware of the importance of breeding and good standing. He is very erudite, and he reads the newspapers avidly. He knows all about the political intrigues of the local gentry, and even of those who rule over us from the Houses of Parliament in London. From our previous conversations I am aware that he has studied the discoveries of the great scientists, and while he is a little suspicious of Joseph's reputation for wizardry, he does respect the skill of my old friend in solving mysteries and inventing new medicines. He will satisfy the needs of my mind, I thought as I looked at him – but will he satisfy my other needs? He is some years older than I am. I wondered what he looked like beneath that maroon topcoat and grey waistcoat, and beneath those black breeches and yellow stockings...

We sat together on the sofa, and he put his arm round my shoulder. I realized that this was the closest to intimacy that we had ever got; we had never kissed. It also struck me that I had not kissed a man in passion since Owain and I enjoyed our picnic and other activities on the cliffs some fifteen years ago.

'Martha, do you know why I have come here today?' he asked.

I almost laughed out loud, but that would not have been kind. So I smiled and replied: 'Why yes, sir. It was not so difficult to discern from the contents of your letter.'

'Good, good. So you were not too surprised when you received it?'

'Not at all. I was touched and charmed by its contents, and I have to say that I have never in my life received such a precious gift as this beautiful ring, accompanied by your red rose.' I showed him the ring on my finger, and he looked very relieved. I took his hand and held it. 'Thank you so much, Ceredig. That was a truly romantic gesture, and it could only have been made by a true gentleman.'

'My mother's, and now yours, Martha. That ring is made of Welsh gold from three different mines. It has been on the finger of the Mistress of New Moat for four generations, and now it is on the finger of the Mistress of Plas Ingli. I dare to hope that it might return to New Moat, as I dare to hope that my affection for you might be reciprocated.'

'Try me, Master ap Tomos.'

He looked shocked for an instant, and then realized that I was inviting him to seek a successful outcome to his mission. He blushed, and cleared his throat, and removed his arm from my shoulder. Then, in the approved fashion, he dropped down onto one knee before me and took my two hands in his. Again, I was tempted to laugh, but I controlled myself, appreciating that this was the most important moment of his life. He looked up at me, reminding me of a puppy which wants its mistress to throw a fetching stick into the sea.

'Martha,' he said at last, 'you must know that I have loved you since the moment I first set eyes on you more than twenty years ago. I have desired you without respite, and that desire has almost eaten me away. Now I can hold back no longer. I love you, and as long as I live I can love no other. You know my estate and I know yours. It is my earnest wish that they should be joined, and that you will allow me the honour of serving and protecting you and your dear family until the day I die.'

'Thank you, Ceredig. We know each other as close friends of long standing. We are both free agents. Our fathers are dead, and we may do as we will. But I must have the blessing of my mother...'

'You have it, Martha, and so do I. Last week I called to see her, and told her of my intentions, and she said that a union between us can only lead to an improvement in your happiness.'

'I hope she is right, Ceredig. But now I will be direct with you. I cannot in all honesty say that I am certain of my heart. You have said that you love me, and I believe you. But I have been harmed by love in the past, and I am still frightened of what might happen to me.'

'I understand perfectly, Martha. I know you and your history better than you may think. You might not love me now, but I beg you to allow me to earn your love. Believe me, I *will* earn it, for I will never be fulfilled until you are happy.'

I smiled, and knew that there was no going back. 'Master ap Tomos, you speak with honeyed words. For a man who thinks himself shy and reserved, you are clearly practised in the art of wooing.'

'You are wrong, Martha. I have never been on bended knee before, and I hope I will not need to again. My words have been carefully composed, and rehearsed a thousand times before my bedroom mirror. My servants think that I am quite mad.'

'As indeed you are, Ceredig.' I laughed. 'Only a raving lunatic would pursue the moody and erratic Mistress of Plas Ingli, with her reputation for sailing through life blissfully unaware of the destruction and mayhem left in her wake!' He laughed too, and I saw that trapped behind the impeccable manners was a warm and funny soul who might be encouraged to escape. So I said:

564

'Well then. Enough of the preliminaries. What is it, kind sir, that you wish to say to me?'

He swallowed hard, and said it. 'Martha, I love you, and wish to give my life to you. Will you consent to be my wife?'

I thought long and hard, as one is supposed to do. Then, on an impulse, I said: 'Before I decide, sir, I ask you to stand up, and take me in your arms, and kiss me.'

I let go his hands, and rose to my feet. He looked bemused, and then flustered, but he was in no position to refuse my request. 'Do not worry, sir,' I continued. 'It is perfectly permissible, and indeed desirable. I promise not to gobble you up.' I closed my eyes and opened my lips, and awaited developments. I heard him getting to his feet, and then I felt the soft touch of his lips on mine. Then I felt his arms round me, and I held him tight. Our kiss became more intense, and I suddenly sensed that he was not very experienced. So I gently encouraged him, and before we knew it we both had to gasp for breath, and Ceredig said, 'Martha *cariad*, how long I have waited for that moment! But I thought you said you would not gobble me up. Much more of that in the days and months to come, and there will be nothing left of me! And your answer?'

'Yes, Ceredig. Lead me to the altar if you please, and make an honest woman of me.'

'You are quite perfect as you are, Martha. And now may I give you another kiss as a reward for your excellent taste in matters matrimonial?'

I consented, and we kissed again, long and hard, and more than once. At last we went down

565

to the kitchen and announced our betrothal to the household. Sara insisted that we should open a bottle, or two, or three, of the best Portuguese wine in celebration, and in truth we all got a little tipsy. Then Ceredig mounted his horse and went home just before darkness fell. I trust that he got back to New Moat without falling off and doing himself an injury. Now that I have satisfied myself that he is in proper working order, I do not want to marry damaged goods.

3 July 1822

The arrangements are all complete, and the wedding will take place in St Mary's church on the 21st day of August, which is the same date as my wedding to David in the year 1796. We have had discussions with Curate Maggs, and he promises to get Rector Devonald back here for the occasion. The banns will be read out according to the agreed schedule, and I trust that nobody will object.

Lewis Legal has had several meetings with Ceredig and myself, and with another attorney from Narberth, and the marriage settlement is agreed and signed. With the hay harvest occupying the greater part of June this year, because of very changeable weather, I have had little time to think of the future. But the more I see of Ceredig, the more attached to him I become. He may be unpractised in the arts of love, but he is very firm in his opinions and very decisive when discussions need to be concluded. I will accept his guidance, and go along with his wishes, for the weariness which I still feel over the management of the estate and the launching of Sara and Brynach into the wider world has not gone away. I need to share my burdens, and I need to share them soon. Some I will happily pass in their entirety onto Ceredig's broad shoulders.

The new man in my life is proving to be charming and attentive, and even funny. He has a talent, never noticed before by me or anybody else, for making me laugh, and his reserve appears to be lessened with every day that passes. Sara says that that is all down to my influence, but I doubt that. He is also rather more passionate than I ever dared to hope, and that augurs well for the night on which he will first share my bed.

The only thing that creates a flutter of consternation in my breast is Ceredig's insistence that New Moat will be the marital home. I know that Sara and Brynach love the Plas, and will be distraught when we have to move, but it is their destiny to fly away from the nest and I cannot prevent it. In Brynach's case, I want him to fly back again and take over Plas Ingli, and provision is made for this in the marriage settlement. But I love this place with every ounce of my being, and I love the old blue mountain and its wide skies and guardian angels. I once made a vow that I would never leave, except in a coffin. So I am torn between happiness and *hiraeth*, and the one is currently a long way from the other. Oh, that the two might coincide.

Full Circle

5 August 1822

The final arrangements for the wedding are in place. The guest list is prepared, and the celebration will be one of the grandest affairs of the year in Pembrokeshire. Ceredig does have social pretensions, and has insisted that some of the big gentry should be invited. I have gone along with his wishes, although I do not think we should overreach ourselves. Even Lord Cawdor and his lady have received invitations, and have gracefully accepted. The feast will be lavish indeed. Ceredig will pay for it, although at my insistence it will take place at the Plas. Ceredig wanted it at New Moat, but I refused to agree. We will have fireworks and torches, and musical entertainments, and dancing in the barn. Billy is not amused at the prospect of an invasion by the upper classes, and wonders if he is expected to scrub the yard with soapy water and polish the pigs.

Brynach has returned from school, and I have had many long conversations with him and Sara together. They have reassured me over and again that marriage to Ceredig will ensure my future serenity, even though I sense that they will be sacrificing their personal happiness by moving to New Moat. Just now, Brynach wants to make music and travel in Europe, and follow the usual pursuits of young gentlemen, but I have managed to persuade him to concentrate on the future for a few minutes at least, and he accepts that, as he is heir to an enlarged estate, our expectations of him are also enlarged. After the wedding we will take him out of the grammar school in Haverfordwest and send him to Oxford. And when he is twenty-one he will take over as Squire of Plas Ingli. In the meantime, I have convinced Billy to continue to farm the Plas as tenant for the next few years. He is perfectly capable of it, although in the past he has fought shy of responsibility. Betsi and Ioan came to see me yesterday, and I showed them the marriage settlement, which makes ample pro-vision for them and their children born and as yet unborn. I asked for their blessing and was given it unreservedly.

So all should be well. Ceredig becomes ever more attentive and passionate when we meet, and I have to say that I am flattered to be at the very centre of his world. But I am more than a little frightened by his ardour, and feel that his love is almost too intense. I have admitted to him that there is uncertainty in my heart, and perhaps that is what spurs him on to ever more generous and ostentatious gestures of affection. He will not admit it to me, but he is very frightened that even now he might lose me. I have told him over and again that I have made my promise, and that – God willing – I will keep it.

What is the will of God? I wish I knew. I trust that his angels watch over me, but there is, as ever, a part of me that anticipates the intervention of cruel fate. I cannot stop myself from looking for omens and portents in all things, and although I have had no premonitions of disaster in past weeks there is one sign that does cause me concern. This morning, when I walked alone upon the mountain, I climbed up among the blue rocks with the intention of visiting my cave. I did not reach it, for in a hollow surrounded by boulders as large as hovels I came across the signs of habitation. Beneath one boulder there was a pile of sticks and broken branches, and nearby I found the ashes of a fire. There were a few scraps of food among the stones, and when I looked at the mosses and grasses on the ground they had clearly been flattened by somebody sleeping or sitting upon them. I put my hand into the ashes, and found that they were still warm. I was too upset by this discovery to continue to my cave, and I returned immediately to the Plas. As I walked, I tried not to turn something innocuous into something momentous. The ashes and the traces on the ground could, after all, have been left by some vagrant, or even by one of the travelling harvesters.

When I got back to the house Bessie was just placing dinner on the table. I waited until everybody was seated, and then I addressed my housekeeper directly. 'Bessie,' I said, 'you know, and everybody else around this table knows, that the creature called the Nightwalker has caused me great trouble in the past. I have not seen him for more than five years. You gave me an assurance that I would never see him again. Are you still certain of that?'

'Why yes, Mistress, as certain as may be. But why do you ask?'

'I have found traces of habitation up on the mountain, on the south side overlooking the Plas. Somebody was staying there last night, for the ashes of his fire are still warm.'

At this, I saw Billy and the other men exchanging nervous glances, and Bessie herself looked shocked. Then Sara piped up. 'From what I have heard, Mother, the Nightwalker does not leave traces. If there is somebody hiding up on the mountain, it must surely be some vagrant who is up to no good. I think Brynach and the other men should get up there among the rocks to find him, and send him packing.'

They all agreed to this course of action, and off they went. When they came back, three hours later, they looked well pleased with themselves. 'We found him, Mother,' said Brynach. 'Some old vagrant cowering among the rocks up near the summit. He was harmless enough, and very scared. We told him to leave, and he will not return. He will be out of the parish by nightfall, and he knows that if we find him anywhere near here again we will give him a thrashing and hand him over to the constables.' And that was that, for they changed the subject and talked of the harvest instead.

Greatly relieved, I took a walk at dusk down the lane towards Dolrannog, to see how the harvest was getting on. There I met the Irish harvesters, including Michael O'Connell. We greeted each other warmly, and they congratulated me on my impending marriage to the Master of New Moat. 'We wish you great happiness, Mistress,' said Michael. 'You deserve it after all your misfortunes.

571

Mind you, we will be sad to see you leaving the Plas. The place will be empty and lonely without you.'

'Oh, I will be coming and going. And Billy will look after it well, of that I have no doubt.'

I confirmed with Michael that I would have work for his group at the Plas round about the time of the wedding, and explained that I wanted no barley in the barn until the wedding dance was over and done with. We talked of music, and Michael and his musical family members agreed to play for us. 'Excellent!' said I. 'It is high time that the North Pembrokeshire gentry learnt how to dance Irish jigs. Now, have any of your people been sleeping rough on the mountain lately?'

'Oh no, Mistress,' said Michael. 'They would never do such a thing, for the mountain is haunted. That creature they used to call the Nightwalker has returned. Dressed in a big black cloak and wide-brimmed black hat, he is. We have seen him several times lately, standing up among the rocks, looking down at the Plas.'

21 August 1822

The fateful day has come and gone, and I am still here to tell the tale. So much has happened that I hardly know where to start, and my emotions have taken such a battering that I am quite drained of energy.

I will start almost at the beginning. Yesterday, the day before my wedding, guests began to arrive from all over Pembrokeshire. It was a very hot day.

We suspended harvesting activities so that we could concentrate on one thing at a time, although in truth we had concentrated on little other than the wedding for two weeks beforehand. We now have good relations with almost all of the local gentry families, and the squires of Trefach, Pentre Ifan, Cwmgloyn, Bayvil, Llwyngwair, Gelli Fawr and even Henllys had all agreed to put up guests from far afield. In the past, some of those grand houses were inhabited by the most evil of my enemies, who are now thankfully dead and buried. Ceredig slept at home, since it would not have been seemly for him to stay at the Plas before the wedding, but he spent much of his time rushing hither and thither, arranging things. As grand coaches deposited weary travellers at their various destinations, he tried to welcome them all personally. I told him that that was unnecessary, but he was quite insistent, and as the day went on he became more and more frantic and nervous. He turned up at the Plas several times during the day, apparently to calm us all down, but his visitations had quite the opposite effect.

As best we could, we proceeded with the arrangements. We had invited all ninety of our guests to the Plas for evening refreshments and entertainments as a prelude to the wedding itself. Betsi came over from Cenarth and moved in for the night, and I could not have managed without her calm efficiency. She, Bessie and Liza worked wonderfully well together, and we had extra help with baking and cooking from Hettie and Patty who came up from the Parrog. I would have grieved for the absence of my long-lost daughter,

Daisy, but there was no time for grieving. Around midday Ellie, Mary Jane and Catrin arrived with their families, and then Morys and his family arrived from Brawdy with my mother, who was excited, hot and very bothered. All of the gentlemen and children were sent off on healthy walks in the searing heat while the real work was done in the kitchen. It was even hotter inside than out, as bread rolls and cakes, puddings and pies, fish and fowl, jellies and joints were prepared and cooked and put away in the pantry. Sara and Brynach took on responsibility for keeping me out of the way, and for the most part they succeeded in their endeavours, so that when Ceredig arrived at six of the clock I felt rested and well prepared for the excesses of the evening. I had to calm him down, for he was like a cat on a hot slate roof, but at six-thirty we were both stationed on the front doorstep as coaches started to arrive.

By seven-thirty the Plas was filled with happy, laughing, chattering people. The kitchen was out of bounds for guests, but the cream of the Pembrokeshire gentry was crammed into the parlour, the office, the dining room, up the stairs and along the passageways, and even into the old nursery. Since we were blessed with a calm warm evening people spilled outside onto the lawn in front of the house, and from there into the garden and the orchard. Billy and the other men had placed so many candle lanterns in the trees that in the dusk the Plas must have looked, from the summit of the mountain, like a glittering fairyland. There were introductions galore, and I spent the greater part of the evening anchored to Ceredig's arm, smiling and curtsying. Lord Cawdor and his lady were of course the centres of attention, with many guests vying for the opportunity of a few words with them, by which means they might be uplifted by an inch or two in the estimation of their neighbours. I thought it all very silly, but I did not mind, for it took a little pressure off Ceredig and myself. The Earl spent a good while talking to the two of us, and I was very flattered when he said, 'Why, Mistress Martha, the Plas is every bit as delightful and as well appointed as has been rumoured! I can well imagine that nobody who comes to live here ever goes away again! And you, my dear lady, are clearly thriving, and grow more beautiful with every passing year.' Then he turned to Ceredig, and said: 'My dear Master Ceredig, you are greatly blessed. It will be a true privilege for you to have the second most beautiful woman in Wales as a wife. Take care of her, for I dare say there are crowds of young fellows seeking to snatch her from you!' And having thus flattered both his lovely wife and myself, and Ceredig into the bargain, he wandered off chortling to himself, with a gaggle of fawning admirers trailing after him. Joseph was not far away, and he caught my eye and gave me a very obvious wink. He was clearly as amused as I was by the antics of both the greater and the lesser gentry, and I found it hard to suppress a giggle.

Ceredig was delighted by the attention and the flattery lavished upon us by the Earl, and felt that his status had been considerably enhanced as a result of it. But not for the first time, I sensed a tension within him when the Plas was mentioned in glowing terms, and it crossed my mind that maybe he resented the beauty of its location and its reputation for hospitality as compared with his own rather sombre mansion up in the hills. I wondered briefly whether he even resented my love for this place of blue stones.

There was no time for pondering on the sensitivities of my betrothed, for my brother Morys, who was in charge of the proceedings, clapped his hands and called the assembled company to order, since it was time for musical entertainments. Most of us clustered into the parlour, which had been almost cleared of furniture for the occasion. Those who would not fit settled on the steps and on the lawn, and the windows were opened wide. My beautiful Sara sang a sweet love song, very nervously, and then several others with musical skills or musical pretensions gave us little performances on the pianoforte and the clarinet. I insisted on an Irish folk tune or two from the O'Connells and their friends, and felt sad that there was no room for dancing. Never mind, I thought, for we can dance the night away in the barn tomorrow evening. Then Ceredig sang something doleful by Master Schubert in his strong bass voice. People clapped and cheered, and I became aware that all eyes were directed towards me. 'Cariad,' said Ceredig at last, 'they want you to play something on your instrument.' I demurred, and pretended that my fingers were too stiff and that my palms were too moist, but they would have none of my excuses, and at last I was prevailed upon to call for my Celtic harp.

Bessie brought it to me, and I was thankful that

I had practised on it only the day before, in anticipation of a demand for a little performance. Silence fell upon the room as I set about the task of tuning. I frowned as I realized that the strings were very much out of tune, for I could not understand why. 'I am sorry, ladies and gentlemen,' said I, 'but tuning is not easy this evening. The heat, or the moisture in the air, must have something to do with it. Please bear with me.' So I continued, plucking one string after another, tightening some and loosening others. But as the minutes passed, and a gentle murmuring began among the guests, I still could not complete the task. So I became flustered and in truth made matters worse instead of better, since I could not listen properly to the pitch of each string. I fear that I was close to tears when Bessie came up to me and said quietly, but loud enough for everybody to hear: 'Mistress, do not worry. There is a fellow out in the kitchen who came to the door a few minutes since, begging for some food. He overheard your tuning efforts, and says that he knows how to tune a harp. He will help you, if you will allow it.'

'Why, yes please,' said I, as a wave of relief swept over me. 'Anything to save me from this embarrassment! Please show him in.'

The guests laughed and clapped, and shared in my relief. So Bessie went and fetched the vagrant from the kitchen. He would not come into the parlour, so Bessie gave the harp to him, and he sat at the bottom of the stairs and started on his task. From where I was sitting, I just caught a glimpse of him. He was quite tall, but stooped, with a shock of white hair and a thick white beard. He was dressed, so far as I could see, in a rough woollen jacket and ragged trousers. Vagrants sometimes have their uses, I thought, and sometimes hidden talents too. And as the vagrant worked and plucked at the disobedient strings, so the rest of us got back to chatting. Glasses were refilled, and soon the room was humming with happy conversation again. Ceredig and I got caught up in a discussion about the complexities of the Celtic harp with my mother and Rector Devonald. The minutes ticked away.

Then I heard the faint strains of harp music above the babble, coming from the foot of the stairs. Bit by bit the conversation in the parlour became hushed, and then stopped altogether. The old vagrant had not simply tuned the harp perfectly, but he was now playing it as only a master could play it. The tune was 'The White Lilac Tree' ... and the player was Owain, returned from the dead.

His fingers, my tune. I knew it instantly. The colour drained from my face, and I sat as still as a marble statue. I must have gripped Ceredig's hand, for he said: 'Martha! What is the matter?' I could not reply. With complete silence in the room, and all eyes upon me, I got to my feet and walked across the room to the door. I went out into the passage and faced the harpist as he sat on the bottom stair, with his eyes closed and his fingers gliding across the strings. On the second finger of his left hand was the ruby signet ring given to him by the Fentons all those years ago. He opened his eyes, and they were as blue and beautiful as ever. He gave a faint smile, which I could just make out through his white whiskers, and said, 'Hello, Martha. Do you remember me?'

At that point the full horror of the situation struck me, and I fainted. I came to a few minutes later to find myself on my bed, with Joseph leaning over me and waving a bottle of smelling salts under my nose. Betsi, Bessie, Liza and Sara were crowded round the bed, and as I blinked in the bright light they were joined by Morys and my mother. Then I wept, and the one who was most conveniently to hand was Joseph. I sat up and flung my arms round him, and flooded his collar with my tears. 'Oh, Joseph,' I wailed, 'what shall I do? What shall I do? Do you know that that man is Owain? Oh, what shall I do?'

He could say nothing for a while, for I was sobbing hysterically, but at last I calmed down, and he whispered into my ear: 'Simply do what your heart dictates, Martha.'

I wept again, and through my tears I saw that all of the other women in the room were weeping too. But I managed to compose myself, and Joseph forced all of us to smile when he said: 'Come, come, ladies. This is all very dramatic, if I may say so. Nobody has died, and indeed somebody we all love has come back to life.'

'That may be so,' I intervened, 'but this is a tragedy none the less. Where is Owain now?'

'He is still at the bottom of the stairs, Martha,' replied Morys. 'He is being tended by one or two of your guests. I fear that he has a fever, and is very ill.'

'Oh, no! The poor, poor man. And Ceredig?

Where is he?'

'He is still sitting where you left him, and in a state of deep shock. He will not say a word to anybody.'

I knew then that this was a situation largely of my own making, and that I was the only one who could put matters right. I also knew that my actions over the next few minutes would cause terrible pain, and that little else would be talked about in the grand houses of Pembrokeshire for months to come. But I could not hide away for a moment longer. I stood up, and wiped my eyes with Joseph's large white kerchief. Mother tried to say something, but I stopped her. I would not take advice from anybody, since Joseph's advice was all that I needed. Liza tidied me up, and then I swallowed hard, made my way onto the landing, and set off downstairs.

Owain was still sitting on the bottom step, and the harp was still in his hand. I took it away from him, and handed it to Bessie. Then I took his hand and pulled him to his feet. Looking back on it, seldom can a more incongruous sight have been seen at the bottom of the Plas Ingli staircase than the mistress of a thriving estate, dressed like a queen, holding hands with a battered and filthy vagrant. 'Owain,' I said, 'I never answered your question. I do indeed remember you. And you and I have unfinished business.' I knew perfectly well that scores of people were listening in, and that every word of mine would be reported far and wide. But that was the least of my concerns, and in truth I was beyond caring.

'Are you all right, *cariad?*'

'Much better for seeing you, Martha. But I fear that I am actually quite ill.'

'I can see that. Your eyes are pained, and your hand is shaking and very hot. But will you excuse me for a moment? I have to speak to Ceredig.' He nodded, and let go of my hand.

I walked into the parlour, which was crowded with guests and so noisy that I could not have made myself heard even if I had shouted. I pushed my way through to where Ceredig and I had been sitting a century ago. As I did so people realized that I had returned from my room, and fell silent. I knew then that my conversation with Ceredig was going to be very public indeed. But it could not be avoided.

He was sitting perfectly still on the sofa, apparently oblivious of everything that was going on around him. I stood in front of him, and he lifted his eyes to meet mine.

'Ceredig?'

'Yes, Martha?'

'You know that Owain has returned?'

'Yes, I know it.'

'I am very sorry,' I whispered, as tears started to roll down my cheeks again. 'I am truly very sorry. But in the circumstances, I think it best that we call off the wedding.' I could hardly articulate the words, and I am not sure that Ceredig heard them, let alone anybody else. He nodded, and there was a very long silence in the room. 'Do you want your ring back?'

There was another interminable silence, as he looked at the floor. Then he shook his head. There was nothing he could say to me. He did not meet my eyes again, but got to his feet and strode out of the room. His face was expressionless, and there were no tears in his eyes, for a gentleman does not weep in public. He pushed his way through the crowd in the passageway, went out through the front door, and disappeared from my life. Afterwards, Billy told me that he went straight to the stable, saddled his own horse, and galloped off into the darkness with only the faint moon to light his way.

I stood rooted to the spot in the middle of the parlour floor, shaking with emotion. At last somebody sat me down, and I was given a glass of water. The room erupted around me into a pandemonium of excited conversation. Never in the history of Pembrokeshire, I dare say, has such a thing been seen before, and I pray to God, for the sake of all concerned, that it will never be seen again. I was incapable of rational thought. Suddenly my intended husband was forgotten, and Owain was the centre of attention. Everybody wanted to talk to him, and Joseph and Morys and his brother James had to protect him from the crush. Mary Jane, his sister, who had refused for so long to accept that he was dead, was overcome with emotion just as I was, and clung to him as she wept.

Things at last became quieter, and while I could not get anywhere near Owain myself, I noticed that his hand became steadier and that the flush upon his cheeks was reduced. Morys engaged him in earnest conversation for a while, and then held his hand up for silence. 'My dear ladies and gentlemen,' he announced. 'This has been a most difficult evening for all of us, and especially for my sister Martha and for Master Ceredig. I personally cannot imagine what has gone through their minds. But what we have witnessed has not been a tragedy but a miracle. A dearly beloved gentleman has returned from the dead. Fifteen years have passed since he disappeared out in the bay, but now he has returned. He tells me that tales of his abduction by fairies or mermaids were greatly exaggerated. He also tells me that he is suffering from malaria, which manifests itself through feverish attacks without warning. But he appears now to feel a little better, and if it is your wish, he might enlighten us as to where he has been all this time.'

A great cheer went up around the room, and Owain was pushed towards the sofa which I now occupied. He looked embarrassed, and was clearly some way short of being hale and hearty, but he managed to tell his story. I will retell it as accurately as I can, but not now, for I am utterly exhausted. I will write it down tomorrow, maybe when Owain is asleep.

22 August 1822

Not for the first time, Owain is asleep in my bed, and not for the first time I am outside it. I am watching over him like a fierce guardian angel, and I will not allow anybody but Joseph to come anywhere near him. He has been ravaged by a high fever for most of yesterday and today, but now he is calmer and is breathing easily in his sleep. We

583

have burnt his filthy clothes, and washed him, and shaved him, and cut off most of his snow-white hair. He still looks a good deal older than his forty-two years, but at least he is recognizable as Master Owain Laugharne, Squire of Llannerch.

This is his story. He said that when he was far out in Cardigan Bay on that fateful day in May 1807, he was a man in love and celebrating life. He rowed far out, and quickly, for he felt that his body was surging with energy. He was headed for a special ground, known only to himself and a few other fishermen as a place where mackerel may always be found early in the summer season. It was uncommonly hot, with the sea flat and the sun searing down from a cloudless sky. He was almost out of sight of land when suddenly a plank sprang out of the bottom of his boat and water started pouring in. He frantically tried to fix it back into position, but then another plank sprang out, and then another. He had no tools on the boat, and his frantic efforts made matters worse, and soon water was coming over the side as well. He realized that he could not save the boat or himself, and that he must write a note to me. Frantically he poured out the cordial from the bottle which he had carried with him, tore a page from his notebook, and scribbled some words onto it, though he cannot now remember what he wrote. He stuffed the message into the bottle, pushed the cork back into the neck, and flung it away from the sinking boat. Then the little craft went down, in a tangle of nets and lines and other debris, in less than five minutes. He had two net floats on board, and he had the presence of mind to bind them together, and to himself, in order that he might prevent himself from sinking.

He was alone on a wide sea beneath a relentless sun. He tried to swim back towards the distant coast, but he realized that that was nigh on impossible with the two floats attached to him, so he decided that he might as well allow the tides and the currents to take him where they would. The water was very cold, and he thrashed his arms and legs about frantically now and then, in an attempt to keep warm. He knew that the tide was ebbing, and that he would be, carried further and further towards the north-west. By mid-afternoon he was out of sight of land. By evening, with dusk falling, he was quite convinced that he was going to die, for he was becoming lethargic and he could feel the cold seeping through his veins. He looked round and could see nothing but the greasy flat surface of the sea. There were no ships, for they were certainly all becalmed, and there were not even any seabirds to be seen. He thinks that he lost consciousness for a while, and then suddenly he came to his senses and realized that the water was frothing and boiling around him, and that the air was filled with crying seagulls. He was surrounded by leaping and diving porpoises. They nudged him and pushed him, and at first he thought they were going to eat him. But then he realized that they were trying to save him. They were talking to each other and to him through high-pitched pinging sounds, and at times he thought they were singing.

Then another sound came to his ears – the sound of splashing oars. A rowing boat was approaching from the north-west, silhouetted against the last glimmer of light in the evening sky. There was a man with a lantern in the bows, and he was clearly attracted by the churning of the sea and by the clouds of white seagulls overhead. Then, he said, a peculiar thing happened, for in the spreading darkness he became aware that the sea around him was glowing with a green phosphorescence. He had heard of that before, from old sailors, but never seen it himself. And now he was in the middle of it, glowing green himself, with the porpoises threshing the water to a green foam around him. Then they were gone, and so were the gulls. He still did not know, he said, whether that episode was a fantasy, or a product of the delirium of a dying man. He looked at Joseph with a question in his eyes. 'It was real,' said Joseph. 'You may be sure of it.'

He must have lost consciousness again, and when he came to he was in a bunk on a sailing ship, still feeling terribly cold but with a dry nightshirt next to his skin and warm blankets piled on top of him. There was a rough sailorman looking down at him. He held a lantern in his hand, and addressed Owain in a language he did not understand. He could feel that the ship was under way, on a calm sea at first, but then with a rising wind above and short choppy seas below. Within an hour or two the ship was caught in a fearsome storm, and he spent the greater part of the night being violently sick in his bunk. At last the storm subsided, and he began to feel better. The dawn came, and he worked out that the ship was tacking westwards against big seas. He wondered why the captain did not run with the wind and the sea, and thought that the ship was perhaps too close to the Bishops and Clerks, or to the Smalls. But then the waves reduced in size, and the wind swung round to the north, and the sailors began to relax. He found a fellow who spoke a little English, and discovered that the vessel was Portuguese. Owain quickly realized that this was a smuggling vessel which had dropped off a cargo between New Quay and Aberaeron, and was now intent on getting clear of the Welsh coast with all haste. The captain had not the slightest intention of putting him ashore, and the sailor simply indicated that he would have to take his chance with them. He resigned himself to spending a fortnight at sea and then making his way home from Oporto or some such place.

He quite enjoyed his time on board, and learned a good deal about seamanship. He even learned a little Portuguese, and got on well with the captain and the crew of five.

After an uneventful passage across the Bay of Biscay and down the Portuguese coast, the captain reduced sail and warned that the glass was falling sharply. Another storm was coming, this time from the north. It struck with terrible force. There was nothing for it but to run before the wind and the waves, with the smallest possible amount of sail and a sea anchor trailing. For three days the storm raged, and all those on board were in fear of their lives. It was impossible to take sightings, so the captain had no idea where he was. The ship began to take in water, and then, in the middle of the third night of the storm, Owain heard a new sound – the sound of mighty waves crashing onto a rocky shore. The ship ran aground, and in the maelstrom all the men were thrown into the sea. Owain thought that they would all die. They scrabbled in the midst of the chaos for anything that would float. Something bumped into Owain, and he grabbed hold of it. He did not know it at the time, but it was a seaman's chest which was locked tight and somehow kept enough air inside it to provide buoyancy. Then he and the chest were flung onto the rocks by a foaming breaker and left there, high but not dry. He was terribly injured, with a broken leg and a broken arm, but he dragged himself higher up onto the reef before he passed out because of the pain.

He woke up and thought that he was in Heaven. He was in the shade of a tent, with a high sun just visible through the tent fabric. He could smell some sort of incense burning in a vessel nearby. Three beautiful women were looking down at him, dressed in loose-fitting blue garments. He thought that they looked friendly enough, but his head was swimming with the pain of his broken limbs, and one of the women poured something bitter down his throat. He lost consciousness again. He drifted in and out of sleep, and realized that his rescuers were trying to repair the damage. They used bits of timber as splints, and he recognized the wood as having come from the wreck of the lost smuggling ship. Gradually he recovered, and found that he was a celebrity. He worked out that he was somewhere on the Moorish coast of Africa. He was the only one to have survived the shipwreck, and after some days his rescuers showed him where the six Portuguese sailors had been buried in the sand. He was in a tented village of perhaps forty people – men, women and children of all ages. There were some camels tethered nearby, and the place was overrun by smelly goats. They fed him, as he recovered, on camel's milk and goat's milk, and a sort of white rancid cheese, and on dates and other fruits which he did not recognize. Then they struck camp, and gathered up their belongings, and set off inland, into the great desert. He had to go with them, for there was in truth no alternative.

He stayed with the Moors for two years, learning their language and their ways. His arm and his leg mended well, much to his surprise. The tribal people never quite accepted him as one of their own, but he developed a great affection for them and a respect for their culture and their religion. He wondered at first why they had shown him such compassion, but in due course the chieftain explained that they thought he must be a king, for the chest that was thrown up onto the rocks along-side him was half full of golden guineas. This, he realized, must have been the captain's chest containing the proceeds of the ship's last landing of smuggled goods. 'Keep it,' he had said to the chieftain. 'It is yours, in gratitude for your kindness.'

In due course the tribe returned to the coast near the Straits of Gibraltar, and Owain found a vessel that would take him across to the other side. He and his adopted Moorish family parted with a good deal of sadness, and he said that they all wept. But he told them that he had to try to get back to Wales; and, in recounting this, he turned to me and said that there were many occasions on which his love for me was the only thing that kept him going. He would not go into further detail, and I knew that there had been great danger and great hardship during his time in Africa. He wanted to send a letter to me from Gibraltar, but there was no ship that could carry it to England or Wales. He then travelled across Spain without a single gold coin in his pocket, and determined that he would walk and work his way northwards, or else throw himself upon the mercy of those he met. For a year he wandered across Spain, trying to work out where he was, and learning the language. He thought that he would try to reach the north coast and find a trading vessel that might take him home. But the country was in chaos, with armies marching hither and thither, and spies everywhere. Some were working for the Spanish generals, and some for the French, and some for the British. But then there was a lull in the fighting, and some brave merchants from England and Wales started to visit Spanish ports again. Owain reached Bilbao, and in one of the sordid inns close to the harbour he happened upon a sailor who hailed from Newport. The two men got talking, and Owain would have sought a chance to work his passage home, but that he asked first for that which he most craved: news of Mistress Morgan of Plas Ingli. 'Ah yes!' said the fellow. 'Mistress Morgan, the black-haired and brown-eyed beauty who makes one gentleman after another mad with love. A very merry widow indeed. They do say that she is tamed at last. When last I heard, she was betrothed to be married to Master Ceredig ap Tomos of New Moat. I dare say that by now they are man and wife.'

When Owain reported this, I could not restrain myself, and burst out: 'But that is preposterous! I was never betrothed to Ceredig all those years ago, let alone married, and I was certainly not merry!'

All of the listeners in the room laughed in spite of the tension. Owain put a restraining hand upon my arm, and smiled. 'I am simply reporting what this fellow told me, Martha. It may or may not have been true, but at the time it was all the information I had.' And so he continued.

This news, he said, broke his heart, and he decided to make a new life in Europe in spite of the troubles caused by Master Napoleon. He travelled again in Spain, and then moved across France. He had no difficulty in travelling about, for he spoke both Spanish and French fluently. At last he met up with a unit of the British army, and was introduced to General Picton. The two men, both from Pembrokeshire, got on well, and Owain became a spy for the Duke of Wellington. Twice he was captured, and twice he escaped. He was at the Battle of Waterloo in 1815, caught up in the thick of the fighting; indeed he saw General Picton die. He was himself injured in the spine by a musket ball probably intended for the General, and spent several weeks in a field hospital. The ball was removed, but his injuries became infected, and he almost died. He was also suffering intermittently from malaria, which had first afflicted him in the southern part of Spain some years before. At this time, he said, his spirits were at a very low ebb. He was still in love with me, and thought of me every single day, but he was injured and sick, and he was not sure that he had long to live. He thought that if he returned to Wales he would find me happily married to Ceredig, and that he would be plunged even more deeply into despair as a result. So he decided to continue wandering in Europe until the Grim Reaper caught up with him. Better to let things be, he thought, and better for me and his family to think him dead, so that we might all proceed with our lives.

As he talked, his voice cracked, and I found that I was not the only one in the room dabbing my eyes. I squeezed his hand, and after some moments he continued.

He travelled to Italy, then to Greece, and then back to Italy again. He worked as a professional musician in Venice and then in Verona for wealthy families, and became fluent in Italian. He taught French and music to various bothersome children, but was well paid. He crossed to North Africa again, and met up with his Moorish friends. They had a joyous reunion, and he talked to a female soothsayer who looked at him and said: 'I see, Welshman, that you are still mad with passion for your woman in Wales.'

'That I am,' Owain had replied, 'but she is no longer free. She is married, and she has forgotten me.'

'Wrong, Welshman. She is not married, and she still loves you. Go to her before it is too late.'

This was about six months ago. The Moorish family insisted that the soothsayer was never wrong, and they all said that he must go. So, against his better judgement, he agreed. He crossed once again to Gibraltar, and there he found an East Indiaman in harbour, picking up fresh food and water for the last leg home. He had no money, but persuaded the captain to give him a passage, and he took the place of a sailor who had died off the coast of West Africa. When the ship arrived in London he found another ship that was heading for Bristol, and worked his passage on that. In Bristol, at the beginning of July, he thought of walking home, but he was enfeebled by a bout of malaria. So he wandered along the quayside and found a ketch with the name *Carningli* painted on the side, and he thought that this must be an omen. He went on board, and discovered that the captain was there, waiting to load up with luxury goods ordered by a merchant called Master Skiff Abraham. He was a Parrog man himself. 'Well well, Captain,' said Owain, in Welsh. 'Master Abraham is an old friend of mine. I too am a Pembrokeshire man. Will you give me a passage home? Skiff owes me a favour or two.'

'And who are you, sir?'

'They call me Neifion Jones, because many years ago I came from the sea more dead than alive. Will you take me home?'

'Yes, Neptune Jones, if you will work your way.'

'Agreed, then. I know how to sail a ship, and it is my earnest desire never to fall into the water again. One further thing. Mistress Morgan of Plas Ingli. Married, I dare say, or moved to some faraway place?'

'Good gracious no. Unmarried and unhappy, so I hear. But she is betrothed to be married to

Squire ap Tomos of New Moat. He is a good kind man, but I doubt that he will manage to drag her from the Plas.'

Three days later the ship set sail, and arrived at the Parrog around the end of July, after various stops along the way. Owain did not know the date of the wedding, and feared that he might not reach Newport in time. When he arrived, he said his farewells to the captain and crew of the *Carningli* and found out where Patty and Jake were living. He was in the middle of another bout of malarial fever, and he was very weak. He told them who he was, and they could hardly believe their eyes or their ears. But they put him into a room in Hettie's lodging house and looked after him. He pleaded with them not to divulge his identity to anybody. But he *was* very sick, and Patty insisted that Joseph should be sent for in order to treat him. Joseph arrived, and gave him some foul potions, and became a part of the plot.

Owain would not divulge to the assembled company what passed between himself and the others, but he devised a plan by which he might ascertain whether or not I still loved him, without jeopardizing my future happiness. I am still un-certain, as I record this story, how many of my family and friends were involved in the conspir-acy, but I am certain that Bessie was one accom-plice. It can only have been she who destroyed the tuning on my harp, and devised the story that a harp-tuner had arrived in the middle of our celebratory evening, just when one was needed.

Having laid his plans, and having secured the collaboration of various of my friends, Owain recovered from his fever and decided to live rough on the mountain. He borrowed an old hat and a cloak from Hettie, for the nights were cold. He met Joseph a few times during the month of August, and was told that my love for Ceredig was by no means certain. This, he said, caused his heart to leap for joy, but it sank again when he realized that my old love for him might well have died away with the passing of the years. He watched the Plas on various occasions, longing for a glimpse of me. Then one day he did see me, coming up the mountain towards the place where he was hiding. He managed to scurry away between the rocks, and was mortified when I discovered the traces of his habitation. He tried to escape, but in his panic he was overtaken by another bout of fever and collapsed near the summit. Then Billy, Shemi, Will and Brynach came hunting for him, and leapt upon him when they found him. He feared for his life, he said, but then he told them who he was, and swore them to secrecy. They took him down to the Parrog and deposited him once again in Hettie's lodging house, having extracted a promise that he would not emerge again until the day before the wedding. He promised to obey that instruction, and obtained a promise in return that if I did not react to his playing of the harp on that night, they would let him go and would never divulge to me the fact that Owain Laugharne was still alive.

'And what would you have done, Owain, if I had not reacted as I did this evening?'

'I really do not know, Martha. I suppose I would have walked out through the door a broken man. I am broken enough as it is, and I might well have come to the view that there was nothing left to live for...'

His voice trailed away, and he sat there with his shoulders hunched, looking like an old man of ninety. He had been listened to in complete silence. And now the silence continued, broken only by the sounds of blowing noses and gentle sobs. I became aware of tears flowing down my cheeks, and I am now reliably informed that there was not a dry eye in the room. It was two o'clock in the morning. At last we all brought our emotions under control. I wanted to ask Owain a thousand questions, and so did everybody else, but we could not, for we all realized that he was quite exhausted by the telling of his story. Then Joseph took control of the situation. 'Ladies and gentlemen,' he said, 'we have heard a most extraordinary tale of heroism and constancy, and we can but marvel at the courage that Master Owain has displayed over the course of fifteen long years. But now he is exceedingly tired, as indeed is Mistress Martha. We must also remember Master Ceredig, who is gravely suffering. May I suggest that we now all retire to our various homes or lodgings, and give these fine people some peace?'

Everybody agreed, and over the next hour there was a hum of conversation, and a clattering of hooves in the yard, and a crunching of carriage wheels as one party after another went on its way. Somehow we got Owain up the stairs, and undressed, and into my bed. He was asleep, I think, before his head sank into the pillow. And I was asleep in an instant, as soon as I settled into my deep chair at his bedside.

23 August 1822

On the day which should have seen my wedding, Owain was very ill indeed, and we all feared that he might die. Joseph spent many hours at his bedside, trying to calm his fever and administering various remedies. At times he placed his hands upon his patient and gave him healing, and at the end of the day my dear friend was so exhausted that he collapsed, and we had to put him to bed downstairs. But Owain survived the crisis and began to recover.

Joseph would not allow me to stay in the bedroom during daylight hours, and although I disobeyed instructions and looked in very frequently, I had to cope with the consequences of the cancellation of the wedding. Thank God I had Morys with me. He dealt with a constant stream of visitors throughout the day, all of whom enquired earnestly after Owain's health. Many of them stayed for an hour or two, chatting and enjoying refreshments in the shade of the garden, and speculating endlessly about the details of my dear man's story. The pantry was full of food, and while some of it would keep, a great deal of it had to be eaten. So I gave instructions that we should be as hospitable as possible, and Catrin, Nansi, Betsi and the rest acted as attentive and sweet hostesses. Many of my guests wanted to leave behind the wedding gifts that they had brought with them, so that they might be transferred to Owain and myself, but I absolutely refused to contemplate any such thing, on the grounds that this would have been a betrayal of Ceredig, and I insisted that all gifts should be returned to the donors.

Sometimes during the day I felt sociable, and had the energy to meet my guests, but at other times I was overtaken by exhaustion and had to lie down. It was uncommonly hot. Sara and Brynach, bless them, monitored me closely, and they shepherded me through the day, ensuring that I did not allow free rein to my obsession with etiquette. They spoke for me where necessary, carried messages back and forth, and showed common sense far beyond their tender years.

By dinner time my worries about the health of Owain were compounded by worries about Ceredig. I realized that hardly any of our guests were concerned with his welfare, and that he had been transformed from the centre of attention one day to an afterthought on the morrow. This angered me, for I realized full well what a terrible tragedy had befallen him. He was by no means a laughing stock, for I had tried to ensure through my words and deeds that his good reputation would not be tainted in any way. But he had suffered a most appalling indignity, and I was concerned that with no family to support him he might never recover from it. So after giving the matter some thought, I penned the following to my former fiancé, in the hope that it might do something to ease his agony.

Plas Ingli, on the 21st day of August 1822

My very dear Ceredig,

Today should have been the day of our wedding, and like you I am still reeling from the consequences of recent events. I am confused and drained of energy myself, and I fear that your misery must be a thousand times greater than mine.

I trust that you know me well enough to appreciate that in the circumstances it was inappropriate and indeed impossible for me to proceed with you to the altar. Owain was drawn back to the Plas by love, and once I knew that he was alive I could never have survived within another marriage – not even within a marriage to a dear kind man such as yourself. The consequences would have been misery for us all.

Please be brave and do not be too concerned about the repercussions of what has happened. I sense that there is a great sympathy for your situation, and you may be assured that your peers will still hold you in the highest esteem. Indeed, your behaviour yesterday evening was exemplary, and can only have enhanced your reputation as a fine and worthy gentleman.

I dare to hope that the pain will pass, and that our friendship will not be at an end. I cannot simply cast away my affection for you, and I will value your constancy and your love until my dying day. The Plas is still open to you, and neither Owain nor I bear any ill-will towards you. Please write when you have a moment, and I trust that before long we three will be able to meet and put sadness behind us while confirming our loving friendship.

Your affectionate Martha

I did not show this letter to anybody, and I folded it in a clean sheet of paper and gave it to Billy. Then I asked him to ride to New Moat and give it personally to Ceredig accompanied by friendly greetings. I told Billy that he should not expect a reply. However, I dare to hope that the man who might have been my husband will reply in friendly terms just as soon as he has recovered from the appalling humiliation which has been visited upon him.

24 August 1822

Things are returning to normal. All of the wedding guests have gone home, and over the last two days my own dear friends, and the members of my family from Brawdy and Castlebythe, have set off from the Plas to look after their own domestic and estate affairs. I was sad to see them all go, for we have shared a time of momentous events which none of us will ever forget. I could not have managed without their support and their love, and the bonds of kinship and friendship which may have been loose through inattention are now bound a good deal tighter.

Joseph, who has been sharing Billy's room downstairs, went rushing off this morning, having received a message that a patient of his is close to death. He had to go, of course, but we were all sad to see him leave, for he has been on sparkling form, and is almost as delighted as I am to see Owain around the Plas again. He says he will be back soon, for he is still delving into the mysteries surrounding Owain's years in foreign parts. He says that he requires detailed information from the dear man on the medicinal skills of the Moorish people, and I dare say that will be just the start of a long and detailed interrogation.

Owain is still here, and is miraculously cured. He says that that is the way with malaria, but I put his recovery down to Joseph's ministrations, to four days of decent food, and to the healing properties of love. Tomorrow he will go to Pontfaen, for he has many legal matters to sort out with his brother James and various attorneys. When somebody returns from the dead, there are many repercussions! He cannot go back to Llannerch, for there is a tenant called Will Morgan now in residence, and James cannot simply tear up the fellow's tenancy agreement and throw him out into the yard. I still think of Owain as the Squire of Llannerch, but there are wills and other documents to be consulted, and complications lie ahead. That may present a problem for Owain, but in truth it matters not a jot to me, for all I want to do is carry on where we left off and rearrange a wedding between the two of us. Morys says that it would be insensitive to do that too quickly, and of course he is right. In deference to Ceredig we will wait for some weeks before making any announcement. In any case, we must both learn to know each other again, for we are different people now, and we have each been changed by fifteen years of living. I think I recognize him as the same beloved person that I knew, and he says the same of me, but we both have a great deal of digging to do, and the things that we unearth will not always be pleasant.

I have ordered the restart of the harvest, and I thank God that the weather has held. The barn is now full of itinerant harvesters, and I am leaving everything to Billy. So many of our neighbours have volunteered to help that we cannot use them all. I suspect that out on those shimmering hot cornfields there will be more talking than harvesting for a day or two. Let them talk; it will soon pass.

I have received no news of Ceredig, nor any reply to my letter. I trust that he is well, and that his sadness will have been buried by the demands of his own estate. He harvests late at New Moat, but he told me himself some days since that his barley is ready for cutting, and I know that he likes to supervise everything in person. Just now, as I sit here at my dressing table with quill pen in my hand, I trust that he is relaxing in his parlour with his servants, with a well-deserved jar of ale in the hand that might have led me to the altar.

I do not know why I have filled this page of my diary with tittle-tattle, for I should have been concentrating on a far more important matter. In truth, I have been procrastinating. Should I betray myself in writing? Have I become demure and cautious with the passing of the years? Heaven forbid. I have been rash before, and I hope that I can be permitted a certain rashness again. For better or for worse, I will commit the secrets of my heart to my Dimetian chronicle. They are, after all, the memories which may well sustain me in years to come.

This morning, with Owain so much better, and

the white-hot sun searing its way into the heavens, I thought that both he and I should get away from the Plas for a little while. I determined upon a picnic. I prepared everything early in the morning, and packed up a little wickerwork hamper with items which matched as closely as possible those which Owain had packed for our picnic on the fourth day of May in the year 1807. I put in a linen cloth, silver cutlery, delicate china plates and crystal glasses. Then I put in a bottle of good Portuguese wine, freshly baked wheat bread and salty butter, slivers of smoked salmon, cold cooked potatoes, and slices of cold ham and mustard. Finally I added an earthenware pot of gooseberry cream and custard.

Owain came down rather late for his breakfast, wearing only a very large nightshirt which he had borrowed from Billy. He looked comical, with stubble on his chin and his white hair close cropped. He concluded that something was afoot when he saw the picnic hamper on the table. 'Master Laugharne,' said I, 'you are late for breakfast, but I forgive you on the grounds that you have been abroad for too long and have lost your ability to interpret the sounds of the kitchen. In any case, you need rather more sleep than the rest of us just now. Eat up your porridge, if you please, for you will need all your strength today. I have an expedition in mind. As the Mistress of this grand mansion, it is my privilege to invite you to a ramble and a picnic.' Sara and Brynach were sitting at the kitchen table at the time, and said that they would love to come too, but I would have none of it, and told them that their place was in the barley field with the harvesters, bending their backs and perspiring beneath the midday sun. They made a great show of moaning and protesting, but in truth they knew that I wished to spend time alone with Owain, and they respected my wishes.

Before we set off on our adventure I took Owain by the hand, led him up the stairs, and into my dressing room. He realized, as did I, that he had no clothes, since his filthy vagrants' garments had been burnt. I opened up the large wardrobe against the west wall and took out a clothes hanger which held a white shirt, a pair of breeches, a gentleman's undergarment, and a pair of yellow stockings. Then, from the drawer underneath, I took out a pair of men's walking shoes. 'Your clothes, and your shoes,' I said. Owain looked quite amazed.

'Are these the very ones...'

'Indeed they are, *cariad*. The very clothes which you wore on our last picnic together. Shall we see if they still fit you?'

He nodded, and quite unselfconsciously pulled off his nightshirt and dressed in the clothes which I handed to him. I watched, and saw that his body was very wasted. The garments did not fit him perfectly, but we agreed that they would do. He was so moved by the thought that I had kept them that he could not speak a word. He gave me a little kiss on the cheek, and I noticed that he had tears in his eyes.

I decided that Owain was not strong enough to walk all the way to Aberrhigian, so we took two of the horses. Owain got them and saddled up, and while he did so I went and changed my clothes. I would not let Liza help me. In my wardrobe I found the same lime green dress, the same yellow bonnet and the same white woollen shawl as I had worn at our last picnic. I put on my lightest and shortest stays. I decided to leave my riding habit behind, and after much thought I also took off my undergarment. Authenticity was everything, and I knew that on our last visit to the seaside, fifteen years ago, I had worn no undergarment, for they had not at that time been either respectable or fashionable. Would Owain be aware of the niceties of female fashion? I doubted it. But when I went out into the yard to meet him, he recognized the dress and the bonnet straight away, and told me that I looked more beautiful than ever.

We rode down past Parc Mawr and were greeted with cheering and waving from the harvesters. We waved back, and immediately felt a surge of support and goodwill. Owain was very touched. 'My dear Martha,' he said, 'I had forgotten what a blessed place this is. You are here beside me, and that is magic enough, but then the magic is compounded by the Plas and its people. Today I am truly under a spell, and I wish the spell may never be broken.' I smiled, and we trotted along the Cilgwyn road to Newport and then out along the Fishguard road before taking the turning down through the woods to the quiet cove of Aberrhigian. Of course there was nobody there, for at this time of year, when the weather is bright, every pair of hands in the parish is employed on the harvest. We tethered the horses near a small pool in the river, where they could get at water to drink and foliage to eat. Then we walked up the path at the edge of the cove, climbing higher and higher above the beach. Owain insisted on carrying the hamper, but there was a flutter of consternation in my heart when I realized that he was struggling for breath and walking with a slight limp. 'Don't be alarmed, Martha,' he said. 'The musket ball that went into my spine passed through my lung before it got there. And this old break in my right leg still gives me pain. I will be all right as soon as I sit down.'

Then we reached the little grassy ledge high on the cliffs, overhung by golden furze bushes and quite hidden from the world. I had not been here in the fifteen years since Owain's disappearance, and it had not changed at all. The vegetation was a little higher, and now, because it was late summer, there was no thrift and sea campion, but the furze was still in bloom and its heavy scent of tropical islands still hung in the air. 'There now, Master Laugharne,' I said. 'Your secret den! May I have your permission to share it with you for a little while?'

'Indeed you may, Mistress Morgan. Since I was taken away by the fairies, this is all that is left of my kingdom, and I have vowed to make a present of it to the first lady who will kiss me.'

'But sir, if you have been living with the fairies, and have eaten fairy food, it is written in the ancient chronicles that a kiss upon your lips will cause you to disintegrate into a pile of grey dust, which the wind will sweep away.'

'Try me, Mistress Morgan. If I am indeed a king of the *Tylwyth Teg*, and that is my fate, at least I shall die happy.'

So I took Owain in my arms, and for the first time in fifteen years I kissed him on the lips. He did not dissolve into dust, and as we embraced and our kiss turned from something gentle and tentative into something wild and hungry, I realized from the hardness in his breeches that he was considerably more alive than dead. 'Cariad,' I whispered at last, 'are we still here in your secret den, or are we in Heaven, or in fairyland?'

'I think I will call this place Heaven from now on, for like the early Christians I have frequently dreamt of reaching it at the culmination of my struggles.'

'My goodness, Master Laugharne, you are in a very theological mood today, if I may say so.'

Undeterred by my flippant remark, he continued. 'For fifteen years I have dreamt every day of you, Martha, and of this blessed place, and of returning to it one day for...'

'For unfinished business?'

He nodded and smiled. Then we stood apart, and Owain took the blanket out of my bag and spread it on the ground. By mutual consent, the picnic could wait. He sat down, and motioned me to sit beside him. I did as he wanted. Then he put his left arm round my shoulders and touched my lips with the fingers of his right hand. I closed my eyes, and for an age he traced the outlines of my cheeks, and my nose and forehead, and my eyebrows and my ears. How I loved it when he touched my ears! I felt the passion rising within me, and then his fingers were gone from my face and they were on my body instead, and his lips were upon mine. His tongue was inside my mouth, exploring and probing. We kissed for so long that my head started to spin, and at last I had to stop and gasp in the fresh breeze off the sea. I removed his hand from the inside of my dress, where it had been firmly clamped upon my breast.

'Owain,' I laughed, 'you have waited fifteen years and three months for that particular encounter, so you can quite well wait for a few minutes more for the rest of your feast. Before you touch the main course, there is a certain tradition that must be followed. Whenever I sit here on this grassy bank in the sunshine, it is required of me that I should examine your injuries and check if you are healing.'

'I have the greatest respect for tradition,' said Owain. 'Where would we be without it? Swinging about in the trees, I dare say, like the apes that I once saw in Gibraltar. Carry on with your task, Mistress Martha, and wake me up when you are done.' And he flung himself down upon the rug and lay flat upon his back, feigning sleep. Undressing him in those circumstances was not at all easy, but I set to with a will. I managed to pull off his shoes and his stockings, and then unbuttoned his shirt. It was tucked into his breeches, and he tensed his stomach muscles so as to prevent me from pulling out the tails. So I had to pummel his stomach, and then kiss it, and then tickle it in order to get him to relax, and after he had been reduced to hysterical giggles I succeeded in my task. In truth I was reduced to hysterical giggles too, and in my efforts I tore his shirt. 'Help! Help!' he whispered. 'I am being violated by a fearsome female! Help, help!'

I shut him up by kissing him on his lips, and then continued with my task. With further struggles, and by tipping him over, I managed to get his shirt off his back. Then there was the complicated matter of his breeches. I unbuckled his belt and pulled it away. Then I unbuttoned the flap on the front, pulled for all I was worth at the trouser legs, and away they came. His under-garment followed, although removing that was not easy, because of the strange and beautiful anatomy of the excited male. But at last he lay there at my mercy, entirely naked and very aroused. Then he coughed again, and I saw a spasm of pain cross his face. 'Owain,' I said, 'you have aged, and war and disease have taken their toll. But you still have the body of Adonis, and I still love every inch of it. May I kiss your injuries?'

'Heal them if you will, Martha.'

So with my fingers and my lips I traced the scars across his chest, which were still visible almost sixteen years after the cuts were carved out by John Fenton's knife. There was a new scar beneath his ribs, where a musket ball had entered his body and a surgeon had sought to remove it. There was a slight bend in his right arm, and some scar tissue, where he had broken it during his shipwreck, and I saw that the muscles were somewhat wasted as compared to his left arm. I examined his right leg, and there was a lump on his shin where the broken bone had healed out of alignment. I thought it a miracle that after that injury he had walked thousands of miles, back and forth across Europe, in the years of his absence. I turned him over and examined his back, and was appalled to find that that was marked too. There was a vertical scar close to his spine where an army surgeon had removed the musket ball that almost killed him, and I was horrified when I discovered a multitude of scarred lesions across his back. 'Oh, my God. You have been whipped without mercy, and it is a miracle that you are still alive. When?'

'Twice, when I was captured and interrogated by the French.'

'The devils! What else did they do to you?'

'I will not talk about it, Martha.'

He was still lying on his front and could not see my face, but now I felt tears welling up in my eyes. So I kissed the scars, and anointed them with my tears, and dried them with my hair. As I did so, he coughed again, and I felt his body tense as a spasm of pain passed through it. 'My poor dear Owain,' I said. 'You have been your old playful and irreverent self today, and you have encouraged me to joyful frivolity too. But has everything been a pretence? Are you in constant pain?'

'No. It comes and goes, as does the malaria. I am in truly sparkling form, so long as I do not over-exert myself. I hope that you do not expect me to pay for my keep by scything three acres of corn when we get back to the Plas.'

At this, I had to laugh, and I turned him over onto his back again. He looked up at me, and I thought that there was laughter as well as pain in his eyes. And love. I was reminded, if reminding was necessary, that this beloved man, horribly injured and diseased, had kept himself alive for fifteen years when others might have died, sustained by a flame of love that warmed his heart. Love for me. But for how long? Would he be taken from me again – by the injuries to his body and by the disease which might consume him from within? I could not bear to think about the future, and so I concentrated on the present.

As he lay on his back and watched me, still greatly aroused, I stood up and began to undress in front of him. First of all I took out the clips from my hair and let it fall free. I took off my simple silver necklace and the bracelets which I wore on my wrists. I undid the ties on the front of my cotton dress, and pulled my arms through the sleeves, and let it fall round my waist and to my feet. Then I loosened my outer petticoat and stepped out of it. I struggled with my stays, as one does. Owain laughed at my impatience, but at last I loosened the bows, pulled the wretched things away from my body, and threw them onto the grass. Finally I let loose the straps of my most intimate petticoat and let it fall, exposing my breasts and then the rest of me as I pulled it down over my hips. I stood naked before him.

I wanted him there and then, but Owain smiled again and said, 'Stand there, if you please, Martha. I have waited fifteen years for this. Let me love you with my eyes.' And his eyes roamed up and down my body, caressing me, for what seemed like an age.

At last I began to feel embarrassed by the act of exhibiting myself, and said, 'Please, sir, may I come a little closer? I am too far away from you, and I am feeling cold.' That was an absurd remark, given that it was just after noon, and the heat of the August day was at its fiercest.

'Then I had better do my duty and warm you up,' said Owain, taking his hands from behind his head and stretching them towards me. I took his hands, and he drew me down onto the blanket beside him. I closed my eyes and let him roam all over my body with his fingers and his lips. He was infinitely tender and patient. Then I did the same with him, and tried to be gentle and restrained, but a white-hot passion was rising within me, and patience became a vice instead of a virtue. Then our mouths were together, and he embraced me with such power that the breath was almost forced out of my lungs. Now our hands moved not with exploratory tenderness but with serious intent, and I held his manhood hard as his fingers caressed me. He was on top of me, but even in the midst of my surging passion I realized that some of his gasps were of pain rather than ecstasy. His broken arm and leg, never properly healed, were hurting him terribly, of that I was sure. So I took the initiative, and rolled him over onto his back. He said nothing, but smiled, and let me have my wicked way with him. I dared not let down my weight upon him for fear of causing him even more pain, but I tried to support myself with my arms and my knees.

Neither of us could wait for a moment longer, but he suddenly said, 'Martha, are you sure?'

'After fifteen years of waiting, I am very sure.'

Then he was inside me, deep and hard, and he gasped. 'Oh, Martha! How I love you!'

I gasped too, and said, *'Cariad,* at last, at last!'

My resolutions of tenderness were quite forgotten, and his pain was forgotten, and in a wild frenzy we rose to the peak of our loving, and sighed and shouted together.

Exhausted and aglow, I rolled off him and lay by his side. We held hands, and as the mad pounding in our hearts was gradually stilled we looked at the sky, and the gulls that wheeled far overhead, gleaming white in the August sunshine. 'I am sorry Owain,' said I at last. 'My enthusiasm got the better of me. I hope I did not hurt you.'

Owain laughed. 'Last time I had something to apologize for, and now it is your turn. Do not worry, dearest. I am quite unharmed.'

'Thank God for that. I must not be greedy, but preserve you like a crystallized fruit, and enjoy you a little at a time.'

'Ah, rationing, rationing. A basic female instinct in these hard times. You are not very good at rationing, Martha, whatever your instincts may be. And you have a large appetite.'

'I admit that freely, Owain. The last time I knew a man was in February in the year 1805, and that was dear David, on the night before he died. Seventeen years is a long time in a woman's life.'

'I can well imagine, Martha, what miseries of abstinence you must have suffered, with gentlemen and rogues fighting to find their way into your heart and your bed. And yet you waited for me.'

'And did you wait, Owain? Before today, were you still a virgin?'

'No. I cannot lie to you, *cariad*. Twice I have known other women in the years when we have been apart. On the first occasion, I was in a

Moorish tent, broken and battered after the shipwreck, being looked after by a young woman who should have known better. She gave me something that made me drowsy and eased my pain, and then she climbed between my sheets and took possession of me. I was only vaguely aware of what was going on, and was filled with remorse afterwards. Then, years later, when I was at a very low ebb, having been given the false information about your betrothal to Ceredig, I met a young war widow in Spain who was sad and very lonely. We fell to talking, and one thing led to another. But it was a strange experience, for when I looked at her body I saw yours, and when I kissed her I tasted your lips, and when we came to the climax of our loving I sighed, "Oh, Martha! Oh, Martha!" and she became very angry, and threw me out into the street.'

At this I collapsed with laughter, and so did Owain, although I dare say he had not previously found the episode funny at all. Then, still giggling, I said: 'Master Laugharne, one sort of hunger is assuaged, but not another. It so happens that I have here a most delightful picnic, and if we leave it any longer it will be rotted in the heat and attacked by flies. May I invite you to join me in a little celebration of our love?'

'I accept with pleasure, Mistress Morgan,' said he, and he sat up and watched me as I unpacked the hamper and laid everything out in fine fashion on our blanket. It was very hot, and it did not occur to either of us to put our clothes back on. Owain was again moved almost to tears when he saw that I had duplicated, down to the smallest

614

detail, the picnic which he had prepared for me in that fateful year of his disappearance. And so we sat on our hidden grassy bank beneath the clifftop, looking out over the wide bay that had taken him from me so many years ago. The sea surface was disturbed only by the gentlest of breezes, breathing in from the west. There were five white sails on the horizon, and rafts of puffins and guillemots sitting quietly on the water. Beauty was everywhere. I feasted my eyes on his body, as he did on mine. We ate and drank and talked endlessly about the things that had happened in both our lives over the last fifteen years. It was but a start, and there would be many more hours of reminiscing, storytelling and questioning ahead of us.

But one question could not wait. I had to ask him whether he had worked out who had been responsible for the sabotage of his boat on the fateful day of his disappearance. 'Squire Price of Llanychaer, of course,' he replied. 'Who else had a reason to wish me dead?'

'Joseph and I have long since come to that conclusion,' I said. 'But we have never found absolute proof. And the two men who did the work, Maldwyn Biggs and Freddy Cobb, are both dead. Should we pursue Master Price and bring him to justice for attempted murder?'

'From what I hear, Martha, he has had a life of tragedy and pain from the day of that foul deed. It is almost as if he has been cursed. Let him be. He has surely suffered enough, and I am minded to forgive him.'

Then I was suddenly moved to ask Owain about the Nightwalker. 'Did I ever tell you about

615

the creature in black that haunted me over a good many years?'

'I am not aware that you ever did, Martha.'

'Well, he has been absent for a long time, but then he reappeared on the mountain, looking down at the Plas, at the beginning of this month. He was dressed in a long black cloak, and he had a wide-brimmed black hat on his head. When Brynach and the servants jumped upon you near the top of the mountain, were you by any chance wearing those particular items of apparel?'

Owain laughed and said: 'Yes, Martha, I was. That was my little joke. When I was in Hettie's lodging house she told me about the mystery of the Nightwalker. I thought that if I dressed as he was dressed it might cause some confusion, and since he was supposed to be a ghost it might prevent brave fellows like Billy and Will from trying to catch me. So Hettie got me the cloak and the hat, and I acted out my little charade.'

'And are you the Nightwalker?'

Again he laughed with abandon. 'Good gracious no, Martha. How could I have been? I have been in Africa and Europe, and I have the signs on my body to prove it. What would have been my purpose, anyway, in prancing about on the mountain, year after year, come rain or shine?'

'So if you are not behind all of these sightings, who is? Do you know the identity of the Nightwalker?'

'I have no idea who he is, *cariad*. If I did, I would certainly tell you, for I will hide nothing from you. Now then, no more black thoughts on this most beautiful of days.'

And he finished his little bowl of gooseberry cream and custard. Then he downed the last drops of red wine from his crystal glass, and sighed with contentment, and stretched himself out on the blanket. I busied myself with packing everything away into the hamper, making sure to wrap up the crystal glasses and china plates with soft woollen cloths. As I worked, I hummed a little tune to myself, and realized too late that it was 'The White Lilac Tree'. I assumed that Owain had snoozed off, but when I glanced at him he was wide awake, watching me with a smile on his face. And he was very aroused. He said: 'Mistress Martha, I thought of having a little siesta, but I have thought better of it. Come here, if you will.' And so I obeyed, and we loved one another for a second time on our grassy bank, as the sun started to slip towards the west. This time it was a gentle loving, but it was no less wonderful, and we felt that we were soaring with the white birds towards the sun and the stars. Afterwards neither of us apologized, for there was nothing to regret.

When we got back to the bay we bathed in the warm sea, and then dried ourselves with the woollen blanket. The afternoon was far advanced when we collected our irritated horses and set off for the Plas. Owain suddenly looked worried, and said, 'Martha, you are still young enough to bear children. What if...'

'Do not worry, Owain. I have finished with childbearing. I know it with absolute certainty.' My certainty was rather less absolute than I pretended, but now was not the time to worry about that. I did not articulate it, but I had faced an enforced wedding before, and now I was prepared to take the risk of facing one again.

When we arrived back I was tired myself, and Owain was exhausted. He had several coughing sessions as we rode through Newport and up Greystones Hill, and I realized that his leg gave him great pain when he was on horseback. But he did not complain, and he brushed aside my comments and my questions. We looked a scruffy pair indeed when we arrived home, with Owain sporting a ripped shirt and me with matted hair still damp and salty after our swim. Sara, bless her, met us on the doorstep, and was as honest as ever. 'Oh my, Uncle Owain,' said she. 'You look tired, and your shirt is all ripped. What have you been doing?'

'Oh,' said Owain with a grin. 'We have been having exciting adventures, and for me it has been a very hard day.'

I could hardly suppress a giggle, and I added, 'You should have seen him, Sara! Today he has been into dark caves, and he has investigated unexpected nooks and crannies, and has climbed to unimaginable heights!'

Sara is quite old enough to know what I was talking about, but she is somewhat naive in the ways of the world. She pressed me for elaboration, but I would not oblige.

25 August 1822

Today, soon after dinner, Joseph rode into the yard on his black pony. I was sitting in the shade of the garden at the time, feeling just a little lonely, for Owain had gone back to Pontfaen in his brother's coach. My dear friend looked serious, and I knew that something was wrong when I saw the grim set of his jaw. He dispensed with his usual greetings, and simply said: 'Martha, I bring you very bad news. Ceredig is dead.'

The bright day was instantly transformed. I was standing up when Joseph spoke to me, but now I felt the colour drain out of my cheeks and I became dizzy. Joseph caught me before I fell, and carried me across to my garden seat. He laid me out on it and placed his coat beneath my head. I gazed up in absolute horror at the leafy canopy above me while Joseph knelt at my side. 'I am sorry, Martha,' he said. 'That was misjudged. I should have broken the news more diplomatically.' I closed my eyes and breathed deeply, until I was composed enough to look at Joseph. I was too shocked to cry.

At last I was strong enough to sit up. Joseph sat down beside me, and put his arm round my shoulder. 'He took his own life?' I whispered.

'Yes, Martha. There is no doubt about it.'

'Oh, may God have mercy upon his soul. The poor man. May I ask how it happened?'

'You may ask, but I will spare you the details. With a shotgun, in the woods near Farthings Hook Bridge. They found him this morning. He had been dead for twenty-four hours.'

'Oh, Joseph, what misery he must have endured! It must have happened just when Owain and I were on the cliffs yesterday, rediscovering the joys of love...' And I looked at him with a wild panic in my eyes, and clutched at him as guilt flooded through my veins.

He smoothed my hair, as a father might with a small child. 'Martha, you must not reproach yourself, for you have done nothing wrong. Your conduct over these past few days has been exemplary, and I have been proud to call myself your friend.' But in spite of his reassurances I could not hold back my tears. And so, not for the first or the last time, I wept upon his breast as he tried to console me.

When I had recovered the capacity to speak, I sobbed, 'Poor Ceredig – he must have gone through four days of Hell. And no family to console him or advise him. Why did he not come and talk to me? Why did he not summon you and ask for your advice? Was he so lonely that he had no-one to turn to in his hour of need? Oh, Joseph, I wrote to him! I wrote him a letter, in the hope that I might help him. And he received it and read it! Billy told me so!'

'I know, Martha. Here it is. It was lying at his side when they found him.'

Joseph handed me the letter which I had written on the day that we were to be married. It was creased and battered, as if it had been folded, and opened, and folded again, on many occasions. And it was splattered with blood.

'Forgive me, Martha, but I have read it. When the men handed it to me, I thought at first that it was a note from him to the world. People who take their own lives often leave farewells behind them. Then I recognized your writing. I have to say that your letter was quite beautiful. It could only have been written by a very tender-hearted lady.'

His voice cracked, and I realized that Joseph too was crying. So Joseph Harries, the Wizard of Werndew, the man reputed to be devoid of emotion, wept into my hair, and we clung together, and gave each other consolation, in the shade of my white lilac tree.

26 August 1822

Yesterday Joseph and I talked far into the night, and since he would have risked life and limb on a ride over the common back to Werndew, we found a bed for him. He has taken the death of Ceredig far harder than I might have imagined, and I now realize that it might have been a consequence of seeing the body, or what was left of it. Even a man such as he, who has seen death in a multitude of forms, is still humane enough to be shocked almost out of his wits by that particular death, so close to those he loves. And he probably feels guilt too, for he is one of those who connived in the plan to bring Owain to the house and to humiliate poor Ceredig.

Today we have all talked, in spite of the fact that the harvest has still been going on around us. The kitchen has seen a stream of harvesters throughout the day, and Bessie and Liza have been hard pressed to maintain the supply of food and cider required by the workers. There have been five wagons in use, two of them our own and the other three hired from Skiff, carrying wheat sheaves to the rickyard and barley to the barn. The talk has been of little else but the death of Ceredig, and I have had to endure a constant stream of visitors offering their condolences. Without exception they have said that I must not blame myself, but in my present mood I am not minded to take their advice, for I feel guilt more strongly than anger or grief. And the burden of it is heavy indeed.

I have talked more with Joseph, and with Sara and Brynach, and even with Bessie, for she is my most trusted female friend. But she has been frantically busy in the kitchen, and more serious conversation with her will have to wait. This afternoon Betsi came over to the Plas from Cenarth, for news travels fast, and she found out about Ceredig only a little later than I did. She knew that I needed her, as indeed I did, and she has worked miracles in giving me comfort in the midst of a situation that threatens to drive me mad. Joseph has gone home, and Betsi is staying tonight. I dare say that Owain might come tomorrow, for by now he too will have heard the news. He will also be blaming himself, for we are all caught up in a tangled web of horror the like of which none of us has ever encountered before.

There will be an inquest, and Owain and I are due to be questioned by the magistrates. But that may be some days off. After that, Ceredig will be buried in the grounds of his mansion at New Moat. The Rector refused to give him a church funeral, or a place in the graveyard. He had no family, so everything has to be arranged by his housekeeper. My poor, poor Ceredig – miseries pursue him, even after death.

This evening, as I sit at my window, lights are

flickering down in the *cwm* and the sky is crackling with stars. Later on, a new moon will make a shy appearance. The air is still, and I can hear the faint sound of a wistful tune on a tin whistle, coming from the barn. The Irish usually fiddle and dance at the end of a day's work, but not tonight, for they have picked up on the prevailing mood.

Why did he do it? Because he was mad with love for me, that is for sure. And because he was rejected, and cast aside because of my love for another man. Perhaps he could not understand how I could walk away from a life of comfort and security and towards the uncertain promise of a future at the side of a wanderer with no house, no land and indeed no inheritance. From what he could see, Owain was destitute and sick, and might not even live to see the year out. But Ceredig must have known, surely, that my love for Owain was matched by my love for the Plas and for the mountain. I think he knew, in the deepest corner of his heart, right up to the moment of truth, that he would never drag me away from this place. Poor, poor man!

But perhaps, alongside the love and the rejection, some small part of what killed Ceredig was the death of his own self-respect. I should have realized that on the fateful evening, but I did not. He loved me, but he also wanted my estate and my seven farms, because through marriage the New Moat estate would then have extended to ten farms, with land in the mountains and near the sea. What esteem he might then have enjoyed! Ceredig was not a vain man, but I fear that he did place too high a value upon the opinion of others. When he walked out of my parlour and out of my life, I believe he was so ashamed that he could never bear to look another man in the eye. Oh, Ceredig, you dear fool! What a shame! What a waste!

I cannot, and will not, absolve myself from responsibility for Ceredig's death, and neither can Owain. But those guests who sighed and gasped and wept and cheered on the evening of the wanderer's return should also hang their heads in shame.

In Spite of Appearances

29 August 1822

Full circle. As on so many previous occasions, my hand is shaking with emotion as I write, and I am not sure that I will be able to keep my composure until I have recorded what is in my head and my heart.

Two evenings since, on the final day of the harvest, I was in no mood to eat supper, or to join in the celebration of harvest home. I left that to Sara and Brynach to organize, for they need to take more responsibility and they supervised the tradition of carrying *y wrach* back to the house when the last of the barley fields was finished. There was a good deal of horseplay from the servants and from the twenty or so harvesters who have helped us this year, but with Ceredig dead and not yet in his grave, I was in no mood to take part. The whole place has been so crowded with people, and echoing with such a babble of conversation, that I had to escape. I told Liza that I would go for a walk, and she encouraged it, for she could see that I had had enough.

Since dusk was not far off, I took a lantern and a tinder box with me. I told Liza that I might well stay out all night, and that she need not send out any search parties for me unless I was still absent at breakfast time. She raised her eyebrows, but said nothing, since she is well used to my eccentricities. I wrapped a cloak round my shoulders, and set off up the mountain. As soon as I was clear of the Plas I felt better, for the evening was calm and mellow, with a touch of autumn about it. As the light faded, bats and moths flitted about my head, and tawny owls called to each other across the valley between Gelli Wood and Coed Ty Canol. Lights started to flicker here and there, and the smoke from cottage chimneys sank back to earth, as it often does on late summer evenings, instead of rising to heaven. I stopped at Ffynnon Brynach and anointed myself, and after catching my breath I continued my climb. As I followed the faint sheep tracks through head-high bracken I could hear music drifting up from the Plas. The Irish were at it with their fiddles and tin whistles and drums, and I knew that there would be good dancing and jollification in both the barn and the kitchen until the early hours. I smiled, and was happy to leave them to it. The best of luck to them, I thought, for they have worked hard, and they have little enough in the way of relaxation. They all have shillings in their pockets, and food in their bellies...

Twenty minutes later I stood at the entrance of my cave. I thought that I might sleep there, for I had never done so before. There was just enough light to see the outlines of the flanking rocks and the ferns and dry grasses which made the entrance slit invisible. Away to the west, over Dinas Mountain, there was a hazy sunset, with the last reds and purples fading into blackness. How I loved this place! Every time a new sky, a new texture on the rocks, a new scent on the air. And yet at the same time immeasurably old, and unchanged. I ignited my tinder and lit my candle lantern, and crept in through the cave entrance. I went to my familiar bed of moss against the back wall, and placed the lantern on the ground before me. I sat down and pulled my knees up to my chin. I closed my eyes, and tried to empty my mind, and peace washed over me.

I do not know how long I sat there in the quietness. Maybe I was there for an hour. Then I heard the faintest of sounds from somewhere outside, on the side of the mountain. I was immediately alert, with my ears pricked and my heart pounding. I did not move, but sat there with my face illuminated by the faint glow from my lantern. The sounds came closer. I could hear irregular footfalls, and several times there was a clatter as a stone or boulder was moved. There was a deep rumble as one large stone was dislodged and went crashing down the slope. That was followed by complete silence for several minutes. Then came the sounds again, drawing ever closer. A boot scraping on a rock surface. The rustle of a loose garment. A dull thudding noise, possibly made by a staff or some other wooden item struck against the rock. Then, most terrifying of all, the sound of rasping breaths. Some person or creature was just outside the cave entrance, fighting for breath. I was petrified, and threw my shawl over the candle lantern in case the intruder should see the glimmer of light through the slit in the rock. I pressed myself against the innermost wall of the cave. When my eyes had adjusted to the darkness, I could just discern a gleam from the starlit sky outside, but then even that dim light was blocked off. Somebody, or something, was standing at the entrance, and as my panic reached a peak he – or it – started to squeeze between the entrance pillars.

I closed my eyes and curled into a ball, covering my head with my arms. I was so terrified that I might have been whimpering like a small baby. Then I heard breathing very close, and knew that the creature was inside the cave, and standing over me. For several minutes I stayed there, too frightened to cry out, or to open my eyes, or to move an inch. I became aware of movement within the cave, and then even though my eyes were closed I knew that my shawl had been lifted off the lantern, for a glimmer of light penetrated my eyelids. Something touched my arm, and somebody whispered, 'Mistress Martha?' I was shaking like a leaf, but eventually I opened my eyes and lifted my head.

I saw, no more than twelve inches in front of me, the face of the Devil. In an instant all the terrors of my life washed over me and transported me into a living hell. I screamed, and screamed again, until the vision of that face was obliterated by a merciful blackness...

30 August 1822

It is early morning, and too cool and wet to work outside. I must continue with my narrative, for last night I was so moved by the recollection of my encounter with the Devil that I had to stop.

At last I recovered consciousness, and took a while to work out where I was and what was happening to me. I realized that I was on the ground, covered by my cloak. The lantern was still flickering on the ground, just a few feet away from my head. I felt that I had not been interfered with, and I sighed with relief on that account. Then I saw a figure huddled up on the other side of the cave, and I became aware of a strange choking and sobbing sound. Somebody, some man, was weeping. I was absolutely confused. Did the Devil weep? Did ghosts weep? Or could it be that this was at last the Nightwalker, and that he was human enough to sob like a small child? Then I saw a black wide-brimmed hat on the ground, and saw that the figure huddled against the cave wall was covered in a black cloak. It was confirmed. This, I knew, was the encounter that he had planned and that I had half expected since my first fateful sighting of him near the Plas, many years ago.

Now, in spite of the fact that I was still afflicted by a cold fear, I could not resist my instinct for compassion. So I crawled across the dusty floor of the cave and touched his shoulder. 'Why, sir, are you weeping?' I asked.

Gradually he composed himself. With his head still covered by the cloak, he whispered: 'Mistress Martha, I weep for the world, and for you, but mostly for myself.'

'Look at me, sir, if you will.'

'Will you scream again?'

I swallowed hard, and said: 'I will endeavour not to, sir.'

'And will you talk to me? I have much to say.'

'I promise it. But you need not whisper, for there is nobody to hear.'

There was a strange sound from under the cloak that might have been laughter. 'My voice, Martha, has gone before me to Heaven or Hell, having taken its leave of me five minutes before noon on the tenth day of August in the year of our Lord 1806. It is a miracle that I can still manufacture a whisper.'

I swallowed hard, and felt apprehension grip my heart. 'I did not know. Please forgive me.' There was a long silence, and I thought that the figure beneath the cloak nodded. So I continued. 'Now, sir, please uncover your head and look at me, and be assured that a minute of whispers from a gentleman is more blessed to a woman than an hour of boastings and bluster. Are you a gentleman?'

'That I am, madam, in spite of appearances.'

And with that, he sat upright just a foot or two in front of me, and let the cloak fall away from him. I looked for a split second, and then closed my eyes again, for I had great difficulty in controlling myself. I opened my eyes once more. The man before me had lost his right arm. His right eye had also gone, and there was virtually nothing left of his right ear or his nose. He had only a few wisps of hair on his head. He had no eyebrows. His face and his scalp were covered with raw and inflamed skin coloured red and purple, and there were streaks and patches of scar tissue across his features.

When I had recovered from this appalling revelation, all I could do was whisper: 'Oh, you poor thing. I am so sorry...'

The man made a strange noise, and I saw that he was laughing. 'This whispering business is contagious, as I have found on many previous occasions over the years. Speak loudly if you will, because my hearing is somewhat damaged. But rest assured, Mistress Martha, that a whispered sentence from a beautiful lady is the most perfect balm for a troubled soul.'

The ice was broken, and I laughed too. 'I too am a troubled soul,' I said. 'But my troubles are as nothing when set alongside yours. How did this happen?'

'I was in charge of a line of field guns in a skirmish with the French not far from Boulogne. One of the guns would not fire, and I was called to assist. My mind was not fully concentrated on the task in hand, and the gun exploded a few feet away from me. Three gunners were killed, and I was thrown back by a fireball. I daresay it is a miracle that I survived. I was treated by a naval surgeon at first, and then shipped back to England with other casualties. For almost five months my life hung by a thread. But somehow my wounds started to heal, and I begged to be discharged from the hospital and from the army. I was given my pay and my papers. Then I falsified a letter to my parents, with the help of a kind commander, saying that I had died honourably on the field of battle. I thought that was the best thing to do, in the circumstances.'

'And now, sir, who are you?'

'Iestyn Price of Llanychaer. I dare say you do not recognize me.'

I sat in silence on the floor of the cave for a long time, trying to come to terms with this news, my mind seeking wildly to connect together small fragments of memory from the past. Then I said bleakly: 'But he is supposed to be dead, and Squire Price and his family grieved for his death.'

'That was my intention. And now, with my mother and sister gone, my father has had to come to terms with the fact that I am alive. And soon he will have to grieve again.'

'You mean...'

'Yes, I am dying. The Grim Reaper has given me, in his infinite wisdom, a considerable reprieve. But now I have an incurable infection which is eating me away. Even the Wizard cannot cure me.'

'You have consulted with Joseph Harries?'

'Of course. For many years he has been the best friend that a man can have. When I might have died, in the hard winter of 1807–1808, after I had to flee from Cwmgloyn, he took me in and kept me warm and fed. I was at a very low ebb, as you might imagine, having to contend with hysteria and mob rule at the same time.'

Memories came flooding back, and what he said began to make some sense. But there was one question that I now had to put to him. 'May I come to the crux of the matter, Master Iestyn, by asking why you have returned to this area with your strange and protracted nightwalking charade?'

'There are several reasons, Martha, but before giving them I want to say I am dreadfully sorry for the fact that things have not always turned out as planned. I fear that I have terrorized you, and that was far from my intention. My bunch of daffodils was, as you might have appreciated, a peace offering. Sadly, my planning of this business was rather better than my execution of it. Now then, to reasons. First, I loved my home area. *Hiraeth*, they call it. You know about it, and I know about it too. I could not keep away, in spite of my injuries. Second, I loved you, and still love you...'

'Oh, no!' I was appalled. 'Is there no end to this? Ceredig, and now you as well?'

'I heard about Ceredig, and I am horrified. But I am not entirely surprised. Martha, you are wise in the ways of the world, but I sense that you are also very naive in certain matters. You have more power in you than a whirlwind, and part of that power comes from your beauty, which drives men mad.'

'Oh, my God. I have heard that before, and I am terrified by it. But you of all people, Iestyn? We hardly knew each other when we were young.'

'We kissed six times, as I recall. And you had magic in your lips.'

'But those were the furtive kisses typical of a youthful flirtation. Surely they cannot have meant anything to you?'

'They meant the world to me, Martha, and still do. From the moment our lips first touched, I have been besotted by you. I have loved you through fire and brimstone, through joy – when I could find it – and through pain. When I approached that field gun I should have known that it would explode, but I was thinking of you at the time.'

Then *I* exploded, and said with my eyes blazing: 'Iestyn! That remark was very cruel! Is it supposed to make me feel better, or is it supposed to make me feel guilty? I have had enough of guilt! It has chased me around like a shadow, and will not let me be! How could you have been so stupid? You foolish, miserable man...' And my voice trailed away, as the tension of the situation became too much for me. I am ashamed to say that I dissolved into tears. Iestyn put his one arm round my shoulder as I sobbed, and at last I recovered.

'I apologize for that, Martha. I seem to specialize in stupidity, and you are right: it was very insensitive of me.'

'Very well. Let us forget it. You were telling me about the reasons for your charade. Have you finished?'

'No, there is one more thing. The last reason for my determination to stay close to this place, in spite of all the risks involved, is the love which I bear for my son Brynach.'

At this I was rendered totally speechless. I could not laugh, I could not cry, and I could not even move. I think that even my mind stopped working. I could not look at Iestyn, and I gazed at the flickering flame in my candle lantern instead. But after a protracted silence, Iestyn gave a strange sound that might have been a chuckle. 'Mistress Martha!' he whispered. 'I count it as an achievement that I have reduced you to silence. I count it as a further achievement that none of your friends have betrayed either me or Brynach over all these years, in spite of the pressure that you have put upon them.'

'You mean that they all knew?'

'Of course they did. Meredith and his wife Jane first, and then Patty, and of course Jake, next Joseph, Bessie, and then my father, finally Billy and your other servants...'

'So that was the conspiracy, and the reason for their comings and goings, and their whispers in dark corners, and their clandestine meetings one with another?'

'I dare say. Wonderful, faithful friends, all of them. Martha, you are very lucky to have around you people who will love you, come what may, and protect you from anything that might harm you.'

'Thank you for reminding me, Iestyn. Of course I know it. But I have to tell you that this charade of yours has placed an almost un-bearable strain upon my relationships with my friends and servants. There are times when I have felt abandoned and betrayed, and times when my love for my friends has almost turned to hate.'

'I cannot believe that, Martha. I do not think that it is in your nature to hate your enemies, let alone your friends.'

Then I frowned, and asked the obvious question. 'But why, Iestyn, if Brynach is your son, did you not leave him with his mother? Did she die in childbirth?'

'No. She is very well, and I gather she is also happy.'

'So the child was born out of wedlock?'

'Correct.'

'So why, if neither you nor she wanted him, did you not take him to your own family at Llanychaer and seek the assistance of your parents? Your mother might have been pleased to give him a home.'

'I doubt that, Martha. They thought I was dead. If I had turned up at Plas Llanychaer, looking as I do, with a bastard child in a basket, my mother would have gone out of her mind. She was a strange, sad and inadequate woman, in any case. And my father was an unkind and bullying fellow who was very short of tenderness. He could hardly cope with Fanny's whimsies, and would at that time certainly not have managed with a newborn baby and a half-dead son in the house. Brynach would have had a truly miserable life. And if I had asked Patty to deliver the basket with the baby in it onto the doorstep of Plas Llanychaer instead of Plas Ingli, my father would have immediately transferred it to the Overseers of the Poor, and Brynach would have ended up in a hovel somewhere, kept alive by contributions from the poor rate. I doubt that even a pleading letter purporting to have come from me would have made any difference to his attitude. Remember that I used to be able to write with my right hand once, Martha, but now I have to scribble as best I can with my left, in a style that is quite impossible for any of my old friends or family to recognize.'

'So you thought that Brynach would have a better life at the Plas?'

'I knew it. I knew that as a widow you had troubles enough, and that I was placing another massive burden on your shoulders, but my instinct told me that you would cope. And I thank God that you did. I could never have anticipated the love that you have shown towards my small and innocent child, Martha, and the fierce and yet gentle protection that you and your servants and family have given to him over all these years. Thank you, thank you from the bottom of my heart. I count it as a privilege that I have been able, every now and then, to see him as he has grown up into a young gentleman, and to see you and your other children, and to hear from my friends how you have all been getting on...'

He stopped, and I could see that he was shaking with emotion. Tears, I realized, were impossible, but they would have come, if only he had not been so terribly damaged. I went and sat next to him, and put my arm round him. I kissed him on his scarred and inflamed cheek.

'And I suppose that your choice of the Plas had nothing to do with your affection for me?'

'I have to admit that that did enter my mind. Do you remember once, Martha, when we were very young, and I was rather drunk, I swore to you that one day you would carry my child? You slapped my face, I think.'

I laughed, and so did he. 'Yes, Iestyn, I remember it well. It must be very gratifying that your prophecy came to pass, although not in the manner that you might have wished.'

I had more questions for him, so I sat down again and faced him, finally getting used to his appalling injuries as revealed in the flickering light of the lantern. 'How did you know about my cave, and how'd you come to find me here this evening?'

'Observation, Martha, and a good spyglass. Long ago, and more than once, I watched you coming up onto the mountain and disappearing. I thought there must be a cave, and so one day, when you had gone home after a visit, I searched for your tracks, found them and followed them to the entrance. This is a very special place, and I knew it was special to you, so although I have visited it often over the years, and have slept here many nights, I have never lit a fire here, and I have always been careful to leave no trace of my visits. I have found much solace on your bed of moss. I am sorry if you feel that your sanctuary is now defiled.'

'Far from it, Iestyn. It has been defiled once, but not by you. I will not talk about that. Now then, I am intrigued by your decision to dress in black, and to create the fantasy in the minds of others that you were a phantom, or even the Devil doing his mischief. Why did you do it?'

'Partly because it was necessary,' he whispered. 'Looking as I do, with half a face and half a body, I had to choose garments that hid the extent of my injuries. I could not exactly amble about in public and melt into the crowd. And I did not want to be chased. You might not realize it, Martha, but the loss of an arm is a great hindrance when it comes to running or leaping about on the boulders of this beloved mountain. Also, I have had little enough amusement in life, and I quite liked the idea of being a ghost, to keep people away from me.'

'But how did you manage to move about without leaving any tracks? Billy and the others were quite convinced that you were a phantom who flew through the air, as indeed was the old lady who bumped into you on the Parrog.'

'Oh, that was the easy part. I learnt about tracking in the army, from an old fellow who had been a scout in the American War of Independence. When you learn about tracking others, you also learn how to leave no tracks yourself. When there was snow on the ground, I wore snowshoes, and swept snow across my tracks with the end of my cloak. When the ground was wet, I wore soft shoes called moccasins, which a friend made for me out of calfskin to a design used by the Red Indians. I never stepped in soft ground, and always took care to walk on hard surfaces, or rocks or stones which leave no traces. I never wore boots – I knew that if I had, that terrible fellow called Joseph Harries would have been onto my trail like lightning!'

I shook my head, and grinned, and wondered at the simplicity of it. 'And why did you come and go as you did? Sometimes you were here at the Plas, and sometimes elsewhere, and sometimes you did not appear for years on end. I have thought long and hard about your movements, Iestyn, and can discover no rhyme nor reason in them.'

'My movements may have appeared complicated, but in truth they were not. My first visit to the mountain was made before Brynach was born, for I knew even then that I would have to find a good home for him. My accident in France destroyed any prospect of my being a suitable father for the child. So I came and looked, and thought at first that my old friend Meredith Lloyd might take the baby. But he and his wife were distraught at the imprisonment and impending execution of his brother Matthew, and in no fit state to think of anything else. Meredith let me stay in secret in the hovel once used by Matthew and his family. I was there for about six weeks, and it was bitterly cold. It snowed a lot, and I could never get warm. The only people who knew I was there were two servants, who had been told only that the place was inhabited by a good man who had some catching illness. They left food for me on the doorstep, and never came inside. I never went out in daylight, except when it was snowing and I thought I could move about without being seen.

'By the end of January in 1807 I had determined to leave the baby at the Plas. All that I heard about you from Meredith was complimentary, and I was even pleased when I heard of your betrothal to Owain, for I knew him to be a good man. I came several times and observed the Plas, and Llannerch too, seeking to work out the comings and goings of family and servants and friends. If truth be told, Martha, I was also seeking to get a glimpse or two of you, so that you might transmit a little brightness into my dark life.'

'That may be, Iestyn. But you terrified me into the bargain.'

639

'Again, I can only say that I am sorry. That was not my intention. Then I discovered your friendship with Patty, and found out more about her from Meredith. I called on her one dark night, when Jake was away at sea. She was very afraid when she saw me, as one might imagine, but when I explained who I was, and offered her a guinea, she agreed to help me. She was hard up, and needed the money, but in truth she is a soft and gentle woman and I think she was driven above all by compassion. I swore her to secrecy. She agreed that if I would deliver the baby to her at dead of night she would carry it to the Plas and place it on the doorstep. Then in the middle of April I received news of the baby's birth, and went away to fetch him. I hired a wet nurse and a carriage, and took two days to travel back to the Parrog. On the night of the twenty-fifth of April – I remember the date well, for it was the last time that I kissed my little son – I handed the child over to Patty, and she took him to the Plas as planned, very early next morning.'

'Oh, you poor man. I can hardly imagine the anguish you must have felt when you let him go.'

'It was not easy, Martha. For most of the spring I stayed on the Cwmgloyn estate. I met Patty occasionally to hear news of little Brynach. Then we got careless, and that led to the incident on the Parrog in July which almost cost Patty and Jake dear. Things were moving on apace, and I got out of the hovel in Cwmgloyn just in time, before it was burnt to the ground. When that happened I was hiding in the woods nearby, frightened out of my wits. In fairness to Meredith, I had to move on, and he advised me to go to Joseph and ask for his help. I lived rough for a while, and then I knocked on Joseph's door. Blessed man that he is, he took me in immediately, and tried to do something for my wounds, which were weeping. He had some remedy involving sulphur, and many other potions and ointments. He dressed my wounds several times a day, and I declare that at the time he did little else. His other patients were sadly neglected. I stayed at Werndew over the winter of 1807–1808, except for the mild spells when I lived rough. Sometimes I was very ill indeed. I had a few close shaves, especially when you once descended on Werndew without warning. After the winter I felt better, but Joseph warned me that any further visits to the Plas might lead to the collapse of all my plans, and he said that you were obsessed with discovering the Nightwalker's identity. Much as I longed to see you and my little boy again, I agreed that I would stay away. In the spring I was bored, and I took it into my head to see how things were at my old home of Llanychaer. I thought that I might see my father, my mother and my sister, and that this might give me some consolation. Unfortunately they saw me and got very frightened. Then I was appalled to discover from Joseph that my father was intent upon hunting me down. My own father! There was nothing else to do but flee, for Joseph warned me that every inch of territory hereabouts would be scoured by hounds, and by men driven by the prospect of a cash reward.'

'So where did you go?'

'I walked, always at night, all the way to Swansea. It was a long journey, but the summer weather was good. I thought that I would never see you, or Brynach, or the Plas, again. I chose Swansea because the place is always full of people who have been burnt in the furnaces. There are disfigured and maimed men on every street corner. I put away my cloak and muffler and hat, and took on a new identity. I worked in the smelters and on the tramroads, and sometimes in the docks. I made many friends, and the exercise did me good, for I somehow contrived not to die. I exchanged various letters with Joseph, Meredith and Patty, and they told me how my son was getting on. The years passed, and at last I was driven by a mad desire to return to Pembrokeshire in time for Brynach's tenth birthday. So I took a risk and wrote to Bessie–'

'Indeed you did. I remember it well.'

'–and I pleaded with her to help me. I needed an accomplice within the walls of the Plas. I said that I would go to Werndew at the beginning of April in 1817, and that I would hope for news of what might happen on Brynach's birthday. I told her that Brynach was my little boy, and promised her that I would harm no-one. Luckily she believed me and did as I asked, and so I did get a glimpse of you and your happy family as planned, in spite of the mist around Carn Edward. I gather that that got poor Bessie into considerable trouble.'

'You are quite correct, Iestyn. And you almost turned me from a woman with iron resolve into a quivering wreck.'

'Then, later in that same month, I was horrified when Joseph told me of my mother's death. I attended the funeral, at a safe distance, and the raindrops did my weeping for me. I was utterly distraught, for I loved my mother dearly in spite of her shortcomings and her nervous disposition. On that day I was soaked to the skin, and caught a chill. Joseph was hard pressed to keep me alive. Then I heard that Fanny had taken her own life. I was frantic to go to Llanychaer, but Joseph would not let me out of Werndew until I was well again. At last, on June the twelfth in the disastrous summer of 1817, I decided to go to Llanychaer and make a reconciliation with my father. I thought it was time to tell him everything, now that Brynach was growing up. Joseph agreed to help, but only on condition that I put away my hat and my cloak and promise never to play the part of the Nightwalker again. He had had enough of my tom-foolery, and said that he was no longer amused by my efforts to frighten the living daylights out of innocent people. In any case, he said, some day I would be captured, and the truth would come out, and that would lead to distress all round. So I agreed that it was time for the Nightwalker to die.'

'And not a day too soon. So Joseph took you to your father?'

'He did, after dark, later in the month of June. The servants were all away in Newport, attending *Ffair Gurig*. Father was in his office, and Joseph invited himself in and told him to prepare himself for a shock which would at the same time bring him unimaginable pleasure. And he pushed me into the room, and left Father and me to our own devices.' Iestyn's whisper trailed away again, and he became very emotional. I waited a few minutes while he composed himself.

'And then?'

'It was a very difficult time, Martha. But I discovered that my father was a changed man, chastened by guilt and by the tragedies that had afflicted him. He embraced me and welcomed me home.' He paused for a long time, as if he was fighting for breath. I was alarmed, but then he continued. 'We devised a plan. The essence of it was that I was dead, and should remain dead. Three of Father's oldest and most faithful servants were told that there was a new arrival at Llany-chaer – Thomas Price, a distant relative who had been burnt in an accident in a Swansea furnace, and needed a peaceful place in the country in order to recuperate. I was given Fanny's room, at the end of the west wing of the house, well away from prying eyes. And there I stayed.'

'But did you not wish to get out and about? And did none of the other servants wonder about your identity? And how is it that I and the other gentry families heard nothing of the presence of a stranger at Plas Llanychaer? Nothing stays secret in these parts.'

'It was not easy, I have to admit. I have been very sick for most of the last five years, and confined to my bed. Joseph has called in often to see me, as have my other friends, including your servants. My father has been a pillar of strength, and the servants at Llanychaer have been very discreet. You will have noticed that the Squire has withdrawn from public life, to a very large extent, during these past few years.'

'I had noticed, and wondered about it. But he

has made overtures of friendship towards me and the Plas, and I have to admit to being suspicious as to his motives. Does your father know that Brynach is your child?'

'I did not tell him at first. But then I took him into my confidence, on condition that he should never lay any claim to Brynach, or do anything to disturb his happiness at the Plas, or reveal to him that there was any blood link with Llanychaer.'

'He agreed to that?'

'Of course. And you can trust him. He has, I think, come to love the Plas, and your family and servants. To him it represents everything that has been missing from his own life.'

There was one other matter on which I required an explanation. I told Iestyn that I had expected an appearance from the Nightwalker on the occasion of Brynach's fifteenth birthday. Had he not been tempted to catch another glimpse of his son? Yes, he admitted. He knew that there would be another picnic at Carn Edward. Although he was very sick at the time, and although it meant breaking faith with both his father and Joseph, he took out his Nightwalker's cloak and hat from the chest at the end of his bed, put them on, and crept away from the house by a back entrance early on the morning of 7th April. He got close to the rocks, and was settling down to wait for the arrival of the picnic party when he was leapt upon by Billy, Shemi and Will. He was so weak that he was incapable of resisting arrest, but he said that my three faithful servants got a fearsome shock when they stripped away his muffler and knocked off his hat and saw the extent of his deformity. There was nothing for it but to come clean. He told them everything, and to their eternal credit they agreed to keep the secret and to tell me nothing. He was very ill, and had been further damaged during the ambush. The three men carried him home to Llanychaer, handed him over to the Squire, and then had to go and fetch Joseph because they were afraid he might die.

'And now here we are in the month of August, Iestyn, and you are still very much alive. You have a remarkable instinct for survival.'

'Instinct maybe, Martha. But I am not well. It almost killed me to climb up here to your cave today. Joseph has done what he can, but after tonight you will never see me again. And I will never see Brynach again. The Grim Reaper is waiting for me outside this cave, and I am grateful to him for not coming inside and disturbing our conversation.'

'Rubbish, Iestyn. You must not talk like that. I will get you home, although I can see that my candle lantern will not keep alight for very much longer.'

'Never fear,' he whispered. 'Mine is outside on the grass. And soon we will have the light of dawn to guide us. Perhaps it is time to go...' And he made as if to struggle to his feet.

Then I realized that there was one question I had not asked him. So I asked it.

'And who, Iestyn, is Brynach's mother? I must know.'

'Oh, Martha. Have you not guessed? It is your sister Elen.'

I felt as if the roof had fallen in on me and

646

crushed every part of my body. Elen? How could that be? What sort of insanity was this? Was Iestyn playing a cruel joke on me, just for his own amusement? Elen had been in Bath, more than a hundred miles away from here, before she went off to America. And how could she have known Iestyn, let alone borne his child? Then I noticed that he was making that strange noise that passed for a chuckle.

'Do not look so surprised, Martha,' he whispered. 'I am not insane, and this is neither a wild fantasy nor a cruel joke. I met Elen in the summer of 1806, at a ball, when my regiment was based in Bath. I had met her before, of course, just as I had met you, when we were young. I found her very beautiful and I think she liked me well enough, and we were swept along by alcohol and passion. We talked a little, danced a great deal, drank too much, and ended up in the same bed. We loved each other with a good deal of enthusiasm. Next morning, we were both filled with remorse, but we hoped that all would be well. We talked about you, Martha, and I was horrified when Elen told me that David was dead and you were a widow. I never loved Elen, but I have never fallen out of love with you since the day you first cast your spell on me as a sweet sixteen-year-old. I dared to hope that if I could return to Pembrokeshire there might be hope for me if I could make my way to the Plas and declare my love. I planned it all, but then I was chosen for this raid on France. I had to go, but I dare say I was a hopeless officer, for I was obsessed with thoughts of you.'

'Please, Iestyn, spare me the details.'

'Then came my accident. In December a letter reached me in hospital. It was from Elen, saying that she was with child and that I was the father. I was struck with panic, but as soon as I got out of hospital in January I rushed back to Bath, wearing a wide-brimmed black hat, and a muffler over my face, and a black cloak round my body so as not to attract too much attention. I found her at a friend's house, confused and terrified at the prospect of bearing a bastard child. She was even more terrified when she saw the extent of my injuries. I offered to marry her, but she became almost hysterical. At last her friend Bella and I managed to calm her down, and between us we conceived a plan. I promised Elen that I would find a good home for the child, and you know the rest. Before I had determined that I would leave Brynach at the Plas, I had grave concerns about the fact that you were all alone as a hard-working widow, but I thought that you would soon be married to Owain, and that he would make as fine a father as could be imagined. So I decided, and when I got the message from Elen that the child had been born, I went back from Pembrokeshire to Bath to collect him. I did not tell Elen where I was taking the baby. I have not told her to this day, and I promised her that I would not divulge to the new parents the name of either the father or the mother.

'But now, Martha, so close to my death, I have come to consider myself free from my pledge to Elen, and I think it important that you should be in possession of the truth. At some stage in the future, when you and they are ready, you may say what you will to both Elen and our beloved son.'

Now I was weeping again, for this poor brave man who had endured so much over so many years because of his love for me and for his baby son. Motherhood I understand, but fatherhood has until now been a mystery to me. Perhaps the two are not so different after all.

There is not much more to tell. Iestyn was clearly growing weaker by the minute, and as I observed him I became very worried. I insisted that I must get him back to Llanychaer as soon as possible. Outside the cave, the light of dawn was spreading across the eastern horizon. There was already just enough light to see by. Somehow I managed to get him out of the cave and down off the rocky mountainside into the area covered by high bracken. Both of us ended up very bruised, scratched and dirty. I got him down as far as Ffynnon Brynach, and washed him as best I could with some of the healing water. He was barely conscious, and I knew then that I could not possibly get him back to Llanychaer all by myself. 'Iestyn,' I said, 'I must go and get help. I will fetch Billy and the other men, and between us we will carry you home. Will you be all right if I leave you here for just a few minutes?'

He nodded, and then held out his hand towards me. I grasped it with both my hands and held it to my breast. 'Martha,' he whispered. 'I think I am slipping away. I fear that I shall never see you again. Before I go, will you kiss me and tell me that you love me?'

So I kissed him gently on his rough scarred lips. Then I said, 'I love you, Iestyn, for you are the father of my son. You have given so much love in your life that you will surely obtain your reward. Now sleep in peace.' Then he gave the slightest of smiles, let go of my hand, and slipped into unconsciousness.

I was overtaken by panic. I placed my ear close to his lips, and found that he was breathing steadily. Then I ran all the way down to the Plas. I knew that I must not wake Sara or Brynach, but I thought that I was safe on that score, since there was little chance of young people waking up before ten of the clock without drums and bugles. I entered the house as quietly as I could, for it was still not five. I managed to rouse Billy and Will, and cursed the fact that Shemi had gone home to Sian and their children for the night. They stirred reluctantly, for the harvest dancing and drinking had gone on until the early hours, and they had sore heads. But to their eternal credit they moved quickly and quietly, and we were soon out of the sleeping house and on our way to Ffynnon Brynach, carrying a short stepladder on which to transport the unconscious Nightwalker. We took two hours to get him to Plas Llanychaer, and we left him there, still fast asleep, with his father. We all knew that he would not wake again.

1 September 1822

Today, after a delay of a couple of days caused by showers, I rang my handbell from the front door of the Plas, signalling to the people of the *cwm* that the gleaners could come. They have been into all ten of the harvest fields, with sixty-five women and children scrabbling about for every ear of wheat, barley or oats, and gathering up every bit of straw left behind by the carters or the harvesters. According to tradition, men, horses and carts are strictly banned. The gleaners have been hurrying back and forth between the fields and their cottages and hovels with their hessian sacks and wicker baskets, and I trust that their gleanings will help to keep them and their families and their animals alive over the coming winter. Now they are all gone, and the Plas is quiet again. There is a blessed peace here, and I need it, for the pandemonium of the harvest, and the events surrounding Owain's return and the death of Ceredig, have left me exhausted. And I am still shaking from the revelations made by Iestyn during our night together in my cave. But I have slept for fifteen hours, and I am somewhat recovered. And gradually I am coming to terms with what I now know about Brynach, and Elen, and Iestyn, and about all those of my family and friends who have been conspiring to keep things from me.

I must soon close my diary and attend to the world around me. Since I started on this volume, some sixteen years ago, I have truly learnt a great deal about courage and constancy, and about the capacity of brave men such as Owain, Ceredig and Iestyn to give love until they have no more left to give. Saints, each of them, in their different ways – one alive, one dead, and one asleep. I admit to having been cynical and even arrogant about the ease with which men might be manipulated and pushed into doing silly things. But I have had to learn hard lessons as the years have passed, and I have had to learn a great deal about myself. It has been no bad thing for me to have been almost the last person at the Plas to learn the truth about the Nightwalker, and I am touched and humbled by the manner in which all my family and servants have sought to protect me from horrors sometimes real but mostly imagined.

And I am struck by the fact that from the beginning to the end of this history no man of my acquaintance has inflicted serious injury upon another. I pray to God that I will never forget that fact until the day I die, and that I will learn to give trust to good men, where trust is deserved.

4 September 1822

Iestyn lasted until Brynach went back to the grammar school in Haverfordwest. That was a mercy, for it saved me from explanations or lies.

In spite of Joseph's best efforts, the sleeping saint never recovered consciousness. He stopped breathing, with his father at his bedside, two days ago. By his own wishes, there was no lying in an open coffin, and no funeral. He was laid to rest in a grave in the corner of the Llanychaer walled garden, under a simple cross and an inscription which read as follows: *Here lies Thomas Price, metalworker, late of Swansea. Died of his injuries, 2 September 1822.*

As the coffin was lowered into the grave, Squire Price, Owain, Joseph and I stood together, with our arms around each other, and wept.

GLOSSARY OF WELSH TERMS

Bach: 'little one' (a term of endearment)
Bara brith: literally 'speckled bread', traditional currant cake
Cariad: darling
Cawl: traditional broth made of mutton, leeks and other vegetables
Carn: heap of stones, rocky hill summit
Cnapan: old ball game, thought to be a forerunner of rugby football
Coed: wood or trees
Cwm: valley or hollow in the hillside
Duw: God
Dyn hysbys: literally 'knowing man', wise man or wizard
Ffair Gurig: the Fair of St Curig
Ffynnon: spring or water source
Foel: bare hill, summit
Gambo: a flat two-wheeled cart with no sides
Gwahoddwr: a bidder, engaged to announce a forthcoming wedding
Gwlad y Tylwyth Teg: fairyland, under the sea in Cardigan Bay
Gwylnos: wake night or vigil, before a funeral
Haidd: barley. **Parc Haidd** means 'barley field'
Hen Galan: the old New Year, 12 January
Hiraeth: longing or belonging. Refers to a

region or a special piece of land

Ingli: probably an old Welsh word meaning 'angels'

Parrog: flat land along a shore or estuary (Newport's seaside community)

Pibgorn: old wind instrument once popular in Wales

Plas: big house or palace

Rammas: a doggerel verse used in a bidding before a wedding

Simnai fawr: big chimney, large open fireplace

Toili: phantom funeral, interpreted as an omen of a death to come

Tolaeth: a death omen, usually heard as the sound of coffin making

Twmpath: jolly evening of song and dance (literally tump)

Wrach: witch or hag (**y wrach** is the name given to the last tuft of corn cut during the harvest, carried into the farmhouse and stored until the start of next year's harvest)

The publishers hope that this book has given you enjoyable reading. Large Print Books are especially designed to be as easy to see and hold as possible. If you wish a complete list of our books please ask at your local library or write directly to:

Magna Large Print Books
Magna House, Long Preston,
Skipton, North Yorkshire.
BD23 4ND

This Large Print Book for the partially sighted, who cannot read normal print, is published under the auspices of

THE ULVERSCROFT FOUNDATION
